Interesting Enough

A Wren Island Novel

Laura Joy Lloyd

Windy & Yaiyu Publishing

Advance Praise

"*Interesting Enough* whisks readers away to the charming small-town atmosphere of Wren Island, where island life, meddling elderly aunts, and an unexpected romance prove that even the most stubborn heart can't resist love in bloom."

-Lauraine Snelling, award-winning and best-selling author

"Laura Joy Lloyd writes in familiar yet wonderfully refreshing ways about pain, hope, and the loyalty of friends."

-Bill Myers, best-selling author, award-winning filmmaker

"Wren Island is so endearing, I felt nostalgic for this enchanting place when I finished reading. The delightfully eccentric aunts and the quirky personalities of the characters brought the charming coastal community to vibrant life."

-Holly Varni, award-winning author of the Moonberry series

"Laura Joy Lloyd's *Interesting Enough: A Wren Island Novel* is more than enough, from beginning to end. Lloyd's debut will hook readers, and her witty dialogue, beautiful setting, and intriguing storyline won't let go. You'll want to move in and stay awhile, just like her character's quirky family members."

INTERESTING ENOUGH

-Robin W. Pearson, Christy Award–winning novelist

"Laura Joy Lloyd is a fabulous writer with a keen understanding of prose that cuts straight to the heart. I'm so glad she's gifted us with *Interesting Enough: A Wren Island Novel*. Within these pages, you'll find colorful characters and a setting you won't want to leave. Laura is definitely an author to watch."

-Brandy Vallance, award-winning author of *The Covered Deep* and *Within the Veil*

"This is the kind of story that gently restores something inside you. With humor, heart, and a cast of characters who feel like family, *Interesting Enough* invites you to believe—maybe for the first time in a long time—that you are already worthy of love, rest, and belonging."

-Tonya Kubo, community strategist, host of the *Find Your Freaks* podcast

Published in the United States of America by Windy & Yaiyu Publishing.

First Edition June 2025

Cover by KUHN Design Group | kuhndesigngroup.com

Wren Island map by Tessa Burns | tessaburns.com

Author photo by Suzanne Rothmeyer | suzannerothmeyer.com

ISBN (paperback) 979-8-9988968-0-4

ISBN (e-book) 979-8-9988968-2-8

Library of Congress Control Number: 2025909708

For media inquiries and Wren Island updates, visit the author's website.

laurajoylloyd.com

For the reader giving life her best.
And for those who love her.

I

Only the dogs

"How can you be any good at songwriting without also being a singer?" Allison repeated the question out loud, not that anyone but the dogs could hear. Or maybe she said it out loud *because* no one but the dogs could hear.

Easing her thirty-foot sport boat out of Reclamation Island's sheltered marina, she glanced at the fencing supplies she'd stowed on deck. All tied down securely. Both the dogs were in their life jackets, so it was all systems go, as some people say.

Did people say *all systems go* about boating? Next time she was looking for an interesting topic to discuss with herself, she'd look up the answer online.

That young pushy guy she'd just met in the pub reminded her of her ex. She could almost hear Tank asking that guy's question. *How can you be any good at songwriting without also being a singer?* Tank would have listed every reason Allison was unqualified to be a songwriter. Then he would have turned the reasons around to show how qualified *he* was.

Oh boy, was she glad those days were over. She rolled her eyes at ever being charmed by a braggart who bestowed his own nickname during his testosterone-boosting phase.

Beyond the marina, choppy water in the strait, typical for the Pacific Northwest, indicated a rough trip home. Allison steered into the stronger current. "I ask you, Louise, where's the rule that says you have to be able to sing to write music?"

The only answer was the dog's thumping tail.

"You can do anything if you put your mind to it. Take boating, for instance." Allison patted *Buttercup*'s wheel. A year ago, she didn't know the difference between a grapnel and a plow anchor. Now, after watching a bunch of YouTube videos and passing the licensing exam, she was piloting through the Salish Sea in a custom Ocean Sport Roamer—painted her favorite color, bright yellow. Sailing over sleeping volcanoes, intricate kelp forests, and hundreds of species of fish.

Allison turned an ear toward *Buttercup*'s stern. The engine sounded funny. Maybe. Or a current was running hard against the hull. Probably nothing. Just another boating quirk she hadn't encountered yet.

Anyway, why shouldn't Allison Theodore, not a singer, write music? Or anything else she wanted to.

One of these days, she was going to do something really interesting. And important. It couldn't be something she could buy, because with all the money she had now, that would be too easy.

She still liked her first idea. Rescuing a bunch of homeless dogs. Really important stuff! Who knew the animal shelter restricted adoptions to just one dog at a time unless the dogs were a bonded pair?

Allison glanced at the larger of her life-jacketed dogs. The shelter staff said Louise and Lokita weren't bonded when they arrived. But by hovering protectively, Louise convinced everyone she and the smaller, blind Lokita needed to stay together. "You're a loyal friend, Louise."

Having two dogs wasn't as interesting as having fifty dogs would have been, but it was better than having no dogs.

The next really interesting idea, songwriting, had stuck so far. With a single hit, Allison Theodore could rock the world. All those childhood piano lessons could finally be made use of. Doubters could watch and see how you can be good at songwriting without also being a singer. Naturally, success might take time. These days, she had all the time she wanted. How many forty-five-year-olds could say that?

The middle of the strait had its own weather system. Wind barreling down from Canada, waves slamming against *Buttercup*'s bow. Even from the enclosed pilothouse, watching spray shed from the windshield made her feel woozy. Sure, islands were in sight, but if she and the dogs ended up in the frigid water, land would be a lifetime away.

But there was no need to feel nervous. She could take those square-shaped breaths she learned about in therapy, after the divorce. Imagine moving along a square's four sides, one at a time, like a dance. One, two, three, four. Breathing in on the odd side, out on the even. Repeat.

When *Buttercup*'s motor sputtered, Allison kept her eyes ahead, willing continued forward movement. Wren Island would be in sight soon.

With a cough, *Buttercup*'s engine died. The current, running strong under the brisk north wind, immediately began pushing the boat back. Allison reached for the radio's handpiece. A nearby boater might lend help.

Then again, did she really need to call for help?

She replaced the handpiece, rummaged around belowdecks, and dug out the manual the guy at the sales office stamped with his contact info. What section should she search in?

Oh, here. Troubleshooting.

The fuel filter, maybe. She found the spare, replaced it, and tried to restart the engine. Still no power.

After searching through the manual again, she suspected trapped air in the fuel lines. With step-by-step guidance from a YouTube video, she bled the lines, then retried the engine. Woo-hoo, look at that! *Buttercup* was up and running. Allison's fist-pump into the air set Louise dancing. Lokita joined her.

The boat swept past neighbor islands until Allison's own private paradise came into view, the beach on Wren Island's south side. Allison angled *Buttercup* around the island's forested western point and slowed, keeping one eye on the sonar to avoid the underwater boulders littering the approach.

Drifting past her boathouse, she glanced inside the roll-up door. All co-pacetic. The boathouse and pilings were original to the property, but the dock's new composite decking allowed light for fish below. She turned off the motor. Then she tied up, port side. Home again.

"Whew."

Impatient Louise wiggled her entire back end while waiting for her life jacket to be unfastened, then leaped over the gunwale to the dock and galloped toward the beach. Allison unfastened Lokita's tiny jacket, opened the walk-on loading door on *Buttercup*'s port side, and led Lokita to the dock, careful to keep the leash short.

"Now we're on the dock," Allison sang. "We are on the dock. So be careful where you walk. Careful where you walk."

She sang it the same way every time so Lokita would know exactly where they were. The people at the animal shelter said it was helpful to give a blind dog lots of audible cues.

Ahead, Louise sniffed the line of debris zigzagging the beach after high tide, then ran into the forest, probably after a squirrel or rabbit. No need to worry. The dog could run for acres and stay on her home turf.

Allison walked slowly with Lokita, letting her navigate driftwood, rocks, and clumps of seaweed at her own pace. They climbed the slope of dune grass and the rocky path above it, passed between the pair of concrete lions stationed as imaginary lookouts, and met a panting, happy Louise at the sheltered front door.

"Come with us to the service door, Louise."

Allison followed Lokita, who was straining at the leash now that the cozy warmth of home was within a few sniffs. At the service entrance, Allison toweled off Lokita and watched her amble through the mudroom toward the water bowl.

"Louise!" Allison hollered outside toward the front of the house. "Come inside this way!"

No Louise. Allison closed the service door and walked through the house to the front door. Opening it, she found Louise waiting, tail wagging, tongue hanging out of a wide grin.

"It wouldn't hurt you to come through the service door, you know." Allison toweled her off. "Why must you enter and leave through the front door?"

Dry and clean, Louise headed for the water bowl, then slumped into her enormous daytime bed next to Lokita's small one.

Allison drank from a glass of water at one of the kitchen sinks, then headed back outside. She grabbed a wheelbarrow from the shed and pushed it to the dock. Unloaded the fencing supplies. Lined them up near the mostly finished fencing at the back of the house. Gathered tools from the garage.

Once the remaining sections were in place, the new fence would keep Lokita safe and contained. Louise could use the fenced area too, instead of gallivanting through every mudhole in the forest. Organization and convenience. Keys to sanity when caring for dogs.

As Allison stapled the final wire sections into place, the wind picked up. She hosed off the wheelbarrow and tools, then laid them to dry in rows on the garage floor. Even with the neat way she positioned the tools, the garage looked cluttered. When she came back out tomorrow morning, though, each tool would be exactly where she'd left it. A nice bonus to living alone. You didn't have to worry about another person messing with your stuff.

She tweaked the tools until they were lined up just right.

Back inside the house, she flipped on lights and sent Lokita and a reluctant Louise outside to the newly fenced area. Louise made a quick dash of it and ran back in, always afraid to be outside in the dark. No matter. Louise had the bladder of a camel.

Did camels have large bladders? There was another interesting topic to look up online next time she wanted to have a conversation with herself. Maybe over dinner tonight.

When Lokita was ready, Allison sang her back inside, inviting the dog to follow her voice and be as independent as possible. "Little Lokita, come to me. Here you are, right with me." Both dogs followed her into the kitchen.

Allison was halfway through a bowl of ramen noodles when the power went out. And she'd used up significant battery life researching camels! (They had small but efficient bladders, it turned out.) Nothing to do now but call it a day.

In her bedroom suite, Allison closed Lokita into her crate before showering by the light of a camping lantern. She pulled on pajamas, then climbed into bed next to a sprawling Louise.

Raindrops pelted the floor-to-ceiling windows. Wide awake, Allison tried to remember whether she had latched the back door when she came in. Had she closed the garage tight? What about the shed door?

The house creaked as the roar of wind blasting through the evergreens outside grew louder. One tree crashing down in the wrong direction would be—

A sweep of raindrops washed across the wall of glass. Louise, ever on guard, tensed. Listening. For what? What more could this storm possibly throw at them? Holding her breath, Allison pulled the sheets up over her head.

Okay, time for square breathing. She could practically feel the house swaying now, and everybody knew houses didn't sway. They weren't supposed to, anyway. She closed her eyes. Sway, sway, sway. Surely the house had seen storms like this before, being so near the sea.

Oh no! She'd left *Buttercup* tied at the dock instead of pulling her into the boathouse. The boat would be damaged—or gone—for sure.

Another roar of wind blasting through the surrounding trees. More swaying of the house.

Was this how life would end? She and the dogs pinned under a tree in a crumpled house? How much time would pass before anyone thought to check on them?

Instead of being remembered for having done something important, Allison Theodore might not be remembered at all.

2

A lopsided sign

The next morning, Allison woke slowly. No more storm, and the house was still standing. Had *Buttercup* survived? The charismatic little boat might be sunk or drifting to Canada by now.

In the early light, Allison pulled on clothes and walked through the house, checking for storm damage.

Every single leaded-glass pane on the south side of the house was intact. Woo-hoo about that! The fireplaces were all dry, and there weren't any strange noises coming from anywhere. The power was still out, though. She plugged her phone into a portable charger and tucked it into her vest pocket.

When the dogs woke up, Allison snapped a leash on Lokita and stepped outside into a dimly lit morning fresh with salt air. Louise bounded ahead, scattering the brown birds hopping between low-lying branches.

The storm had washed new kelp and driftwood up the beach. And, just as Allison had feared, her boat was gone. What if *Buttercup* was floating into rocks, grounding or sinking, leaking gasoline or oil into open water? She'd alert the authorities, take responsibility for any damage. If only she'd thought to put *Buttercup* under the protective cover of the boathouse.

Walking along the dock with the dogs, she sang. Not in a *real* singer's voice, just in a regular girl's voice. "Now we're on the dock. We are on the dock. So be careful where you walk. Careful where you walk."

She sat at the end of the dock, dangling her legs over the water, amazed at the changes one year had brought. She'd been working at a day job, pushing herself to be extroverted far more than she found comfortable, eating microwave dinners off a folding table older than she was. Now, she had this serene life, thanks to those five miniature paintings her mom had picked up for fifty cents each at a yard sale.

What if Mom hadn't thought those paintings would look cute in her bathroom? Or if Allison hadn't tacked up the paintings in her own closet-sized bathroom after her mom's funeral? Or if her coworker hadn't stopped by to deliver a secondhand television, used the bathroom, and suggested getting a professional opinion on the paintings?

All Allison had dreamed of the day before the appraisal was receiving sufficient funds to pay for car repairs. Wasn't that funny? A new transmission was the best perk she could think of.

The day after the paintings went to auction, she could have bought every car dealership in the county. Instead, she did something she'd always wanted to do. She took a day off work and went on a whale-watching tour.

And what if she hadn't been on a tour boat weaving through picturesque islands? She wouldn't have noticed a lopsided real estate sign. Wouldn't have seen a massive English Tudor house peeking out from the woods, fronted by an expansive beach of driftwood and boulders. Wouldn't have done something else she'd always wanted to do and bought property. A fortress hemmed in by acres of forest and its own beach. Perfect for an independent girl desiring solitude. Her mom would have loved this place.

Across the quiet morning, the sound of a gong resonated, the signal that whales could be heard through the Wren hydrophone scientists used as a tool to understand whales, especially the endangered Southern Resident orcas. People at the commune up the hill behind Allison's house always monitored the hydrophone, ready to hit the monastery-style bronze disk as a friendly, low-tech way of alerting neighbors to tune in when whales could be heard.

Allison patted the dogs at her side and watched the water. There. A pod of three orcas traveling close to shore, toward her boat dock. All females, from the size and shape of their dorsal fins. Probably related to each other, because female orcas lived in family units for their entire lives.

The orcas surfaced several times in a row to breathe, then dove deep, arching their backs and straightening their tails. A dive like that meant they'd stay underwater for several minutes.

Gong, gong, gong.

This was worth using battery power for. Allison pulled up the app on her phone and listened as the orcas she'd seen talked and sang to each other.

A puff of air burst from the water near the dock. One orca, emerging to breathe. Then more puffs as the rest of the family surfaced.

Allison tilted her head. "I heard you girls singing. Encore?"

Another deep dive. More of nature's incredible music.

When the orcas moved on, Allison tucked away her phone and battery pack. No more gonging came from up the hill, but a bobbing sound came from nearby. Like a boat bumping lightly against a dock.

Wait a minute! Allison stood, walked the length of dock to her boathouse, and poked her head through the side door. *Buttercup*! Tied up nice and neat!

Must have been Ralph Wesson. Once again, her neighbor had been helpful—despite his usual pretense of *not* wanting to be helpful.

Back at the house, outside the service entrance, Allison hosed the dogs clean and toweled them dry. Lokita ambled inside and settled in her bed. Allison walked through the interior and opened the front door to Louise.

"Maybe we could teach you to ring the doorbell."

Dogs settled inside, Allison collected the dry tools from the garage and stored them in the shed, each in their designated places. One of these days, she was going to order a label maker and mark where every tool should go. Talk about fun! Like throwing a party for herself.

Exactly at noon, she gave each of the dogs a cookie—the kind that wouldn't crumble into a mess with every crunch.

When the power and internet came back on, she microwaved a mug of water and steeped one tea bag, careful not to drip amber liquid on the pearl-white countertop she'd chosen with spotlessness in mind. She returned the tea to the cabinet, straightening the box to be in line with a canister of sugar. Then she opened her laptop to find out what the rest of the world had been up to.

READ NOW was the subject of the email from Aunt Macy.

All the capital letters weren't worrisome. That style seemed just like Macy Johansson. What worried Allison was that her mom's sister was emailing her at all. What emergency could possibly be going on that involved Allison? It's not like she knew Aunt Macy well. Or any of her aunts. Her mom said the sisters remained close as young adults, then drifted apart. And since Allison had grown up not knowing her aunts, meeting them for the first time at her mom's funeral had been awkward.

Aunt Shasta had traveled all the way from where she was volunteering for a nonprofit. (Was it South America or somewhere else?) She'd worn yellow leggings and giant daisy-shaped earrings the entire time they celebrated her sister's life.

Sensitive Aunt Amelia, the youngest sister, had used up an entire box of tissues during her visit, dabbing her teary eyes and drippy nose. She had hair almost identical to Allison's except silver gray.

Bossy Aunt Macy, talking in all capital letters all the time, coordinated the details of the memorial service on behalf of her sisters. In an impressive effort at circularity, she prepared rainbow sherbet punch from a recipe dating to their mother's baby showers. The hundred white doves released were so clean they seemed fairylike.

It had been nice for Allison to see the sisters' love for Mom up close from a front-row seat. It had also been nice when they returned to their own homes. The aunts were a bit much all together and all at once.

Allison hadn't heard from any of them since. Maybe the aunts had been glad to get back to their own lives. Maybe, like her ex, they didn't consider Allison interesting enough.

At a pounding knock from the service entrance, Allison jumped. Louise slinked to a watchful position in front of Lokita's bed. After peeking through a side window, Allison swung the door open and greeted her neighbor.

"Brought your mail." Ralph gave Louise a wary glance.

Allison turned to see Louise demonstrating one of her signature smiles, a raised right upper lip. It could be interpreted as the start of a snarl if her whole back end wasn't wiggling too.

"Thanks. And thanks a lot for bringing in my boat last night. I completely forgot to."

"Your plastic fantastic would be at the bottom of the ocean by now."

Ralph, proud owner of a seventy-three-foot mechanized landing craft used during the Vietnam War, had made it clear he held little regard for a customized sport boat with all the bells and whistles. Still, he'd pulled the plastic fantastic into the boathouse for safekeeping.

She smiled at him. "I mean it, Ralph. Thank you."

Muttering, he rubbed his graying beard. "All right. Here's your mail, then." Allison accepted the envelopes. "But you're going to have to pick up the rest yourself." Despite his arguments otherwise, Ralph was spot-on dependable about bringing mail and small packages over from the mainland. Large items, however, needed advance arrangements.

"What have I got that's still waiting to be picked up?"

"Aunt somebody."

Allison blinked. "You're kidding! My aunt's over there? Is it Aunt Macy?"

"How am I supposed to know which one is which?" Ralph gave her a pointed look. "And I don't get paid to provide passenger service."

"Right. Thanks for the mail and the message."

Sending another uncertain glance in Louise's direction, Ralph shook his head. "Something's not right about that dog."

After he left, Allison shut the door. "Don't listen to him, Louise. There's nothing at all wrong with you. In fact, you're extra special."

She tapped her phone awake and clicked open her aunt's message. It didn't say much.

THERE TOMORROW AND MORE

Loud and cryptic, like Aunt Macy. Since the message was sent yesterday, it explained why Aunt Macy was waiting to be picked up today.

Too bad she hadn't given more notice. The house had plenty of bedrooms, but the same couldn't be said for furniture. Allison had balked at ordering a bunch of furniture just for herself. She liked the minimalist look. Simple lines. Having only what is useful and beautiful. No clutter made it easier to keep things clean.

She crossed the kitchen to the sunroom and tweaked the single chair to be at a forty-five-degree angle to one corner. How would she keep Aunt Macy entertained? Lots of chats, probably. With Aunt Macy unloading opinions at every opportunity. Oh well. For a few days, it would be fun to get to know one of her mom's sisters.

In the mudroom, she pulled on boots and a jacket. "You're in charge while I'm gone," she whispered to Louise. The dog opened one eye, briefly.

Allison tapped a reply to Aunt Macy's email.

On my way to get you. Look for a bright yellow boat arriving where short-term visitors tie up, at the end of Dock A.

3

Not just a visit

Seagulls wandered close to the bench where Amelia Theodore rested. The birds hoped for a handout, maybe. Not that Amelia planned to offer her donut. Chocolate glazed was one of her favorites.

In the marina ahead, a ferry, painted white with green trim, approached its berth. Efficient attendants lowered and secured the loading ramp, then motioned it was safe to disembark. Bicycles and motorcycles rolled off, followed by trucks and cars. Empty, the ferry sat higher in the water, exposing more of its green hull. Then, as one vehicle after another drove into the hold for the next passage, the ferry lowered with the added weight.

All those people and vehicles, traveling to and from Pacific Northwest islands. But Wren Island was too remote to be serviced by Washington State Ferries. Did people on Wren even drive cars? Just what were she and her sister Macy getting themselves into by moving in with their niece?

Amelia pulled off her prescription sunglasses and squinted up at her sister. "Are you sure Allison definitely said she wants both of us to move in with her?"

"Of course Allison wants us to live with her. Who would turn down free caretakers? Plus, we're family. That poor little girl, all alone in the world since our dear Anne departed. But not alone anymore! Now Allison has *us*. She needs us, and you need a place to live and me to take care of you."

Amelia frowned at the recurring message behind her sister's words. *Poor Amelia Theodore.* "This time it's not just me that needs a place to live, though, right? You need a place too. Don't you, Macy?"

"If our very own millionaire niece doesn't have room for two aunts and four pieces of luggage, I can't imagine what this world is coming to. What's the problem? I'll tell you what the problem is. There's no problem at all."

Of course Macy hadn't answered the question. Expertly changing the subject was one of her specialties. As the oldest and self-proclaimed wisest sister, she always gained steam during arguments. Eventually, you ended up wherever Macy had decided you were going—and you got there together, so that was something.

Gulls made ha-ha-ha sounds as they came near for the few bits Amelia pulled from her donut and tossed their way. She lifted a corner of the blue gingham cloth covering the birdcage next to her on the bench. "Kitty and Matt look cold."

"Kitty and Matt are cold, you're cold, I'm cold. We all scream for ice cream. Perk up, Melia."

Easy for Macy to say. Amelia eyed her sister's trendy orange sneakers, fitted yoga pants, and green smoothie drink. Macy and Shasta were the most energetic and shaped-up of the sisters. Shasta would probably still be bungee-jumping off bridges in Australia after the rest of the world was dead and gone.

Anne, Allison's mother, had always been more like Amelia. Not weak, but cautious. Amelia remained a Theodore because she'd never married (and all indications were she'd stay unmarried forever). Anne married but didn't change her name. Allison too. One less detail to sort out when the marriages ended.

Amelia *almost* felt like Anne's daughter could have been her own, even though they'd never lived close or spent time together. It wasn't just that they all three were Theodores with first names starting with the letter *A*. Amelia and Anne had been completely connected—heart, mind, and soul—in childhood and as young adults. Even later, when the general weightiness of life edged in, Amelia had felt connected to Anne. There'd been no falling out or major grievance between them. Just little practical challenges, adding up unnoticed. Pushing increasingly weary sisters apart.

Oh, how she missed Anne. If only she could telephone Anne right now. If only Anne were here to be part of this season of their family. Anne would be thrilled to see two of her sisters eagerly waiting to hug her daughter. About to live together under one roof! All thanks to Anne having raised a gorgeous daughter with a bigger heart than any the sisters could hope for. Swallowing tears, Amelia adjusted the cloth over the birdcage.

Macy hopped forward. "There she is, I bet. In a bright yellow boat, just like she said. Melia! Here comes our Allison!" Macy galloped off.

Amelia finished her donut and flicked whatever crumbs might remain on her fingers to the gulls. She replaced her sunglasses and looked out across the marina, filling in the gaps between what she could see and what she'd learned reading about the place. Blurry in the distance, islands blanketed in evergreen forests rose from the depths. Much farther north in the Salish Sea, toward Canada's Gulf Islands, Wren Island wasn't even in sight. To get there, they'd follow a strait north, then veer west to wind around more islands.

Closing her eyes, Amelia listened to the bustling marina activity. "I hope I get to see a whale."

Next thing she knew, Macy was tugging on her arm. "Melia, listen carefully. Allison didn't know we were coming. She knows I'm here, of course. Go surprise her with the additional news you've come along too."

"I thought you said—"

"I decided it best not to unload everything on our Allison all at once, so I didn't mention details yet. Off you go, then. Introduce yourself. Or reintroduce yourself. But whatever you do, Melia, don't mention any details."

By *details*, did Macy mean Amelia wasn't supposed to mention their need for a permanent home? Or Amelia's recent diagnosis? Had Macy asked Allison if it was okay to move in? Or had Macy just shown up with her cringe-worthy sister in tow, hoping for mercy?

Amelia picked up the birdcage and made her way toward the yellow boat, which wasn't at all hard to see, even for someone with her fading abilities.

"Aunt Amelia?" Allison's beautiful smile lit up her entire face. Those perfectly straight teeth were thanks to Anne and the orthodontics she'd put teenage Allison through. The whiteness of those teeth, though, was a more recent improvement.

Amelia melted into her niece's hug. "I'm here too, Allison. Can you manage with both of us? We'll find another option if we're going to be a bother." Amelia looked around. What other option? Sleep on that bench over there?

"You have a bird!" Allison reached for the covered cage. "I'm glad you and Aunt Macy came for a visit."

A visit. So that's how Macy had presented it to Allison. Amelia squinted back at her sister, who was doing those up-and-down stretches she said were effective at fighting off free radicals.

"*Two* birds!" Allison was peeking under the cloth. "Australian zebra finches, right? What are their names?"

"Miss Kitty and Marshal Matt Dillon. Like on *Gunsmoke*—that's an old television show you probably never saw. Macy got the birds for me." *After my most recent outpatient procedure*, Amelia almost added—but that probably fell into the category of details Macy didn't want mentioned. "You don't have cats, do you?"

"Two dogs. No cats. Your birdies will be safe and happy on Wren Island."

Truly, her niece's smile was pristine. How did she keep it that way? Amelia closed her lips over her own crooked, yellow smile. Macy had always said Amelia should take better care of her teeth. Now it turned out Macy was right about that too.

4

Patting a lion's head

When her niece pulled her boat up to a long dock with an immaculate building off it, Amelia thought she might be in a half-imaginary, half-real dream. Beyond the dock, a wide beach sloped up to a grassy dune and—wonder of wonders—a fairy-tale castle in the woods. Wouldn't Anne have loved it?

While Allison and Macy collected the luggage, Amelia gathered the birdcage and her snacks. Allison and Macy chattered off the dock and on down the beach. Amelia took her time, navigating driftwood, rocks, and clumps of seaweed.

Allison stopped walking and pointed to where the far edge of the forest sloped down to the water. "Look at the bald eagle's nest in that tree. My neighbors say a pair has built several nests on Wren. I'm hoping the eagles will use this one next spring. Watch your step along here. These rocks create an uneven path."

They climbed stone steps, then stood between two concrete lions as stately as the house they seemed to guard. Amelia patted one lion's head, then the other.

"Here we are." Allison set down Amelia's suitcases and reached to open the red, arched door.

Amelia was the first to step inside. She'd always remember that. Always remember that she got to view the magnificent entry with no one ahead of her. No one blocking her view. It was almost as if the house welcomed her. (Welcomed *her*, Amelia Theodore!)

First, she was in an alcove where a low ceiling sloped down to wrought-iron candle holders on either side. Then, she was stepping into an illuminated circle. Onto an elegantly patterned hardwood floor warmed by a thick, round rug, its deep blues complimenting curving walls the shade of a robin's egg. An ornate, dark wood stairwell drew Amelia's attention up one wall.

Oh! The ceiling! A perfect dome, with a glittering chandelier dropping from its center.

Next to Amelia, Macy thumped their suitcases to the floor and sank into a ladder-backed chair. "Goodness. Isn't this something?"

Allison grinned. "Wait until you see the rest of the house."

The rest of the house? Amelia peeked at what she could see. One room off the entry boasted two-story windows, a fireplace surrounded by an elaborately carved mantle, and a grand piano. On the other side of the entry, another large room, another large fireplace, another wall of windowpanes. Other than the piano and the chair Macy was sitting on, not a stick of furniture.

A big brown dog was creeping, shy, across the sculpted entry rug. Amelia set down the birdcage and reached out one hand. The dog crept close. Sniffed Amelia's hand and the top of the birdcage. Wagged into a sit and gazed up at Amelia with an adoring smile.

Allison laughed. "Louise must think you're a-okay, Aunt Amelia."

"A pleasure to make your acquaintance, Louise." One of the nicest things about animals was that they accepted you the way you were. They cared less if you were the prettiest or brightest and more if you were comfy enough to relax with.

Allison straightened their suitcases to be in line with the wall. "There's another dog around too. Let's leave the luggage for now and get you two refreshed. Would you like a glass of water with lemon? A cup of hot tea?"

Amelia followed her niece and sister along a corridor lit by wall sconces. When Amelia stopped to peer into a cozy room with a television and a sectional, the big dog next to her stopped too. Then they caught up to the others in the kitchen.

The kitchen! A clean, white counter topped a wide, long island. On one wall, built-in glass cabinets hovered over more gleaming countertops. Ceiling beams ran the length of the room. Where did that door at the end lead? A sunroom with a concrete floor, nearly empty of furniture.

While Allison and Macy chattered, Amelia chose a seat at the kitchen's round, weathered wood table. Could it get any better? It could, because she was pretty sure she was sitting smack dab in the middle of a turret. (Amelia Theodore in a turret!) Beyond the curved wall of windows, nuthatches scampered through vines crisscrossing a boulder that anchored the upward sloping forest behind the house.

"Close your mouth, Melia. Do you want to catch flies?" Macy clunked mugs onto a tray and continued her conversation with Allison. "So we said to ourselves, why not come by and see how our Allison is getting along? How *are* you doing, sweetheart?"

Allison carried the tray with the teapot and three mugs to the table, diamond stud earrings sparkling along the edge of her ear. "The renovations on the house were a hassle, but they're finished now, and I stay busy with my work."

"Work?" Macy added napkins to the table and sat.

"I'm writing songs." Allison poured tea and set a mug in front of Amelia. "Or trying to."

"How sweet." Macy patted Allison's arm. "And since you don't need money, it won't matter if you're successful or not."

Allison wiped the edge of the teapot. "It's true I don't need to sell my songs to pay the bills. But I'd like to write something that mattered to someone."

"Aren't you lucky, though?" Macy patted Allison's arm again. "You'll never have to worry about money again. You'll always be able to take care of yourself. And you'll always be able to take care of everyone you love."

At this, Amelia set down her mug of tea. Finally, they were sharing the details with Allison. "What Macy's leading up to, Allison, is that—"

"I wasn't leading up to anything." Macy flapped a napkin at Amelia, shushing her. "I was simply stating that our Allison is completely independent. And isn't that nice for our Allison?"

So, big sister Macy was directing the conversation again. In the direction big sister Macy wanted it to go. Which, if history repeated itself, was probably for the best.

5

Ocean view or forest view

Allison threaded her way through the forest on one of many trails between her property and the commune up the hill. She'd left her aunts poking around the kitchen, where they'd already broken a ceramic bowl.

Aunt Amelia wasn't the most coordinated person. Neither was Aunt Macy. The stacks of bowls in the cabinet were going to look uneven until Allison ordered a replacement. Mismatched. Off-kilter. Not how she liked her kitchen at all.

Oh well. The aunts would only be here for a few days.

The damp, clean-smelling forest felt hollow without Louise barreling through it, but there'd been no convincing the dog to leave her post where she was monitoring the aunts. Very little got past Louise. Her vigilance kind of made up for Lokita missing so much.

So. Why were Aunt Macy and Aunt Amelia here on Wren Island? Mom would be thrilled. She'd always grieved their distance, both geographic and proverbial. Wished her sisters lived close enough for Allison to know them.

But why were the aunts visiting *now*? Anne was gone, and Allison had grown up and established her own life. Did they feel the need to make amends? Mom had never indicated any rift existed. Allison's financial advisor had warned her of a situation that hadn't seemed to apply to her at the time. Previously unknown family turning up. Did the aunts want money? Did they need money?

The forest trail curved past a rocky outcropping before it opened to a meadow. The commune sat on a sloping hill directly above Allison's property, in a clearing with a view of the Salish Sea below. Allison ducked under the rustic archway of twisted branches marking the property entrance and walked past several outbuildings, scattering chickens and ducks as she went. In the courtyard of the main building, Ed Piper soaked reeds in buckets of water. Allison slowed her approach and admired the finished woven baskets surrounding him, the kind of productive creativity she aimed to tap with her songwriting.

Ed had called the two of them simpatico, since both had taken an early retirement. Fed up with the city's rat race and diagnosed with the dangerously high blood pressure that killed his father and grandfather, Ed had vowed to ease up by growing his own food, enjoying nature, living simply—goals he considered met by living at an unnamed commune of like-minded people on the same remote island in the Pacific Northwest that had drawn Allison.

The serene smile Ed greeted her with said he created intricate baskets just because he liked to. Whether or not anyone else appreciated his efforts. "Hey, Allison!"

"Hi! Could I borrow a couple of cots for my aunts to sleep on? They're visiting and I don't have any guest beds."

Ed motioned for her to follow him inside the main building. They passed by the fountain in the foyer and through the large dining room to the end of a hall, where Ed creaked open the door to a storage area and pulled out two cots. "I'll drive them over in the Polaris later."

"I'd really appreciate it." Ed driving the cots over in an all-terrain vehicle would be much easier than her carting them down the trail on foot.

Back at the house, Allison found her aunts and their suitcases teetering halfway up the back stairs. She reached for their luggage and led the way.

At the landing, she turned to them. "Sleep in the same room? Or in separate rooms?"

"Same," the aunts replied together.

Allison climbed the final steps and turned to them again. "Ocean view or forest view?"

"Goodness." Aunt Macy reached for Aunt Amelia's hand. "Wherever you'd like to put us, sweetheart."

"Forest view, then. That room is larger and has two bathrooms off it." Allison pulled the suitcases to the room at the end of the hallway. "A neighbor is bringing over cots later. I hope you'll be comfortable. I guess it'll be okay for a few nights."

Her aunts busied themselves by unzipping suitcases and hanging clothes in the closets, their few belongings standing out in the otherwise empty room. Well-worn shoes, a curling iron, plastic bags holding toiletries. More cardigans than necessary for a few days' stay. Polyester shirts printed in geometric patterns for Aunt Macy, clothing in pastel shades for Aunt Amelia. The clutter sent a tremor of unease through Allison. She squashed it. Wasn't it about time she offered one of her many additional bedrooms to overnight guests? Until now, no one had wanted to visit. She'd been so competent at isolating herself, she hadn't let anyone get close enough to ask.

She helped Aunt Macy stash the empty suitcases in a closet, then joined Aunt Amelia at one of the floor-to-ceiling windows.

Aunt Amelia smiled. "I can hear the wind in the trees. And this room smells like pine."

"When it's warm, I open all the windows at this end of the house. If you get cold, we'll use the fireplace." Allison ran her hand along the cedar beam mantel as she moved to the doorway. "For dinner, how about macaroni and cheese with bratwurst?"

Aunt Amelia's face lit up. "Is that what you eat?"

"It is tonight. We don't have any restaurants here on the island, but we have a grocery market. The owner, Virgil Tagaloa, bakes the best muffins you've ever tasted. Rotates through a gazillion varieties." There was sure to be flavors her aunts would enjoy. "In the morning I'll pick up a few for breakfast."

Downstairs, in the butler's pantry, Allison prepared a serving platter for tomorrow's muffins. With any luck, she could duck in the market in the morning, grab muffins and leave payment, then duck out without drawing attention from Virgil. The last thing she wanted right now was the attentive market owner asking questions.

She pulled a folding table from the butler's pantry and set it up in the sunroom for the birdcage. While Aunt Amelia fed and watered Miss Kitty and Marshal Matt Dillon, Allison pulled bratwurst from the fridge and calculated how much macaroni and cheese to make for three. Aunt Macy clomped in and began setting the table. Lokita wandered in as the macaroni was simmering and the bratwurst was sizzling.

"Little Lokita, come to me," Allison sang. Lokita wandered close, Louise nudging her from behind. Allison picked up the snuggly white dog, tucked her under one arm, and turned to her aunts. "This one is Lokita."

"Oh my." Aunt Amelia stepped forward. "What happened to her eyes?"

Aunt Macy put an arm around Aunt Amelia. Allison stroked Lokita's soft, silky head. "She had an eye disease. It got so bad both eyes needed to be re-moved."

Aunt Amelia's mouth dropped open.

"The animal shelter didn't have money for the surgery, so I paid for it and adopted her—and Louise because she's Lokita's best friend."

"You *chose* to bring home a blind dog?" Aunt Amelia's eyes were wide.

"*And* her friend?" Aunt Macy's voice cracked.

Allison snuggled her face between Lokita's soft ears. "Uh-huh."

Aunt Amelia shook her head. "Macy, we have to tell our niece why we're here. The whole story. All the details."

Aunt Macy reached for Allison's arm. "Allison, sweetheart, I think we'd all better sit down."

6

Start something new

That night, the forest beyond Allison's bedroom windows draped itself in darkness. Above the trees, stars would be glittering against the black sky of a new moon. Didn't the people at the commune say a new moon was the best time to start something new?

Lokita snored rhythmically from her crate. On the bed next to Allison, Louise twitched in her sleep, dreaming. Chasing a squirrel, rabbit, or flock of seagulls.

In a dream, you could run like the wind, as fast as you wanted to without needing to see where you were going. You could run on the beach, smell the kelp, crunch sand and clamshells under your feet, leap over slippery logs. You'd hear the waves rolling higher up the beach and know you were perfectly safe.

You could be carefree in dreams. But not in real life.

Allison had known, as soon as she'd heard what was going on, that she wanted Aunt Amelia to live with her. Aunt Macy too, because the two sisters seemed like a package deal. Like Lokita and Louise. But how exactly was all this going to work?

Aunt Amelia would need continuing medical care for her macular degeneration. As the aunts aged, they both might need more medical care. Allison could finance all that, of course. But without dependable ferry service, how were they going to get back and forth to the mainland for medical appointments? Especially on days when the weather didn't cooperate for boating.

Would the aunts be comfortable in this lost-in-the-woods house? They might prefer living in a more populated area with easier access to amenities.

Allison rolled over and laid a hand on Louise's warm side. Could she leave this house? This magnificent home she'd created for herself?

And there was the other part of it. Was it wrong that she didn't *want* to share her life? Didn't want to find another's unrinsed tea mug staining the sink. Smell unfamiliar shampoo in the hallway outside the bathroom. Wonder if she'd be the first to tiptoe into the kitchen tomorrow morning.

A knot tightened in her stomach. What had she become? A forty-five-year-old recluse? Years of loneliness stretching ahead of her? If her mom were here, she'd insist on sharing the house. Her mom would say keeping family close was more important than keeping a neat and tidy home. Far more desirable than maintaining privacy and distance.

For now, Allison would make things as comfortable as she could for her aunts. They should sleep in real beds, not cots borrowed from the commune. They might want to choose a different bedroom or sleep in separate bedrooms. Might want a room with an ocean view instead of a forest view.

With macular degeneration, how much longer would Aunt Amelia be able to see distant views?

Allison wiped tears.

Her aunts might need other things too. They might like more clothes and shoes. Did Aunt Amelia enjoy reading? You could easily enlarge the print of e-books. Or listen to audiobooks. Were there audiobooks with music sound-tracks?

There was an idea! Compose soundtracks for audiobooks. When Allison hummed a new tune, Louise woke up. Shifted her position. Drifted off again, taking Allison with her.

The next morning, the sky was deep blue with the first hint of dawn when Allison walked along the gravel road to the island's grocery market. Louise raced up the steps and curled into a cushioned bench on the porch. Allison stepped inside.

Virgil Tagaloa was nowhere to be seen. Allison released a sigh of relief. Jax, Virgil's fourteen-year-old son, greeted her. "Morning, Allison."

"Hey, Jax. Have you got any muffins yet?"

"Straight out of the oven." Jax pulled out a pan and set it on a cooling rack.

"I'll take six of whatever flavors you want to give me."

Allison moved through the market quickly, choosing fresh eggs from the commune hens, then bacon and butter from a farmer on the north side. Her bill paid, she stashed her groceries in a cloth sack, thanked Jax, and ducked out, collecting Louise from the porch.

At home in the kitchen, she prepared the bacon—on low heat and with a towel handy for splatters—while Aunt Macy threw raw vegetables into the blender for a smoothie. Aunt Amelia scuffed in wearing a pink bathrobe and gray bunny slippers and sat down at the table.

Allison wiped a few drips off the counter from around the blender, added the finished bacon to the scrambled eggs and muffins on the table, then sat next to Aunt Amelia. "Here's what I've been thinking. We'll live here for now. But we'll plan to move so you can have easy access to high-quality medical care."

Aunt Amelia shook her head. "I don't want to move. I like it here. And I don't want you to leave your home."

"Be reasonable, Melia." Aunt Macy sat and sucked her vegetable drink through a metal straw. "It's not about liking things. It's about you needing to be taken care of."

Aunt Amelia sent a pointed look toward Aunt Macy's drink. "You have your green drinks you like. I would like to stay here. Eating bacon and a peach almond muffin in a turret."

Wiping drips of bacon grease from the table, Allison breathed around all four sides of a square, one at a time. Truly, it was difficult to know which of the aunts was least coordinated. "Why don't we agree to make one decision at a time? We'll figure it out as we go. What size mattresses do you want? And what kind? I'll order two beds today."

"Two beds? Hmm." Aunt Macy clinked the metal straw around in her glass. "I wonder. Should we order an extra?"

"An extra bed?" More bacon grease slipped from Aunt Amelia's fork to the table. "Whatever for?"

"Your next boyfriend." Aunt Macy chuckled and patted Aunt Amelia's hand. "Close your mouth, Melia, unless you want to catch flies."

Allison wiped the table. As far as she knew, Aunt Amelia had never been married. Put another way, Aunt Amelia had made smarter relationship decisions than Allison.

She glanced at the hair curlers and fuzzy pink collar. Aunt Amelia didn't seem like the type to attract boyfriends. Neither did Aunt Macy. And it's not like tons of eligible bachelors were hanging around Wren.

"Our room has plenty of space for three beds." Aunt Macy sipped her green smoothie. "We'll pile stuffed animals on the extra bed just like we used to when we were kids. A whole bed for stuffed animals. You'd like that, wouldn't you, Melia?"

"Sure I would. But I don't think we need to buy an extra bed just for—"

"It's settled, then! Right, Allison? Three matching beds, because Melia wants one for her stuffed animals. We're doing this for you, Melia."

Allison stopped wiping drips and studied her aunt. The bossy one directing the conversation. Two beds, three beds, what did it matter? She wanted her aunts to be comfortable, right? So, okay, she'd order three.

Two for the aunts, one for the stuffed animals—or any boyfriends that might turn up, as unlikely as that might be.

7

The credit card

Later, they all headed to the beach. Louise chased seagulls. Aunt Amelia, with Lokita on a leash, investigated shells and driftwood.

Standing next to Aunt Macy, Allison watched the waves roll in. "Since you and Aunt Amelia are going to be living with me, I'm giving you a credit card."

"A credit card?"

Allison nodded. As far as she was concerned, her aunts could max out a couple of credit cards every year for the rest of their lives if they wanted to. Still, it might be smart to offer guidelines. "If you want to order clothes, shoes, books, or whatever, just do it. If you want something big—"

"Something big?"

"Ask me if you're not sure if it will be okay."

Aunt Macy stuffed her hands into her pockets. "Could I get a new jacket? The wind jumps right through this one. And Melia says her socks aren't soft anymore."

"That's exactly the kind of thing you can order on your own with the credit card. Let me know if you want help." Allison pulled her jacket collar up against the wind. Pushed by whitecaps, *Buttercup* bobbed at the end of the dock. "I wish we had a more reliable way of getting people to the mainland. And a general physician here on Wren full time."

"Aren't there any medical people up at that commune?"

Allison shook her head. "It's a real puzzle. I don't know what they're thinking up there. It's wonderful that they live sustainably. That they're conscientious about taking care of the land. But most of the members have lived here for years. They're getting to an age where they might want to be under a doctor's care instead of trusting their health entirely to herbs and supplements. What's going to happen when someone at the commune experiences a medical emergency?"

"Don't they have a boat?"

"They don't need one. My neighbor Ralph Wesson brings their supplies, and we all help cart it up to their property."

Ralph's reluctance to be the island's unofficial ferry service was one reason she'd stopped ordering furniture for the house. His pride and joy, the flat-hulled *Lucy Jo*, had the capacity to carry a few vehicles at once. But oversized cargo had to be unloaded on the beach, because Wren didn't have a crane of adequate size on any of its docks.

Running *Lucy Jo* up on the beach usually included a lot of shouting and swearing on Ralph's part. Then the cargo still needed to be carted down *Lucy Jo*'s loading ramp, up the sandy beach, over the dunes, and to its final home. Allison's house was the closest to the beach. Everyone else had to haul their supplies by truck or all-terrain vehicle over bumpy roads. Most Wren Islanders preferred making do with what they already had.

Until now, it had been easy for Allison to live with minimal furniture. And the blank space, free of clutter, helped her to think creatively. Which she hadn't done in a while.

"Do you mind if I head back to the house and work?"

"Work?"

"Songwriting."

"Of course, sweetheart. I'll bring Melia and the dogs back when they're all played out. You go have fun with your ditties."

Allison cringed. Ditties? Why would her aunt assume she was writing fluff? Neither aunt had heard any of Allison's songs—primarily because she hadn't written any yet. Once she got going, though, she was going to compose *real* music.

"Oh, Allison?" She was halfway up the beach when Aunt Macy called. "Would an airplane ticket be considered something big on the credit card?"

An airplane ticket? Did Aunt Macy already want a vacation? It would temporarily cut down on the number of people making messes in the house. "Want to go somewhere warmer for the winter?"

Aunt Macy shrugged.

Allison's first real song awaited. "Sure, that's okay."

Inside the house, she headed upstairs to her office. Calling the cozy den an office made it sound like important work was being done there. She sat at her desk. When she bumped the mouse, the computer screen lit up, then the electronic keyboard beeped. She pulled open the drawer housing the computer keyboard and opened all the apps she'd need. Then she put her hands in her lap.

What to write? Start with lyrics? Start with a tune?

The view out the window behind her computer screen would inspire anyone to create something beautiful. A symphony maybe. Or a film score. A pop single.

She drummed her fingers against the desk. Stood, paced, sat down again. Watched the cursor blink, blink, blink in a rhythmic tempo. How about a tune, though?

The muffled sounds of her aunts returning with the dogs reached her. Aunt Macy caused a scuffle trying to boss Louise into entering through the service door.

Allison walked to the top of the circular staircase, above the entry, and hollered. "Louise doesn't come inside through the service door! You'll have to let her in at the front door!"

When Aunt Amelia appeared below, shuffling across the round rug, Allison lowered her voice to a more normal tone.

"Aunt Amelia, will you please wipe Louise's paws before she runs in? There's a towel draped across the back of that chair."

Aunt Amelia grabbed the towel and shuffled toward the front door. Louise appeared on the rug a moment later, cleaned off but not as thoroughly as Allison would have liked.

Oh well. She headed downstairs to sweep up the mess herself. Meant to be composing music—a song just at the tip of her fingers, ready to burst out—she was sweeping sand instead.

Maybe she should hire a housekeeper. No, then she'd be cleaning up after one more person.

By the time she was back gazing out the window in her den—not her den, her home office, where important and interesting stuff ought to happen easily but rarely did—any twinge of inspiration she'd felt when looking out earlier was gone.

"Allison!" Aunt Amelia's voice wafted up from the kitchen. "We're making dinner so you can keep working on your next song!"

Her *next* song? Writing the first one was going to be a major accomplishment.

The cursor blinked its steady beat. Allison tapped her fingers on the desk. An awful lot of clattering was coming from the kitchen. What were those two cooking for dinner? Oh no. It sounded like they'd found the spaghetti sauce in the freezer, and you had to unwrap those packages just right or red tomato bits splattered everywhere.

"Doo do doo do doo," she sort of sang, in a losing battle to write a real song, pressing the electronic piano keys into a chord.

Lokita wandered past the doorway.

"Little Lokita, come to me." Allison sang the dog close. "Here you are, right with me." Scooping Lokita into a cuddle, Allison let her voice lilt any way it wanted to. "You are sweet. You're a treat. Best of all, you're mostly neat."

8

A grand opportunity

A few days later, Amelia was sitting at the table in the kitchen turret. She called this one the kitchen turret because it turned out there were other turrets in the house. The entire circular entry was a turret, for one. Another turret flanked one end of the mouse room.

The mouse had been there for a while, flattened under an unburnt log in the fireplace. Amelia called it the mouse room only in her thoughts. She was pretty sure spick-and-span Allison wouldn't want to hear there'd been a mouse in her house.

A mouse in the house. See, those were the kind of rhyming words Allison could use in the marvelous music she composed. What a prolific songwriter Allison was! New songs being sung every time you turned around! And every catchy tune easy to remember.

Quietly, Amelia sang a personalized version of the song Allison often sang to Lokita. "Little Amelia, come to me. Here you are, right with me."

And how about the dock song that kept everyone safe? Amelia tapped her feet to it. "Now we're on the dock. We are on the dock. So be careful where you walk. Careful where you walk."

When Macy bustled into the kitchen and began clunking glass bowls from the fridge to the counter, Amelia pointed to the catalog page she'd been squinting at through a magnifying glass. "Is an espresso maker something big?"

"Why would we want an espresso maker? None of us drink espresso."

When Allison breezed into the kitchen, Amelia pointed to the photo and tried again. "Would an espresso maker be something big on the credit card?"

"Oh wow. I've heard they can be fun to use but expensive. It might take up too much counter space." Allison began wiping the expansive counters.

Amelia scanned them. If you asked her, she'd say Allison was a tiny bit overprotective of her countertops. Plenty of space for an espresso machine! Next to the cabinet with the vintage dishes Allison had saved from Anne's things, or in the corner beyond the main sink, or near the smaller hand sink, or at this end of the counter nearest the table.

What was that expression Amelia had seen on tee shirts and mugs? *Not before coffee.* Espresso could be Amelia Theodore's whim for the new year. "I'd drink espresso every morning if it came out of a fancy machine like this."

"Be reasonable, Melia." Macy clunked more bowls on the counter. "You have to spoon finely ground coffee beans into those things. You have to tamp it down just so. You have to boil water—hot, scalding water—and pour it just right. There's no way you'll be able to do those kinds of tasks. Don't go complicating things for the rest of us even more than they already are."

Another list of tasks Amelia—or *Melia*, as Macy insisted on calling her—couldn't be expected to do. Sighing, she turned the catalog page.

"Allison, sweetheart." Macy squeaked the palm of one hand across the counter. "I've already cleaned this."

"You have?" Allison bent down to scrutinize it at eye level. "I'll just go over it again and make sure we've gotten every last crumb."

Amelia watched Macy and Allison moving through the kitchen. Macy making messes, Allison following behind, cleaning. When Macy pulled out a cutting board and began pounding raw chicken breasts on it, Amelia steadied the rocking kitchen table. "What are you making for dinner, Macy?"

"Chicken cordon bleu."

"I don't think so." Allison wrung a dishcloth into the sink. "I don't have any cheese or ham."

"Yes you do, sweetheart." Macy sounded pleased. "I purchased supplies from your nice young grocery man. That credit card you gave us comes in handy."

Allison draped the dishcloth over a rod. "When were you at the market?"

"Earlier. I met Mr. Virgil Tagaloa and his son, Jax. A stunning pair."

Amelia had heard the tone in her sister's voice often, and recognized what was happening. Macy believed she'd landed on pertinent information others may or may not be aware of yet. In this case, the quality of the Tagaloa family.

Allison didn't know yet to ask Macy for more analysis. Or maybe Allison didn't *want* to ask for more. Cool and indifferent, she leaned against the counter. "Speaking of the credit card, I'm going to cancel that one and give you a different one. Someone must have gotten the number. There's been a few weird charges."

"Weird charges?" Macy dumped breadcrumbs into a pan.

Allison swept stray crumbs into the sink. "International airfare, for one. To New York from Sydney, Australia."

Amelia propped her elbow on the table and leaned her chin into one hand. "Our sister Shasta lives in Australia."

Looking up, Allison eyed Macy. "I thought Aunt Shasta lived in South America."

"You know what, Allison?" Macy's tight tone indicated she wanted to be large and in charge. Probably Allison didn't know yet to recognize that tone either. "You gave me responsibility for the card, so you should let me be the one to straighten it out. You want me to know how to do that sort of thing, don't you?"

The conversation was well within Macy's control now. Amelia smiled in admiration.

Allison rinsed a bowl and stuck it in the dishwasher. "There were other charges too. Domestic flights. And get this. A bunch of charges in Green Bay, Wisconsin—including tickets to an NFL game. Is the Green Bay football team the one with the fans who wear those odd-looking yellow hats?"

"Made of foam and shaped like a giant cheese wedge." Macy tossed chicken pieces into the pan of breadcrumbs and slogged them around. "What will people come up with next?"

Returning her attention to the catalog, Amelia studied another page. Popcorn makers. Now that would be fun. For movie nights. Or football games, if Shasta ever came to visit. Especially when the Green Bay Packers, Shasta's favorite team, were playing. "Our sister Shasta loves watching the Green Bay Pack—"

"Melia!" Macy rushed over. "Look what you've done. Spills all over your shirt! Allison, hand me a clean towel please."

Amelia squinted down. "I've spilled? I don't see it."

"Right here. Everywhere. Don't move. Don't even talk, because when you talk, you move." Macy accepted a towel from Allison and swished it back and forth across Amelia's shirt. "So anyway, Allison, I'll call the credit company right away. You leave it to me."

"I guess that'd be okay, if you really want to." Allison loaded the dishwasher. "What else should we buy to help you two feel at home here? More clothes? Let's make things comfortable for you."

Amelia shooed off her sister and the flapping dish towel. "It already *is* comfortable, Allison. We don't need anything else."

Macy tugged at Amelia's shirt again. "This is your grand opportunity, Melia. Ask for anything you want. Tell us what you need so we can take care of you."

There it was again. *Poor Melia needs help.*

Standing, Amelia glared at her sister. "Why don't *you* tell me what I need? You seem to have it all figured out already."

She headed for the sunroom, pulled the single chair close to the birdcage, and sat. "Here, little birdy, birdy, birdy." Kitty and Matt hopped from perch to perch.

The voices of her niece and sister in the kitchen grew quieter. Amelia stretched her legs. So what if they were talking about her? Big whoop. Probably it was all about Amelia needs this, Amelia needs that.

She closed her eyes and listened to the wind whispering through the pine trees outside. Kitty and Matt settled. The voices in the kitchen ceased. All that remained was the sound of Macy clanging pots and Allison turning the faucet on and off. If Amelia leaned down a little, she could hear Lokita, curled on the floor nearby, snoring.

Leaning a bit farther, Amelia knew she was falling from her chair as it was happening. Somehow it happened fast and also in slow motion, so she didn't cry out until after she hit the floor. Immediately, she regretted crying out, because the pain in her side grew worse. Fierce enough to take her breath away.

"What happened?" Allison appeared, knelt, and took Amelia's hand. "Are you all right?"

"Melia! What have you done?" Macy scurried close.

"Oh-h. I fell off the chair." Amelia tried to breathe. Ouch! She tried to take a deeper breath. Settled for shallow panting.

Allison touched her lightly. "Can you get up? Can I help you?"

Slowly, Amelia crept up on all fours and made her way back to the chair. Taking a careful breath, she winced. "It hurts."

"Aunt Amelia, can you tell me where it hurts?"

She took another tentative breath. "My side. And my shoulder, a bit."

"You've got to stop falling, Melia." Macy's voice had risen. "How many times have I said it? One of these times, you're going to get hurt."

Amelia could have hollered at her sister—she really, really could have. Oh how she wanted to. *I am hurt this time! Do you think I wanted to fall out of a chair and land on a concrete floor?*

But she hadn't hollered at her sister in years. And she wasn't about to start now—not in this house. Anyway, the pain in her side wouldn't allow it. The only sound was her shallow breathing and the click of toenails on the floor as Louise drew near. Amelia let the dog lick her fingers, her hand, her arm.

The birdcage was undisturbed, at least. It would have been awful if she'd knocked it over as she fell. But there were Kitty and Matt, hopping from perch to perch, twittering and happy.

So that was nice, wasn't it? Life would go on for the finches just like it always did.

9

Sharing air

Lying on a bunk belowdecks, in one of Allison's stylish, pristine cabins, Amelia shifted into a more comfortable position. Earlier, on the trip to the mainland hospital, the choppy water had bounced the boat around so vigorously Amelia nearly passed out from pain. Now, after anti-nausea and pain medication, the trip home to Wren Island was bearable.

Amelia touched the ice pack at her side and pictured, inside her eyelids, the radiographs she'd seen. Two cracked ribs. Not broken, though, so there was that to be thankful for.

Up the stairs, in the pilothouse, Allison was chatting with Macy. "Over there is Reclamation Island, where I go for supplies I can't get on Wren."

"Look at those cliffs." Macy's voice was full of awe.

"The south side of Reclamation is called Wail Point. Not whale like the animal. W-A-I-L."

"Isn't that something?"

The rocking boat, the warm blanket. Even though Amelia was lying down, safe from another fall, she opened her eyes and kept them open. Not that keeping her eyes open helped orient her to the surroundings much. Maybe she was just tired today, but her eyesight seemed worse.

"Oh look! Over there." Allison sounded excited. The boat engine grew quieter as it slowed, then stopped.

"Melia." Macy's head appeared in the doorway. "Come up on deck. A pod of orcas is heading right toward us."

"I'm going to see whales?" Amelia moved as quickly as she could, but that wasn't saying much. On deck, she peered in the direction Allison pointed. "Where are they?"

"They just passed us." Allison's voice was hushed. "Oh *wow*."

Amelia pressed her lips into a thin line. How had she missed seeing orcas pass right in front of her? Were they still close enough to see? Close enough for *her* to see? Scanning the blurry water, she listened to the waves rhythmically meeting the side of the boat. Then, bursts of air erupted several yards from the boat.

Whales! Right here with her!

She turned her face and pretended to see everything she was missing. When more bursts of air erupted, she felt the spray on her face. And that was really spectacular, to think she'd felt the breath of an orca. She'd even smelled it. Kind of a fermented fishy smell that stuck to the roof of her mouth.

She took another breath. Sharing the same air as an orca seemed like an extra-special thing to do.

Later, at home, Amelia drank the chicken broth Macy placed in front of her. With Allison's help, Amelia ascended the back staircase and crawled onto her cot. Then, alone in the dark, snuggled under the blankets, she called on the imagination that had never once, in sixty-seven years, disappointed her.

Allison's bright yellow boat glided over a glassy surface, water so clear you could see all the way down to boulders on the sea floor. Porpoises waved hello as they bobbed past. One squeaked at her. *Good afternoon, Amelia!*

Then the orcas arrived, with elegant dorsal fins and crisp markings of black and white on their shiny skin. When the orcas dove deep, Amelia could still see them all those fathoms below. And since this was imaginary, she jumped in the water with them. When they all swirled to the surface to breathe, Amelia was close enough to touch an orca. But she didn't. She wanted all orcas, even the ones in her imagination, to stay wild and free.

Instead of touching, she climbed back into the boat. And drank hot choco-late with marshmallows—as much as she wanted, because imaginary cocoa was nutritious. Until she was back in her bed in a fairy-tale castle where a dog's cold, wet nose bumped her hand.

As Louise drifted off with a heavy sigh, Amelia did too.

10

Another delivery

On the day the new furniture was due to arrive, Allison pulled on warm layers and headed for the beach. The winter sun, cutting across the horizon, created a satisfyingly blue sky over the beach's pale sand.

When Ralph's *Lucy Jo* came into view, Allison joined the other islanders gathered at the landing. People from the commune, several farmers, and other neighbors pitched in to help unload and carry furniture up to Allison's house. Sofas and tables into the room with the piano. Comfortable chairs and desks into the other room off the entry. Two recliners into the television room. Bedroom furniture upstairs. A rolling birdcage into the sunroom.

The work of unloading lasted until lunchtime, when Allison and her aunts served sandwiches they'd already prepared. After everyone returned to their own homes, the humming house fell quiet again.

Allison tucked her exhausted aunts into their new recliners and placed the television remote within reach. She transferred Miss Kitty and Marshal Matt Dillon to their rolling home. Using a tape measure, she verified the new furniture was positioned exactly where she wanted it.

Then she scrubbed floors and vacuumed rugs. Tidied the kitchen and ran the dishwasher. Disinfected the bathrooms, wiped the switch plates, ran a clean towel across the smudged walls. Washed two loads of laundry. Swept the entrance areas.

Finally, it felt like her own house again. For the first time since the aunts had arrived, her home felt balanced. Two aunts, two dogs, two birds.

She peeked into the television room. The aunts were sound asleep, the dogs snoozing around them. She pulled on her boots and a warm vest and headed for the beach.

The hydrophone gong sounded as she walked. She scanned the horizon, climbed to the top of a boulder, and waited.

There. A pod of four orcas traveling parallel to shore. Rhythmically emerging in sync, breathing nearly as one. When the orcas dove deep, Allison pulled out her phone and listened until their songs grew distant.

The sun was setting when Ralph pushed *Lucy Jo* onto the beach again. Two deliveries in one day! Allison climbed down the rocks and walked toward the landing.

Ralph—the same Ralph who claimed he didn't get paid to provide passenger service—helped someone off his boat. The passenger wore a puffy coat over leggings striped with green and yellow. On her head sat a wildly knitted cap with loose strings coming off at all angles. When the woman stood on tiptoe to whisper in Ralph's ear, he chuckled.

Look at that. Ralph had gotten himself a girlfriend. She seemed kind of familiar, though.

"Allison!" Ralph waved and pointed at the woman. "Want me to carry this delivery up to your house too?"

Why on earth would Ralph do that?

"I'm here, Allison!" The woman wiggled with excitement. "Let the party begin!"

Recognition brought a sinking feeling. Allison walked closer.

Aunt Shasta smooched Ralph on one whiskered cheek and batted long, false eyelashes at him. "You've been fabulous. Fabu-*lo-so*."

She pulled a yellow hat out of a bag—a foam hat in the shape of a cheese wedge, no doubt purchased on Allison's credit card—and popped it onto Ralph's head. Then she turned her attention to Allison.

"And you, chickee, look absolutely stunning."

If Allison's mom were here, she'd be crying tears of joy. She'd be warm, generous, hospitable. She'd send Allison a familiar look.

You can do anything if you put your mind to it.

Smiling, Allison leaned into the arms reaching for her. "Aunt Shasta! Welcome to Wren Island."

II

Splash landing

Sitting at a desk generously purchased by her niece, Macy scrolled through an online shopping site. Through the open window, a light breeze, scented with the season's first blooms of heather, drifted into the quiet house.

Once her sister Shasta had arrived on Wren Island, winter's frigid hold immediately loosened to allow spring. A fitting welcome for twirling, carefree Shasta Jenkins, who was probably flirting with Ralph right now.

As for Allison, she was out again, disappeared to wherever she went afternoons now. Melia and Louise were dots walking on the beach. Macy patted Lokita on her lap and returned her attention to shopping.

Beachworthy sandals for Melia—that's what she was after today. Size 10 wide. Canvas, not leather, so they could get wet. Thick soles, arch support, covered toes. Poor Melia. She'd always been clumsy, and now she stubbed her toes even more.

Macy studied the options and found shoes that were returnable if Melia didn't like them. She pulled out Allison's credit card, completed the purchase, and tucked the card away for safekeeping. Wouldn't want to be careless with Allison's money. Their niece was really something, wasn't she? So exceptionally accommodating. Even giving them a credit card so they didn't have to ask for money.

Shasta had purchased more than Macy and Melia put together. Framed movie posters for the television room. An outdoor popcorn maker. A rolling drinks cart for the upper level.

Not that they ever put anything alcoholic on the cart. Talk about being exceptionally accommodating. *Everyone* had been supportive of Macy about that.

All of it added up to the biggest sense of relief she'd ever known. Relief she and Melia knew where they belonged now, because Allison cared enough to take them in. Relief Shasta had finally arrived from halfway around the world—even if Shasta might decide, as she often did, to not stick around.

Mostly, Macy felt relief she need never fear living alone again. Any recovering alcoholic would agree too much solitary time could be unhealthy. Here on Wren Island, she was surrounded by people who knew not to leave a stray bottle of wine in the pantry.

Of course she'd initially been appalled when Shasta asked, right away, if Macy had been attending regular Alcoholics Anonymous meetings. The first question out of Shasta's mouth! And Macy *had* been attending AA meetings. Not in person—Wren Island was too small and unpopulated—but online.

She'd balked when Shasta insisted Macy tell Allison everything. The loss of her driver's license, job, and marriage. Shasta showing up unannounced one night, seeing the worst, then hauling her angry, bleary-eyed sister into rehab.

Macy realized she was hunching and sat up taller at her desk. It had felt satisfying to report she'd been sober for two years, five months, and nine days—especially remarkable given that Melia had been diagnosed with macular degeneration the same week Macy was released. They'd limped along for a while—Shasta off to Australia by then. Was it any wonder that when Allison came into money and bought this big house, it had seemed their only solid hope might be found on Wren Island?

Allison agreed they were meant to be on Wren. All of them. If Anne could see her daughter today, she'd be so proud.

Pulling out her cell phone and texting Allison about Melia's new sandals, Macy kept it short.

SANDALS CHECK

Minimal words. All caps. No punctuation. Why bother with more? Just send the essential info and wait for Allison to reply. Not that Allison was likely to. So far, Allison had disappeared every afternoon this week. Her boat was tied up at the dock, so she was probably on the island. Maybe she turned off her phone. Or maybe she saw Macy Johannson's texts and ignored them. Did Allison ignore everyone's texts?

The online ordering complete, Macy carried Lokita downstairs and tucked the little dog into her kitchen bed. The kitchen felt much more homey now that they kept essentials on the counters instead of hidden behind cupboard doors. Coffee and tea in metal tins. A rack of hanging mugs. The new espresso machine gleaming from one corner. Several loaves of bread—they all liked different kinds—and Melia's breakfast cereals. You didn't notice the crumbs unless you went searching for them—which Allison did, regularly.

The whine of a small airplane in the distance came closer. Much closer. At the sound of a splash, Macy dashed outside.

"Mace!" Shasta waved to her from the beach.

Macy joined her sister as a little white airplane eased up to Allison's dock. The pilot hopped from one float to the dock. Ralph helped tie up.

Shasta threw a kiss in their direction, then turned to Macy, her red hoop earrings swinging. "Ralph's son is visiting."

Macy squinted. Tanned and muscular, the pilot looked like he'd materialized from a magazine. No resemblance at all to hunched, grouchy Ralph Wesson.

"Hey there, ladies!" The pilot pulled off aviator shades and swaggered toward them.

Shasta, in full flirt mode, reached to pat Hack's broad shoulder. "Impressive landing, Hack. Mace, meet Wren Island's newest eligible bachelor. Hack, my sister Mace."

Macy tried not to wince when Hack's handshake nearly crushed her fingers.

"Two knockout girls in one family? Too bad I can't stay longer. I'm headed to Alaska for the summer, piloting for a crew shooting aerials for a television show you'd recognize if I named it—but I won't, because my livelihood depends on keeping secrets." He flashed a twinkle smile at Shasta, longer than what might be considered appropriate.

After Hack sauntered off with Ralph, Macy huffed out the breath she'd been holding. If ever a man was a player, Hack was. *Two knockout girls in one family?* Surely he didn't expect a couple of middle-aged women to fall for a line like that. She turned to her sister. "You already know Hack?"

"Met him earlier today with Ralph." Her starry-eyed sister sighed. "One desirable dude."

Macy's intuition kicked into high alert. "Please tell me you're referring to Ralph, who is much nearer your age."

Shasta laughed. "No, silly. Hack. He's perfect for Allison."

"Oh Shasta, I don't think I like where this is going." Whenever Shasta got involved in someone else's love life, the whole situation went south. With collateral damage. "Don't push romance on Allison right now. She's got a lot on her plate."

Shasta laughed. "All the more reason to help her lighten up."

Lighten up? Macy shook her head. "This is a small island, Shasta. Everyone knows everyone else. If a romance breaks up, things could get awkward for all of us."

"I guess we'll see, won't we?" Shasta twirled off.

Macy trudged back to the house. For as long as she could remember, Shasta had suggested Macy needed to lighten up.

But someone needed to keep a steady head around here. They couldn't all run off to the other side of the world whenever they wanted to. Jump into on-and-off romantic relationships whenever they felt like it.

Macy was still recovering from the time Shasta convinced her to get involved with that postman who collected socks with cats on them. How was Macy to know the man would be offended by socks with dogs? That he'd throw a temper tantrum worthy of a two-year-old, right there on a public park bench?

"No, thank you," Macy said out loud to a fling that might turn sticky for her niece.

At the house, she turned to look back at the beach. Shasta was dancing in the foaming surf, oblivious to any care in the world.

Yes, her sister annoyed her. Both her lighter-hearted sisters did. But really, who was she kidding? Most days, she was mostly annoyed with herself.

12

Nice things to wish for

On the beach, far from the water's edge, Amelia sat in the sand and sorted shells. The long brown shells of razor clams in one pile. Smooth white shells in another. Crab shells and broken bits in a third pile. So far, she hadn't found a whole sand dollar. But finding one was on her list of nice things to wish for.

Virgil Tagaloa's son, fourteen-year-old Jax, said late summer would be the best time for sand dollars. After a string of warm summer days, you might find a whole one in an exceptionally low tide. So there was an optimal chance that this summer she'd be marking off at least one item from her list of nice things to wish for.

Jax knew lots about the Pacific Northwest's natural features, thanks to his dad, who was basically a modern-day mountain man. At the grocery market, Virgil could be all business if needed. But he seemed most comfy outdoors, with binoculars around his neck and hiking shoes on his feet. If Virgil lived in a city, would he leave his long dark hair free or tie it back?

Jax said they'd lived in a city before his mom got so sick she chose taking drugs over having a family, even one as stupendous as him and his dad. On Wren, it had always been just the two of them.

Part of Amelia hoped Allison and Virgil might get together. Wouldn't they be super together? But just because Amelia lost out on romance a lifetime ago during her own spring season, she didn't need to conjure up other romances.

Spring was unfolding *so* slowly here on Wren. In January, the magnolia trees had started to stretch. Then little green tips poked up in the bulb beds around the house. The willow trees softened. Now, fragrant heather blooms buzzed with honeybees. Birds twittered everywhere.

Allison said a pair of bald eagles was nesting in a tree near the water at the east edge of the forest. Amelia was keeping her binoculars handy. Seeing a baby bald eagle take flight for the first time was also on her list of nice things to wish for.

Wonder what Macy would make for dinner tonight. Hope nothing messy. It was altogether disorienting to see Allison walk back into the house all refreshed and happy, then see her face fall at the state of the kitchen. Allison had done so much for all of them, and now it almost seemed like Allison was being crowded out of her own home. The problem was simple to Amelia. They all needed Allison, but Allison didn't need them. *Allison is perfectly capable of taking care of Allison.* That's what Virgil said once. In a tone that indicated he admired her for it.

Up the hill, the gong sounded. There'd be whales singing into the hydrophone. If Amelia owned a cell phone, she'd listen in.

Tucking her shell collection into a fabric bag Macy made with her new sewing machine, Amelia walked toward the house. Every few paces, she stopped to let her cracked ribs catch up with the rest of her. The ribs had healed, but still reminded her to be careful. Stepping around a section of driftwood, she kept her eyes focused on the ground in front of her.

Inside the house's service entrance, she navigated the shoes and bags her sisters left lying around, handy for when needed next, and made her way into the kitchen. She sat at the round table, then reached for a large-print book and flipped on her lighted magnifier—both purchased by Shasta on Allison's credit card.

Shasta joined her. "Let's get you an e-reader, sis. You can make the font as big as you want and adjust the brightness. You can even use it to listen to audiobooks."

More ideas for Shasta to spend Allison's money. Before Amelia could protest, she sneezed. "Are you wearing a new perfume, Shasta?"

"Spell on You." Shasta pulled out a mirror and crunched a short spike of highlighted hair into place. "That's the name of it. Spell on You."

Wiping her nose, Amelia pushed her own soft curls behind her ears and returned to her book. "Thanks for thinking of an e-reader for me. But I don't want Allison to have to buy me e-books."

"You can borrow them from the library." The mirror clicked closed.

Amelia looked up. "I could put library books on an e-reader?"

Shasta pulled out a shiny tube of lipstick and reopened the mirror. "Of course, silly. And let's get you your own cell phone and laptop. Then you could be on social media."

Her own phone? A laptop? Entertain one simple idea of an e-reader for library books and then, whammo, more purchases were bundled in. "I don't want to be on social media."

"You like YouTube," Shasta said around the lipstick application.

"Because I like learning. And YouTube doesn't cost anything. Hey Shasta, does that glittery stuff feel funny on your lips?"

Shasta closed the lipstick and mirror. "Not once you get used to it. YouTube is social media, sort of. You could have your own channel and post videos. All you need is a phone with a decent camera, then you can go around videoing whatever you want. It can all be in large font so you—" Shasta dropped her makeup to the table. "Oh, tiddlywinks! I see another mouse."

"Ack. You get it this time, Shasta." Amelia lifted her feet off the floor while Shasta swept her way to the back door. "Wow! You made that look like the easiest to sweep out yet."

"Practice makes perfect. And we're getting lots of practice around here." Shasta propped the broom in the closet, sat back down next to Amelia, and twiddled with a false eyelash. "Right then and there, that could have been material for your Wren Island video channel."

Amelia laughed. "People don't watch stuff like that. Do they?"

Shasta's sparkling lips blew her a kiss. "With a girl as sweet as Amelia Theodore posting? Sure they would."

13

An entire symphony

Allison ran her hands around the smooth, orange-colored trunk of the arbutus tree on Virgil's front lawn. Five afternoons of peace in a row! They'd been worth missing Ralph's son arrive in a floatplane yesterday and Ed's delivery of firewood from the commune with his Polaris the day before. She heard all about the action from her aunts during dinner anyway, and listening to them describe their afternoons was nearly as entertaining as if she'd been present.

She held the tree and shifted her feet, crunching dried berries and thick green leaves. Closing her eyes, she listened to the wind whisper a melody through the pines. This was why she stopped to visit the arbutus tree each afternoon. Nature, more than anyone else, knew how to write a song.

Inside Virgil's cabin, Allison unpacked her bag and set up her laptop. She turned on the light at her desk, plugged in the electronic keyboard, and waited for everything to connect.

Now she could be thankful for the day Aunt Macy had insisted everyone take a fiber supplement and Aunt Amelia spilled a jug of orange juice and Aunt Shasta propped up three more foam cheeseheads next to the television. (Those cheeseheads were the final straw. This wasn't even football season!) And she could be glad, though still a little embarrassed, about fleeing to the forest for a must-have cry and running into Virgil, who'd done what he always did—asked questions.

She was still surprised she'd blabbed out all her frustrations instead of shutting him down. Even more surprised that Virgil hadn't run away but, being Virgil, had asked more questions. Until, pretty soon, after thinking through things with Virgil—he'd been so *kind* about it all!—she'd felt more optimistic.

Like Virgil pointed out, it wasn't that she didn't love her aunts. She *wanted* to take care of them and share her home with them. But all together and all at once, her aunts could be a little much. (Virgil agreed this was true.) Thanks to more questions from Virgil, she'd figured out what was frustrating her the most.

It wasn't the sticky messes on the kitchen counters or that another aunt popped up every time Allison finally thought she might be alone for a few minutes. She wasn't worrying about the future. Or feeling overwhelmed coordinating her aunts' medical care. No, it wasn't any of that.

What frustrated her most was that she was losing grip on her pursuit to do something important. Live an interesting life. Be someone. Her dream of songwriting was getting lost in all the chaos. She was getting crowded out of her own space.

With all the electronics required for music composition, she couldn't easily sit on a log in the forest and work. Virgil's offer for her to compose in his cabin on the afternoons he and Jax were managing the grocery market was ideal—and generous.

He'd gone a bit over the top in ordering an electronic keyboard so she didn't have to haul hers over. And Jax was as generous, digging a lamp out of the attic and saying he hoped she liked the dragonfly shade. Allison smiled now at how its intricate stained glass contrasted with the rest of the commonsense cabin—and at how optimistic she felt putting money into an account for Jax's future education.

She sat at the keyboard and tapped out a melody. Added in a few chords and a supporting harmonic line. Tried a few words around the melody.

"Dragonfly, if you'd like to try to fly, come along with me to see what's beyond the sky and sea."

Just another ditty.

Poking around in her software, she figured out how to add different orchestral parts on the screen. Look at that. She could write an entire symphony for a complete orchestra. Or could write a movie soundtrack, maybe. Win a Grammy!

She deleted the rinky-dink lyrics. When she tried to add music for a brass section, she stalled. Gee, this felt a little overwhelming, trying to write a soundtrack for an entire orchestra. But if she ever wanted to write an important song, she'd have to come up with better material than a ditty.

When the setting sun angled through the west-facing windows, she saved her work, packed up her laptop, turned off the desk lamp, and closed up the cabin. Walking back to her house, she hummed.

After an afternoon like this, she could handle anything. Another fiber supplement? Bring it on. More spilled orange juice? No problem-o. One more cheesehead in the television room? Go team! Although, if she saw Aunt Shasta sneaking Ralph Wesson out the kitchen door one more morning this week, she might lose it. Seriously! Aunt Shasta and *Ralph*?

If she ever got together with someone again, she sure wasn't going to sneak him around. And next time—if there ever was a next time—she was going to make double-dog sure she was interesting enough.

She could picture it, crystal clear. A formal gathering celebrating her latest musical success. A handsome man fascinated by her, waiting for an introduction to the intriguing woman behind the music. With her busy composing schedule—new songs by Allison Theodore being highly anticipated—she wouldn't have time to fit him in, but eventually he'd win her over with his persistent adoration.

The only problem was she'd have to figure out how to *stay* interesting enough for him.

The next relationship couldn't be allowed to fall apart like when she and Tank returned home from her second in vitro fertilization treatment. Like Tank saying the moment they walked in the door, *Allison, you're not interesting anymore.* As if he were changing brands of breakfast cereal. Just like that, she was alone and uncertain of what, if anything, had made her interesting in the first place.

So far, she hadn't been interesting enough for anyone else. Unless you counted the aunts. And unless you counted Virgil. But just because Virgil had almost kissed her didn't mean he thought she was interesting.

It was just one of those perfect storm kind of things. Virgil coming back to the cabin early because the market's credit machine had run out of tape. The two of them chatting (because Virgil asked questions) and then not chatting (for whatever reason they stopped). Virgil looking at her intently and her thinking *Oh boy, here we go.*

Then Virgil remembered he needed to take red pens back to the market with the machine tape. And thanks to Virgil not making a big deal about the almost-kiss, she was free to keep using the cabin—as long as she skedaddled home before the market closed.

That had been too close of a call, though. Because if anything like that ever *did* happen between her and Virgil, she'd have to find another place to write music. And at the rate things were going at her house, she might as well find another place to live too, if she wanted to keep her sanity. Maybe she could join the commune and leave the house to the aunts.

No, she wouldn't fit in at the commune. Too young.

If she ever did get together with someone again—and the odds of that were dwindling, since even Virgil Tagaloa wasn't interested enough to follow through with a kiss—she wasn't going to sneak the guy around like Aunt Shasta was with Ralph. And she was going to stay interesting enough to keep the guy. She'd be such a famous songwriter he'd never *want* to leave her!

And it definitely wasn't going to be Virgil. The almost-kiss had happened before she'd seen his grocery stockroom. The moment she laid eyes on all that inventory stashed helter-skelter any which way, she'd known she and Virgil could never have a future together.

14

Being extra nice

When he finished sweeping the market's porch, Virgil used the broom to nudge the low basket into place near the door. Depositing the broom in the storage closet inside, he retrieved the bag of assorted toys he'd collected for dogs to gnaw on while visiting the store. Allison's dogs especially. As he tossed the toys one by one into the basket, he heard himself sigh like a lovestruck puppy.

Not only was he out of practice courting a woman, he'd never been genius at it to start with. He could thank mutual friends for introducing him to his ex-wife. Could thank youthful eagerness to shape his future for falling in love fast and never seeing the red flags, never listening to the whispers of instinct. He still believed vows were meant to be kept—even in the worst of times. And despite the worst of times, he'd done everything possible to build a shared life.

Drug addiction doesn't listen to anything but its own voice, though. It buries the truth under misperceptions, twists reality into the unknown, and, on the worst of days, blots out any hint of hope. He would have kept trying to save his wife, though, if their wreck of a marriage was only breaking the two of them.

Picking up the stainless steel bowl that held water for canine visitors, Virgil stepped inside the market, threw the bowl in the dishwasher, and found a clean replacement. One glance at Jax, conscientiously counting the money from the register for a second time, was all the reminder Virgil needed that his son's arrival, a medical miracle due to his mother's drug use, was the best day of Virgil's life. It had added another hard angle, though. Made divorce eventually necessary for Jax's protection.

Virgil dropped his head. For a long time, that necessity felt like a massive failure. What kind of father removes a child from his mother? What kind of man can't lead his family to the other side of dark days?

Now, he recognized guilt had kept him trying to stay in touch with his ex. Until the day he realized she hadn't asked about Jax in years.

Back on the porch, he set the clean bowl of fresh water near the door where dogs expected to find it. Scanning the beach and looking to the horizon, he straightened. Relocating to Wren Island and purchasing the grocery market was the best decision he ever made. And he had to admit, as his eye fell on their docked boat, that he'd had fun sinking his remaining money into the thirty-eight-foot SAFE Full Cabin. He felt no shame in springing for 1,350 horsepower. With little else going the way he'd wanted, he figured he should at least be able to count on his boat's performance. A top speed of sixty knots would do (he'd only gone to fifty-two, once, for eight seconds). Plus foam-reinforced collar with performance wings, black substrate, weather-tight cabin. He'd focused on substance over style for transporting his most precious cargo then, four-year-old Jax.

A neighbor and frequent customer passed by with a wave, and Virgil nodded back with a wide smile. On Wren, surrounded by nature, new friends, and a peaceful environment, he and Jax thrived almost immediately and continued to do so. Thanks to Virgil's experience as a grocery manager and helpful advice from friends, the market usually ran at a small profit.

At first, he told himself he was being extra nice to Allison Theodore because she was a newcomer to Wren Island. That during the renovation of her house, when she'd come into the market to order supplies, it was basic business know-how that he notice what she was wearing. Skinny jeans and an athletic pullover, or a short dress and flipflops, or a yellow puffer jacket and yoga pants. But what was his excuse for noticing how she'd push curls away from her face and glance around the market, pretty brown eyes sparkling, like every visit was her first? Maybe, if he'd really been focused on business, he would've acted on her comments about how difficult it must be to keep track of all the inventory, not to mention expiration dates. Answered her questions about his system for tracking stock levels. When he laughed off those topics, she looked confused and maybe disappointed.

Also at first, he thought she was riddled with nervous habits. Standing at the cash register, she'd straighten the card reader. Click ballpoint pens closed. Wipe a smudge off the glass showcase of muffins. Brush crumbs into the trash. Just when he was about to put his foot down—enough with the fidgeting already!—he realized she fidgeted whenever they were talking about an area of life she felt she was losing grip on. The house renovations. Her songwriting efforts. The privacy she obviously valued.

She fought so hard to appear composed and independent. Put together, capable, self-sufficient. Plus, she was more gorgeous than he'd ever dared to imagine any woman could be.

But no one can be entirely independent, right? No one needs no one. Yet there she'd be, brilliantly beautiful, fighting hard to remain emotionally distant. Revealing a glimmer of vulnerability, then bringing down the curtain again over those pretty eyes. All while a friend was standing right there willing to help.

It was one of the most fascinating things he'd ever witnessed.

He'd figured Allison Theodore, recent heiress of millions, would lose interest in living on an island in the middle of nowhere. When her aunts arrived, he thought for sure they'd all pack up and move to the city. Instead, they hunkered down. Which was fantastic, of course, because Wren Island was the best place in the world to be. Also fantastic because he got to keep seeing Allison Theodore. But the island was too small to give her space if their relationship got bumpy.

Relationship? See how easily he got ahead of himself? Somewhere in there he realized he loved Allison Theodore. When he saw how she cared for her aunts, maybe. Or even earlier, when she brought home shelter dogs no one else wanted.

Hidden under all her fidgeting and uncertainty is a kind, extraordinarily embracing heart. Now, whatever Allison cares about is on his radar too. Whoever

Allison welcomes he's glad to see. And anything that challenges her challenges him.

Like the day Allison mentioned she'd stopped the renovation crew from chopping down a tree. The big old walnut on the corner where her driveway met the road. How could he not admire a woman who'd stand up to a foreman about whether an incoming tower crane needed more room? A woman who'd insist they work around the tree and not so much as bump into it with a wheelbarrow if they wanted to keep their jobs?

She still thought she'd won that argument. But she might not have if the construction crew hadn't gathered around tables in the market's café at the end of their workday, eating sandwiches, drinking beer, talking about chopping down the tree early the next morning, before Allison knew it was happening.

The look Ralph Wesson sent Virgil from where he sat nearby, drinking a Pepsi and eating pistachios, indicated he'd heard and didn't like it any more than Virgil.

It took every ounce of restraint Virgil could muster to only step up to refill their drinks and quietly ask, "You guys talking about that walnut on the edge of the Theodore property?"

"Yes sirree."

He'd locked eyes with the foreman. "Nowhere near a good idea to take it down."

The foreman had laughed. "You got a sacred attachment to that tree?"

People often make that mistake about Virgil Tagaloa, because of the color of his skin, the shape of his eyes, and his wildish hair. Plus he was defending a tree. It wasn't surprising he was stereotyped, though his ancestors weren't native to the Pacific Northwest. They came from a tiny island in the South Pacific. And Chicago.

Having stopped by for a snack and a snooze near the market's entrance, Allison's dog Louise picked up on the change in atmosphere, sat up, and fixed the foreman in one of her signature stare-downs. Virgil could've hugged Louise right at that moment—and he did later.

Virgil could've hugged Ralph too, for what he muttered from his seat across the room, loud enough for the crew to hear. "Taking out that tree would be a mistake. Big mistake." Ralph was handy to have around when the chips were down.

That foreman hadn't known Ralph's reputation or wouldn't have asked "What's that, gramps?" The low growl Louise let out when the foreman started to laugh again had surprised the man. Virgil too. He'd never heard her do anything like that before. But there she was that day, growling on cue. The dog no one but Allison had wanted, saving the day.

As far as Virgil knew, Allison never learned about the thwarted plan and still believed what he and Ralph said when she asked why they seemed to be keeping watch on the tree. They thought it was home to nesting wrens. It helped their credibility when the excuse they came up with on the fly turned out to be true.

Would Allison ever find out the walnut was still standing thanks to Ralph and Louise and Virgil? Probably not. That was okay. Allison Theodore wanted to feel like she was taking care of everything herself. Virgil wanted Allison Theodore to be happy.

He finally understood what his mom tried to drill into him years ago about true love. *It's when you love her for her, not for you. If you'll still love her even if she never loves you back, that's true love.*

For the first time in his life, he loves a woman for her, not for him. If Allison Theodore never loves him back, he'll still love her. He knows that right down to his core.

She's smart, beautiful, capable, and resourceful. Everyone stands taller around her. Feels more optimistic. Breathes deeper. Feels more connected. She brings that out.

She. Is. Incredible.

Moving at the speed he was the day he almost kissed her would've been a big mistake, though. Eventually she'd have brought the curtain down again. Shut him out, maybe forever, afraid to be vulnerable. Allison needed to see him that way on her own time. To feel like their forward movement was within her grasp.

Would he be okay with just being friends? If that's what she wanted, he would. That didn't mean he wasn't hoping for more. In addition to world peace and becoming a better man, he was praying for opportunities to show Allison Theodore she could trust Virgil Tagaloa. If the answers to his prayers included another opportunity for a kiss, even better.

15

Marching orders

Macy pulled another decorative pillow from the clothes dryer. She'd had to scrunch the pillows in, but they tumbled out easily now. After checking each seam, she punched down the stuffing. The pillows had definitely shrunk. But what did it matter if an eighteen-inch pillow was now sixteenish inches? Eventually it'd get smashed by a rear end.

Carrying the stack of pillows, she teetered to the television room, where she found her sisters lazing on the upholstered sectional, dogs nestled around them. Like bumps on a log.

"Shasta, remove your feet from the coffee table. Melia, please turn off the television. Allison's out again this afternoon, and we all know what that means. I'm in charge."

"Well, aren't you the hoity-toity-froity-poo?" Shasta slid her feet off the table.

"We're supposed to be caretakers of this house, not freeloaders. Shasta, I want you to clean the bathrooms. Melia, I want you to—"

"Why do I have to clean the bathrooms?" Shasta scrutinized painted fingernails, fire engine red today. "We should hire help. It's not like Allison doesn't have money to spare."

"We *are* the help, sister."

Shasta mumbled to little Lokita in her lap.

Macy tapped her foot. "Would you care to share your comment with the rest of us?"

"All I said is people advertise for caretakers if they want them. They don't just let any garden-variety people who show up uninvited."

"*Garden-variety* people? We're family!"

"Un-wad your panties, Mace."

Standing, Melia yawned and stretched. "I thought Allison left Louise in charge."

"Be reasonable, Melia. Allison *said* Louise was in charge. But everyone knows a dog can't be the boss. Louise, move! You're blocking the exit."

The dog didn't budge. Macy shuffled her sisters around Louise, out of the room, and into action. "Whatever you do, Shasta, don't let on that Ralph is staying over nights. Makes no difference to me now that we each have our own bedrooms. But Allison seems about ready to flip. Finding out Ralph sleeps in your bedroom might send her over the edge, if you know what I mean."

Shasta twirled, counting out a few dance moves. "I think she already knows."

Macy pointed down the hall. "Bathroom duty, Shasta. Melia, you're vacuuming. Make sure you get all the corners. Okay, then. We've got our marching orders."

Melia tapped Macy's arm. "What are you going to clean?"

"Windows. All those little panes at the front of the house." Macy shooed off her sisters and collected towels and cleaning solution.

She started in the big room off the entry. The room with the piano nobody played. Should she drop hints about not letting hard-earned skills go to waste? Anne hadn't enrolled her daughter in piano lessons just so Allison could ignore a Steinway grand.

A wall of windows faced south. Two more tall sections of windows flanked the fireplace. It all added up to a lot of windows, but Macy had said she'd do windows, so she'd do windows.

She pulled a ladder from the garage and set it up. It reached halfway up the wall. Once she'd climbed up, she was in front of a million little panes of glass.

Breakable glass. Maybe this wasn't such a smart idea. Maybe she should settle for cleaning the panes she could reach from the floor. She climbed down.

Without a ladder, she could reach five rows of panes. And those were the rows you looked through anyway, right? After all, she was a free caretaker, not a paid one. She got to work. Scrubbing, scrubbing. Taking care of Allison's house.

Right away, a pane cracked. Just cracked all on its own for no good reason at all!

Maybe that pane had already been loose. Maybe it had been ready to go as soon as the next person touched it, and the person happened to be her. So now there was a visible line through the pane. The window was still in place. So it wasn't all that bad, right? One cracked pane was hardly noticeable. She went on scrubbing the others.

When the second pane cracked, she almost didn't notice, because Melia was roaring the vacuum cleaner around upstairs. Honestly! Was there a racetrack for vacuum cleaners up there?

Macy touched the second cracked pane. At least this one was located in a corner. Less noticeable. She fingered the towel in her hand. Was it not soft enough? Was her cleaning solution wrong? She'd cleaned a lot of windows in her lifetime, and none of them had cracked. Why were these so touchy?

Allison wasn't going to be happy about the broken panes. Not at all.

What if Allison regretted asking her aunts to stay? What if Allison decided Melia could stay but Macy's help wasn't needed anymore?

Macy continued cleaning, careful to not press too hard.

The racetrack for vacuum cleaners came nearer as Melia circled toward her. Macy wiped a few more panes, gently, but another pane cracked. Three cracked panes! The vacuum quieted.

"Uh-oh, Macy. Were those always broken?"

Macy turned to see Melia staring wide-eyed at the windows.

Bouncing down the stairs, Shasta skidded to a stop. "Yikes, Mace."

"I didn't mean to break them." Macy heard the panic rising in her voice. "They must have been weak. All the others are fine."

Shasta came closer and inspected, running a manicured finger along the cracks. "It's because you're so tense, Mace. Glass is no match for your ferocity."

Ferocity. That was a new one. Jitters, tremors, ruthlessness, nervousness, atrocity, monstrosity. She'd heard all of those before, from Shasta or one of a dozen other people she'd hurt. But ferocity was new. She swallowed. "Maybe Allison won't notice."

Shasta tapped a cracked pane. "You'll have to tell her what you've done."

The sound of the service door squeaking open reached them.

"She's home," Melia whispered.

"Hey, everybody!" Allison popped into the entry and nodded at the vacuum, then the sudsy bucket and rags. "We're cleaning! Woo-hoo!"

Slowly, Melia and Shasta parted from Macy.

Allison, sweetheart that she was, looked refreshed and optimistic—until she saw the cracked panes. Expressions crossed her face like a bad movie Macy couldn't unsee.

Disbelief first. Then disappointment.

A hint of anger.

Finally, worst of all, an expression Macy had never seen on her niece's face. Would have given anything never to see.

Crushing overwhelm.

16

Learn to be okay

Before the sun was up, Allison pulled on her favorite vest—bright yellow with extra pockets in front—and an orange hat Aunt Shasta had knitted for her. She called Louise and snapped the leash on Lokita. In the rising light, she walked through the dune grass to the beach, where Louise took off, scattering seagulls. Lokita, tugging on the leash in excitement, sniffed through clumps of drying seaweed.

Farther down the beach, Allison stopped and looked back at her magnificent home. Purchasing the house and property had felt like the right thing to do partly because she'd known her mom would have loved it. And if Mom were here, she'd be sharing the home with her sisters.

Safe, loved, and welcome, her aunts were thriving on Wren.

Why wasn't Allison Theodore thriving? Why did every day bring more of a sense she was hurtling closer to losing control, shattering apart, fractionalizing like the glass panes Aunt Macy tried to clean yesterday?

Was *fractionalizing* a word? Back in the day, which wasn't all that long ago, even though it felt like a lifetime ago, Allison could have discussed that question with herself over a bowl of ramen noodles. Asked the dogs for their opinions. Looked up the answer online and relayed it to the dogs.

When she'd first settled on Wren, she had thrived. The house renovations had been all-consuming, like putting together a complicated puzzle. And when the work was complete, she'd created a grand home.

How empty it had felt, though! A few pieces of furniture. A kitchen with just the basics. No espresso machine, motorized recliners, framed movie prints. No Miss Kitty and Marshal Matt Dillon.

Allison didn't miss that emptiness. But she did miss her independence. The sense of being an individual—just her, Allison Theodore—instead of the helper everyone needed for material problems.

These days, she was getting lost in all the clutter. Yes, that's exactly what it felt like. Like she was fractionalizing into nothingness.

Calling Louise, she collected Lokita. From this distance, the broken windowpanes weren't noticeable. The leaded, iron-framed windows—original to the house—had survived renovations and who knows how many storms. But they couldn't survive Aunt Macy.

Oh well. One could either laugh or cry about it. Allison breathed around a square. One, two, three, four. If the panes weren't replaceable, she'd leave them in place and learn to be okay with it.

About the state of her kitchen, however, it was time to take a stand. Clutter everywhere. Crumbs left on the counters. Drip marks across the floors. At this rate, they were going to end up with an ant problem. (Or would it be an *aunt* problem? Ha!) Plus, she could never find anything, because nothing was ever where it was supposed to be.

She'd implement the solution she came up with last week. Labeled storage containers. Labeled shelves too. First in the kitchen, then near the service entrance. It was all happening as soon as Ralph delivered her next shipment of supplies—label maker included.

After Ralph arrived later that morning, with three wheelbarrows of deliveries plus Hack, the aunts sorted through packages. Allison headed to the garage to rearrange tools. Whenever Hack was around, the room temperature seemed to go up several degrees. (Good thing *he* wasn't staying long on Wren.) When the guys finally left, each aunt disappeared upstairs with her own deliveries, and Allison went to work organizing the kitchen.

Cereal, rice, and beans went into clear, airtight containers, all labeled. Same with the other dry goods. Aunt Macy's gazillion cake and brownie mixes took up an entire shelf, so Allison tapped out *Baking Mixes* and attached the label to the shelf. Another cupboard held a lifetime supply of instant coffee packets. When were they going to drink instant coffee, now that they were using an espresso machine? She tapped out *Instant Coffee* and tucked the container into the cabinet with the powdered fiber supplements Aunt Macy sometimes added to her smoothies.

When Allison finished, the aunts were still upstairs. Whatever they'd gotten delivered must be keeping their attention. Wonderful.

Eyeing Aunt Macy's newest appliance, now neatly stored on the shelf labeled *Pressure Cooker* in the butler's pantry, Allison remembered Jax once mentioned it was possible to bake a cake in one. She set her laptop on the kitchen counter—pristine now that it was clear of the usual clutter and crumbs—and scrolled through recipes.

Forty-five minutes later, a dense round of brownies was cooling on a rack. After cleaning the pressure cooker and other utensils, Allison returned everything to their labeled places. She sprinkled powdered sugar across the cooled brownies and transferred the dessert to a vintage plate her mother had treasured. Easy-peasy, and she might have time for a few minutes of undisturbed peace.

She was enjoying a latte when her aunts clomped into the kitchen.

"Say something, Allison." Aunt Amelia held up a cell phone.

"Are you recording?" Allison waved at the camera. "Hi, Aunt Amelia!"

"Shasta helped me buy a cell phone." Aunt Amelia sank into a chair next to Allison and looked around, disoriented. "Where did everything go?"

"Now *this* is a kitchen!" Aunt Macy was already poking through cabinets. "Matching containers. Everything clearly labeled. We look like professionals!"

Allison stood and joined her aunt. "Can we try to keep it this way?"

"Of course I'll keep it this way." Aunt Macy beamed. "You'd better keep this kitchen neat and clean too, Shasta. And if Ralph gets himself coffee, he'd better clean up after himself. Melia, it's understandable if you make a mess and need our help."

Straightening the basket of cloth lunch napkins Aunt Macy had bumped, Allison glanced at Aunt Amelia, who was staring at her phone screen. Was Aunt Amelia listening to the conversation? Was she okay with her sister relegating her to near helplessness?

"Mace." Aunt Shasta leaned against the counter. "It's not fair for Amelia to be the exception. Allison's got this kitchen set up so nicely none of us have any excuses. Amelia, you're going to clean up after yourself like the rest of us do, right? Whoever drops the crumbs cleans up the crumbs. Same goes for drips. Use your magnifier and headlamp."

Aunt Amelia held her phone up, ready to record. "Say it all again, Shasta."

Aunt Shasta repeated the instructions while Aunt Amelia recorded.

"Got it." Aunt Amelia's voice took on a reporter's tone. "And with fewer crumbs, we might have fewer *uninvited* kitchen guests, large or small, *if* you know what I'm getting at." Beaming, she tapped the phone and tucked it away. "Can we eat this chocolate cake now?"

"It's a brownie I made in the pressure cooker." Allison pulled little plates from the shelf labeled *Little Plates*. "With a secret ingredient."

"Mm-mmm." Aunt Amelia smiled around her first bite, then took another. "It tastes buzzy."

"Buzzy?" Aunt Macy sniffed a brownie and narrowed her eyes. "You didn't put liqueur in these, did you?"

"Of course not." Allison reached for Aunt Macy's arm. "Keep guessing."

Aunt Shasta's bracelets clinked as she raised one hand. "Winning answer right here. Coffee."

"Right! I also found a recipe that uses instant coffee in frosting. Next time I make these brownies, I'll frost them."

"Wow!" Aunt Amelia pulled out her phone and began recording again. "So what we have here, folks, is a new idea for all you who love using a pressure cooker. Allison's buzzy brownies—a phenomenon sure to sweep the country. Stay tuned for the frosted version in a future episode."

Savoring a bit of the rich dessert, Allison closed her eyes. She could do this. Life with her aunts. For as long as they needed her. You could do anything if you put your mind to it.

17

Listening

The next day, Allison followed the ascending forest trail toward one of her favorite overlooks. When Lokita grew tired, Allison picked her up and carried her, calling Louise to stay close. Trails could end abruptly at a cliff. If you weren't paying attention, you'd go right off the edge.

Was there any music more lyrical than a symphony of songbirds on a spring morning? And it all happened naturally—no software or electronics required.

Allison walked across soft beds of fallen pine needles as the trail, narrow and shadowy under the trees, opened into a sunlit clearing. When Allison veered east toward the ledge with the best view, Louise ran ahead—right toward the cliff. "Louise!"

The dog circled back. Allison set the wiggling Lokita on the ground, checked the leash was clipped, and guided both dogs through the remaining steps.

Allison sat on a log, Lokita climbed into her lap, Louise sprawled in the sunshine. In the distance, the snowcapped Olympic Mountains gleamed. Dozens of islands dotted the Salish Sea. North of Reclamation Island, a freighter traveled west. A cruise ship cut a path across the strait, toward Seattle.

"I should come here more often," Allison said out loud, not that anyone but the dogs could hear. "Get away from the chaos at the house."

She shifted on the log, petting Lokita. "There's one thing I don't understand. Well, I don't understand lots of things. But here's one. How do you break three windowpanes in one afternoon? Don't you reevaluate your technique after the first break?"

Sighing, Allison petted Louise when she, too, drew close. "What do you guys think of the *stuff* everywhere now? Shoes and bags strewn around every entry. It complicates navigation for you especially, Lokita. And all those arcade games! If Aunt Shasta orders one more—"

"Shasta's ordering arcade games? As in Pac-Man?"

Allison startled but knew the voice without turning to look. Virgil.

"Sorry," he said. "I'm probably disturbing you."

She glanced at him and sighed. "Disturbance is a regular occurrence in my life now."

Looping his binoculars around his neck, he dropped his head and stepped back. "I was watching a barred owl snooze when I heard your voice."

Watching an owl snooze? Talk about being easily entertained. To judge from the clean scent that reached her, the plaid flannel shirt he wore was freshly washed. Or maybe the scent was shampoo lingering in all that hair. She waved for him to sit on the log—but not close to her. No need to risk another almost-kiss. Not that Virgil would be interested.

Louise moved to lean against him. Allison played with Lokita's ears. "I was talking to the dogs."

Virgil scratched Louise's back. "Mind if I listen in?"

Allison sighed again. "So far, we have full-size arcade versions of Pac-Man, Donkey Kong, and Frogger in the garage. Aunt Shasta's talking about ordering a disco ball too. You should have seen her eyes light up when I suggested—joking, mind you—she build a brick oven out there for pizza."

Virgil laughed—long enough to make her laugh too. The situation *was* kind of funny. Viewed from a distance. With someone next to you casting a different perspective.

When Virgil reached for Lokita, Allison handed over the little dog. "I feel like I'm on the edge, Virgil. Right on the edge of losing my mind. The worst of it is, I feel like I'm disappearing."

Virgil petted Lokita. "How so?"

Allison twisted a long strand of grass. "Before the aunts came, I knew what I was about every day. I'd get up in the morning and start checking things off my to-do list. The dogs would be fed at regular times. The house would stay clean. I knew where everything was. Now? It all feels jumbled."

"And that makes you feel like you're disappearing?"

She thought for a moment. Virgil was being Virgil again, asking lots of questions. But his questions usually helped her figure things out.

"Maybe I feel this way because I'm running around, busy, but not doing what I really want to."

"Which is?"

"Write music. A song that matters. Pursue *my* dream instead of helping everyone else with their problems. I don't mind taking care of my aunts. I love that they live with me. But I'm not getting any songs written except the bits I do at your place. I'm grateful to use your cabin, but even when I'm alone there, I'm not in my own space. I don't feel like I'm able to just be me."

The sun inched higher, scattering the ocean's surface with glitter. A distant sailboat left a hint of a widening wake. The silence stretched. Maybe Virgil was thinking up more questions.

Or was he desperately searching for an escape from a boring conversation?

"You know what might help." Virgil stretched his legs, in no hurry to leave. "Get away by yourself for a while. Really get away. Not here on Wren. Maybe take your boat somewhere."

She twiddled the dry grass. "Overnight?"

"Why not?"

Valid question, genius suggestion. In twenty-four inspired, uninterrupted hours, she'd be free to write a dozen songs. A hundred songs if entirely undisturbed for one week.

She sat straighter. "Where's the rule that says I can't go off on my own for a while? I'd have everything I need on my boat." She sagged. "But what if my aunts need me?"

Virgil repositioned his ball cap. You'd think he'd give up trying to stuff all that wonderful hair under a hat.

"Wren Islanders will look out for your aunts. Jax and I will stop by regularly. We'll help them install a new soda machine and a Whac-A-Mole game in the garage."

Allison burst out laughing. Imagine Virgil Tagaloa in cahoots with her aunts!

"And there's no rule that says you can't."

What a look Virgil was giving her! Like he'd seen inside her and was celebrating her. Like he found her to be enough. *More* than enough.

Had anyone ever looked at her that way before?

No matter. Leaning into a look like that would end in pain far too familiar. Desertion. Rejection. Another monumental effort to start over again on her own. This time by building even more fortified walls. And she didn't have the strength to do all that again.

She scrambled to her feet, collected the dogs, and waited until she was several yards down the trail before calling over her shoulder.

"I'll think about it. Thanks for everything, Virgil."

18

Best-case scenario

Well, that conversation didn't go anywhere near how it seemed it might. Virgil pulled off his ball cap. Ran his fingers through his hair and tugged out a few tangles. Did what he could to reposition the ball cap, then drummed his fingers on tree bark.

Allison had laughed at his offhand joke about the soda machine and Whac-A-Mole game. How thrilling to come up with a line to make her sparkle!

Why didn't his comment about there being no rule get a laugh too? He'd thought it would, since she was so preoccupied with doing things right. Instead, presto chango, she was off and running like a scared rabbit.

He readjusted his cap, then tapped his fingers on the bark again. Allison liked talking about rules. So why had that comment changed everything?

And how could the most fascinating person he knew feel like she was disappearing?

She did acquire her aunts, and a much more complicated life, overnight. In addition to a convocation of eagles, a parliament of owls, a charm of finches, and a gaze of raccoons, Wren Island was now home to a hodgepodge of aunts, who often acted like a bunch of kids. And Allison helped her aunts feel they were spectacularly special in every way, which they were.

Would Allison Theodore ever think of Virgil Tagaloa as spectacularly special? Could she ever love Jax like family?

There he went again, hoping for something in return for loving her.

Best-case scenario at this point, he and Allison would become better friends. He was already her friend who sometimes asked helpful questions and sometimes came up with a line to make her laugh. Also, he was the market owner who could order any supplies she might need for herself, her aunts, her dogs, or her property. And he could put a rush delivery on them so she didn't have to wait longer than necessary. Every once in a while, he could help in ways she didn't know about—like saving a beloved tree, bathing her muddy dog, stocking up on hard-to-get supplies.

So, actually, he was living the best-case scenario already. Virgil Tagaloa, friend of Allison Theodore. Around if needed. Ready to help. Available for conversations here and there, like any friend would be.

Yep, best-case scenario, already happening.

He would've liked to punch or kick something, but he didn't want to hurt anything—even a tree. Because who knew? Maybe trees felt pain too.

Standing, he looked over the log he and Allison had sat on a minute ago, close enough to touch each other if they'd both wanted to. He'd read that water and nutrients continue to pulse through a fallen tree until the log eventually decomposes and becomes part of the forest floor. The fallen tree might even sustain a new tree. This tree fell two winters ago and was well on its way to forgetting pain.

He kicked at the decayed bark until the log's smooth interior revealed itself. Instantly dismayed, he ran his hands over the fresh wound, hoping his touch might ease the pain. He let his hand linger, because maybe that did help the tree feel better.

Then he headed back down the trail to the market, where everyone knew Virgil Tagaloa would be reliably helpful and friendly. Available when needed, out of the way when not.

19

Ideal departure time

Early the next morning, Allison gathered supplies for a few nights alone on
Buttercup, then checked the weather forecast and tide tables. If she wanted
to travel with the currents, now was an ideal departure time. *Come on, aunts.*
Upsy-daisy so I can say goodbye.

Finally, she grabbed a pen and a sheet of paper and wrote a note.

Headed out for fun and supplies. Planning to stay a few nights on my cruiser.
Will text and email when I can, but don't worry if you don't hear from me.

She underlined the last part so Aunt Macy wouldn't be tempted to send out
a search party. After signing off with a few *x*'s and *o*'s, Allison tucked the note
under a plate of frosted brownies on the kitchen counter.

Then, like a teenager dodging curfew, she slipped out of the house. Louise
started to come along, saw the inky blackness outside, and changed her mind.

"You're in charge while I'm gone," Allison whispered.

On the beach, she nearly whooped. Freedom! No aunts, no dogs, no messes.
As she eased her boat away from Wren, a bald eagle called to its mate. One day
soon, she and Aunt Amelia would watch the fledgling take its first flight.

The sky was lightening to blue as she entered the strait. Calm water this
morning, and the current pushing her. Wonderful. She cruised along, blasting

top hits from a radio station in Canada, letting *Buttercup* carve the water in a graceful dance.

Nearing Reclamation Island, Allison opened the marina's booking app and requested a guest slip with port tie. Helpful for loading supplies, should she purchase any, which she didn't plan to do. She eased into the assigned slip and tied up.

Look how simple life had become. No dogs to strap in and out of life jackets. No Louise insisting on an ice cream cone. This time, maybe she'd buy herself an ice cream.

In town, the pub was humming with the breakfast crowd. The door to the tea shop next door was open. Classical music spilled out to the boardwalk. Allison stepped inside.

Neat white shelves housed colorful skeins of yarn. Pale blue walls met a warm, wide-planked wood floor. A grand piano, much like the one at her house, filled one corner. The entire shop smelled of herbs and spices.

Allison breathed deep, walked forward, and sat at the counter next to a frail-looking older woman. Two women working behind the counter sorted loose tea into glass jars. They were using a label maker!

"Hello, Allison." A woman behind the counter greeted Allison with a smile. "I'm Gemma Campana. We met when you first visited Reclamation Island."

Gemma motioned to the young woman working with her. "This is Stef, and next to you is Violet. What can I get you this morning?"

Allison chose a chai latte and settled in for a chat. Why hadn't she thought of doing this before? Getting away, all on her own, was exactly what she needed.

When she'd finished her latte, she said goodbye and headed outside. On the boardwalk, she stopped to admire a sparkly pink scooter.

"It's a ton of fun." Gemma joined her, watering the potted flowers.

Allison smiled. "Is it yours?"

"It is. My husband and I both ride scooters between town and our house on Wail Point. Have you ever ridden?"

"Yes, and I've actually thought about getting a scooter." Allison shook her head. "But the roads on Wren are mostly dirt and gravel. A scooter would never hold up."

Gemma set down her watering can. "You need an off-road motorbike. I've got one at the house I'm not using. Have you got a way to get it back to Wren? You could borrow it."

Allison looked toward the marina. With *Buttercup* moored on the port side, it'd be a simple matter of rolling the bike on deck.

But she couldn't borrow a motorbike from a person she hardly knew. Or could she?

Islanders often banded together to share resources. And borrowing a motorbike from Gemma would be a lot simpler than waiting for Ralph to deliver a new one.

"How about I rent it from you?"

"Sure. Come back to the house with me and try it. If you like it, you can take it back to Wren and have fun with it."

Allison did like it. She knew that as soon as she roared out of Gemma's driveway and circled back through a forest trail. And the bike was a one-seater, so there was no room for anyone else to tag along. Room for independent Allison Theodore only.

Gemma walked her to the dock, helped tie down the bike, then turned to her. "Safety first, sister. Keep your eyes open. Wide trail? You're good to go. But if the trail narrows, slow down. These island trails can end all at once."

Allison nodded. Like the forest trails on Wren that dropped off into nothing.

"Narrow trail, slow down. Got it."

20

Smiling ladybugs

Spring sunshine streamed through the bedroom windows as Amelia tucked her bathrobe and slippers into the closet. The room's pink walls glowed. She'd always wanted a pink bedroom. Now, thanks to Allison, she had one. And her own bathroom. And her own fireplace. Her sisters had the rooms they wanted too. Allison's house was that magnificent.

Amelia's pink walls were accented with hand-painted bird tracks, large and small. An occasional feather, painted black, white, brown, blue, red. Amelia touched a tiny mottled feather that seemed to be drifting to the floor. One of these days, the baby bald eagle living on Allison's property would take flight.

Did a baby bird know how to fly automatically? It would be awful if it had to fall first before learning.

Amelia pulled on stretchy pants and a soft cotton shirt. She layered a zippered coat over the top, then stood in front of the full-length mirror. Did these pink and yellow clothes go together okay? Only one pattern, so she was okay there. Shasta would say she needed bling. Amelia dug through her bathroom drawers and found a headband with smiling ladybugs on it, plenty bling.

Downstairs, she fed Miss Kitty and Marshal Matt Dillon, then returned the birdseed to its labeled, airtight container. She wiped the counters, checking for stray seeds. No more mice. Allison would be pleased to know it. But since Allison hadn't known about the mice before, it wouldn't be any fun to tell her there were no more mice. Like Macy always said, *What Allison doesn't know won't hurt her.* It turned out Macy was right about that too.

Oh look. A note. Amelia held it up close. From Allison. Going away, getting supplies, having fun. Hooray for Allison.

Amelia reread the note. Away for a few days? How many? What if they needed her here? What if Allison needed *them*?

Virgil would say that was unlikely to happen. *Allison is perfectly capable of taking care of Allison.* He ought to know, seeing as he was quite capable himself.

When Macy and Shasta walked into the kitchen, Amelia handed over the note. "Allison's gone away for a few days."

"Away? A few days?" Macy read the note. "What an odd communiqué. Is it only that she wants to have a little fun, do you think? I hope it's not that she doesn't like us anymore. Or doesn't want us here anymore. Melia, you've got to stop dropping crumbs. Allison's probably tired of cleaning up after you."

Amelia rechecked for crumbs, then rinsed the dishrag and wrung it out in the sink. She hung the rag to dry, perfectly straight—the way Allison preferred, even though Allison wasn't around to see. What more did Macy want Amelia to do?

Slicing a sliver of frosted brownie, Shasta threw a look toward Macy. "I wouldn't blame Allison for wanting a break from us."

The brownie Amelia sliced for herself was larger than Shasta's. This was breakfast, after all. Once she'd cleaned up her crumbs and a few others she was unflinchingly certain weren't hers, she headed outside to the sunshine.

Biting into the brownie, she smiled. Coffee in the frosting too. Allison's buzzy brownies were getting better and better. Amelia finished her breakfast and pulled out her phone to record honeybees on a blooming rhododendron.

"Melia?" Macy called from an open window. "Can you go to the market and let Virgil know we need dog food? We don't want Allison to find the house gone to pot when she returns."

Amelia headed for the market with Louise at her side.

As it turned out, Virgil happened to have the right brand of dog food in stock *and* the time to carry it back to the house. And he wasn't surprised to find out Allison had gone away for a few days. Almost as if Virgil already knew Allison might go away. Like they'd had a private conversation about it, away from the hearing of nosy aunts.

All signs pointed toward Virgil possibly being interested in Allison. Maybe even in love with her! After what Virgil's ex-wife had done to him—so many ups and downs, even after the baby arrived—Virgil would be nothing less than courageous to love again.

So far, though, Amelia didn't have anything concrete to go on. Just little things like Virgil stocking Allison's preferred brands. Virgil was such a nice guy he probably did as much for everyone on Wren.

As Amelia walked up the driveway with him, she pulled out her phone and played a video she'd made of Louise chasing sticks on the beach. "I've recorded a lot more videos too. What could I do with them?"

Virgil shifted the dog food from one arm to the other. "What are your ideas so far?"

Before she could answer, she tripped on a tree root—and regained her balance all on her own! That was another nice thing about Virgil. He was there if you needed him, but he wasn't obvious about it. Like reaching an arm out when she tripped, but not insisting she hold on.

Steady on her feet again, she considered his question. "I was thinking I could put the videos on social media in case people were interested in life on Wren Island. Should I have a plan first?"

Virgil smiled. "You could start with a plan. Or you could just start posting videos for fun and figure out a plan later. Down the road, you might even earn money from the venture."

"You're kidding!" Amelia stopped walking. "I could earn money from making Wren Island videos?"

21

On her own

Clear of Reclamation Island's no wake zone, Allison opened up the throttle. Just a girl on her own now. With her bright yellow boat, bright yellow vest, and bright yellow motorbike. Matchy-matchy. Woo-hoo!

North of Reclamation and Wren, she steered toward a group of small islands. As she drew closer, she slowed and checked her navigation charts. None of the islands were inhabited full time, so the area might be a nice place to drop anchor for a few days.

Rounding the north side of one island, she came upon a pod of orcas milling below a rocky cliff. She put *Buttercup*'s motor in idle and engine in neutral, then turned off the depth finder, minimizing interference with the orcas' own highly developed biological sonar.

The orcas, seven of them, emerged and submerged. With each breath, a puff of air burst from the water, attuning Allison to nature's rhythm. In the water below, there'd be a song running wild and free.

She pulled out her phone. No signal. Probably no hydrophone around here either. She slipped her phone into one of the big front pockets of her vest and went to zip the pocket closed, but the zipper stuck. As Aunt Macy would say, they don't make things like they used to.

The orcas moved closer to shore. *Buttercup* drifted with them. Then into the exact place Allison needed! A hidden cove, sheltered by the land in a way that you had to be *in* the cove before you knew it existed.

Again, the orcas emerged, arched their backs, and lifted their tails up from the water for a longer dive. In the silence that followed, Allison took in the island's forested bank, rocky shore, sandy beach. And wood dock? Someone must spend time here, even if they didn't live here. The orcas emerged again, punctuating the cove with their rhythmic breaths.

When the orcas moved on, Allison inched *Buttercup* up to the dock.

First things first—check for sturdiness. Wouldn't want to wake up tomorrow morning and find out she'd tied up to a failing dock.

She dropped the motor into idle and made her way to the bow of the boat. Leaned over to peer at the pilings. Heard a plop in the water. A fish jumping?

Oh no! Not a fish. Her phone! There it went, sinking along the piling.

Should she go in after it? The phone was totally out of sight now. She'd be down there in murky water alongside who knows what else. A neglected crab pot, tangled fishing line.

No, going after the phone wasn't worth becoming caught. Unable to surface. Unable to breathe.

Wasn't that funny? Not long ago, she would have panicked at the idea of losing her cell phone because she couldn't afford to replace it. Now, she was hardly batting an eye.

Still, why hadn't she gotten a floating phone case like every other boater used? When she ordered herself a new phone, she'd order a floating case for it. And one each for the aunts' phones too.

It wasn't like she'd be unable to send a communiqué, as Aunt Macy liked to say. With her new satellite hotspot, Allison could send emails from her laptop.

She tied up and walked the length of the dock. Old and rickety, but sturdy. This perfectly hidden cove would be home for the next few days. The island would be fun to explore too.

And, hey, look at that!

A trail. Leading from the beach into the forest. Plenty wide for a girl to buzz through on a motorbike.

22

Winging it

Look out, world! Amelia Theodore was now on social media.

Sitting in the sand at the high-tide line, she practiced her narrative voice. "Check out the Wren Island channel, folks, where there's lots to see. Shells and waves are easy to record. Birds are harder, because they scatter whenever Louise runs around."

Amelia was recording dry seaweed dancing in the breeze when footsteps jogged up behind her.

"Hey, Amelia! Whatcha doing?" Hack wore a too-tight tee shirt and too-short shorts. Revealing clothing seemed to be the theme of the century, at least with city folks. And tourists. Which Hack seemed to be, even though he was Ralph's son.

Amelia hit the button to stop recording. "I'm making a video about seaweed. Louise, your paws are in the video *again*."

"Whatcha gonna do with the film?" Sitting next to Amelia, Hack straightened his aviator shades.

"Add it to my YouTube channel."

"Want to make a movie about me?"

"Sure." Amelia held her phone up in front of him. "What do you want to talk about?"

"Let me think."

While Hack thought, Louise followed a butterfly, then returned to Amelia's side. Still thinking, Hack tossed a stick. Louise didn't go after it but laid down at Amelia's side, blinking.

Finally, Hack shrugged. "I'll wing it."

"Okay." Amelia hit record.

"Hey everyone! Hack here, with my new friend Amelia on Wren Island. Never heard of Wren? Check your navigational maps. Middle of the Salish Sea. Tiny island, home to . . ." He looked at her, eyebrows raised. "How many people live here?"

"I don't know."

"Home to I don't know how many people. And to me for a few more days before I head to Alaska." Hack wrapped an arm around Amelia's shoulders and pulled her into camera range. "Home to this lovely lady. And her two sisters. Also her hot babe of a niece. Oh, and my dad and other people and a couple of strange dogs. So there's a hey from Hack on Wren Island. See ya!"

He hit the button to stop recording. "What's your channel called?"

"So far, I've come up with the super creative name of *Wren Island*. Thanks, Hack. Your video will add variety." Amelia put her phone away and glanced at him. Could she bring herself to ask? "Do you really think Allison is a—"

"Hot babe?" Grinning, Hack stood. Just popped up without having to get on his hands and knees first. The benefit of young muscles doing whatever you asked them to and right away. "Would I say it if I didn't think it?"

He jogged off. Amelia patted Louise. Imagine having two men interested in you at the same time. If anything romantic developed here on Wren, she'd document it with her new camera. The recordings should probably remain a mouse-in-the-house secret, though.

Later, sitting at the table in the kitchen turret, Amelia added subtitles to a video of Allison singing to the dogs, then uploaded the finished product. Was it odd that nobody had viewed her YouTube channel?

When Shasta twirled in, Amelia asked her. "Wonder why people aren't watching my videos."

Shasta glanced at the screen. "You haven't made the channel public."

Amelia peered at it. "You're right! I'll figure out how to do that. But first, another video."

She positioned a frosted brownie on a pretty plate. Set the featured item on the kitchen table. Pulled out her phone and aimed the camera.

"Here you go, folks. The frosted version of Allison's buzzy brownies, an original recipe from Wren Island. Stay tuned, and I'll make another video so you can see what all goes into them." Amelia stopped recording.

"You're really getting into this, aren't you? Making videos about life on Wren." Shasta smeared cream cheese on a bagel.

Amelia bit into the brownie. "All I've got to do now is figure out how to make my channel public. Virgil says I might even earn money from it."

"Oh, Virgil again." Shasta laughed.

"What's funny about Virgil?"

"Just that we seem to have a love triangle going on."

"Huh?"

"Virgil's falling for Allison, whose denying she's got the hots for Hack, who likes anyone in a skirt. And you're crushing on Virgil."

"I am not! I like Virgil for Allison." *Because he reminds me of the man I loved,* Amelia almost added but didn't. *And there's nothing nicer I could wish for Allison.*

"Anyway, Shasta, you've got your math wrong. With all that going on, *if* it's going on, it's much more complicated than a triangle."

23

The motorbike

Yet again, *Buttercup*'s custom portside gate proved itself worth the additional cost. No need for Allison to haul the borrowed motorbike onto the dock in an undignified manner. Risk dropping it into the water below—like she'd lost her phone. Just open the gate, roll the bike onto the dock, and everything was all systems go. Maybe tonight, over dinner, she'd finally look up the appropriate way to use the phrase *all systems go*.

She strapped on the helmet Gemma had insisted she take. Too loose, but she wouldn't need a helmet while riding through a deserted forest—unless she crashed into a tree, which she didn't plan to do. She tugged the straps as tight as they'd go.

The bike rumbled to life under her, the sound of the revving engine cutting into the peaceful cove. She was off! Making a few donuts on the beach.

Seagulls scattered, just like they did when Louise came at them. Woo-hoo! Allison gunned the engine and followed the trail into the forest. A wide trail. Other people must bike here too. (Because it was such a great spot!) She picked up speed, climbed higher, circled around.

Near a giant cedar, she pulled to a stop, cut the engine, and parked. The view from up here was amazing! She pulled off the helmet, ran her hands through her hair, sat on the trunk of a fallen tree, and listened to the music of the forest.

There was the moon, already rising ahead of the setting sun. The people at the commune said a waning moon was the time to release things. She breathed deep, releasing tension.

Tonight, back at the boat, she'd set up the Wi-Fi and email a quick message to the aunts. She'd look up *all systems go*. Microwave a frozen burrito and eat it under the stars. Sing herself a new song.

But first, there were more trails to explore! She hopped back on the bike and strapped on the helmet. *Safety first, sister.* She revved the engine and took off. When the ascending trail widened, she sped up. When it narrowed, she slowed.

The trail widened, and she picked up speed. It narrowed, she slowed.

Wide again, so she blasted along. Narrow here, with the brush encroaching. But she pushed through because right up ahead was a clearing like the one on Wren, with room to do wheelies in. And she was independent and *free* today!

She flew along the narrowing trail—until she saw her error. Her monumental, frightening error.

Not racing toward a clearing. Racing toward a cliff.

Panicked—she had seconds to either stop or reroute—she squeezed the brake too hard. The bike skid, then shot over the edge with her clutching it, her arms looped around the handlebars, her legs wrapped around the frame. As if the bike might fly her upward to safety, not hurtle her into a dark abyss.

She closed her eyes. Felt the rush of wind, the last bit of earth she might ever know. Hoped Virgil would check on the aunts. And the dogs.

Let go, Allison.

When she did, the motorbike, heavier than her, dropped away faster, snapping tree limbs. Free of the encumbrance, she felt lighter. She'd be like a bird if she wasn't falling to the—

A flash of pain, a diminishing shudder. Then . . . nothing.

24

A moment

Virgil added the last case of canned chili to the stockroom shelf and positioned the expiration dates to easily be seen. Hard to argue that wasn't being more organized.

Glancing around, he spotted an empty shelf, unusual with the way he and Jax crammed things in. Had the supplies kept on that shelf been moved elsewhere? Or were they sold out?

He checked the supply list, printed eons ago. Scribbling blocked out most of the original information, so out-of-date it served as more of a suggestion than a guide. He'd make a note to print an up-to-date list.

As he reached to grab a pen, a searing flash of pain pierced through him, ripping from head to toe, swirling around his racing heart. He staggered to a wall and leaned against it.

A dizzy spell? Panic attack? Muscle spasm? All he'd been doing was the usual market stuff.

Heart thumping, he stood there, catching his breath.

"Dad?" Jax's voice reached Virgil from the cashier counter up front, as if this moment were like any other. "Ed Piper's here. He wants to know if we have chicken wire in stock."

"Be there in a moment." Virgil rubbed his chest.

A similar experience happened once before. When Jax's mom overdosed on cocaine, two hundred miles away, in a different state. Later, Virgil learned his own wrenching, unexplained pain had occurred at the same time. A defining moment from another lifetime, when he deeply loved his wife.

The only person in this world he was that connected to now was his son.

Virgil poked his head around the doorframe. Jax was sucking on a licorice stick, chatting with Ed. All normal there.

Did that mean . . . ?

Heart racing for real now, Virgil pulled out his phone. No new messages. Had Allison called to let anyone know where she was and how long she'd be gone?

Probably not. She was Allison Theodore, perfectly capable of taking care of herself. On a getaway encouraged by her friend Virgil Tagaloa.

He tapped out a text. *Hey, how's it going? Enjoying your getaway?*

After hitting send, he stared at the screen for an unreasonable amount of time. Drummed his fingers on a shipment of cereal boxes. Willed a reply to pop up and put his mind—and body—at ease.

"Come on, Allison. Just a quick reply."

A few words would let him know she was okay. That he'd just experienced an arrhythmia or spike in blood pressure. Even a heart attack would be more desirable than a supernatural response connected to something horrific Allison was enduring.

Squeezing his eyes closed, he breathed in. Exhaling, he nearly broke into a sob from the force of an overwhelming longing. For Allison's safety. For her protection. For her to continue being everything she was, always, forever. Free, independent, beautiful, capable.

He wasn't too proud to beg. He'd done it before, many times. Would do it again, as often as needed.

Please, God, keep her safe.

25

Try to fly

Dragonfly, if you'd like to try to fly . . .

Eyes closed, she floated up to join the symphony of birdsong in the treetops. The birds had invited her. Included her. Asked her to be part of their glorious music.

She took small, careful breaths. Little breaths hurt less. No need to sing right now. The others can carry the tune. Encircle her with grandeur.

Someday, she'll be brilliant like the birds. She's a songwriter! She's never written anything as spectacular as this, though. Her name is . . . Allison Theodore. Yes, that's her name! She lives on Wren Island with her aunts. Three sisters. Macy, Shasta, Amelia. Their sister Anne—Mom—gone now.

A careful breath, a small sigh.

Listen. A bald eagle calling. The entire forest symphony hushed. Everyone camouflaged in place, motionless and quiet. Then a flapping of wide wings, a whisper of swaying branches, the dripping scent of pine.

Allison opened her eyes.

Could it be? An eagle perched in the tree above her?

Allison Theodore was under the weight of an eagle. Wasn't that interesting?

Was it interesting enough? (Interesting enough for who?)

The air shifted, the eagle lifted. A scattering of pine needles tickled her face. The little birds, safe again, resumed their symphony.

Little birds, little breaths, little wings, little lives.

Dragonfly, if you'd like to try to fly, come along with me to see what's beyond the sky and sea.

26

Unicorn colors

Macy rinsed the ceramic lunch bowls and stacked them in the kitchen sink. Best to let those soak before adding them to the dishwasher. Detouring around Louise, who was sprawled across the kitchen floor, Macy spotted food bits under Melia's chair and pointed.

"Look, Louise. Free crumbs."

The dog ignored the suggestion. Louise didn't seem to dislike Macy, but she rarely followed through on anything Macy asked of her. Which made Louise the newest member in the growing club of individuals annoyed with Macy Johansson. Led by founding member and president Macy Johansson.

Just as Macy tackled the crumbs around the toaster, Shasta twirled in, pleased as punch with her colorful self.

"Shasta! What on earth have you done to your hair?"

"Unicorn colors. Aren't they fabu-lo-so? Let's do it to your hair too."

Gaping, Macy scrutinized the pink, green, purple, and yellow colors blending through Shasta's short hair. "Your head looks like a pom-pom."

"Best compliment I've gotten yet!" Shasta twirled into a sit at the table.

Oh, to be the woman who could color her hair any which way just because it might be fun. The woman who could interpret a comment about her head looking like a pom-pom as a compliment.

Macy lifted the heavy pot she'd used to make eggplant parmigiana. Perched it on the edge of the sink. Allison didn't like eggplant, and Shasta had suggested they make the most of their time while Allison wasn't around. Make the most of their time!

But it wasn't as if Allison was the warden and they were criminals on the lam. Caretakers of the house—that's what they were. Just because the homeowner wasn't present didn't mean they could get away with—

The heavy pot just slipped out of her hand! Crushing the ceramic bowls in the sink to smithereens.

Macy turned off the water, set the pot aside on the counter, and poked through the rubble. How many dishes had they lost this time?

Shasta tsk-tsked. "Your ferocity again."

Macy whirled to face her. "If you make one more comment about my *ferocity*, I'm going to dunk your pom-pom in this greasy water."

"Macy!" Eyes wide, Melia reached for Louise, who had scrambled to her side.

Macy gazed at her baby sister. Today Melia wore a coral-colored cardigan over a white cotton blouse. Pink polyester pants had probably been chosen to match the cardigan but didn't. Melia's hand was halfway to her mouth with a half-eaten oatmeal raisin cookie, the bewildered look on her face one she'd often had decades ago in childhood.

Had anything about Melia changed in all these years? Had Melia lost any innocence, even over all the lifetimes they'd lived?

"I wouldn't really dunk her head, Melia." Macy eyed Shasta. "Even if it does look like a pom-pom."

Returning her attention to the dishes in the sink, Macy picked out the broken pieces and tossed them in the garbage.

Just for once, it'd be fun to be irresponsible again. Take off whenever she wanted to. Dye her hair whatever color she wanted. Drink whatever she wanted.

"How come you're all aflutter, Macy?" Melia's voice was quiet.

"Someone's got to keep this house from going to pot."

She was shaky inside again. Not from a desire for alcohol. But from worry about Allison having gone away. Not just that, but *how* Allison left. A note scribbled on scrap paper! One corner tucked under a plate on the kitchen counter. Gone before the sun was up—like she couldn't get away fast enough.

It'd be no surprise if their niece had tired of them. Look how they'd disrupted her life! Did Allison regret asking them to live with her?

Macy set the dirty pot in the sink. Oh, if only she could ask Allison. Right now! Knowing how Allison felt would be better than all this wondering. All this worrying. Macy squeezed the pot's handles. Knowing would be better than rereading and refolding the note in her pocket, searching for assurance that wasn't there.

"Maybe we ought to email her. Or call her. Just to check in."

"Check in? With who?" Shasta's face screwed up in confusion.

"Allison! Our niece? The one who lets us live with her?"

"Oh, I'm sure Allison would think that's the bee's knees, Mace. She finally gets away, and there you are, still bugging her. She's been away a few hours and you want to send the Mounties after her. Take a chill pill, sis."

Tilting her head, Melia squinted. "The Royal Canadian Mounted Police do water rescues?"

"It doesn't matter if they do or not, Melia." Macy sent a pointed look at Shasta. "Because we're not in Canada."

"We're close to Canada, though. Maybe Allison took her boat over there."

"You think she left us for another *country*?" Macy nearly dropped the pot again. Wiping her hands on a dish towel, she followed Shasta to the door. "Where are you going?"

"Out. And you do know you don't have to wash all those by hand? They've improved on dishwashers since the Dark Ages." The service door slammed behind Shasta.

Melia started collecting the dirty dishes. "Do you want these in the sink or the dishwasher?"

"Straight into the dishwasher, I guess."

After Melia loaded the dishwasher, wiped the table, and pulled on a fuchsia jacket, Macy stepped up to straighten the chin loop of her sister's wide-brimmed hat. "Where are you off to?"

"To make videos on the beach. Want to come along, Louise?" The dog padded out behind her.

Returning to the kitchen sink, Macy scrutinized the greasy pot. She picked it up and squinted at the tiny print on the bottom. *Dishwasher safe.*

Well, why not live on the wild side? Macy threw the pot in and started the cycle.

When Lokita stood up in her little bed in the corner and stretched, Macy kneeled to pet the dog. Scooped her up for a cuddle.

Ahh. Down went her blood pressure. What was that ditty Allison liked to sing to Lokita? "Little Lokita, right here with me. Aren't you sweet, right here with me?" Or something along those lines.

Such a cute little song. Calling it a *ditty* had gotten a funny look from Allison, though. So there was another question Macy wanted to ask her niece. *Allison, do you call them ditties or something else?*

There were lots of questions she'd like to ask her niece. *Allison, what do you enjoy about songwriting? How did you get started? Why is it so important to you? How can we help you reach your dream?*

Why hadn't she asked? Intent on taking care of the house—and, let's be honest, mostly wrecking it—she'd overlooked taking care of her niece.

Didn't she love her niece more than anything in this world? Didn't she love her niece and her sisters like her very own life?

So, there it was again. That feeling of being mostly annoyed with herself.

27

Here comes Louise again

On the beach, Amelia pulled out her phone and recorded the circles of shells she'd arranged on the sand. "Here you go, folks. The smooth white ones are clams. The purples with funny hair are mussels. And look at these twisty delights—once homes for hermit crabs and snails."

Louise's nose and paws wandered in and out of the picture. Amelia patted the dog's big brown head, stopped recording, and tucked her phone into a pocket. Maybe instead of calling her YouTube channel *Wren Island*, she ought to call it *Here Comes Louise Again*.

Walking along the beach, she followed the high-tide line so her feet wouldn't get wet. The tide was rising quickly this afternoon. You could tell that by the sound of the waves rolling around on top of each other at the waterline.

She stopped to listen. The booming waves settled, then whispered back out to sea, taking a quick breather before they pushed close again—wilder, deeper, stronger.

Amelia walked on, navigating around a huge piece of driftwood—practically an entire tree trunk. How dramatic it would have been to see the ocean toss *that* onto the beach! Like an invisible giant tossing aside a toothpick. She would ask if Allison ever thought of driftwood that way.

What was Allison doing at this moment? Was she cozied up around a camp-fire with a captivating novel? Enjoying an iced tea with a new friend? Eating a tuna salad sandwich in the sunshine?

Wow! Look at all that orange foam left at the waterline by the last roll of waves. Amelia walked closer. Jax said foam on the beach was caused by algae decaying offshore, a sign of a healthy ecosystem.

Look at all those bubbles at her feet, popping in the sunshine. And look at the tiny clamshells! What might a person do with so many? She leaned over to pick up a gleaming half.

Oops. An incoming wave got her feet wet. (And turned her toes to ice!) Holding the shell, she backed up. One of these days, she was going to check that whole sand dollar off of her list of nice things to wish for.

Also soon to be checked off, hopefully, was seeing the baby bald eagle take its first flight. Amelia squinted up at the tree where the eagles were nesting. Not much activity up there today. Maybe the parents were hunting elsewhere. Maybe they'd found another island to visit. Maybe they were visiting Allison! Soaring above Allison's bright yellow boat. Wouldn't Allison think that was fun?

Louise ran close, sniffed the foam on the sand, and sneezed. Amelia patted the dog's head and bent to pick up another shell. This one was extra pretty because—

The wave caught her by surprise. The smashing force of it!

Knocked off her feet, she swirled with a million grains of sand. Submerged, she tried for footing and almost found it—until another wave crashed into her. And there she was, in the middle of the same water that could toss a tree like a toothpick.

The water would rest eventually. It had to. It would need a breather, a moment to ease back out to sea. But what if it took her out to sea with it?

First, she needed to come up for air and *breathe*. She would explode if she couldn't take a breath!

She scrambled to right herself. Almost there. Whoosh. Another wave crashed into her, over her, around her. Which way was up? How long could she go without coming up for air?

Was that a dog barking? *Don't come in after me, Louise. I don't want the waves to grab you too.*

The water pulled back, gathering itself, depositing Amelia in the soft, wet sand. Louise, still barking, ran in circles around her. Against stiffening joints, Amelia hauled up to drier sand. Up to the high-tide line. Up to the shrub line, where she finally caught her breath.

She was soaked in ice water. Covered in sand. Shaking so hard she might already be crying and not know it. But she wasn't a goner. *No need to worry, folks. Amelia Theodore is still with us.*

Breathing more steadily, she sat on a driftwood log—yet another tree tossed aside like a giant's toothpick. Macy had always warned her not to get too close to the surf. Now it turned out Macy was right about that too.

Footsteps ran close. Ed Piper from the commune. "Amelia! Are you okay?"

"I'm fine." Her voice sounded weak. She tried again. "I'm okay. Just wet."

Ed draped something warm around her. A blanket? No, his own coat. When Ed sat on the log next to Amelia, Louise nudged his hand for a pat.

"Sure glad *that* didn't get recorded." Amelia pulled the soaked, sandy phone from her pocket. "Uh-oh. Can it be saved, do you think?"

Ed reached for the phone and wiped it dry. "Maybe. Submerging it in a bowl of rice will draw out the moisture."

Amelia pushed her dripping hair away from her face and looked toward the house—not that it was anything but a blur. Had anyone up there seen what just happened? "Macy's going to blow a gasket when she finds out."

"About the phone?" Ed rolled it along the bottom edge of his flannel shirt.

"About me getting caught in a wave. She'll think I shouldn't be allowed on the beach alone anymore."

Ed patted Louise. "Would you like me to drive you over to the commune? You can warm up there. I'll bring you back whenever you're ready."

Teeth chattering, Amelia glanced at Ed's all-terrain vehicle parked on the beach path. Her pants felt like sheets of ice against her legs. Her cracked ribs, mostly healed, ached from the setback.

Not only would Macy blow a gasket, she'd up her efforts to hover over Amelia even more than she already did.

Amelia half shivered, half cringed at being that much more restricted.

"Sure, Ed. I'd appreciate the help."

28

Where she landed

In a flood of warmth, Allison opened her eyes.

Above her, pine branches waved. She squinted against the sunlight slanting through them, piercing her head.

She must get back to her boat. Back to Wren Island. The aunts. The dogs. Kitty and Matt. How long had she been lying here? *Hope Virgil remembered to check on everyone.*

One inch at a time, she tested her body. Right hand and fingers? Moving. Right arm? Moving but sore. Left arm?

A line of fire zinged up from her arm, through her neck, into her head. Sucking in a breath, she lifted her head for a look.

Ick. Her left arm was coated with blood and dirt.

Easing her head back to the ground, she realized Gemma's helmet was still in place. *Safety first, sister.* She inched toward the idea of testing her lower half. Something didn't seem right down there. When the pain stopped swirling, she'd try again.

The eagle returned, quieting the forest. Another whisper of swaying branches, another scattering of pine needles. Another shifting of the air as the eagle lifted, then the symphony of birdsong resumed.

Okay, time to get moving. Upsy-daisy. When she sat up, pain shot like burning embers through her left leg and hip. That might not be a positive sign, all that burning on her left side. Could she move her toes? Yes. Could she stand? Oops. Not yet.

When her head stopped spinning, she scrutinized her arm again. What a mess. If today was Halloween, she could pretend to be a zombie.

Wait a minute. Was today Halloween?

No. It was springtime.

Using a broken branch for support, she hauled herself up, stood, wavered, kept her balance. Woo-hoo, she kept her balance!

Oh boy, it hurt. She'd call for help.

No. Her phone had sunk in the murky water by the piling. She wouldn't be sending any messages out to the world until she got back to the boat.

Uh-oh. Look where she landed. Halfway down the bank, halfway up. Gemma's yellow motorbike had nearly disappeared in the shrubbery below.

Allison studied the rough terrain to it. If the bike would still run, she could use it to get back to the boat. One wheel had come off, though, and landed way over there. She'd have to climb down the ravine, collect the wheel, repair the bike, haul it out of the ravine.

She glanced at her arm, tested her hip. Getting to and repairing the bike was probably not going to happen. Not today. Maybe Gemma would be okay with having a new bike as a replacement.

Onward and upward, Allison Theodore. She could follow that deer path up the slope. Use the stick as a crutch.

Partway up the bank, she leaned on the stick and studied her left leg. It felt awfully strange. No bones jutting out, though.

The pain in her hip was gone. No feeling there at all anymore. Was that a sign of improvement?

Well, whatever she did, she wouldn't sit down. She might never get up again. *Keep going. Soon you'll be back on the boat.* Could that be a song? It sure could!

Soon you'll be back on the boat, sister. Walk on, walk on, walk on, sister.

29

Whales among us

Standing in front of a full-length mirror at the commune, Amelia fingered the linen shift her new friend Judy had loaned her. "It's so comfy!"

Folding the sleeves to the right length for Amelia's arms, Judy smiled. "Organic cotton, certified fair trade. We try to make conscientious clothing choices here."

"I like that it's baggy and lets me move freely." Amelia ran her hands across the fabric. "Do you wear a lot of clothes like these?"

"I only need a few outfits, because they're well made." Judy pointed to her own linen shift. "I've been wearing this one every Thursday for the last six years."

"You're kidding." Amelia sat and pulled on the warm socks Judy offered her. Wool, hand knitted. "So when you wake up on Thursdays, you already know what you're going to wear?"

Judy handed her a soft cardigan. "Every week, I rotate through the same six outfits—except on Saturdays, when I choose different clothing based on how I feel. Here at the commune, we try to simplify our lives. Not wondering what to wear every day frees our minds to think about other interests. Gardening, art, music. Caring for nature, our livestock and crops. Helping each other. We're not exactly minimalists, but we enjoy living simply."

Amelia glanced at Judy's tidy closet. Open space separated every outfit, allowing a place to rest your eyes before looking at the next outfit.

In her own closet at home, Amelia was constantly digging for items she thought she remembered having but couldn't find. Pushing through clothes she'd never been thrilled with. And her clothes closet wasn't the only burgeoning space.

The entire house was getting buried under clutter. With all the purchases Shasta had made on a whim. The food Macy had stockpiled for doomsday. The magnifiers and other gadgets Amelia had collected. How many items had she and her sisters acquired since moving in with Allison? One chair was all there'd been in the entry the day they arrived.

Maybe she could suggest to her sisters they stop buying so much stuff. Would that be asking too much, though? Amelia knew as well as anyone that feeling limited wasn't much fun.

Her hair almost dry, she fluffed the curls around her face. She liked the shampoo she'd used. In bar form, same as the soap. Both made right there at the commune. Judy said plastic packaging took a toll on the environment and endangered wildlife. After one more glance at the tidy closet, Amelia followed Judy outside.

In the courtyard, Ed and Louise were playing a game. He hid a treat under one of several small wood boxes and let Louise guess which box the treat was under. Louise's rear end wiggled with excitement, just like it had during the drive over to the commune in Ed's all-terrain vehicle.

Amelia peered at Ed's flannel shirt and well-worn jeans. Did he wear the same outfit every Thursday?

"Might be wise to give your phone more time." Ed motioned to the bowl of rice. "While we're waiting, do you want to see the rehab aviary?"

"You help injured birds here?" Amelia fell into step with him.

"We're an official wildlife rehabilitation facility, although we mostly take in birds."

The path curved around the main buildings of the commune, then stretched along the edge of a sunny meadow. Evenly spaced posts, connected by sections of rope, acted as a sort of fence. As she traveled, Amelia ran her hand along the sections and counted in her head. Four, five, six, seven. The rope ended at the twenty-third post.

"Here we are." Ed guided her inside a large building with a solid roof and canvas walls. They passed through an intake area. Charts on one wall indicated times for feeding, watering, cleaning, and medication. A separate room held storage bins of food and additional supplies.

In the main care area, potted trees and shrubs provided the feeling of being outdoors. Cages separated individual birds from each other physically and visually. In one cage, a medium-sized bird shifted on its perch.

Ed spoke softly. "This mourning dove has an injured foot."

While Amelia studied the bandaged leg, the bird cocked its head to one side and blinked back at her.

"Over here, we have robin babies." Ed led Amelia under the low-hanging branches of a blossoming potted tree, to a table where someone was dropping mealworms into three gaping beaks. At another table, Ed handed Amelia a tiny cup woven with grass and bits of dry moss. "Have you ever seen a hummingbird nest?"

Amelia gazed at the intricately woven, thimble-sized home in her palm. "Where are the babies?"

"I'll show you."

Back outside, Ed pointed to the hummingbirds zipping to and from a liquid feeder on a nearby branch. "All grown up and independent now."

Amelia sighed.

They traveled the path back to the main building, Amelia counting fence posts in her head. Fourteen, fifteen, sixteen. At the twenty-third post, Amelia headed for the courtyard and collected her phone. She turned it on and opened a couple of apps. "It's working! Thanks so much, Ed."

"Would you like me to drive you home now?"

Before Amelia could answer, Judy stepped into the courtyard. "Entertaining stuff happening on the hydrophone. A pod of Southern Resident orcas with lots to say. Amelia, would you like to ring the gong?"

Amelia glanced at the large bronze disk suspended from weathered beams, then back to Judy. "You'd let *me* ring it?"

A solid felt mallet was placed in her hands. "Give it all you've got so everyone on Wren hears. Three big whacks."

Amelia took a deep breath and swung. GONG! The sound reverberated through her.

Judy flipped on an outdoor speaker, and the sound of singing orcas filled the courtyard. "Whack it again."

The mallet met the disk, sending a sweeping thrill through Amelia. *Whales! There are whales among us, everyone!*

Judy swapped the mallet in Amelia's hands for a pair of binoculars. "See the orcas over there? Subtle markings on their backs and dorsal fins identify each individual. This is a pod of endangered Southern Residents. Let's listen for another few minutes, then hit the gong again."

Amelia fiddled with the binoculars until the vision became crystal clear—a real treat for someone who usually viewed the world blurry! Five sleek orcas emerged, dipped and disappeared, emerged again. She could see individual drips in the air when the orcas breathed!

Nearby, several buoys bobbed on the water's surface. "Are those crab pots they're swimming around?"

"Unfortunately, yes." Ed sounded sad. "Fishing gear poses a real risk for marine animals. They can become entangled in the ropes and be injured—or even die. A tragedy any time, and especially regarding Southern Residents. Only about seventy remain in this world."

Amelia watched the creatures emerge and submerge. Every time the orcas dove deep, their music filled the courtyard. Amelia whacked the bronze disk again, then watched the orcas until they moved on.

Back at Allison's house, just inside the service entrance, Amelia stumbled through scattered shoes and bags. She layered her damp clothes into the washing machine and closed the lid.

"Did you just put wet clothes in the washer, Melia?" Macy appeared at her side. "What on earth are you wearing? Two of you could fit in that—if the wrinkles were ironed out."

"I fell down while walking on the beach." True, if not the complete story. "Then I visited the commune. That was me hitting the whale gong just now! I borrowed an outfit from Judy, who wears the same outfit every Thursday." At that information, Macy's eyebrows rose higher.

Amelia fluffed the curls at the back of her neck. "Did you know the people at the commune use shampoo in bar form? Solid like a bar of soap. They make it themselves. No plastic packaging required. So anyway, I think I'll go to bed early tonight."

After Amelia left the laundry room, she heard the washer click off and the lid squeak open. Her sister, peering in. Poking around.

The washer lid squeaked closed. The cycle resumed.

Business as usual here at Allison's house. Macy keeping a close eye on everything. And everyone.

30

Going over

Limping, Allison pushed through thorny shrubbery. It didn't matter if she got more scratches on her arms. She was already a bloody mess. The primary goal—in fact, the only goal at the moment—was to get herself back to the boat. Preferably before dark.

Up ahead, the shrubbery thinned to reveal a trail. A wide trail. The same trail she careened off? Would it lead her back to the dock? How far had she traveled on the motorbike before she went over the edge?

Wasn't that *so* funny to think about? She told Virgil she was on the edge—the aunts driving her to the edge of losing her mind. Then she did go over! Not the proverbial edge, but a *real* edge. Went crashing right over. Would Virgil find that funny too? She said she was about to go over the edge. And then she did! Ha ha ha!

Oh, her head. Wobbly.

It wasn't her aunts' fault. They didn't send her over the edge. Her dear, dear aunts. They love each other. Love her too.

Yes, they do, Allison Theodore. They love you. Words for a new song!

Her dear, dear aunts. They're so *special*. She loves them so *much*! She'd like to drink one of Aunt Macy's green smoothies right now. Dear, dear Aunt Macy.

Allison limped to a clearing off the trail. What a view. The moon was rising, though, so better keep going. Got to get back to the boat before dark.

Soon you'll be back on the boat, sister. Walk on, walk on, walk on, sister.

She sang to herself until it grew dark. And colder. A night spent in the forest wouldn't be *that* terrible. She was alive, so she had that much going for her. If she wasn't alive, things would be worse, for sure. If only it were warmer tonight. The forest would be much nicer if it were warmer. Much, much nicer.

She sank to the ground under a cedar tree. *Rest. Move again when it's light.* What would the aunts be eating for dinner tonight? *Light. Tonight.* Rhyming words. She was Allison Theodore, a songwriter.

The aunts were probably in the kitchen—the *warm* kitchen—right at this very moment. If she was there with them, she wouldn't even bother cleaning up after them. Crumbs, crumbs, bring on the crumbs.

An owl hooted, peaceful. Owls hunted at night and dozed during the day. Virgil watched an owl sleep once. He said so. Virgil said so, not the owl.

Did the owl on this island have a family? In a dry, cozy nest. Where nobody's hip was smoldering in hot lava. Nobody's arm felt like cooked spaghetti. Nobody's head was about to explode.

Allison's eyes stung. She would not cry, though. Owls don't cry. Sea turtles do, but owls don't. Or do they?

Hope Aunt Macy isn't bossing Louise. Hope someone remembers to warm up Lokita's bedtime blanket. Wouldn't it be sooo nice if Mom were here, to tuck Allison in at bedtime? With a warm blanket. Like when Allison was just a kid. And if she didn't feel well, Mom would bring her graham crackers and peanut butter and fizzy pop.

Allison sighed. Did she ever thank her mom for all that?

She'd like to tell her thanks now.

For tucking her in with a warm blanket. And for everything else too.

31

Caretaker

Macy warmed a mug of herbal tea, brought it to the kitchen table, and flipped off the overhead lights so the under-cabinet lighting would create a soft glow against the darkness beyond the windows. She found a favorite streaming music station—Frank Sinatra, Dean Martin, and Perry Como—and sighed into a seat at the table.

Earlier, she'd opened the clothes washer and discovered Melia's clothes smelling of salt. Swishing among grains of sand. The question was whether Melia had intentionally been in the ocean. Or had it happened by accident?

The way Melia scurried away from anything cold, it was unlikely to have been intentional. So there had been a close call while Macy wasn't watching. Maybe while she was sewing that new snack bag for Louise.

Macy sipped her tea. She ought to keep closer tabs on Melia. Her sister's eyesight wasn't going to get any better. It was up to the rest of them to look out for her. And by the rest of them, she meant herself. Their sister Anne would have helped, but dear, dear Anne was gone. Allison shouldn't have to worry about looking after Melia.

Shasta padded in, wearing a tiger-print nightie, matching robe, and sequin bonnet. If the day came the family needed Shasta to take over, she'd probably just recommend keeping calm and adding glitter.

Setting down her mug, Macy sighed. "We should keep a more careful watch on Melia."

Shasta leaned across the back of a chair. "Mace, you don't have to be in charge all the time. We're adults. We're capable of looking out for ourselves. And anyway, I've been meaning to tell you I'll be heading out soon."

"Heading out?"

"Away. This place is closing in on me. All the you-can't and you-must rules. As soon as I decide where I want to go, I'm getting myself a plane ticket out of here."

Tensing, Macy pulled her hands from the mug. "Getting yourself a plane ticket with what?"

"The credit card."

"*Allison's* credit card?" Macy's blood pressure shot up. "You can't use Allison's money to leave. You can only use Allison's money to stay here. To keep building on *this*."

"There you go again. Making rules for everyone. It doesn't matter. Ralph will help me. Or Hack. He's quite resourceful. And *he* doesn't have scruples about spending money."

Macy stared at her sister. The one willing to flirt with a man half her age. "You'd go with Hack? He's leaving tomorrow, isn't he? Shasta, please don't go."

Shasta put a hand on Macy's shoulder. "Mace, I thank God every day that rehab worked for you. You're an amazing person with all kinds of talents. But you've got to let people live a little. You've got to let *yourself* live a little." She gave Macy a quick hug before disappearing down the dark hallway.

Taking a deep breath, Macy wrapped her hands around the warm mug. Rules. Scruples. Rehab. *Let yourself live a little*. Did she even know how to? Not anymore. Throwing that greasy pot in the dishwasher without first scrubbing it clean might be as wild as she got now.

Why was this happening? She'd poured everything she could into life here on Wren Island, and now it was all falling apart. Allison had left. For what she said was a quick getaway, yes. But what if Allison's getaway was a test run? What if Allison wanted to spend more time away from Wren Island? What if Allison figured out she didn't need her aunts?

And now Shasta was talking about leaving. With Hack! *And he doesn't have scruples about spending money.* For goodness' sake! Why shouldn't people be careful with money? Even Allison, a millionaire, was scrupulous. Macy huffed through another sip of chamomile tea.

Would Melia want to leave too? Even if she wanted to, she had nowhere else to go. Melia would always need her big sister. That was one consolation, though bittersweet.

As usual, Shasta was off her rocker. Recklessness didn't get you anywhere. It was way, way overrated. Macy swallowed another sip of weak tea.

At times like these, she was really, really glad there was no alcohol in the house. Avoiding that recklessness would be a monumental effort even for Superwoman.

Macy held her cooling mug, then called her AA sponsor. Talked, listened, talked and listened more. Until she was strong enough to end the call. Prep ingredients for tomorrow morning's smoothie. Do a few up-and-down stretches in front of the floor-to-ceiling windows.

The house quieted under a wash of stars. Macy let Lokita outside while Louise, unwilling to go out after dark, watched. Wasn't Allison smart for creating a safe fenced area off the service entry? Allison knew keeping the ones you loved close was important.

A caretaker—that's Macy Johansson now. No longer a raging alcoholic, but a recovering alcoholic. No longer a wife, but a strong woman being a caretaker for everyone she loved. Her sisters, her niece, and everyone *they* loved.

Lokita finished her business and tootled back inside. Louise greeted Lokita with a wagging tail—and gave Macy's face a quick lick when Macy scooped up Lokita.

Running a sleeve across her face, Macy eyed the big dog. "Getting to be better friends, are we?"

While Louise wagged her tail, Macy snuggled Lokita. The dog's little ears were so cold! Just from being outside for a few minutes?

Macy checked the electronic weather station. Wind building from the northwest tonight. There'd be frost on the ground tomorrow morning.

Cuddling Lokita, Macy walked through the house and made everything snug. Warmed a blanket and tucked Lokita into bed—just like Allison would have. Whispered goodnight to Louise creeping into Melia's dark bedroom. Said a prayer for Allison—their very own Allison—wherever she was.

In her own room, Macy slipped under the bedcovers. She aligned her spine into the position least likely to wake her with a backache, closed her eyes, and placed one hand over her heart. Then she visualized a path to sound sleep.

Tonight, she followed two spotted fawns through a meadow flitting with butterflies. Sleep would be found under a purple-misted waterfall beyond the meadow.

Tomorrow, with all its responsibilities, waited somewhere beyond.

32

No answer

At 1:00 a.m., Virgil was tossing and turning. Wracking his brain to figure out why, unless it was because he was just plain cold. He bumped up the thermostat and checked the weather forecast. Frigid temperatures tonight and into the morning hours. Even after burrowing deeper under the blankets, he still couldn't sleep.

Had he drank coffee late in the day? Eaten spicy food? Too much adrenaline pumping through his veins? No, unless abundant adrenaline was the result of worrying about Allison, which was now starting to feel like physical torture.

He was an idiot to suggest she go off on her own. *Get away by yourself for a while.* Who suggests that to someone they want to protect? Who encourages the woman they love to leave?

He thought he was offering a helpful suggestion. And maybe going off on her own was exactly what Allison needed. Knowing Allison, she was making the most of her independence. Enjoying life unhindered.

Unless she didn't actually want to be all that independent. Unless she *really* wanted to be taken care of, treasured, held close. Had she found someone else to be with? Was *that* why his body ached?

At 2:00 a.m., he sat in the leather chair that'd always been predictably comfortable. Now it failed to console. He searched his Bible for an instant answer that wouldn't be there—except to pray, which was always an answer of sorts, so he did.

At 3:00 a.m., the day was about to begin anyway, so he switched on a soothing music playlist. Then mixed up a batch of apple streusel muffins. Because last time he made them, Allison said she liked them.

With the freshly baked muffins cooling on a rack, he pulled on a knit hat and his warmest jacket and stepped out to the covered porch. An owl hooted from the pine across the road. A barred owl. Virgil waited for a reply.

None came. The owl's mate must be off hunting. Did owls worry when out of contact with each other?

At 4:15 a.m., he remembered Allison had installed an AIS transponder on *Buttercup*. The automatic identification system tracked a boat's movements, assuming the vessel operator left the transponder turned on.

He thought about that for a minute. Knowing Allison, she wouldn't be comfortable sending public updates. Not to mention, commercially minded Ralph often ranted about pleasure crafters jamming the airwaves unnecessarily.

Pulling out his phone, Virgil opened the app, which indicated Allison Theodore's thirty-foot Ocean Sport Roamer, *Buttercup*, hailing from Wren Island, last sent a signal from the island's south side, a few hundred yards away. Maybe she arrived home late last night. He strode off the porch and down the road.

At the beach, early morning light revealed Allison's dock was vacant. He knocked at the boat house. When there was no answer, he unlatched the door and poked his head in.

No *Buttercup*. No Allison.

He closed the boathouse door with more force than necessary, annoyed with his own overprotective actions. Allison was an adult. She had a right to her privacy. If she wanted to turn off updates to her boat's whereabouts, okay.

But if she needed help, how would they know where to find her?

Overhead, a bald eagle swooped past the dock. Landed on a tree branch that swayed under its weight. Seven years ago, there'd been a nest in that tree.

Bald eagles often returned to the same nests. They raised one fledgling at a time and kept their young close for a couple of years. Even without binoculars, Virgil could see this eagle's intelligent-looking eyes scanning the shallow waters off the beach. The majestic creature, top dog in the bird world, was a gorgeous reminder the world was full of mysteries. Mystery upon mystery.

Breathing another prayer for Allison, Virgil trudged back to the market, pulling his coat collar up against the brisk air. The collar also hid his scowl at finding Ralph and Hack on the front porch.

Ralph, Virgil was fine with seeing anytime. Hack, not so much. Hack always made him feel insufficient. After age fifty, a little softness around the middle was inevitable, wasn't it? Apparently, working out eight hours a week wasn't enough—not if Virgil were being compared to the beefed-up Hacks of the world. Every girl in the room perked up whenever Hack sauntered in. Every girl. Including Allison.

Virgil pulled his attitude together. "Coffee, guys?"

They sat at a table in the market's café. Near the fireplace, which wasn't the only thing heating up as Hack yakked on about spending summers in Alaska—something Virgil had always wanted to do, but he'd never had the opportunity. Virgil wished Hack would pack up all that excess machismo and head to Alaska already.

Ralph was quiet, as usual. It was strange, though, how he kept shutting down Hack's efforts to draw him into conversation.

"We've had some memorable times, haven't we, pops?"

Ralph glared. Annoyed at being called *pops*, maybe.

As Hack rambled off again about fishing for Chinook salmon, Virgil studied the unexpected expressions on Ralph's face. Resignation. Sadness. Shame?

Shoot. If Virgil were to ever feel that way about Jax, things would have to really sour between them. Maybe that's why Ralph had never spoken of his son before.

Hack stood. "Well, I better go pack. I'll be leaving later this morning." He shook Virgil's hand with a killer grip. "Thanks for holding down the fort here, my man."

As if Virgil needed Hack's approval to live his own life here on Wren. He pulled back his hand and flexed it, relieving the irritation. "Bye, Hack." *Hit the road. Flight path. Whatever.*

After Ralph and Hack left, Jax woke up and helped Virgil work through the familiar routine of opening the store for the day. The rising sun lit the sky dimly at first, then hid the stars. It was going to be another bluebird day on Wren. Especially if he heard from Allison.

There he went again, expecting things he shouldn't.

She enjoyed having space. Her space had been overrun by aunts. Her trusty friend Virgil Tagaloa had suggested the brainiac idea she get away on her own. She was an adult and perfectly capable. A logical progression of events had unfolded.

But what about the incident yesterday in the stockroom? The pain he'd felt was real. And what about his growing unease? Was it reasonable or just impatience?

Hadn't he learned anything by now? Love her for *her*. Love her for who she's destined to be—not who he'd like her to be. Not who he longs for her to be to *him*.

He huffed a crate of fresh oranges to the produce display. Sorted the fruit into bins before allowing himself to check his messages again. Nothing.

Once the morning got in full swing for everyone—not just an up-with-the-owls grocery guy choosing flavor-of-the-day muffins—he'd visit Allison's aunts. See if they needed anything. Ask if they'd heard from Allison.

Old reliable, being a friend, same as always.

33

Bumblebee socks

Waking to the house heater rumbling warm air, Amelia stretched under the covers, then creaked upright. After standing a while in front of her open closet, she sighed.

The clothes were so crammed together she could hardly pick out options. Her wardrobe was suffering from random patterns and colors. Shirts that matched only one pair of pants. Shorts that may or may not fit well. If she'd designated a Friday outfit, she wouldn't be standing here feeling overwhelmed.

Simplify. That was the best way to approach this problem. She pulled out the same linen shift she'd worn yesterday and her favorite blue cardigan. Then chose a cute pair of yellow bumblebee socks from her dresser. If Shasta called for more bling, Amelia would point to the sparkly pink hearts trailing each bumblebee.

While dressing, she listened to another chapter of *David Copperfield*. One nice thing about audiobooks and e-books was they didn't take up physical space.

Ready for the day, she leaned against the closet door and wedged it closed. Watched it for another few seconds to make sure it didn't pop back open.

Downstairs, she fed Miss Kitty and Marshal Matt Dillon, careful to wipe up the seeds spilled on the counter and floor. She stepped outside with Lokita to the fenced area and spotted sparrows and juncos breakfasting from the bird feeder at the forest edge. And a little gray bird running around on the ground.

Amelia squinted. Not a bird. A mouse. Well, as long as the mouse stayed outside, they'd be a-okay—to use a term of Allison's. Not that anyone was going to tell Allison about a mouse. This time or any other time.

Back in the kitchen, Amelia was giving the dogs their breakfasts when Shasta flashed in like a neon sign, wearing a pink sequin top—cut embarrassingly low—and black leather pants with rhinestones up the sides. A vivid orange scarf wrapped around her head and trailed down her back. The usual cloud of perfume followed her. Shiny jewelry clinked across her neck and wrists. If Amelia ever mostly lost her eyesight and couldn't see much of anything at all, there was an optimal chance she'd still be able to easily find Shasta.

"A gift from me to you, sis." Shasta handed Amelia a mug tied with a bow.

Amelia squinted at the printed words. *Not before coffee.* "You remembered I liked that phrase! Thanks, Shasta." Amelia fixed herself a bowl of fruity loops cereal with milk, then joined Shasta at the table.

Macy walked in and clunked her phone on the counter as if fed up with it. "Still no message from Allison. Should we call the Coast Guard, do you think?"

Shasta rolled her eyes. "She's hardly been gone a day, Mace. Give the girl a break."

Pulling smoothie ingredients from the refrigerator, Macy sent Shasta a weak smile. "Maybe you're right. Maybe it's just my ferocity coming out again."

Amelia took another bite of cereal, chewed, swallowed, then said what seemed most fitting. "Allison is perfectly capable of taking care of Allison."

Straightening the bracelets on one wrist, Shasta grinned. "She's probably living it up this morning. Eating bagels and lox with a cute new guy. Shopping for fancy stuff. Being adventurous. Hang gliding maybe."

"Hang gliding?" Macy lost her grip on the dish in her hand. Hitting the counter, it broke.

"Tiddlywinks, Mace!"

"I didn't mean to!"

While her sisters bickered, Amelia collected the dirty dishes, lined them up in the dishwasher, and wandered into the main entry. How wonderful it had felt to enter this house the first time! Like the most magnificent place in the world was welcoming her.

When her sisters' barbs against each other grew more animated—more annoying to listen to—Amelia headed outside. What might the bald eagle family be up to today?

She was videoing the frost-edged leaves of a rhododendron when Virgil appeared carrying a brown bag. Full of warm muffins, no doubt.

"Good morning, Amelia. How are things?"

Amelia sighed. "Even a house as big as Allison's isn't room enough for Macy and Shasta to get along."

Sitting on a tree stump, Virgil broke the top off a nearby grass stem and chewed on it. "How's your YouTube channel coming along?"

"I've added lots of videos, but I haven't made it public yet."

"Are you holding off for a reason?"

Amelia fingered the edge of a leaf, melting the frost there. One toggle switch was all it would take for the world to see Wren Island through Amelia's eyes. For some reason, though, it felt like the videos should only be seen by friends. People who already knew and loved Wren Islanders.

She pulled out her phone, found a favorite video, and played it for Virgil. Allison helping Shasta set up an arcade game. Another video, Allison teasing Amelia about making YouTube videos. A special favorite, Allison singing to the dogs in her pretty voice, a row of diamond earrings sparkling along one ear. Those diamonds must have cost a fortune. Allison kept her hair so short you couldn't look at her and not see those sparkly earrings. No one would say Allison was flashy, but when those earrings caught your eye, you knew she had money.

Amelia tucked away her phone. "I guess I'm wondering if the videos are too personal to share. Maybe Allison doesn't want the world watching her sing to the dogs. Or all those other sweet things she does for us. I'll ask her before I make the channel public."

Virgil was studying the water. Short waves half-heartedly rolled onto the beach in a receding tide. If Amelia dared, this morning would be a fitting time to venture near the water alone again. What do you do when a horse throws you? You get right back on. That's what Dad used to say.

"Have you heard from Allison?"

Virgil's unnaturally husky voice grabbed Amelia's attention. He was squinting at the water, not looking at her. Tired? Or a fraction worried?

"No, but she told us not to expect to. Have you heard from her?"

He shook his head and cleared his throat. A couple of times.

Amelia's heart first went out to him for worrying about Allison. Just as quickly, her heart leaped with delight.

Oh, to be cared about like that again! To be loved by a man as rugged as Virgil Tagaloa. With Virgil, Allison would always be safe and protected. She would always be encouraged to be herself, appreciated for being herself. Could there be a better gift to wish for her niece?

Hoping to ease his worry, Amelia repeated Virgil's own claim. "Allison is perfectly capable of taking care of Allison."

The raw expression on his face revealed everything. Yes, he believed Allison could take care of herself. Admired her for it. Supported her pursuit of anything and everything she desired.

But looking from Virgil's perspective, Amelia could now see a negative side to Allison being perfectly capable. To her flourishing competence backed by nearly unlimited resources. Ambition could easily draw her away, over and far beyond an uncrossable chasm.

Allison soaring ahead on her own.

Virgil left where she no longer wanted to be.

34

Smaller than the backpack

The birds came awake one at a time. First a single melody from a sparrow, then another. Robins began chirping. Warblers added their own tunes until the symphony was fully orchestrated.

Allison tried to move her stiff muscles. The pain that had been fire yesterday was now shards of ice. And how did her clothes get so damp? Overnight dew? Was she shivering from cold or because she'd developed a fever? A fever would not be welcome at all right now. Not on top of everything else going on. At least the vest was warm. The bright yellow vest. Matchy-matchy.

Upsy-daisy, you can do it. Whoops. Pain, zinging up and down her neck. Pounding out of her head like a sledgehammer. *Try again. There you go.*

She hobbled down the trail. *Walk on, walk on, walk on.*

Miracle of miracles, listen to that. A boat was approaching the island. Probably pulling up to the dock next to *Buttercup.*

After the boat's engine stopped, voices reached her. A man—and a girl with attitude. Arguing now. Yelling. Oh well. At least it was *someone* to help her back to her boat.

Walk on, walk on, walk on. Crunch, crunch, crunch. Ice shattering inside her hip, fueling hot lava.

The voices got closer, not arguing anymore, and a man came around a bend in the trail. A big guy, wearing appropriate boots for the terrain. He looked able to support her, lift her even. She nearly fainted with relief.

A girl—a teenager maybe—appeared from behind him. She was smaller than the backpack she staggered under. Spotting Allison, the girl halted mid-step. "Whoa."

"Am I glad to see you guys." Allison leaned against a tree trunk. "I had an accident. I'm trying to get back to my boat."

"That your joyride at the dock? How'd you know about this place?" The man looked her up and down. She must be a sight.

"I happened on it." She took a careful breath against her fracturing insides. Or were they *fractionalizing*? "Would you help me get back to the dock?"

He didn't move. Had he not heard her?

When the girl shifted the pack on her shoulders and nearly fell backward, Allison shot a look at the man. He was probably three times heavier than that girl. Why wasn't he carrying the load?

Recovering her balance, the girl looked up. "We've got a cart down at the dock. Maybe we could—"

"Don't need the cart. She's mobile, isn't she?" The man turned back down the trail and called over his shoulder. "What kind of accident did you have?"

Allison watched his retreating back. Lots and lots of help, this guy. About as much support as her ex would have been. Well, she'd always gotten along well enough on her own. She drew herself up. "Motorbike accident. Went off a ledge."

The man stopped. "We better go get yer bike. Might be worth something."

Allison shook her head, but the zinging, punctuated by pops of pain, stopped that. Good grief. Now her heart was thumping around unnaturally. *Scary* unnaturally.

She let her breath catch up. "It's buried in the brush at the bottom of a ravine. I'll come back for it later."

The girl held out an arm. "Want to lean on me?"

If Allison leaned on that overloaded mite, they'd both topple over. "Thanks, but I'm all right."

"You on your own?" The guy continued down the trail.

Limping forward, Allison didn't answer. Out of all the people in the world who might have rescued her, she'd ended up with this clown. The girl with him looked like she needed rescuing herself.

"I asked if you were on your own." He'd turned to face Allison.

She stopped walking and tried to stand taller. Didn't get far. Too painful.

Chuckling, he continued down the trail. When the girl gave Allison a worried look, a weird feeling—a new weird feeling—began swirling around inside Allison. This guy was creeping her out. Or was the weird feeling just from pain? Or from the fever—if she had one?

At any rate, she hadn't been doing *too* badly on her own, had she? Might be best to try to lose this creep. She gathered what strength she could and sent it toward her voice.

"I'm feeling better now. I can get back all right on my own."

He kept going. The girl stopped to hitch up shorts that were falling down and spoke quietly. "What's your name?"

"Allison."

The man spun around. "Allison Theodore? Of Wren Island?"

He'd heard of her. Not entirely surprising. Many islanders knew their neighbors. But she'd remember if she'd met this guy in person. And he wasn't from Wren Island.

She met his challenging look with her own—and accidentally let go of her walking stick. Unsupported, she swayed. Zing up, zing down, zing all around.

The girl bent to retrieve the stick, then straightened an inch at a time under the massive backpack. "Is it okay to give the stick back to her?"

When he nodded, she handed it back, chatting like nothing was amiss. "Here you go, Allison. I'm Mattie, by the way. That's Lester. It sure is nice to finally meet someone out here. We've never seen *anyone* on Seal Rock."

Allison leaned on the stick to catch her breath. Once she was back on the boat, she'd zip away from here. Not that she was comfortable leaving a teenage girl alone with this creep.

"How old are you, Mattie?"

"Old enough," Lester answered. He was far enough away to be useless, but close enough to keep tabs. Mattie just shrugged.

35

Tightening her hold

Macy clicked the pressure cooker closed. Pulled pork sandwiches for lunch, on slices of the fresh bread Jax had promised to deliver from the market. If Allison came home in time for lunch . . .

But Allison would probably still be away at lunchtime. Enjoying herself. Eating in a cute café maybe. Anne used to love discovering new restaurants. Allison was like her mom in so many ways.

Shasta stuck her head in the doorway. "Hack's getting ready to leave."

Macy's heart flip-flopped. Was this the moment she'd have to say goodbye to her sister again? Unkind words still echoing behind them?

"Shasta? Are you leaving too?"

New silver hoop earrings swung as Shasta shook her head. More purchases. Allison's credit card would see relief if Shasta left. Macy's eyes stung. But this was her *sister*. Flawed, yes—weren't they all? And wasn't it better to stick together?

Macy pulled her into a hug. When Shasta tried to wiggle out, Macy tightened her hold and spoke into the pom-pom hair. "Can we stop saying goodbye, Shasta? Please?"

Sighing, Shasta stopped squirming. "For today, yes."

Outside, Macy and Shasta collected Melia and Virgil from the flower beds where they were raking leaves. They all joined Ralph and Hack on Allison's dock.

"Nowhere like Alaska in the summertime!" Hack flexed muscled arms over his head. "Anyone want to come along?"

Shasta elbowed him. "Not this time, Hacky-boy."

Virgil squinted toward Hack's plane. "That little jet handle low altitude well?"

"Like a hot knife through butter. Handy for filming."

Macy glanced at Virgil. Could he be thinking the same thing she was? "Hack? Why don't you fly around the islands and see if you spot Allison's boat?"

"Oh pooh, Mace." Shasta rolled her eyes.

Ralph shook his head. "All you biddies and your worrying. Look up where she's broadcasting from."

"What?"

Ralph nodded toward his own boat. "She's got a web-connected transponder like mine attached to her vessel. Sends a signal showing right where she's at."

Hack pulled out his phone. "Website?" He tapped in the address Ralph gave him. "Name of vessel?"

Macy looked at each of her sisters. Didn't *any* of them know the name of Allison's boat?

"*Buttercup.*" Virgil and Ralph answered at the same time.

"Like the little yellow flower?" Melia's smile widened.

Macy smiled too. With its sleek, high sides, Allison's bright yellow boat did look a lot like a buttercup. Macy sometimes wandered through a field of the blooming yellow flowers in the visions she used to fall asleep.

"Here she is." Hack grinned and held up the phone. "Right here on Wren."

Macy glanced at the screen. A dot on the digital map located *Buttercup* at Allison's dock. "Oh, for goodness' sake, Hack. Obviously, it's not accurate."

Hack's grin faded. "Maybe inside the boathouse?"

"Nope." Virgil shook his head. "I already checked."

Ralph cleared his throat. "She might not want her whereabouts to be public knowledge."

Hack pulled his phone closer. "Wren must be the last location she allowed a signal to be sent. I'll be able to see more if I get in the back way."

"Get in the back way?" Virgil's eyes narrowed.

Hack tapped the screen, then angled the phone toward them. "She's at a little island south of the Canadian border. Seal Rock. Looks like she's been there since yesterday afternoon. Probably relaxing in the sun. Drinking too much." At the taunting look Hack sent her, Macy cringed.

"Can I see that?" Virgil reached for the phone.

"Sorry, my man." Hack stashed it in his shirt pocket. "I've got to leave right away or miss an appointment."

With the whine of an engine and a spray of saltwater, Hack became a disappearing speck in the wide sky. Shasta and Ralph linked arms and ambled toward the forest. Macy joined Melia and Virgil as they headed back to the house.

Sighing, Melia navigated around a clump of dune grass. "I don't think I'd want to spend the summer in Alaska."

"Oh? Why not?" Virgil adjusted his ball cap.

"Alaska can't be any nicer than Wren. Especially with Wren being home to friends who care about each other and look out for each other."

Virgil gave Melia's shoulder a gentle squeeze, then turned to Macy. "Have you heard anything from Allison?"

"She said not to expect to."

"Right. Of course." His jaw tight, Virgil ran his hands through his hair. "Well, Ed and I are putting in fence posts today."

"Fence posts?"

"As a guide along the trail leading up to the market. We'll eventually add them to the forest trails too. Wood posts with rope strung between. Like at the commune."

"Can I help?" Melia propped her rake against the house.

"I was hoping you might." Virgil handed Melia a pair of work gloves. Macy watched them walk toward the market until their chatter about fence posts and the commune fell out of listening range.

Turning to go inside, she almost stumbled over a blinking Louise. "Don't you want to go off and have fun too?" Louise twitched her upper right lip and showed her teeth, her whole back end wiggling. A sure sign she was doggie-happy.

The sound of Ed's all-terrain vehicle approaching the market reached them. When the engine stopped and cheerful voices called to each other, Macy thought for sure Louise would take off, eager to be part of a more charismatic scene. But the dog tilted her head, listening, then blinked back at Macy.

Choosing to stay with Macy Johansson? The most boring person of the bunch?

She patted the dog. "Just for you, we'll go in through the front door."

As Macy prepared lunch, she passed bits of pork to both dogs. That business of Hack looking up Allison's location was strange, wasn't it? Getting in the back way—whatever that meant.

Goodness. Was Hack even his real name? Or had he earned it as a nickname?

Shasta would tell her she was worrying too much. *Take a chill pill, Mace.* But Virgil seemed concerned too. And Virgil wasn't one to worry unnecessarily. Usually, Virgil was as *unworried* as anyone could be.

And what was with Hack's comment about Allison drinking? As if she'd missed the freedom to. Allison had said she didn't mind if they didn't keep alcohol in the house. Macy had believed Allison meant it.

The thought of Allison sneaking away on her own because she wanted to drink freely was enough to . . .

Macy pulled out her phone and tapped a text to her sponsor. After a few exchanges, Macy took several deep breaths. Stretched until Jax arrived with the promised loaf of bread.

When the teenager goggled at the bowl of steaming pork, Macy fixed him a sandwich and sat him down at the table. Once he'd wolfed down the sandwich, she poured him a glass of milk, brought the cookie platter near, and asked him questions—partly to distract herself and partly because teenagers didn't talk much otherwise. In no time at all, she'd learned about all kinds of riveting stuff. Lawnmower engines, muffin recipes, the latest video games.

And Jax was beaming at the attention. She poured him another glass of milk. Slid the cookie platter closer to him.

She was Macy Johansson, caretaker of anyone along her path, teenagers included. Mostly good at it—if you didn't count everything that got broken along the way.

36

A snowplow

On the dock at Seal Rock, Allison peered into the water around the pilings. Her phone was down there. She could dive in after it. That icy water would feel refreshing. Maybe put out the fire rolling around inside her.

Still unhelpful, Lester hopped onto his own boat, a rickety shrimper that must have seen better days long, long ago. "Get in. We'll come back for your joyride later."

Uh-uh. No way was she going anywhere with this guy. She hobbled the final distance to *Buttercup*. Unlatched the portside gate with Mattie's help, boarded, relatched the gate—again with Mattie's help, because Allison's fingers wouldn't work the way she wanted them to.

Inside the pilothouse, she'd be sheltered from the elements. She skipped most of the usual predeparture checklist. Too complicated. While warming up the engine, she lost her balance and crashed to the deck.

Like being crushed under a snowplow—that's how it felt. Not that she'd ever been under a snowplow. But in case she ever was in the future, she already knew how it would feel.

Wasn't that a funny thought? That she knew how it felt to be crushed under a snowplow? Ha ha ha!

Blinking back tears, she waited for the pain to ease.

It didn't.

With Mattie's help, Allison pulled herself upright again. All she wanted to do now was make it home. Make it home to . . . Make it home to . . . Where was she going?

Oh yes. Wren Island.

She threw as much self-sufficiency as she could into her voice. "Untie the last mooring line, Mattie?" The sweet girl complied. "Toss the line on deck. Thanks."

Lester reached for his shrimper's final unmooring. "Get in, Mattie, unless you want to be left behind again."

Shrieking, the girl scrambled off *Buttercup* and threw aboard the final mooring line. She hopped over to Lester's boat just before it rumbled off in a cloud of diesel fumes. Would Lester really have deserted that little girl?

As *Buttercup* bobbed, Allison fought for balance and stared at her navigational equipment. What was she doing, again?

Oh yeah. Driving a boat to Wren Island.

Several hundred yards out of the cove, she passed Lester's idling shrimper. He tossed his cigarette into the water. Littering the ocean. Another demerit.

Then he began trailing her. Was that supposed to make her feel safe? She should radio for help.

How to reach the handpiece, though? For balance, she needed to keep one hand on the wheel. And the other hand was useless. Attached to a spaghetti arm.

She let go of the wheel and swiped at the radio handpiece. Accidentally knocked it off its cradle and sent it swinging. Right, left, right, left. Oh, her wobbly head.

Ick. Look at all that blood everywhere. That was going to be tough to clean up.

From the sound behind her, Lester still trailed her. Could she lose him? Head to a different island? Cruise around until he gave up?

He knew where she lived, though. She was supposed to be going there right now. To that island she called home.

She checked her chart plotter and zoomed out until she could see home. Wren—that's where she was going.

With any luck, that grizzled guy on Wren . . . What was his name? The one who delivered mail? Anyhow, with any luck, that guy would be on the beach swearing when she arrived. That ought to scare off Lester.

Or maybe that other guy would be around. The pilot with the muscles. He could swoop down in his floatplane and buzz the greasy hair right off Lester's head.

That thought wasn't very nice of her. Not charitable to hope for something bad to happen to another person. Hair being buzzed off by a floatplane would hurt. A lot. Gazillions and gazillions of hurt is how it would feel.

Her heart was thumping around again. Strange. Everything inside her felt strange.

Buttercup veered. Allison corrected. Whew. What had happened?

Oops. She'd leaned on the wheel. Probably should try to avoid doing that.

The incessant pounding inside her head threatened to churn into vomit. What a job cleaning *Buttercup* would be. Instead of throwing up, maybe she'd just pass out. Less mess.

Wren Island finally came in sight. Looking at the sonar screen made her feel even more dizzy, so she steered around the underwater boulders by following her gut. Who cared if her boat smashed into a boulder? Shipwreck couldn't be any worse than whatever was going on inside her.

Lester had already arrived at her dock. How'd he get there so quickly?

He disembarked from his boat, barked at Mattie to tie up, and poked his head into the boathouse. Mattie tied up the shrimper, then Allison's boat. Through a haze, Allison watched the girl climb aboard, enter the wheelhouse, and shut down the engine.

Allison looked around. Her boat had a name, a special one. Hadn't she just been thinking of it? If she could remember it now, she'd share it with Mattie.

"That big house up there yours?" Lester strode off the dock, up the beach, toward a massive English Tudor house. Her house.

Where was everyone? No mail guy swearing on the beach. No floatplane pilot buzzing over. No aunts, no dogs. How could they not see she'd returned? How could they not notice her bright yellow boat?

That creep was going to barge right into her house—without having been invited. Of all the nerve. Were her aunts inside? Baking brownies, painting toenails, peering through a magnifying glass?

Time for emergency action. Sound the horn. Five short blasts, the universal boating signal for danger.

"Put your hands over your ears, Mattie. This is going to be loud."

One, two, three, four, five. Allison nearly fainted from the pain shooting through her head. But with only one hand doing what she asked it to, covering her own ears while sounding the horn wasn't an option.

What if no one helpful heard the signal the first time? She couldn't reach the horn anymore now that she was slumped on the floor. The sticky, icky floor. She lifted a hand dripping blood and stared at it. Was it even hers?

"Mattie? Five short blasts again?"

A heavy cloth was positioned over Allison's ears. The horn sounded again, mercifully muffled. One, two, three, four, five.

Mattie bent close, kneeling in the blood that was oozing everywhere now. She removed the cloth and placed one light hand on Allison's back.

"Lester didn't think anybody would be around. Somebody's talking to him now. And people are running over here. You've sure got lots of friends." In Mattie's voice, a wistfulness.

Fading, Allison closed her eyes. Giving in, finally. *Lots of friends.*

Other voices reached her then. People she loved. Coming closer.

37

First in line

As Allison disappeared behind the swinging doors in the mainland hospital's emergency room, Virgil counted the three times in his life, so far, he'd been willing to cause significant physical harm to another person.

Number one was when, after searching for days, he'd finally found his wife in an abandoned building in a neighborhood known for drug trafficking. Sprawled on the floor, surrounded by used needles and syringes, she'd been coherent enough to say she didn't want to come home. To say she didn't want to see six-month-old Jax.

Unwilling to accept that, Virgil got her on her feet and nearly out the door when a peddler buzzed in with loaded needles. The contents of one were in his wife's scarred arm before Virgil could blink. That time, he might have killed the peddler if a neighbor hadn't already noted unusually suspicious activity. Law enforcement officers arriving to check the premises pulled Virgil off a dealer they'd been trying to nab.

Number two happened when Jax and a friend, both three years old, were playing on a swing set in a city park. An out-of-control vehicle swerved from the road into the park, narrowly missing the boys and crashing into a tree. The raging driver hopped out of the car waving a gun. Virgil would have been a hero maybe, if adrenaline from the near miss and the yahoo's hysterical laughing hadn't kept Virgil throwing punches longer than necessary. Now Virgil was grateful a bystander had intervened and redirected his attention to Jax, who was crying not from fear about the near accident but from seeing his dad's fury. That time, the second time, Virgil vowed he'd never again lose control. He went to therapy to make sure.

But, number three, when he found Allison collapsed in a pool of blood, then noted Lester Locum sauntering around like it didn't matter, something entirely different had shifted inside.

In the moment of crisis, he'd focused on the essentials. Staunched the blood. Kept Allison's listless brown eyes focused, kept her talking in case she had a concussion. Alerted the mainland hospital emergency department, coordinated transport. Gritted his teeth when hospital staff told him—all five times he asked—only family was permitted to be with Allison. Shasta pulled herself together in a helpful way for once, keeping him updated.

Sitting on a cold bench in a waiting room far too chilly, he opened his phone's app for vessel tracking. It wasn't difficult to find what he was looking for. *Pinch Hitter* was sending a signal from Wren Island's south side, near Allison's house. Virgil marked the vessel as one to watch.

Finally, a doctor confirmed Allison was going to pull through. She'd be in for a long recovery, yes, but they were more than cautiously optimistic.

Back on his SAFE boat in minutes, Virgil slammed through abbreviated predeparture tasks and fastened on a life jacket. Then he got his money's worth from *Incremental*'s amped-up engines.

He found Lester loafing on Allison's dock under the wary watch of Ralph and Louise, while Jax and Mattie, the young woman who'd helped Allison, scrubbed *Buttercup* clean.

Storming up to Lester, Virgil gripped his coat collar. "What happened?"

Lester brushed him off, tapping cigarette ashes. "Easy, man."

"What *happened*?"

"She had an accident, I brought her back."

"She brought *herself* back!"

"My girl helped her."

Lester was in a headlock in a second. At the very least, Virgil intended to throw him off the dock. Ralph took his time tying up Louise. Then he tapped Virgil's back and pulled him off Lester. While Louise lunged and growled at the creep, Virgil entertained the idea of unclipping the dog's leash and letting her have a go.

He wasn't proud of himself for the headlock or that thought. But Louise tearing into Lester had come into Virgil's mind and played out for a while, whether he liked himself for it or not.

After Lester and Mattie finally shoved off, Macy appeared on the dock with a brown paper bag. She set it near Virgil and Ralph without a word, collected Jax, and headed back to the house. The recovering alcoholic had delivered unopened beers, still cold from the market's fridge. She'd left the receipt in the bag.

It all came over him at once. The grueling wait for Allison to return his texts. Wondering if she was okay, worrying she might not be. The odd physical ache he'd experienced in the stockroom, which he now knew was significant. The sight of the woman he loves, paler than she should be, drowning in her own blood. Her shallow breaths almost disappearing.

Any guy who can handle another guy's tears is worth keeping around. He and Ralph finished the beers and a half-empty bottle of whiskey Ralph kept stashed in Allison's boathouse. Louise kept them quiet company, her head resting on front paws, one eye on the horizon.

Later, Macy wouldn't allow Virgil inside Allison's house. "Jax is playing Monopoly with Amelia. While they finish, go home, shower, and brush your teeth. I'm making you a green smoothie to go. Would you please fast-track me over to the mainland hospital as soon as you feel up for it?"

"In *Incremental*?" Virgil swallowed his surprise. While other islanders routinely complimented his SAFE boat, Macy'd never so much as given *Incremental* a second glance.

"Of course in *Incremental*, although please not incrementally. I want to get there as quickly as possible."

Virgil stayed under thirty-two knots. Macy, one hand holding her hair in place, the other across her heart, seemed impressed enough already.

On Allison's fifth day in the hospital, Virgil stopped visiting. It was clear Allison felt vulnerable, having so little control over her situation. The oxygen mask, IV lines, drainage tubes. The pain medication button she reluctantly pushed with one slender finger. She was Allison Theodore still trying to be perfectly capable of taking care of herself. Every part of him begged to stay at her side and do everything he could, *anything* he could, to see a glimmer return to her eyes.

How did he summon the strength to stay away? Because he loved her for her, not for him.

After twelve days in the hospital, Allison came home to a giant bouquet of wild lilacs in a deep purple color. Virgil had ordered them special.

Maybe there was a faint glimmer in her eyes. "Lilacs are my favorite. How did you know?"

He hadn't. The stars had lined up his way, for once.

Now, watching Allison struggle to get around in a broken body, he couldn't guarantee there'd never be a fourth time he might be willing to cause physical harm. With the way things were going, he was ready to deck any skunk who smelled like half a threat to Allison Theodore. And if Lester Locum ever returned to Wren Island, Louise would have to take a number before having a go at him.

Virgil Tagaloa would be the first in line.

38

Resting

On a lounge chair at the edge of the dune, overlooking the ocean, Allison soaked up the warm sunshine. Her wide-brimmed hat and large sunglasses dimmed the brilliance coming off the water. The cotton blanket Aunt Macy had tucked around warded off the cool breeze.

Little Lokita, curled into a ball across Allison's legs, snored rhythmically. Allison stroked the dog's white fur—clean and sweet-smelling, thanks to Aunt Macy taking charge of bathing the dogs regularly.

In the forest behind Allison, several crows cawed to each other. Raucously chattering, quieting, then raising a ruckus again. Holding court, as Aunt Amelia liked to say. Virgil once said a group of crows was called a murder of crows. Allison had thought he was teasing until she confirmed it online.

Playing with Lokita's soft eyebrows, she watched a sailboat make slow progress toward the west. A boat that size could be piloted by one person. On their own, going somewhere interesting. Like she'd been, not so long ago. Until her independence fractionalized.

The day she'd made her way back to Wren, slumped on *Buttercup*'s deck and not at all certain of anything, Aunt Macy had galloped into boss mode. Allison was whisked off to the mainland hospital in Virgil's reliable SAFE boat with

Aunt Shasta along for support. Ralph was ordered, in no uncertain terms, to keep an eye on Lester—a job Ralph had already willingly taken on. Mattie and Jax were put to work scrubbing Allison's boat deck. So clean you could eat off it, Ralph said. But Ralph might have lower standards than Allison herself in that department.

Because Allison had been out like a light during most of that afternoon, she'd pieced all that together from everyone's reports. All that plus the sad fact that once *Buttercup* was clean and sanitized, Lester had hollered for Mattie, and off they went, not to be heard from since.

There were more memories than Allison cared for of the twelve days spent in the hospital. Staring at the ceiling, waiting for her neck and head injury to stabilize. Taking conscious, careful breaths with a punctured lung. Enduring the achy first days after hip surgery, then the wrenching physical therapy necessary to get her sprained knees in shape to support the new hip.

Every time someone other than Aunt Macy visited in the hospital, Allison scrambled to pull the sheet across her icky, scabbed arm. You'd think Allison Theodore, a grown woman, would be mature enough by now to not be concerned by her looks. True beauty was on the inside, not on the surface, and all that. But there she was, trying to be presentable even in a hospital gown.

When Aunt Shasta noticed Allison's embarrassment, she bought three linen robes with long, wide sleeves—practical *and* pretty. That was the same day Aunt Shasta delivered a bunch of cashmere cardigans and bags of gourmet coffee to the nurses.

Once Allison got home, the real work began. Learning to roll into a seated position with cracked ribs. Inching around the house a little more at a time. Keeping up with the physical therapy someone was always on hand to help with. Staying on top of the pain with just enough medication, but not too much.

Aunt Macy still insisted Allison rest every afternoon. These days, Aunt Macy took care of everything. The dogs, the house, the property. All the meals, unless Aunt Shasta and Ralph got inspired to barbecue.

Taking care of it all was a lot. No wonder Aunt Macy had begun delegating the cleaning chores to anyone who happened by. Like the morning she convinced Ralph, Ed, and Jax to pull the arcade games out from the garage wall, sweep the cobwebs, and even polish the games. Then she handed out lemonade and quarters.

When Allison cried about having lost Gemma's motorbike, Aunt Macy took charge of that too. Got Gemma Campana on speakerphone so Allison could hear for herself that Gemma wasn't at all worried about losing the bike. All Gemma wanted was for Allison to make a full recovery. *We're all pulling for you, Allison.*

Hearing that, Allison had laid back against the pillow and cried more, while Aunt Macy covered for her by chatting away, all upbeat.

Allison smoothed the blanket across her legs and gazed down the beach. One of these days, when the boathouse didn't feel too far away and she could keep her balance better, she was going back to Reclamation Island. She'd bring a gift to Gemma and check on Mattie Conway.

For now, she watched Louise chasing dragonflies in the grassy dune. Aunt Amelia settled into a nearby lounge chair, tugged her pink cardigan into place, and held her e-reader up to her face—reading in large print, probably. Aunt Amelia was a real trouper. Never any complaints. Not a single one.

When the gong from the commune sounded, Aunt Amelia pulled out her phone, tapped the screen a few times, and angled it toward Allison. They listened as nearby orcas sang. When the orcas moved on, Aunt Amelia tucked away her phone and picked up her e-reader again.

All without either of them having said a word.

Lokita burrowed deeper into the blanket across Allison's legs. Tired of chasing dragonflies, Louise came close. Allison did the only thing within reach. She played with the bigger dog's wide, brown eyebrows.

Life slowed and quieted even more.

39

Not snooping

In the sunroom, Macy stepped back from the window so she wouldn't be caught observing. Not snooping, but observing.

Shasta and Ralph were standing around the firepit. Talking, mostly. Shasta's head bobbed up and down, her unicorn-colored hair now faded and dull. And those baggy overalls! The Shasta Jenkins Macy had always known wouldn't be caught dead wearing overalls.

When Shasta stood on tiptoe to whisper in Ralph's ear, Ralph sort of smiled. Then they headed into the forest. Again.

The obvious explanation was that they were *noodling*. But it didn't quite fit. With previous boyfriends, Shasta returned from a rendezvous even more perky and certain of herself. After spending time with Ralph, Shasta looked drawn and worried.

Plus, weren't Shasta and Ralph a little old to be noodling so often? Multiple times a day! Just thinking about it made Macy spin—made her *head* spin, she meant.

She ought to let herself go into all-out sleuthing mode—notepad, binoculars, the whole kit and caboodle—and figure out what was going on. After all, she was in charge of things around here. Allison hadn't said so exactly. But who else was responsible enough?

With Shasta and Ralph disappeared, there was no reason to stand around anymore. Using the edge of her apron, she wiped a damp spot from the windowsill, slobber from Louise. Then she moved to the television room and straightened the remote controls, board games, and foam cheeseheads.

So far, Allison hadn't said anything about the growing collection of fan gear for the Green Bay Packers. Five cheeseheads! One for each of them and one for Ralph. And a bunch of pennants they were all supposed to wave every time the defense got into the red zone—whatever that meant. Macy refolded one of the satiny jerseys Shasta crammed the dogs into every Sunday.

Macy's watch alarm said it was almost time for her AA meeting. Upstairs, she sat in front of her computer, pulled off her socks, and rolled her bare feet across the foot massager.

During the meeting, others shared their successes and failures. Macy nodded sympathetically. When it was her turn, she, too, shared the raw truth.

She'd recently handled unopened beer bottles! Purchased and delivered them to friends. Not only that, but at this very moment, a boatload of painkillers was within easy reach in a kitchen cupboard. She was in charge of dispensing them! But every time she thought about dispensing to herself, one vision stopped her.

Allison, crumpled on her boat's bloody deck, unable to take half a breath without agonizing pain. One measly pain pill would have made a difference for Allison on that awful day.

So yes, Macy was in charge of the pills. And she was guarding them like they were gold. She never ever wanted to see anyone she loved in that much pain again.

When the meeting ended, Macy clicked off. That new girl in the group didn't look much older than the little girl who had saved Allison's life. How'd a young girl like Mattie Conway get mixed up with a loafer like Lester?

During the one afternoon Mattie had spent on Wren, Macy had hinted around every which way, trying to draw Mattie into revealing why she stayed with Lester. But Mattie didn't give up a single morsel of helpful information. Nothing Macy could leverage to convince the girl she could do better.

You had to admit, Mattie Conway knew how to fend for herself. Except that fending for herself had mixed her up with Lester.

Macy pulled on socks—cable knit, Shasta's latest craze—and headed downstairs. Mattie had worn a threadbare tee shirt and too-big shorts that wouldn't get her through winter. Did she even own a warm coat? Lester ought to get her one of those thick, puffy, down jackets. Make himself useful, for once.

In the kitchen, Macy straightened the pressure cooker on the shelf—one less thing for Allison to worry about—and reached for her phone. Time for a communiqué. She scrolled through her contacts, held the phone to her ear, and waited.

"Hello?"

"Gemma? It's Macy. Over on Wren."

"Hi! How's everything? How's Allison recovering?"

"She's fine, just fine."

"She's certainly in competent hands!"

Macy beamed.

"How can I help you, Macy?"

"I was wondering if you know how I can get in touch with Mattie Conway. We'd like to offer her a live-in housekeeping job. Allison said Mattie could have the wing off the sunroom."

"Oh wow! Great idea! But I probably should tell you that several of us here on Reclamation Island have tried to help Mattie and, so far, she hasn't taken us up on our offers."

Deflating, Macy sagged against the kitchen counter. If ever a girl was a candidate for a new start, Mattie Conway was it. Why couldn't the world ever go the way it should?

"Maybe Mattie would like the idea of moving to Wren." Gemma's voice had turned thoughtful. "I don't have a phone number for her, but I'll give her your message next time I see her."

After Macy ended the call, she tapped her fingers on the kitchen counter. If only she were Superwoman! Then she could help everyone in the world. With every problem they had.

What kind of work do you do, Macy?

I'm a caretaker. I solve problems. For anyone who needs me.

A bumping sound at the front door meant it was noon on the button. Macy hurried to the front entry, let Louise inside, and gave the dog a cookie. The no-crumble kind, so Allison wouldn't have to worry about crumbs either.

40

Thumbs-up

Amelia finished a chapter of Shelby Van Pelt's *Remarkably Bright Creatures*. Tucked her e-reader into the zippered, waterproof bag Macy had sewn from oilcloth. Repositioned herself in a more comfy position and draped the blanket over her bare toes.

On the lounge chair next to her, Allison slept. Or maybe rested. Except for stirring to listen to the orcas earlier, Allison had been quiet. Now, the only sounds were Lokita's soft snoring and a murder of crows holding court in the forest.

Listen to that, folks. A murder of crows is holding court this afternoon. Amelia sent the words around her head again. Lines like that could make the difference between amateur and pro on YouTube.

A swirl of dry leaves danced near, coming to rest against a hefty driftwood log. Another toothpick tossed aside by a giant. Amelia pulled out her binoculars and squinted at the three bald eagles perched in a tree on the east edge of Allison's property.

The parents were the ones with the distinctive markings—black feathers everywhere except their heads and tails, which were white. Virgil said the juvenile would keep its muted mottled feathers for at least a year. After that, it might be another few years before the young eagle's feathers became the striking white on black.

Virgil knew a lot about birds. Good thing he'd been paying attention the day the baby took its first flight. With everything else going on, Amelia might have missed it—like Allison had.

Only because Allison was in the hospital, practicing with a new cane and eating a real sandwich for the first time since her accident. A BLT without the bacon or lettuce. Just tomato and mayo, because the smell of everything else made Allison feel sick. But it counted as a real sandwich.

Amelia pulled out her phone, opened the YouTube app, and found her video of that first flight. Both parents taking off. One flying high in circles, the other perching nearby. The poor little baby left on its own. Then the parents calling, whistling, swirling. On and on and on. The baby flapping its wings at the big wide world, scared and excited all at once.

On the video, you could hear the conversation between her and Virgil. She'd asked what she now knew were dumb questions. Virgil was nice about it, but it was kind of the pits that her naivete had been recorded. Another reason to keep her YouTube channel private.

Whoosh. There went the baby. Flap, flap, flap toward the ground at first, then rising. Landing so clumsily on a branch, the parent perched nearby had to flap around and regain its own balance. Amelia had cheered. She smiled now too, watching the video again.

A thumbs-up appeared on the screen.

Huh. Did a thumbs-up appear automatically after you watched a video so many times? Below the thumbs-up, a comment appeared.

Nice shot. With those skills, you'll be raking in the big bucks any day now. The username was Hack Wesson.

Amelia tapped a reply. *Hi Hack. How are you?*

No response.

Maybe a private YouTube channel wasn't all that private. Maybe friends could see it?

Virgil arrived at the usual time, before the setting sun lowered enough toward the water to create a glare and cause Allison discomfort. He threw a frisbee for Louise until Allison woke up, then helped Allison, Amelia, and Lokita back to the house.

Inside, they found Macy pulling a steaming lasagna from the oven. Amelia collected dishes from the cabinets and set the table. All those labels Allison had posted in the kitchen were really helpful, not that Amelia could read them without squinting. But with this many people in and out of the kitchen, it was nice to usually find things where they were supposed to be.

Macy invited Virgil to stay, but he left to have dinner with Jax at his own house. Shasta breezed in as Macy sorted everyone into their places at the table. Amelia passed around a basket of garlic bread.

"Guess what, you guys? I heard from Hack."

Shasta set down her fork. "What? When?"

Macy helped herself to the green salad—and added a generous portion to Amelia's plate too. "What's Hack up to these days?"

Amelia pulled the crusts off a piece of garlic bread. "He didn't say. But he sort of said hi in a comment on my YouTube channel."

"Let me see." Shasta wiped her hands on a napkin and reached for Amelia's phone.

Allison finished chewing a bite. "This lasagna is delicious, Aunt Macy. I thought you hadn't made that channel public yet, Aunt Amelia."

"I haven't."

"Then how did Hack comment on a video?"

"I don't know." Amelia shrugged. "I was hoping Shasta could tell me."

"Me! Why would I be able to tell you?"

"Because you know so much about social media."

Shasta narrowed her eyes at Amelia, then returned her attention to the phone and shook her head. "There's no comment here. You were probably imagining things again."

When Shasta stood and headed for the door, Amelia caught a whiff of Spell on You. Shasta had stuck with the same perfume for a while now. Allison's credit card was probably happy about that.

"Where on earth are you going *now*, Shasta?" Macy clunked her fork to her plate.

"Out." The service door slammed behind her.

Allison sighed.

Macy reached for the salad bowl, clanged a serving spoon to the floor, and nearly toppled a water glass.

Dishes and utensils clattering, sisters bickering, messes being kept track of. Just another evening of the usual activities in Allison's bustling kitchen. Amelia returned the uneaten bread crusts to her plate.

"If we were a murder of crows, someone might say we were holding court."

Wiping salad dressing from the table, Allison caught Amelia's eye and winked.

41

With tags

The next morning, Amelia opened her audiobook app, connected the Bluetooth speaker, and hit play. Brushing her teeth quietly, she listened to Marcellus's thoughts in *Remarkably Bright Creatures.* Imagine an octopus thinking so deeply! The wonderful world of nature.

She rinsed her mouth. Applied the teeth-whitening strips Allison had given her. Wiped the counter around the bathroom sink and dabbed dry the bar of shampoo in the shower. Lavender rosemary. Allison's bar was lemon scented. So far, Allison was the only other person in the house on board with using shampoo in bar form. But the two of them were working on convincing the others.

Standing in front of her clothes closet, Amelia pulled on the same outfit she'd worn last Wednesday. A purple gingham dress with embroidery around the collar. She added a gray sweater and warm tube socks because today's temperature was forecast to be cooler than last Wednesday's. Then she was all systems go, as Allison would say.

Shifting clothes on the rod, she noticed a white cardigan with tags. Never worn. When would she wear a white cardigan? Not for collecting shells. Or taking care of birds at the rehab aviary. Or playing with Louise in a puddle.

She pulled the cardigan off the hanger. Tossed it and a few other unworn items to the bed.

When the audiobook chapter ended, Amelia clicked it off and returned to the bathroom. Removed the whitening strips from her teeth, rinsed, wiped the counter. Leaned close to the mirror and grinned. Look at that! Whiter teeth!

Downstairs, she fed and watered Kitty and Matt. Cornered a mouse (all by herself!) with a broom and dustpan. Let the dogs and the mouse out to the fenced area, where Louise trailed the mouse until it scooted under the wire fence.

Back inside, Amelia found Macy and Shasta preparing a berry smoothie and a bagel with cream cheese, respectively. That was a trick Amelia had learned from watching other people's narrated videos. You said two things about two people, then added *respectively* to clarify who was doing what.

After she fixed herself a bowl of fruity loops cereal with milk, she sat at the kitchen table. Snapping the lid back onto the tub of cream cheese, Shasta waved toward her. "Hey, sis, what's up with all those clothes on your bed?"

"I have too much stuff. Did you know many clothes are made by children working in factories? And they only get paid pennies."

Macy scooped blueberries and Greek yogurt into the blender. "Another problem the world needs a superhero for."

Shasta brought her plate to the table and sat next to Amelia. "Kids as little as five, working all day. I saw it when I was volunteering for that humanitarian group in Vietnam."

"You actually *saw* children working in factories? Why didn't you *do* anything about it?" Macy flipped on the blender and let it whirl, ending conversation for a minute. When the purple-colored smoothie had reached an approved consistency, Macy poured it into a glass.

"Oh, that's rich, Mace. That's real rich." Shasta tapped loose seeds off her bagel. "You *do* know that the problem can be too big for one person to fix—even if that person is as determined as you to run the world."

Amelia listened to the banter. She and her sisters had always fought, especially Macy and Shasta. But now it seemed Macy had lightened up on Shasta. And Shasta had added humor to her barbs.

In a lull, Amelia looked up. "I think I'll donate the clothes I don't need. Someone else can benefit from them."

Macy smiled. "Why don't we *all* go through our clothes for donation? And we'll organize the stuff lying around the entries while we're at it. We don't want Allison tripping."

"We don't want me tripping either." One busted hip around the house was one too many. Amelia collected the dirty dishes and brought them to the sink.

Later, Macy designated Amelia's bedroom as the collection point. Shasta breezed in and threw down an armload of clothing. "We're going to make tons from this stuff!"

Tons of what? Money? As if they needed more. Amelia stacked shirts.

Macy pulled a blouse from the top of the pile and refolded it. "Shasta, what is going on with you? First you bought all kinds of things you didn't need. Now you want to sell it. I want to know what's going on."

"Why can't I sell my stuff?"

"Because it's not your stuff!" Macy threw her arms in the air. "*Allison* paid for it. Allison pays for everything."

Shasta wadded a pair of jeans and tossed them. "Allison's got plenty of money. We bought stuff and now we're selling stuff for a worthy cause. I don't see how there's anything wrong with that. Hang onto those green pants, Amelia. You can wear them to watch Packer games."

"Anybody home?" As Ralph's voice drifted in from outside, Louise raced to the open window and put her paws on the sill.

Leaning out the window, Shasta swayed her hips. "Come on up!"

Macy tsked. "To Melia's *bedroom*, Shasta?"

"Oh pooh, Mace." Shasta headed for the mirror above the fireplace and primped.

At the exasperated look Macy gave her, Amelia shrugged. "I don't mind. It's not like any of us are wearing our nighties."

When Ralph appeared in the bedroom doorway, Shasta motioned to the piles of clothing. "We're selling stuff. We're going to donate the *money* to a worthy cause."

Shasta's emphasis on the word *money* almost made it sound like a secret code. But that was Shasta for you, talking like she knew information you might want to know too.

Amelia returned a skirt to the closet. Red plaid flannel, so she might wear it at Christmastime. When she turned around, Shasta was in full flirt mode with Ralph. Louise was leaning against Ralph's leg, her right upper lip twitching and her tail wagging.

Glancing down at Louise, Ralph shook his head. "Something's not right about that dog."

Amelia paired yellow and green socks together and returned them to her drawer, since Shasta would say to save them for football games. "Maybe it looks like Louise is snarling, but see how happy her back end is?"

"Louise likes you, Ralph. And *we* like you too." When Shasta kissed Ralph on the cheek, Amelia giggled. She couldn't help it. Shasta and Ralph were so funny together!

Ralph grumbled under his breath, then turned to go, Louise padding behind him down the hallway, his voice fading. "I'm not giving you no cookies."

"Give her the kind that doesn't make crumbs!" Shasta hollered after them. "In the yellow-and-white canister next to the toaster!"

Sinking into an upholstered chair, Macy sighed. "Would someone please tell me what's going on around here? Was there a *reason* Ralph stopped by?"

"Maybe he wanted to give Louise a cookie. And say hi to Shasta, of course." Amelia pulled a yellow sweater from the stack and scrutinized it. Keep or donate?

"But why was he here to begin with? Why is Ralph around so *often* now?"

Shasta's bracelets jingled as she looped her arms around Macy's shoulders. "Does he need a reason? Maybe he's just being a sweetie. On the inside so no one sees. Keep that yellow sweater, Amelia. Mace can wear it on game days."

42

Progress

First, Allison walked the stone path around the house. (All in one stretch without having to sit down and rest!) A few days later, she crossed the dunes with only the aid of her walking stick. A week after that, she made a jaunt down to the beach with Aunt Amelia, who kept her promise to not help unless Allison was truly going down. Which never happened, so woo-hoo about that. Now, finally, Allison stood in the doorway of her boathouse.

Buttercup looked fantastic. Mattie and Jax had done a stellar job spiffing her up. You really could eat off the deck—if you swept up the dust first.

Allison closed the boathouse door, retrieved her walking stick, and took a few steps along the dock. Mostly steady today. *Now we're on the dock. We are on the dock. So be careful where you walk. Careful where you walk.*

She crossed the beach and headed for the road, although referring to it as a road was being generous. The unpaved path, just wide enough for Ed to get his all-terrain vehicle through, was littered with potholes and fallen tree branches.

Overhead, a wild wind sweeping clouds across the sky left Wren in peace, not even touching the evergreen treetops. Several little birds scampered around the trunk of a cedar. The crisp scent of burning leaves suggested a farmer was preparing for winter.

Allison followed the fence Ed and Virgil had constructed, a rope strung between posts to help Aunt Amelia keep track of where she was. Counting in her head, Allison knew the post up ahead was the eighteenth from her house.

No more blazing through the forest for this girl, on a scooter or any other way. Not for a while. She passed post seventeen and crunched through the fallen leaves of a birch tree. If Ed Piper were driving Aunt Amelia along here, he'd plow through that big puddle just to hear Aunt Amelia whoop.

At post sixteen, Allison stopped to shed her warm outer layer, tied it around her waist, then resumed walking. Between this jaunt to the boathouse and two sessions of physical therapy, today wasn't a prime time for any other big efforts. Like climbing upstairs to her den—her home office, she meant. Well, it felt more like a den.

Office, den, what did it matter, as long as she was writing music there?

Except that she wasn't writing music there. She wasn't writing music anywhere these days. With all this time on her hands, you'd think she'd be cranking out one hit song after another.

Wow, still fourteen more posts to go.

Back at the house, she waded through the stuff tossed inside the service entrance. Whether the obstacles were shoes and bags or bumpy paths and puddles, it all made a person slow down. She ought to organize this stuff. Label where it was supposed to go. Like she'd done in the kitchen. When she got the energy, she would.

She kicked a gardening basket out of the way, lost her balance, and slid to the tile floor. Just slid down, real slow. It hardly even hurt.

Aunt Macy bustled in while Allison was still thinking about how to get up. "Allison Theodore, sit *down*."

"I *am* sitting down."

"I mean sit down in a chair and *rest*. You are trying to do too much too soon. Are you hurt?"

Allison shook her head.

Scraping a chair close, Aunt Macy helped Allison into it. Then she disappeared through the doorway. The refrigerator door opened and closed. The blender whirred. Aunt Macy returned and shoved a glass at her. "Drink this."

Allison clinked the metal straw around another of Aunt Macy's go-to remedies. "There isn't another fiber supplement in this one, is there? Because I'm good for today."

Ignoring the question, Aunt Macy scooped up loose shoes and bags and threw them into a corner. "Tripping hazards, all of it. We've got three women in their golden years, you recovering from hip surgery, and a blind dog. You wouldn't think this house would allow tripping hazards. It'll be easier to get around once we corral our donations. Drink up, sweetheart."

Allison peered into the glass. It was impossible to tell what all was in it. She drank a third of it and set it aside.

"One of these days, I'm going to get back on a motorbike. A fast, noisy one. And I'm going to *tear it up* all over Wren."

"Oh, for goodness' sake." Aunt Macy stuffed shoes into a basket. "You're not getting back on a motorbike."

"If the roads were better on Wren, riding would be easy-peasy. Gemma Campana rides a scooter all over Reclamation Island. She can because the roads are maintained. Why doesn't Wren have paved roads? We could have, you know, if we organized ourselves."

Aunt Macy inspected a pair of socks and tossed them in the washing machine. "Wren Islanders don't want to travel at the speed of light. Wren Islanders like slowing down."

"It would be helpful for getting supplies delivered. Think how happy Ralph would be if he could pull into a real port instead of hoping a recent tide left a flat spot on the beach."

"A port? Here on Wren? Now I know you're not thinking straight."

"Maybe not a port. Yet. But I definitely think we should improve the roads. I could pay for it."

"With your own money?"

"If everyone wanted it, yes."

Aunt Macy tsked. "Paved roads with higher speed limits would invite riffraff. Visitors would do that thing where they add a hashtag. That's all we need around here."

Allison sipped more of the smoothie. "Just picture it, Aunt Macy. A wide, level road with a neat yellow stripe down the middle. Me buzzing by on a cute yellow scooter."

"Oh, I'm picturing it—and the disaster it'd be if any of us need more of the emergency medical care we don't have here on Wren. There will be no more carousing. No more risking accident or injury."

Allison smiled. "You're being bossy again, Aunt Macy." At least there were intervals between bossiness. Lately, Aunt Macy's edges had been softening. She talked in capital letters less often. Since becoming, in a word, indispensable, she'd also become entirely endearing, even with her rough edges. Aunt Macy would have a ton of fun with a scooter! "You could get one too."

"Get one what?"

"A scooter! We'll get a two-seater for you and Aunt Amelia. I'll even spring for a cup holder so you can bring along a smoothie."

"Oh, for goodness' sake."

Seeing Aunt Macy flush with pleasure, Allison smiled again. Louise bounded in and skidded to a stop in front of them.

"I know, I know. Time for your cookie. Let's go, funny doggie!" Aunt Macy galloped off toward the kitchen, collecting Lokita as she went.

Allison took another sip. Her shiny, clean boat was sitting in the boathouse, just waiting to go out. How satisfying it had felt to be on the water. Far away, on her own. How *free* she'd been, zipping around on Gemma's motorbike. Until she'd zipped over the edge.

Improving the roads here on Wren would be a valuable thing to do. An *important* thing to do. And she could manage the entire project! Allison Theodore, in charge of transportation.

She eyed her nearly empty glass. That would really be something, all right. Because these days, she wasn't even in charge of her fiber intake.

43

A situation

Allison put together an initial proposal for road improvements, left messages with contractors who might want the work, and emailed a request that the topic be discussed at the next community meeting. Then, with a rough estimate of a budget, she called her financial advisor.

"Allison, I was just about to call you." Mark's voice was tense. "We might have a situation."

"What do you mean?"

"One of your credit cards has a suspicious charge on it. It's not for a large amount, and it looks legit. Our office didn't think anything of it until the FBI contacted us."

"What?"

"The payment went to an outfit connected with a case they're working on." He looked up the card number and said the last four digits. "Who all has access to that credit card?"

"My three aunts. But they only have access to the credit card, not the connected bank account."

"Is the credit card saved on any websites?"

"Probably. My aunts use it for online shopping."

"Well, we're not supposed to freeze the card. If we do, whoever's using it will know they've been noticed."

Allison pushed a section of hair away from her face. "This happened once before. My aunt across the country was purchasing stuff and I didn't realize it."

"But those purchases could be explained. They went to legitimate places, right?"

"Right."

"Well, for whatever reason, this one little charge caught the FBI's attention."

"Huh."

Allison mentally ticked through her accounts and their locations. Her aunts' credit card and account were entirely separate. In fact, most of her accounts weren't connected to each other. Early on, she'd set them up that way as a safeguard. Which now proved smart and helpful. Imagine the FBI taking notice of her credit card!

"Do we have to worry about whoever's behind this getting into my other accounts?"

"We'll make sure that doesn't happen. For the moment, the FBI wants you to spend like nothing's amiss. So don't do anything out of the ordinary."

"Like make a down payment on island-wide road improvements?"

Mark's gasp was a clear answer. Recovering, he laughed. "My guess is you're already working on a budget, one that fits well within your overall financial plan. Send it my way when it's ready. But don't reserve a contractor yet. Use your credit cards like normal, but don't move money between accounts. I'll call you back when I've got an update."

When the conversation ended, Allison sat there with a knot tightening in her stomach. It wasn't about losing the money. Her aunts blew through tons every week.

It was that someone would take advantage. A person she didn't even know had helped themselves to her property, not to mention her privacy. They'd used her to get what they wanted. And what could she do about it?

She felt helpless. Like when that creep Lester Locum had headed toward her house without an invitation. Might Lester be involved in this credit card thing?

No, he wasn't smart enough. It was probably being done by an organized crime group. Did that mean her money was paying for drugs? Human trafficking?

Thinking she might throw up, she breathed around a square, all four sides, while she slid her fingers through her hair, which was covering her eyes again. Maybe Aunt Shasta would give her another haircut. The last trim had turned out okay. And it would occupy Aunt Shasta with more than whatever she kept disappearing with Ralph to do.

They could set up a real hairstyling space here at the house, with a shampoo sink and everything. Aunt Shasta would think that was a hoot. They could add a goldfish bowl for tips. Tack the first dollar up on a bulletin board.

Assuming, of course, there was still cash to go around.

Allison tugged at a section of hair. Should she be more worried? Mark had said everything was under control. Was it? If only she could run her worries past someone entirely trustworthy. A friend who could keep a secret. Someone who'd have her back *if* she needed help.

But you couldn't go around broadcasting you were involved in a situation the FBI had taken notice of.

Breathing around another square, she headed for the grocery market. Not for any particular reason—and certainly not because she was hoping to run into Virgil. Only because traveling to the market was manageable. With her hip not ready for a hike through the forest, strolling along her driveway and the road to the market had to be enough.

When a symphony erupted in the branches of a walnut tree overhead, she stopped to listen. The birds were so little, so high up in the tree, she couldn't identify them. Virgil would know what kind of birds they were by listening to their song.

At the market, she climbed the steps one at a time, upsy-daisy. Just that easily, she was on the porch. So, actually, she was making definite progress. Maybe that hike through the forest wasn't far off. First a hike, then a scooter ride. Or a boat trip. She leaned her walking stick against the wall and tested her balance. Actually, an outing on the water might be totally doable now.

She found Virgil in the stockroom, storing shelf-stable oat milk next to whole wheat flour. How did that make any sense? She glanced around the room. More of the same oat milk was stored on a different shelf, next to a supply of bar soap. There was absolutely no organization to the stockroom at all. She sighed.

"Might not make sense to you," Virgil said without looking up, "but it works for me."

She shook her head. "The same product stored in two different places? Less than inefficient."

Straightening, Virgil brushed his hands against his apron and cocked his head. "Are you here strictly in an advisory role, or can I offer you a pumpkin chocolate chip muffin?"

He was teasing her. As if she had any say in how the market was run! If she did, the first thing she'd do would be relocate the fragrant bar soap away from the fresh produce. Then she'd sort the first aid kits by critical expiration dates. Wipe the smudges off the glass muffin case.

She smiled at him. "Pumpkin chocolate chip? Sounds delicious. And a coffee, please. And I want to check the *Almanac*."

"Which one?"

She laughed. Wren Islanders often ribbed Virgil for holding on to past, out-of-date editions of *The Old Farmer's Almanac*.

"The only one that will help me today, Mr. I-can't-part-with-almanacs."

She made her way to the bookshelves wedged into the space under the stairs, no walking stick needed. (Allison Theodore on a roll!) Flipping through the almanac, she found the weather predictions for the current week. A low, wet system might be on its way. But for the next few days, calm, dry weather.

And everybody knew boating in the sunshine was a lot more fun than boating in wet weather.

Almanac in hand, she headed back outside to the porch. Settled on a cushioned twig bench. Watched the ocean for a bit. A flat sea, except in the currents. According to the tide table, tomorrow morning would be perfect for cruising. Ideal conditions for a girl being adventurous again on her own.

Virgil came out to the porch, the screen door swinging shut behind him. He set down a tray, handed her a plated muffin—oozing with warm chocolate chips—and placed a mug of coffee within reach. "Mind if I join you?"

"That would be a-okay."

Virgil picked up his own drink and sat in a wood-planked chair. Between them, the silence wasn't at all uncomfortable. The silence was comforting.

I've got a problem, she wanted to say. *Somebody's stealing my money.*

But the fewer people who knew what was going on, the better. Anyway, Virgil would just ask questions. Lots and lots of questions.

"What breed of dog is Louise, do you think?" Virgil, with another question.

Allison considered. "I don't know. A hound mix?"

"She didn't like Lester. That day you barely made it back to Wren. Lester claimed he'd saved you, when really he'd nearly let you die."

Louise hadn't liked Lester? From Aunt Macy's reports, Virgil hadn't liked Lester much either. Although Virgil had never said anything about it. Allison played along. "What'd Louise do?"

"Nothing, because Ralph tied her up."

"I bet she loved that."

Virgil laughed. "She hated it. She wants to be free and independent almost as much as someone else I know."

Just like that, Virgil was giving her another one of *those* looks. If Allison felt more up to it, she might've encouraged a kiss. Just for fun.

But Virgil might think a kiss meant she wanted more. Which she maybe did. But it was no fun getting going in a relationship like that and then finding out you weren't interesting anymore.

She ate another bite of the delicious muffin, chewed, and swallowed. "We probably don't want Louise loose if Lester's ever back on Wren."

"We probably don't want *me* loose if Lester's ever back on Wren. Next time, Lester will wish *he* was wearing a helmet."

"Oh, Virgil." Laughing, she finished her muffin and sipped her coffee. Looking back, it was funny to realize she'd worn Gemma's helmet all the way back to Wren. The helmet might have saved her life. And not just the helmet. "Mattie

Conway probably saved my life. Maybe more than once. Hope she's doing okay. Hope she's left Lester by now."

Virgil raised skeptical eyebrows over his own mug.

But the sadness behind his eyes felt like it might tip the scales. Cause everything to become too much to bear. The stolen money. The bickering aunts. The daily struggle to move around without help. The thought of a teenage girl caught in a situation she couldn't escape—even when friends wanted to help.

Blinking back tears, Allison studied the flat sea. Anyone with half a raft—or half a healed hip—could sail a sea that calm.

Before she could sail, though, she'd have to convince Aunt Macy to let her go. Standing slowly, Allison tested her legs. All systems go. One of these days, she'd look up where that phrase came from.

"I'd better get back to the house. If I'm gone too long, Aunt Macy will send out a search party."

Virgil helped her down the porch steps and waved goodbye. Allison under supervision. Virgil at this end of her outing, Aunt Macy at the other. On the road between, fence posts to mark her slow progress. What she wouldn't give to get away by herself.

Down the driveway a bit, Virgil jogged up next to her, his dark hair flopping against his back. "I just remembered. Macy wants a bag of brown rice."

Allison stopped walking. Pulled a folded fabric bag from her pocket. Motioned for Virgil to drop in the rice. He did, then unlooped the fabric bag from her hands and resumed heading toward her house.

She followed him. "I can carry a bag of rice on my own, you know."

"Macy also wants my help fixing a faucet leak. And if she sees me coming up the driveway empty-handed while you toil under a load—her words, not mine—she'll put me in the doghouse."

"So I'm doing you a favor by letting you carry it."

"You got it." Humming, Virgil tempered a smile.

44

Putting her foot down

Macy zipped closed a bag of dried currants and stored it in the pantry. Then she returned to the kitchen counter and cut Welsh cake dough into rounds. Transferred the pieces to the griddle, let them sizzle.

Somebody's got to keep an eye on him.

That's what Shasta had said when Macy asked why she spent so much time with Ralph. Somebody's got to keep an eye on him! If that's what they'd come to around here—to *Shasta* keeping an eye on someone—they were in big trouble. That girl needed someone keeping an eye on *her*.

Macy flipped the crisping round cakes.

What on earth was going on around here, anyway? Shasta selling brand-new stuff. Melia wearing the same clothes every day. Ralph hanging around more. Children working in factories and getting paid pennies. Mattie Conway stuck with an ogre. Allison proposing road improvements and a double-seated scooter. For goodness' sake. Someone needed to stop the insanity.

When Allison and Virgil barged into the kitchen arguing about Allison's most outlandish idea yet, Macy put the finished cakes on a rack to cool—and her foot down.

"Absolutely not, Allison. You're not ready to take your boat out alone."

While Virgil filled a glass of water at the kitchen sink, Allison sat at the table and crossed her arms. Delivering the water, Virgil tilted his head. "Your aunt's right this time."

This time? And every other time! But Macy nodded at Virgil, grateful for his support. "You're nowhere near ready to boat alone, sweetheart."

"Just for a morning. I'll buzz over to Reclamation Island and come right back to Wren. You'll hardly know I've been gone."

Virgil grinned at Allison. "Not miss you? I doubt that."

When Allison blushed, pretty and uncertain, Macy's heart skipped a beat. Allison and Virgil were made for each other. Drawn together by an invisible tide—constant in its strength, timeless in its zeal, enduring in its embrace. Virgil clearly knew it. When would Allison see it?

Allison turned her attention to wiping drips of condensation from her water glass. "A guy over on Reclamation Island might bid on our road project. I'll check in with him, deliver a gift to Gemma Campana, ask about Mattie Conway, buy myself an ice cream cone, then come back home lickety-split."

Macy glanced at Virgil. He looked as uncertain as she felt. They both knew Allison was going to do what Allison wanted to do. Virgil couldn't very well order Allison not to go. He wouldn't anyway. Always so gung ho on letting Allison make her own decisions.

It was up to Macy Johansson to lay down the law. The *official* caretaker. Not to mention, if she tagged along, she might run into Mattie Conway.

"I'll go with you."

"I appreciate the offer, Aunt Macy. But I want to go on my own."

Allison had once said Macy had skills at directing conversations. Well, Macy was about to use those skills right now. First she plated a warm cake and slid it across the table to Allison. Butter too. Then she smiled—extra sweetly, she hoped.

"Allison, who knows if I might *need* to pilot *Buttercup* sometime? You said yourself I should learn to drive the boat. What better time than now, right?"

"Great idea, Macy. A win-win for everyone." If Virgil had been holding pom-poms, he could have passed for a cheer squad.

Macy shot him a look she hoped showed her gratitude, then sank into the chair next to her niece. "Let me come along, sweetheart. I'll be as quiet as a mouse, and you don't even have to buy me an ice cream cone."

Allison laughed. "If you go to Reclamation Island, you get an ice cream cone. Rules are rules."

"All right then. We'll go to Reclamation Island together someday."

"I'm going tomorrow."

"Tomorrow?"

"If you're not ready yet, Aunt Macy, I'll go on my—"

"No, no. You're ready, I'm ready. We all scream for ice cream."

Before heading outside, buttery Welsh cake in one hand, Virgil grinned at Macy. "Do me a favor? Bring her home in one piece, no helmet required."

As if a worthy caretaker would permit anything less! This time and every other!

Macy patted her niece's arm. "Home in one piece, no helmet. Okay, then. We've got our marching orders."

45

All still alive

Tuesday morning, Amelia dressed in the same short cotton pants and tunic top she'd worn last Tuesday. She added a wide-brimmed hat. Pulled on Macy's gift of sturdy sandals. Fastened on Shasta's gift of a low-profile life jacket.

The ocean was calm, the air warm, the tide exceptionally low. Jax had described these conditions as perfect for finding a whole sand dollar.

Shasta caught up with Amelia partway down the beach. They waved as Allison and Macy sped off in *Buttercup*. Radio blaring, Allison whooping, Macy probably holding on for dear life.

When it was quiet again, Amelia turned to her sister. "Will you help me look for a whole sand dollar?"

"I'd be honored to help you look for a whole sand dollar."

They strolled along the flat, damp sand, looking for divots. Any disturbance in the sand as the water washed away from it might indicate the presence of a shell.

All they found were little pieces of driftwood and broken clamshells.

"Maybe today isn't the day after all." Amelia shifted her bag from one shoulder to the other.

"What time is low tide?" Shasta bent to pick up something. Another broken clamshell.

"About twenty minutes from now."

"Let's search closer to the water's edge."

Against a flicker of fear, Amelia studied the blur of waves. "It makes me nervous to get that close."

Shasta reached for her hand. "We'll hold on to each other."

Closer to the water, they struck gold. Dozens of whole sand dollars. Maybe hundreds! Each wash of a thin wave revealed more. Amelia picked one up.

Shasta touched it. "Why is it fuzzy?"

"Oh my gosh!" Amelia raised her eyes to her sister. "It's fuzzy because it's still alive. It's an *alive* sand dollar."

"Are you sure?"

Amelia ran her fingers along the purple fuzz covering the front and back. "It must be. They must not bleach to a white color until they've died. Other shells don't turn white until after the critter dies."

Shasta scanned the vast expanse of beach, fluttering with divots. "So these are all alive?"

"If they're fuzzy like this, yes. Let's move higher up the beach. We don't want to crush any of them as we walk."

"Are you going to keep this one?" Shasta touched it lightly.

Amelia cradled the live sand dollar. Lifted it to her nose and sniffed.

Fresh-smelling, like a plant. Reminiscent of lichen growing in the forest. But instead of an earthy scent, the smell of the sea.

She'd always remember that smell. Always remember holding the living, fuzzy critter in her hands. Finding a whole sand dollar was far more extraordinary than she'd hoped or imagined.

She sniffed the creature again, then bent to return it to the sand. Wedged it in the way it might want to be. Felt the fresh emptiness in her damp, sandy hand. She'd held a living sand dollar!

Up the beach, Amelia sat on a toothpick tossed aside by a giant. "When Jax said I might find a whole sand dollar, I didn't know he meant I'd find an *alive* sand dollar."

"It's been a fabulous experience. Fabu-*lo-so*." Shasta twirled before sitting. After inspecting every red fingernail, she looked out at the water and heaved a heavy sigh.

Amelia squinted at her. "Shasta? Is everything okay with you?"

"Huh? Why do you ask?"

How to tell her sister she didn't seem herself? How to say her free spirit seemed dampened? "I guess because lately you seem preoccupied. Worried."

"Me? Worried? Ha!"

When Shasta didn't volunteer any information, Amelia recorded a ladybug making its way along the driftwood log. "Here you go, folks. This late in the year, and we're still seeing ladybugs. One more extra-special thing about Wren Island."

Scooping up sand, Shasta let it run through her fingers. "Is your YouTube channel still private?"

"Yes, because I want Allison to okay the videos first."

"Have you gotten any more comments from Hack? Or anyone else?"

"No."

"Would you tell me if you see another comment?"

Amelia looked up. "Why?"

"I just want to be helpful. If I can be."

Shasta seriously wanting to be helpful? Now that was rare. But why not let her? Life with Shasta was definitely more exciting than life without her. "Okay, you can be helpful. As long as you're not as helpful as Macy tries to be."

Laughing, Shasta put an arm around Amelia. "Mace is going to have a blast with Allison today. I'm glad she's taking a break."

"She'll still be taking care of Allison, though. Even though Allison is perfectly capable of taking care of Allison."

"Virgil's line again." Shasta smiled at the ladybug crossing her hand. "If Allison's not careful, she's going to be swept right off her feet by that man."

"I hope so." Amelia sighed. "Now that I've found a whole sand dollar, Allison and Virgil falling in love tops my list of nice things to wish for."

46

Too tired

Angling wide around the western point, Allison used *Buttercup*'s sonar to make sure she was giving the boulders a wide berth. After pulling into the boathouse—no need to leave the boat at the dock if she wasn't planning to go anywhere soon—she turned off the motor. "Whew."

Aunt Macy helped her tie up, disembark, connect to shore power, and close up the boathouse—one painstaking step at a time. Then sent her a concerned look. "Home for a while?"

Trying not to hobble noticeably along the dock, Allison exhaled. "To tell you the truth, Aunt Macy, that trip to Reclamation took more out of me than I expected it to. I think I'll be happy to stick around Wren for a while."

Closer to the house and back within cell service, her phone dinged several times, announcing a bunch of missed messages. She peeked at the screen. All the calls were from an unlisted number. No voicemails, though.

"I want you to take a nap this afternoon, sweetheart."

"Yeah. I will." With Aunt Macy's help, she worked her way up the grassy dune.

As she was taking another breather, leaning against a concrete lion, her phone rang. Her financial advisor. "Mark? Can you give me a few minutes to call you back?"

She waved for Aunt Macy to go inside without her, crossed the final distance to a bench near the firepit, and returned Mark's call. "What's the news?"

"Not much. Except that the FBI will be getting in touch. And you're not supposed to communicate with anyone you don't know."

Allison rubbed one aching knee, then the other. "You've made sure my other accounts are protected?"

"Of course."

After ending the call, she leaned against the bench's backrest and closed her eyes. Couldn't anything around here be straightforward anymore?

When Virgil sat next to her, she was too tired to open her eyes.

"Trip wore you out," Virgil observed.

"You could say that. Everything okay around here?"

"Yep." Virgil adjusted his ball cap. A move so familiar she knew it without opening her eyes.

When her phone rang again, she ignored it.

"Want me to answer that?"

"Can you look and see who it is?"

Virgil shifted on the bench. "Unidentified number. Probably a salesperson."

Either that or the FBI. The phone stopped ringing. A flock of starlings fluttered into a nearby tree, chattering.

His voice low, Virgil finally asked what she'd hoped he would.

"Do you want to talk about it?"

She squeezed her eyes tighter against the tears. Breathed around a square—one, two, three, four. Waited until she was sure she could speak without crying.

"Aunt Macy asked all around Reclamation Island for Mattie Conway. She wants to give Mattie a job here on Wren, housekeeping for us. Save her from Lester. But we never found her."

"You didn't cover all that ground with her, did you?"

"No. I rested at the tea shop. But Aunt Macy's really *good* at saving people. At helping people when they need it most." When her voice cracked, she swallowed and took another breath. "So I wish she *could* save the world. Or at least Mattie. But things don't always work out the way you want them to. Sometimes you put in all that effort, and all you end up with is a raging headache and an aching hip. And a vanilla ice cream cone."

Her phone rang again.

Opening her eyes, she reached for it and silenced the ringer. Then she sat up and bumped Virgil's shoulder with her own. "We did learn crucial information today, though."

"Oh?"

"Aunt Macy's going to need a lot more lessons before she can pilot *Buttercup* on her own."

47

Up to something

They were at it again. Shasta and Ralph. Heading into the forest to noodle or whatever. Macy pulled on boots, as quickly as a woman her age could be expected to, and darted out the door of the sunroom.

Maybe *darted* wasn't quite the word. She more clomped across the concrete patio like an elephant wearing oversized boots. But Shasta and Ralph hadn't noticed her, so the effect was the same as if she'd darted. In sleuth mode, minus the binoculars and notepad, because there hadn't been time to grab them.

Thank goodness Louise was on the beach, unaware. If she'd been bouncing around, wagging her tail, expecting to come along, she'd have drawn attention.

Following the sound of Shasta's light laughter and Ralph's rumbling voice, Macy continued along the trail, cooler under the thick shade of evergreens. She tripped over a tree root and flailed into the dry branches of a bush, startling a flock of birds—but Shasta and Ralph continued, unaware they were being followed. Macy stepped more carefully as she traveled deeper into Ralph's property.

Into the woods like Hansel and Gretel. She should've thought of them before she started. Leaving trail markers to find her way back home would have been smart.

Was this the craziest thing ever? Snooping on her own sister? Oh well. She'd started following them, so she'd keep at it. In for a penny, in for a pound.

Whatever she discovered out here, though, she was *not* telling Allison. What Allison didn't know wouldn't hurt her.

Several yards ahead of Macy, Shasta moved into a clearing. Sunlight hit the top of her faded unicorn-colored hair. Ralph's head lit up too. In a movie, that would suggest they were angels. Not the case here, obviously. Macy slowed her pace and crept closer to the clearing.

What on earth?

An unfinished building, half constructed. A storage shed? Barn?

Shasta and Ralph came *here* to noodle?

Sitting on the trunk of a fallen tree, Shasta listened to Ralph talk his way around the construction site, though Macy couldn't make out words. Shasta appeared to be in agreement with whatever Ralph was saying.

Then Ralph headed for his truck, leaving Shasta to inspect her nails. The sound of the truck door slamming shut, the turnover of the engine, the crunch of gravel fading as the truck grew distant.

Macy stepped out from the forest. "Shasta."

"Golly!" Shasta's hand flew to cover her heart. "Good *golly*, Mace! You nearly gave me a heart attack."

"Shasta. What's going on here?"

Standing, Shasta planted her hands on her hips. "You're snooping."

"I'm worried about you. Worried you and Ralph are up to something."

"Up to something! Ralph Wesson is a better man than you've ever known, Mace! Much better than any of *your* men have been. You remember that, next time you feel hoity-toity."

Your men. The force of her sister's cutting remark, rooted in ancient history, sent Macy reeling. She stepped back. True, she had picked a few losers. But so long ago! Before her marriage, which had been mostly happy—until she let alcoholism wring out every sweet element.

Certainly, she'd fared better in relationships than Shasta had, with her compulsive need for attention. But when had she and Shasta started comparing themselves to each other? Or had they always, even from the beginning?

Could a sister ever win anything over another sister? If she did, would it be worth it?

"Ralph Wesson is the best man I've ever known," Shasta spat through tears. "I don't care about his past. And I'm *not* going to let anyone take advantage of him."

"Shasta, please." Macy reached for her. "Tell me what's going on."

"Why? So you can fix it? Guess what, Mace? Some things are beyond even *your* superpowers."

Macy felt a little thrill run through her. "You think I have superpowers?"

"Where's your cape?" Giggling, Shasta sank back to the log.

Macy sat and put an arm around one of the sisters she was supposed to take care of, always. Shasta leaned into her. "Mace, I can't tell you what's going on with Ralph. Can't you just trust me?"

"I'm trying to trust you, Shasta. But you have to admit you don't always make smart choices regarding men."

"Ralph's different."

"How do you know?"

"I just do."

Maybe Shasta was right. Maybe she'd finally ended up with one of the good guys. After so many failures, the odds of success ought to be increasing, right? How many times could one person mess up before, finally, they didn't?

She squeezed her sister's shoulder. "Why do you think someone's taking advantage of him? How do you know Ralph's not taking advantage of you?"

"I don't. I have to trust him."

"Oh Shasta. We've been down this path before."

"It'll be different this time. I'm sure of it."

It'll be different this time. Macy had heard those words many, many times. And not just from Shasta. From herself. Usually when part of her recognized she was spiraling out of control, spinning straight toward the danger zone.

Sighing, she pulled her sister closer.

48

Clouds building

On a lounge chair at the edge of a dune overlooking the ocean, Allison pulled a warm blanket close against a chilly breeze. How many more afternoons would be warm enough to sit outside like this? Those clouds building in the west meant rain tonight. Maybe Ralph would offer to pull the lounge chairs into the storage shed before dark.

He angled *Lucy Jo* onto the beach landing, two strangers leaning over the bow. Whatever happened to the Ralph who didn't get paid to transport passengers?

The passengers hopped off before *Lucy Jo* was fully stable. A feat you didn't attempt unless you were confident in your physical strength and balance. Allison repositioned her stiff legs.

Louise raced down to the beach and barked in circles, happy. Dressed in khakis and polo shirts—not the usual tourist gear—the newcomers seemed not to care when Louise put sandy paws on them. One visitor stayed to talk with Ralph, pointing at Ralph's favorite subject, his rig. The other headed toward the house. Visiting who? Was it necessary for Allison to get up and offer a welcome?

No, let Aunt Macy take care of it. Closing her eyes, Allison listened to Ralph's guffawing laughter rise above the rolling waves. Felt herself drifting off.

"Allison, sweetheart." Aunt Macy tapped her arm. "Are you awake?"

"I am now." Fending off Louise's cold nose, Allison squinted against the sunlight. Aunt Macy had one of the visitors with her. "Oh, hello."

"This woman and her partner are here on official business." Aunt Macy's tone and the visitor's serious look sent a flash of awareness through Allison. *Official? As in FBI business?*

Aunt Macy turned to the visitor. "Can I get you and your partner muffins? Glasses of lemonade?"

"Thank you, ma'am, but we won't be staying long."

"I'll leave you and Allison to talk, then."

When Aunt Macy headed back toward the house, the visitor pulled a lounge chair closer and sat.

Allison worked to sit up. "Sorry I'm not more mobile. Or moving quickly. I'm recovering from an accident."

"Yes, I know." The woman smiled and produced a badge. "Special Agent Nancy Sterling, Federal Bureau of Investigation."

Allison eased into a comfortable sitting position. "If my case is hush-hush, why come here? Couldn't you have just called?"

Nancy raised her eyebrows. "We tried. Numerous times."

"Sorry. I haven't wanted to answer calls from unknown numbers."

"Understandable. Thanks for being cautious." Nancy handed her a card. "Put this number in your phone so you'll recognize my calls."

After Allison tapped in the numbers and saved the contact, Nancy pulled out her own phone and called Allison's, verifying the number. Nancy scanned the surrounding area, then leaned toward Allison.

"The prime suspect in your case is wanted on suspicion of bank fraud and might be connected to other crimes as well. You'd be aiding a lot of people by helping us verify his involvement."

Nodding, Allison offered a weak smile. "I'm willing to help however I can."

Nancy opened an electronic tablet and held it between them. "The suspect isn't part of an organized unit. He prefers to play with money belonging to people he knows. Or they think they know him. He goes by many names. Are any of these familiar?" She showed Allison a list while reading the names on it out loud.

"No," Allison said when Nancy paused and looked at her.

More names were offered, from another list.

Allison shook her head. "Sorry. None of those are familiar."

On the third list, one name stood out.

"Hack Smith?"

Nancy's eyebrows went up. "Do you know someone called Hack Smith?"

"I know a Hack Wesson. He visited Wren. His dad is Ralph, the guy who brought you here."

Nancy angled the screen to display a photo. "Is this the Hack you met?"

Allison's stomach muscles knotted. "Yeah. That's him."

"And you met him in person? Here on Wren Island?"

Allison nodded.

"And he said he's related to that guy over there?"

"My neighbor, Ralph Wesson." A prickly feeling crawled up Allison's neck.

Nancy scrolled through data on her screen, then looked up. "Looks like the guy you met here on Wren is our suspect. But he's not related, biologically anyway, to Ralph Wesson."

Allison blinked. "I don't understand. Why would Ralph claim him as his son if he's not?"

Nancy drummed her fingers on the lounge chair's armrest. Tapped and scrolled her screen. Then she stood, pulled out her phone, and strolled forward to the edge of the dune grass. Her partner on the beach distanced herself from Ralph before putting her phone to her ear.

Nancy's voice was low. "Your guy might be connected. Has priors and claims to be the suspect's father." After disconnecting the call, Nancy sat back down next to Allison and gazed out at the view. "Always wanted to see this part of the country."

Was this really happening? The FBI here on Wren? And it sounded like Ralph had a record. The knot in Allison's stomach tightened. "Again, why would Ralph tell us Hack is his son?"

"We'll sort it out." Nancy stood again, waved to her partner on the beach, and turned to Allison. "Don't say anything to anyone about any of this. Talk about it with me only. For now, whatever Ralph Wesson says, act like you believe it."

Allison smoothed the blanket on her lap. Aunt Shasta was awfully tight with Ralph these days. He was hanging around the house more and more. What if he was involved in dangerous activities? With Hack, whoever he was.

"Hack said he'd come back to Wren this fall."

"Ah! Did he? That would be very accommodating of him." Nancy pointed to the ocean. "Look! Whales! I was hoping I'd see whales." She sat back down and smiled. "Maybe I'll stay a while longer."

49

The tell

A bittersweet sense of pride washed over Virgil as the doctor wrapped up Jax's routine appointment on the mainland. Jax had measured two inches taller than the last time Virgil checked. Wasn't it just yesterday he was strapping the kiddo into a booster seat?

They celebrated Jax growing healthy and strong by eating burgers at a favorite mainland joint. While finishing their shakes—chocolate chip cookie dough for Jax, mint chocolate chip for Virgil—they received a dozen messages at once on their cell phones.

Jax was the first to open a text. "FBI's on Wren."

Virgil shot a questioning glance at his son, then answered his own ringing phone.

"We've been noticed." Ed Piper sounded out of breath. "Island's probably crawling with G-men by now."

"Slow down, Ed. Start at the beginning."

"FBI's come to Wren. We don't know why. Or who they're after."

"Well, has anyone asked?"

"They showed us their badges. Said they're investigating clues related to a case and would appreciate our cooperation. I'm losing commune members right and left. Like chickens scattering when the tractor comes through. We don't require ID checks for membership, you know."

Virgil rubbed his forehead. If a commune member was concealing a murky—and possibly dangerous—past, maybe it was better that person go elsewhere. He glanced at the photo Jax was displaying on his phone. A couple of normal-looking people talked with the owner of the farmhouse bed-and-breakfast. "I'm sure things will become more clear in time, Ed."

He ended the call and glanced at the other messages. Everyone seemed to want to be the first to tell everyone else Wren Island had been noticed. Nothing from Allison or her aunts though.

On arriving home that afternoon, he discovered a few old-timers gathered in the market's café, yakking around drinks and chips. He chuckled inwardly at the consensus there were only two agents, not an entire force of swarming G-men. A few islanders were having trouble coming to terms with both agents being women. Virgil frowned at comments about how things had been better "back in the day"—the supposed good old days when men reigned supreme in law enforcement.

To fend off a few islanders trying to buy up staples like the world they knew was ending, Virgil scrawled out a handwritten sign. *No bulk purchases until next shipment arrives.*

Heading out to the porch to install the sign, he nearly stumbled at the sight of the hermit Wren Islanders had given up for gone. Virgil only glanced at the long beard, grimy hair, and ripped clothing. Made eye contact instead, and was rewarded with the hermit's signature lopsided grin.

"Afternoon, Hendrick."

"You got one of those bran muffins I keep hearing about?" Hendrick's voice was more raspy than Virgil remembered.

"Ten-grain okay?" When Hendrick nodded, Virgil plated a muffin. And filled a coffee mug. On the house.

Hendrick studied the muffin, then shifted his attention past Virgil into the store. "Butter?"

Virgil retrieved a couple of squares and added them to the plate.

Rocking back into the market's cushioned twig bench, Hendrick sighed around a bite of muffin. "It's a banner day on Wren."

"Yeah, I guess it is."

Customers purchasing propane required Virgil's assistance. The next time he looked, Hendrick had disappeared. Left his empty plate and mug on a side table.

Considering all that happened within the first few hours of FBI agents landing on Wren, Virgil expected the news that the agents had decided to *stay* would nearly cause the wheels to fall off the island. After the farmhouse bed-and-breakfast owners ordered new blackout curtains for the guest rooms and paid a rush delivery fee, a few café customers made snide remarks about government spending. Joked about worn agents conjuring up a crime to get a paid vacation. When no one owned up to being the reason the FBI had set up camp, rumors flew.

A week later, Parker Johnson rolled over in his tractor, twice. "Survived because my pants' suspenders came unclipped and somehow acted like a seatbelt," Parker told a crowd packed into the market café. "Opened my eyes to a genuine gold bar, stamped 1859, three inches away in the torn-up earth."

Now *that* was worth talking about. Or so the café crowd said even after the umpteenth time Parker recounted the event.

Wren's FBI agents had become old news.

Still, Virgil remained curious. The only fact he knew for sure was the agents weren't on Wren for him or Jax. Nancy and Zelda were friendly enough. Chatty with everyone. Expressed general interest without saying much at all. Engaged in small talk about farming, boating, chickens, fishing, whatever.

Really, the agents could have been doing anything or nothing on Wren. Like anyone else who visited. And no Wren Islander got special treatment from the agents. No one seemed especially under surveillance.

One afternoon while Virgil listened to the agents chatting with a group of islanders in the market's café, Allison stopped in for an apple. He kept extras of her favorite organic Galas hidden behind the checkout counter. She lingered to be part of the group's conversation about a song in the week's top twenty.

"What about you, Allison?" Someone motioned for her to join the group. "When should we expect one of your songs to become a hit?"

She'd hardly finished answering—a brief comment about being a little fish in a big pond—when an agent mentioned a music industry-related scandal everyone was eager to talk about.

When the conversation turned toward the need for forever homes for rescued pets, curious islanders peppered Allison with questions. Quick as a wink, one agent jumped in with photos of her hamsters while the other agent asked everyone—everyone but Allison—about their pets.

Virgil glanced around. No one else seemed to have noticed the agents steering topic after topic away from Allison while appearing to include her. Somehow, the agents made Allison Theodore seem like an average islander.

And that was the tell. Because to pull off making Allison appear ho-hum, you'd need to be intentional. You'd need to coordinate efforts, in advance, with your partner. Plus you'd need significant motivation. A compelling reason to prioritize diverting attention from Allison.

An uneasy feeling swept through Virgil. Whatever the agents were investigating, Allison must be a key part of it. And not as a suspect. Allison was being guarded. As if she needed protecting.

Gritting his teeth, he reached for a broom and swept the market's floor, paying special attention to the area around the group gathered for conversation. He refilled drinks sooner than needed. Delayed working on tasks in the kitchen, which would send him out of earshot, until after Allison had stood, said her goodbyes, and exited through the creaking screen door.

Two minutes later, one agent was still engaging the group gathered in the café.

The other was nowhere to be seen.

50

Necessary

Allison filled large, football-shaped bowls with chips and crackers. Dished up salsa, guacamole, and cheese dip. With one eye on ground beef browning in the skillet, she pulled sprouts and coleslaw from the refrigerator. Checked the pantry for garlic, ginger, soy sauce, and sesame oil. Ingredients for the fried egg rolls Aunt Amelia had requested.

Ralph, Virgil, and Jax were coming over later to watch the Green Bay Packers football game on television. A regular occurrence in an uninterrupted line of ordinary events.

In the weeks since the FBI agents arrived, there'd been no more suspicious charges on Allison's credit cards. No movement around her bank accounts. Nancy and her partner, Zelda, were keeping a close eye on the situation from Wren.

Based on information their team collected, Hack might return to the island at any time. Might follow his pattern of reconnecting with his victims before taking more advantage—although the suspected future threats were never specifically mentioned.

The egg roll ingredients ready for assembly, Allison handed off the finishing touches to Aunt Macy and carried the snack tray to the television room. Set it on the coffee table at right angles. Fluffed the decorative pillows, though the cases had shrunk so much from Aunt Macy's frequent washing, the stuffing was nearly bursting out. Glancing out the windows, Allison felt relieved to see the predictable view, not law enforcement—or, worse, Hack—slipping through the forest. The sooner Hack got caught, the better. It was eerie the way a person could take over your life without even being there.

By kickoff time, Aunt Shasta had crammed the dogs into green jerseys trimmed with yellow, just like the players wore. Where did Aunt Shasta find this stuff?

During a game break, a commercial aired for a television show set in Alaska.

"Wonder if Hack flew the plane they filmed that from?" Aunt Amelia squinted through telescopic glasses.

"Doubt it." Ralph scowled. "Everybody uses drones nowadays."

Allison heard opportunity knocking. "Any idea when Hack's planning to come back?"

Ralph muttered an answer no one could understand.

"Could you please repeat that, Ralph?"

"How am I supposed to know when the kid's coming back?" Ralph's bellowing woke Louise from her snooze.

"Okay, okay." Soothing him, Aunt Shasta refilled Ralph's bowl of Doritos. "Nobody said you had to know."

Everyone settled back into watching the game, but Allison felt like she was being crushed from the inside out, trying to keep quiet about an investigation that threatened her family and possibly involved her neighbor. She'd always found it difficult to keep secrets. Might be one thing that made her so uninteresting.

She set aside her glass of root beer, stood for a second or two until her legs were steady, then headed for the kitchen.

Next thing she knew, Virgil was at her side, peppering her with questions.

"Are you okay?"

"I'm fine."

"You look bothered."

"I said I'm fine."

"Can I help?"

She shook her head. Couldn't Virgil see she'd come to the kitchen to get away? Yet here were more questions piling up in front of her.

"Would you let me know if—"

"Can't a girl leave a room?" She whirled on him. "What's so wrong about wanting a break from *analyzing* things all the time?"

Instead of drawing back, he gave her an odd look. Like he, too, was puzzling things together. Like he was definitely worried. About *her*!

Well, guess what? Allison Theodore wasn't the one to worry about. That was a whack job named Hack Wesson. Or Hack Smith. Or whatever his name was. All those aliases! He could be anyone, anywhere!

Later, when the game had ended and the food had been packed up—no leftover egg rolls, they'd been scarfed down within minutes—Allison stepped outside with Virgil and Jax. Breathed the cooling night air. Marveled at how a full moon could brighten a sandy beach enough for a fourteen-year-old boy to pretend to be under stadium lights.

Before Virgil could say goodbye, Allison offered an apology. "I'm sorry for snapping at you."

Reaching to catch the football Jax tossed to him, Virgil glanced at her. "Remember what I told you about sea turtles?"

"You said they cry. To remove excess salt from their bodies."

Motioning Jax to go distant, Virgil hurled the football. "They also snap. When feeling threatened, that is."

Watching Virgil leave with his son, Allison tried to hang on to the comfort of his perspective. Crying was okay. Even necessary. Snapping too.

Back in the house, she helped Aunt Macy tidy the television room. Maybe Hack would never come back. Maybe he was done with Wren Island, this whole episode a tiny blip moving farther and farther into history. Vacuuming the crumbs on the floor around Ralph's chair, she hesitated.

Could they trust Ralph? Why had Aunt Shasta gotten so protective of him?

Hoping to get to the bottom of things, Allison scheduled a hair appointment for the next afternoon.

51

Some punk kid

The hairstyling space she'd set up for Aunt Shasta included a large mirror surrounded by stage lights, a wall rack for tools, a turquoise-colored cabinet for styling products, and a top-of-the-line shampoo bowl. Allison watched her hair get shorter one section at a time and tried not to wince whenever Aunt Shasta punctuated her animated story with a wave of the scissors.

"So then your mom went straight to the principal. Walked right into his office! Told him the school shouldn't allow bullies in that day and age. That's exactly how she said it. 'In this day and age.' Funny thing for a fifteen-year-old to say. Anne became our hero for that, which Mace never got over, since she likes to think of herself as our hero. Aww, these curls are just like Anne's used to be."

While Aunt Shasta fingered the curls at the back of Allison's neck, Allison let a wave of loneliness wash over her. Even surrounded by her mom's sisters, or maybe *because* she was surrounded by them, the emptiness her mom had left behind nearly fogged Allison in at times.

Wouldn't her mom giggle at cute Aunt Shasta today? Yellow corduroy overalls patched with flowery hot-air balloons. A wad of gum blown into a pink bubble, then popped with satisfaction. What would her mom say about Aunt

Shasta dating a guy who may or may not be involved in a sketchy situation investigated by the FBI?

Aunt Shasta looped Allison's hair behind one ear. "Those diamonds real? Golly, they look fancy."

Allison studied the sparkling gems reflected in the mirror. "They're real, but lab grown. Produced without dangerous mining work. Or forced labor."

"Woot!" Aunt Shasta hopped in place and Allison dodged the scissors. "Hooray for you, chickee. Buying responsibly. We all could do more of that."

While Aunt Shasta spritzed water onto Allison's hair, Allison closed her eyes. Aunt Shasta could benefit from tips about buying responsibly. All those online purchases! Then selling most of what she'd bought.

When the spritzing stopped, Allison opened her eyes to see a worried version of herself in the mirror. "What are you using the money for, Aunt Shasta? From the stuff you sell."

"Oh, I don't know what I'll do with it *exactly*." Aunt Shasta blew a bubble, popped it, sucked it back in. "It'll go to a worthy cause, though."

Allison eased her shoulders out of their tight position. "Like what?"

Aunt Shasta sighed and set aside the scissors. She pulled a rolling stool close and sat. "I'm going to give you the lowdown, chickee. But you gotta keep it quiet. Ralph's in trouble. Like *prison-time* trouble."

The tension returned to Allison's shoulders.

"He did time long ago. Before he got saved and came to Jesus. And now he's being blackmailed."

Allison's mind raced. Was Hack blackmailing Ralph? The FBI knew about Ralph's priors. Why hadn't Nancy said more about Ralph? What if Aunt Shasta had gotten mixed up in this too?

"Ralph hasn't been paying taxes." Aunt Shasta shook her head. "Here on Wren, it's not like there's much for taxes to go toward. No schools, no paid fire department. Golly, not even any law enforcement. Don't you think that could be a problem someday? Anyway, Ralph says he shouldn't owe taxes when he isn't getting anything. I'm not saying I think he's right. I'm just saying what he's done."

Allison tried for a relaxed tone. "Who's blackmailing him?"

Aunt Shasta snorted. "Some punk kid who got the big idea to pretend he was Ralph's son and come here to Wren."

"Hack."

"Right-o, chickee. Hack said he'd keep quiet about the tax money if Ralph would pretend to be his dad for a few days. For what purpose, who *knows*? I mean, the kid's a whack job. Hack the whack job. I'm sorry I ever pushed him on you. You're better off with Virgil. Not as good looking, but much better material." Aunt Shasta took a breath. "Anyway, that's what my money's going toward when I sell stuff. For Ralph to pay off his taxes. He doesn't want to go back to prison. And I owe him. Remember when I almost went to Alaska with Hack?"

It was a lot to keep up with, but Allison nodded.

"Ralph stopped me just in time. Told me what was going on. Can you imagine? Me and Hack and the bears? They have enormous bears in Alaska."

Allison wasn't sure which was worse, bears or Hack.

Aunt Shasta heaved a long sigh. "Thanks, chickee. I feel better already from telling you about it. Talk about a load off!"

While Aunt Shasta swept the hair on the floor, Allison sorted through the new information. The FBI must know about Ralph's record and that he hadn't been paying taxes. Ralph and Aunt Shasta knew Hack was blackmailing Ralph, but it didn't sound like they knew Hack was wanted by the FBI or had involved Allison's money in his schemes.

Maybe *Ralph* knew all that about Hack, but Aunt Shasta didn't. Was Ralph another of Hack's victims or his accomplice?

Then there was Aunt Shasta's comment out of left field—that Allison was better off with Virgil. Definitely a topic for conversation another time. Maybe over a bowl of ramen noodles. With only the dogs listening.

When Aunt Shasta finished sweeping, Allison swiveled the chair to face her. "Are the unpaid taxes the only thing Ralph's guilty of right now?"

"The *only* thing? Isn't that bad enough?" Aunt Shasta removed the slick bib from Allison's shoulders and shook it clean.

Allison stood and brushed off loose hairs. Maybe the FBI would ease the tax evasion charges if Ralph helped bring in Hack. Or did deals like that only happen in movies? "Is Ralph still in contact with Hack?"

"I hope not." Aunt Shasta blew a bubble, bigger, bigger, until it popped across her lips. Giggling, she sucked it back in. "I sure do feel better now that I've told you."

"Thanks for the haircut." Allison stuffed a five-dollar bill into the goldfish bowl labeled *Tips Gratefully Accepted*. She stepped outside, leaving Aunt Shasta dancing around the salon with a broom.

Hairstylists usually became unofficial therapists, listening to and sympathizing with their clients' woes. This time, Aunt Shasta was the one confiding worries.

Allison wanted her aunts to know they were safe with her. Free to do or say anything. But, oh, the weight of the knowledge she must now keep inside! All those pieces of a complicated puzzle rattling around in her mind. One secret after another she couldn't share because doing so might endanger people she loved.

If the FBI never caught Hack, would she always have to live like this? Worrying he'd steal her money again? Worrying he'd steal from or hurt another person? Regretting she hadn't been able to help stop him? Hack had said he'd come back to Wren in the fall. What then?

There was one person she could ask. One person she could talk freely with, who always wanted to know everything Allison knew. She sent a text to Nancy.

Nancy's response came so quick it must have been an autofill option.

Meet at the usual place in 30 minutes?

Allison texted yes while heading for the forest trail.

52

Following the rules

Climbing the ascending trail into the forest, Allison kept a pace that pushed her physically. She wasn't as quick or agile as she'd been before the motorbike accident, but she was stronger than yesterday. Hopefully, she'd be stronger tomorrow.

She stopped to rest at a large arbutus tree like the one at Virgil's cabin. The tree's stunningly red berries more than hinted at winter. As she touched the tree's smooth, orange trunk, a bald eagle circled overhead, its call teetering as if the message that began shakily in the heights must work its way down, step by step, to a more solid understanding. In the distance, another eagle responded. A mate? Parent? Offspring? In still another direction, a third eagle called. An entire family keeping track of each other.

Allison moved on. Nancy would be coming from the opposite direction, from the bed-and-breakfast where she and Zelda rented rooms and helped with farm chores. Picking up the pace, Allison pushed herself. Her mending hip wasn't going to appreciate it. But no pain, no gain.

The meeting spot was a giant oak surrounded by moss-covered fallen trees. A dead zone for Allison's cell phone, but Nancy always got service.

Nancy was counting jumping jacks when Allison arrived. Wow, over three hundred already. Allison sat on a log and waited, mostly ignoring her throbbing hip. Finally, Nancy finished. Four hundred and fifty!

"You've got questions." Nancy wiped sweat from her brow. "Fire away."

"Has Hack really flown for television film crews?"

"We have no record of him doing that. Probably said it thinking you and your aunts would swoon."

Allison nodded. "One of my aunts nearly left with him. Supposedly to go to Alaska."

"Shasta?"

"Yep."

"You can thank your lucky stars that didn't happen."

Allison sighed. "So what's the plan? We just keep sitting around, waiting for him to come back? And then you guys confiscate his laptop and take him in? Nobody's carrying guns around the island, right?"

Nancy stretched. "If we suspect he may be considering violent activity, we'll take necessary precautions to keep you, us, and him safe."

Allison sank her head into her hands. If the FBI was prepared to use guns, did that mean they thought Hack might have a gun? How had she gotten herself into this?

She hadn't gotten herself into this at all. Hack had started it—maybe with the help of her neighbor. Did Ralph carry a gun? He had a record. Allison closed her eyes tighter, curled forward into a ball.

"Allison, hey." Nancy touched her shoulder. "Talk to me."

"I don't know what's okay to say to who. I feel like I've got a million secrets I can't leak out. What are you guys doing about Ralph? How should I treat him now?"

"We're treating Ralph as also a victim in this. Until we know more about his possible connections with Hack, you can treat him the same way you have been. Whatever Ralph says, act like you believe it. Anytime you think you've learned something helpful or concerning, call or text me. Just like you've been doing. Same game, same rules."

It was a lot more than a game, but the part about following rules was easy enough. Rules were straightforward. No negotiation or interpretation required.

Allison sorted through a few more thoughts with Nancy, thanked her, then headed home by the trail farthest from Virgil's cabin. No need to risk running into him. She might end up blurting out words she shouldn't. She might take one look at those searching dark eyes, that single line of concern creasing his forehead, and fall apart. Not okay to do when there were so many secrets to keep.

As she picked her way around a fallen cedar, the whine of a small airplane grew louder above the forest. Hack's floatplane?

She picked up her pace. Anxious to get home. To be with the aunts, preferably inside with the doors locked, when whatever happened that was going to happen.

The plane angled past Wren and continued on. Stopping to sit on a log, Allison caught her breath.

What if Hack was never caught? Went on to hurt another person? Some other girl giving life her best. Wishing her mom was close enough to reach for.

Allison headed home. Back to the grand house that had always protected her—from stormy weather and anything else the world threw at her.

Now, though, the magnificent, unending house spilled over with aunts, dogs, birds, and any friends who happened by. Now the house was filled with treasures *she* needed to protect.

53

Rigmarole

Sorting through supplies in her niece's well-equipped kitchen, Macy planned for both new and traditional holiday dishes. When she discovered a package of vanilla cookies with an expiration date looming, she tore into it. Brewed a large mug of coffee to go with the cookies—real coffee, not decaf. An afternoon pick-me-up worthy of a woman trying to do it all.

By the time she had inventoried the nuts, dried fruit, and chocolate chunks, she was in full flight, buzzing through the kitchen, taking care of things this way and that. Practically a superhero.

Yikes. Were those *more* mouse droppings?

Macy cleaned the area, then scrubbed the entire kitchen and mudroom floors. A lot of mopping, but why not keep going once she'd started? In for a penny, in for a pound. Plus, wood and tile were less fragile than glass windowpanes.

When she'd finished, she was wiped out. She might even be crashing—except superheroes didn't.

She refilled her mug, brought the coffee and cookies to the table, and sat munching. The first cookie was the only real kicker. After that, they stopped tasting sweet.

Energy running sky-high again, she grabbed a pen and paper and jotted menu ideas for Thanksgiving. Roast turkey with stuffing, green bean casserole, gingered cranberries. Would Virgil and Jax join them for Thanksgiving dinner? Ralph? He was kicking around the house so much he'd almost moved in.

Speaking of Ralph, what was up with that half-built storage shed on his property? Macy had hinted every which way, trying to snag Shasta into revealing more. One thing Macy knew for sure. Ralph had better not be taking advantage of Shasta. If he was, he was in trouble—with a capital *T*. And trouble with a superwoman was not a place where anyone should want to land. Not if they knew what was good for them.

Then there was the worry about Allison getting romantically involved with Ralph's son. Isn't that what Shasta had suggested early on? But the other day, when Macy asked Shasta if she still thought Hack would be a suitable match for Allison, Shasta nearly bit off her head.

Just as well. Virgil was the obvious choice. Smart, funny, dependable, kind. Plus he was crazy about Allison. Patient, too, while Allison took her sweet time coming around.

Another cookie, more coffee.

Energy rising again, Macy advanced her planning to Christmas. Imagine the gift giving this year! Shasta would bury them under unnecessary stuff. Impractical gadgets, jeans with holes torn out of the knees, headbands with whirligigs. They'd have to give it all back so Shasta could sell it.

A no-gifts Christmas might not be a bad idea, with Allison acting so strange about money. All that hoopla about making road improvements had gone by the wayside. It wasn't like Allison to announce big plans and then dismiss them.

FBI agents didn't show up every day either. Asking to speak to your niece. Goodness. Was it possible there was a problem with Allison's money?

The miniature paintings Anne bought at a yard sale had brought in a boatload. Much, much more than needed. Like how people sometimes went to prison for several life sentences. If you've only got one life, isn't one sentence more than enough punishment?

Macy frowned. What a comparison to think of! Her brain went every which way these days. Firing on all cylinders or not at all.

Probably she thought of it because of what Shasta said about Ralph. *I don't care about his past.* As if Ralph was a criminal. Or had been. Maybe Ralph was wanted by the FBI. No, they would have nabbed him by now.

After downing another half a cup of coffee, Macy warmed up the espresso machine and popped more cookies. Hot and flustered, she removed her cardigan and tossed it to the back of a chair. Like a rock drummer flinging iconic sticks into the cheering crowd!

Feeling too hot to handle, she turned down the thermostat. Poured a fresh cup of coffee. Added an ice cube because she didn't want to wait for the coffee to cool, not when she felt so thirsty, not to mention hungry. What had she eaten today, other than these cookies? There'd definitely been no green smoothie. The last time she crammed that much nutrition into her had been days ago. Weeks?

What had she come down here to the kitchen for, anyway? Oh yes. To plan for the holidays. The annual rigmarole of commercialism. Everyone on television looking blissful, enjoying family-oriented activities, giving picture-perfect gifts. Like a shiny sports car tied with a giant red bow. Did anyone for real ever wake up to a new car on Christmas morning? No one she knew.

Social media would be overrun with photos of matching pajamas. The latest jewelry styles. Mass-produced ceramic Santa mugs made to appear vintage, perfect for cocoa or cider—with a forbidden nip slipped in. After that, a million sparkling champagne glasses would march past, screaming a new year into place, implying the only path to happiness is to let yourself live a little.

Macy caught her breath.

One day at a time. That was the way to do this. Here on Wren Island, she was surrounded by people who'd help. If she were handed a mixed drink of unknown ingredients, Shasta would straight out question it—in a loud voice. Allison would sniff it for inspection. Virgil would replace the questionable offense with a personalized treat, maybe clean eggnog with whipped cream and a maraschino cherry. Even Ralph knew not to wave an open beer in front of Macy Johansson.

So let another glitzy holiday season throw itself at her. She'd gotten through holidays before, one day at a time. Would get through this one too.

She reached for another cookie. Indulging in a harmless sugar and coffee pick-me-up wouldn't kill her. Not like one sip of alcohol might.

After the first of the year, she'd kick the sugar habit and go back to green smoothies. And exercise. Jazzercise had worked years ago. She jumped up and did a few moves she remembered. Exhausted, she sagged back into a chair.

Holiday meals. That's what she was meant to be thinking about at this moment. How about cheesy potato casserole for Thanksgiving? Pumpkin crunch cake with tons of whipped cream.

Keeping it simple but fun. Taking care of everyone she loved. Following her own path to happiness.

54

The rules still apply

Allison slid a thin metal spatula under a cutout sugar cookie and transferred it to a cooling rack for Aunt Amelia to pipe white frosting onto. Aunt Amelia had yielded spatula duties to Allison after breaking the points off several stars.

Hopefully, baking the cookies would take pressure off Aunt Macy. She outdid herself at Thanksgiving with that brunch of cinnamon rolls, fresh pomegranates flown in from Hawaii, and a scrumptious egg and cheese casserole she called *chilikeesh*. Then a turkey dinner with all the trimmings, plus four kinds of pie.

When Allison's phone buzzed in her back pocket, she first finished transferring the cookies. Washed and dried her hands. Mopped up the drips on the counter and straightened the dish towel. Then she checked her messages. A text from Nancy.

Can we talk? Usual place. 30 minutes.

Precisely one half hour later, under the stark limbs of the now leafless oak, Allison tried to absorb the news that her lifeline regarding Hack was coming untethered.

"You're packing it in? Leaving Wren?" Did the FBI's withdrawal of Nancy and Zelda mean Allison could stop worrying? Would Hack be caught another way, in another place? "So you don't think Hack's coming back to Wren?"

Nancy shifted from jumping jacks to stretches. "He's been tapping into accounts elsewhere. He might have figured out we tracked him to Wren. Don't worry, Allison. We're only a phone call away. Or a text. We'll post an agent nearby."

"Nearby? Here on Wren?"

"Not necessarily. But close. And the rules still apply." Nancy bent to one side at the waist. "Rule number one is?"

"Don't talk about this with anyone."

"Right. Even though we're leaving Wren, it's still an open investigation." Nancy bent to the other side. "Rule number two?"

"Whatever Ralph says, act like I believe it."

"Just like you have been doing." Nancy bent forward, pressing her palms flat against the ground. Such flexibility! "Rule number three?"

"Call or text you if I think I've learned anything helpful."

Nancy shook Allison's hand, then squeezed it and pulled her into a quick hug. Allison sighed as the agent who had become her friend disappeared down the trail. At least an agent would be nearby. But would nearby be close enough?

Allison headed home by the trail near Virgil's cabin—for variety, because she hadn't been on that particular trail for a while. It's not like she was *hoping* to run into Virgil. She just wanted to travel on a different trail.

At an overlook, she sat on a rock, warm in the sun, cool in the breeze. Pulled out her phone and texted Nancy. *Thanks for everything. Hope you get your guy eventually. Enjoy a nice Christmas with your family.*

She swallowed the lump in her throat. It all came back to the same thing again. Allison Theodore wasn't interesting anymore. Her situation was no longer the FBI's hot project.

Allison is boring. She really is. That song, that *ditty*, was all she'd been able to come up with for a long time. How can you be any good at songwriting without also being a singer? Maybe you couldn't. Maybe you couldn't be good at it at all. Maybe all you could do was write dumb little ditties.

Not long after she resumed walking the trail, Virgil appeared, wearing the same old binoculars around his neck. Probably watching the same old bird snooze. The man was the most easily entertained person she'd ever met.

As they walked, he matched her pace. Her *slow* pace, because her hip was aching again.

Virgil came up with a question, of course. "Have you been writing any new songs lately?"

A fair question. But with confidence running low, she interpreted it as an accusation and bristled. "I'm always writing songs."

They continued in awkward silence for a while.

"Allison, do you have a specific reason to be nervous about Hack returning to Wren?"

She whirled on him. "You come up with the most random questions. Lots and lots of questions. I never said I'm nervous about Hack coming back. Why are we even talking about him?"

Virgil met her frustration with a steady gaze. "Every time anyone mentions Hack or anything remotely related to him, it's obvious you're feeling edgy about him coming back."

"It's not obvious! Because I'm not *feeling edgy*, as you say."

Virgil's eyebrows went up.

Allison shifted her gait to ease the tension in her injured leg. Would this stupid hip *ever* heal? She ought to fly to Mexico. Lay on the beach all day, every day, in the sunshine. Nancy Sterling, FBI agent, was leaving Wren. Why shouldn't Allison Theodore, sometime songwriter, leave Wren?

"Virgil, can you please just not ask a bunch of questions for once?"

They walked on. With no questions. For so long Allison started considering whether she preferred Virgil asking random questions or being uncomfortably quiet.

Finally, he put a hand on her arm. "Look over there."

A flock of quail poked through the fallen leaves, peeping as they searched for food. The sight loosened a small part of her that had coiled uncomfortably tight these days. "Aww. Cute."

When the flock zipped into the brush, Virgil pointed at the sky. A bald eagle was circling. The forest grew quieter.

Sighing, Allison detoured off the trail to sit on a log. "You want to know something amazing?"

"I'm always up for knowing something amazing." Virgil sat next to her.

She gave him a sideways glance. *I'm always up for knowing something amazing.* Was Virgil teasing her? He seemed serious enough. Like he really wanted to know.

"When I lay injured on Seal Rock, a bald eagle landed in a tree branch above me. It's kind of hard to explain, but it felt like I was under the weight of the eagle. I know eagles must not weigh much. But it was like the air changed when the eagle was that close. Like the eagle and I had somehow connected."

Virgil tugged loose a stalk of dry grass and chewed on one end. "Some people believe eagles are sacred. Since they fly higher than other birds, they are thought to come closest to the Creator."

"Huh."

"Eagles are sometimes thought to deliver messages from the Creator."

Allison stretched her legs, one at a time. "Being under the weight of the eagle felt comforting. In an unexpected way. And it felt . . ." *It felt like it made me interesting.*

The eagle stopped circling above them and moved on. A symphony of birdsong resumed. The quail family came peeping out from the brush. Allison stood. Stronger now. Ready in case . . . Well, maybe she didn't need to be ready anymore. Maybe this whole mess with Hack was over.

When the trail opened at the clearing around her house, Virgil stopped walking and grinned. "Now I'll tell *you* something amazing."

"Okay." Allison put her hands on her hips. "Let's hear it."

"I'm organizing the stockroom."

"Oh, sure you are. You're probably putting fresh peaches next to dry rice. And cereal next to first aid kits."

"You can believe whatever you want. But I have a question."

"Just one?" When he laughed, she did too. "Well, Mr. I'm-organizing-the-stockroom-and-it's-going-to-be-amazing? What's the question?"

"Can I borrow your label maker?"

When he left a short time later, he held the label maker like a prize, strolling backward up the driveway, grinning at her. Leaving her feeling as if she might actually be interesting—to Virgil anyway. And she was nearly overwhelmed by the impulse to run to him and spill everything. Hand over all the confusing puzzle pieces, all the information she wasn't supposed to share with anyone. Ask him to take it, all of it, and not give any of it back until the fragments were made into a whole.

But being interesting today didn't guarantee she'd still be interesting tomorrow. And it was no fun thinking you'd found someone who would always love you—someone who would always be *interested* in you just because you were you and no one else—only to discover, the next day, you weren't anything special at all.

So she just waved, again, then went inside.

55

Not random

Walking the road back to the market, Virgil tried to sort it out. Allison was so on edge. Back to her old habit of fidgeting. Straightening stuff to ease tension. She probably didn't even realize she was flattening the edge of her shirt sleeve while they talked. Tugging each sleeve over and over. The quail covey's appearance on the trail was timely. Watching and listening to birds can lower blood pressure and reduce anxiety.

Why wouldn't Allison tell him what was bothering her?

He didn't want to push. Would rather she open up on her own timing. But it drove him nuts—bonkers, really—when she started to say something, then didn't finish.

At times it seemed they'd almost bridged whatever gap still separated them. Like if he reached for her, she'd finally surrender. Run into his arms and spill her fears, hopes, dreams, everything.

He imagined holding her close, whispering the right words, feeling her body relax in trust.

Why wouldn't she admit to being on edge about Hack? Could Hack be why the FBI had spent so much time on Wren? Even though Hack wasn't around? Virgil *knew* that guy was fishy! A guy named Hack, getting in the back way to track *Buttercup*'s whereabouts. What else might Hack the hacker have gotten into?

If Allison knew anything, she was buttoned up about it. Ralph might know. But questioning the integrity of a friend's son didn't hold appeal. Ralph never mentioned having a son before. Maybe he never would again. Maybe they'd seen the last of Hack and his bulging biceps.

Allison was sure to attract other interest, though. Not by trying, just by being herself. Unscrupulous people might care about Allison's money more than they cared about her. Would Virgil Tagaloa be fending off phony-baloneys for the rest of his life?

He'd do it. Consider it an honor.

Unless Allison didn't want his protection. Unless she *wanted* to be with someone else. Fell in love with some other guy—better-looking, smarter, stronger. Somebody with more to offer than the grocery guy.

Would he have to watch Allison fall in love with someone else? The thought felt like having his guts ripped out. He shook his head, gritted his teeth. *I love her for her, not for me.* Allison falling in love with someone else was a possibility he should be ready to bear.

Her experience with the bald eagle on Seal Rock was interesting. That was exactly how it felt when a large raptor landed on a branch directly above you. Like you were under its weight. Until now, he'd never heard it described so fittingly.

Did he really ask too many questions? To him, the questions he asked were pertinent. Not random.

Speaking of random, how about her calling him Mr. I'm-organiz-ing-the-stockroom-and-it's-going-to-be-amazing? Her teasing, with her hands on her hips, had sent a thrill right through him. Like he'd shot upward into a sky more brilliant than it ever had been before. He'd like to be teased that way more often.

If she'd allow, he'd like to do a lot of things more often. Protect her. Listen to her. Help her. Understand her. And, especially, hold her. Let her know he's there for her. Will be there for her every day, forever.

Reaching the market, he took the porch steps two at a time, the cherished label maker tucked under one arm. He was under no false impressions. Knew he had use of the label maker only until she got a bee in her bonnet to organize more herself, which could happen at any time.

After checking in with Jax, he headed for the stockroom—and instantly felt overwhelmed. Allison was right. It didn't make sense to store fresh peaches near rice. They were unrelated products and deteriorated at different rates. The market might end up with bugs in the rice or with mealy peaches. It was obvious the inventory was being managed by someone short of genius.

His organization skills were rusty—he'd been okay with passable for too long. But it turned out to be like getting back on a bicycle. As you labeled, your brain started clicking—listening to invigorating music helped—and you knew *why* things went where. Once muscle memory kicked in, you were mostly unstoppable. Having fun, Allison Theodore style.

After freeing up a shelf near the checkout counter, he labeled it *Made on Wren Island*. Amelia could display her handmade crafts. Above the shelf, he tacked nails in the wall for Amelia to display her shell wreaths.

When the new budget kicked in after the first of the year, he'd order stock he never had before. Wren Island souvenirs. Keychains, notepads, stickers, tote bags, hats. What style hat would Allison like to wear?

He spent more than a few moments leaning on the counter, gazing out the window, doing nothing more than picturing Allison wearing different hats. Curls sticking out every which way. Soft eyes focused on him. The hint of a smile, then a real smile. Laughing when he somehow came up with the right line.

It took his breath away, thinking of her.

She'd be beautiful in any hat. He'd order samples of several styles, look them over, guess at her preference. Or he could ask. *Allison, what style Wren Island hat do you want?*

Would she think of that as another random question? She made it sound like he'd nearly used up his quota.

56

Dreary

On a damp, dreary Friday in early January, Amelia pulled the next outfit from her closet. Flannel plaid skirt, leggings, turtleneck, and warm boots. She dressed, returned the empty hangers to the left end of the rod, then slid all the other hangers to the right. Tomorrow's outfit was next in line, ready to go.

After brushing her teeth, she applied the whitening strips Allison stocked just for her. While their magic happened, Amelia listened to a holiday album by Josh Groban.

Christmas had been kind of a bust, if you asked her. Macy swinging between hyperactivity and weariness. Allison startling every time anyone so much as clunked a mug to the counter. Shasta buying a ton of gifts and decorations, then selling most of it. Brand-new stuff!

Amelia was okay with the audio and e-books she received. The pen reader that scanned text and read it aloud could be useful. But a talking first aid kit? She'd never had a problem using the regular kit. Assistive devices, assigned by others to the top of the gift list for someone with low vision, were not at the top of Amelia's list for Santa, had anyone asked.

The worst part? No whales on Christmas day. For the first time ever, she hadn't gotten a line item on her list of nice things to wish for. Maybe the wish was too specific. Too unrealistic. Hoping endangered orcas would show up at a certain time just because Amelia Theodore asked.

One positive bonus had come out of the holidays, though. She'd earned a few dollars. All on her own! Just gathered sticks from the forest, soaked them in water until they were flexible—Ed taught her his technique for softening reeds for woven baskets—and shaped them into wreaths. Then she added shells, lichen, and pine cones.

Since Virgil let her sell her wreaths in the market, they were now hanging all over Wren. And in Annapolis, Maryland! Tourists bought her last five wreaths and shipped them home. Amelia Theodore's shell wreaths decorated houses on the other side of the country. The world was microscopic small, when you thought about it that way.

Allison had helped Amelia set up her own bank account and even put extra money in it, saying she owed Amelia for taking care of the dogs. But anyone would be happy to take care of nice doggies like Lokita and Louise! The money Allison put in the account was more of a handout. Like breadcrumbs to seagulls.

Amelia pulled the whitening strips off her teeth, rinsed her mouth, and wiped the bathroom counter dry. Back in the bedroom, she headed for the collection of stuffed animals on the bench under one window. Time to rearrange for a new conversation.

She positioned the penguin in the center. He knew lots about surviving winter and could teach the others. She snugged the lizard and clown fish close to the penguin. Out of all the animals, they'd need the most support in cold weather. The orcas and polar bear could hang out at the back. They were old pros about winter.

A wash of raindrops splashed across the window, followed by another smattering that sent drips trickling down the glass's exterior. As more raindrops splattered across, Amelia nestled the stuffed animals closer to each other.

Here on Wren, it wasn't snowstorms you had to worry about. It was windstorms. Miles and miles of wind would brew over the ocean for days, then slam into the coast all at once. Add heavy rain, and watch out! *Hold on to your hats, folks.* That's what she'd say if she were narrating a video about it.

She turned off the music and lights and headed downstairs. In the sunroom, she fed Miss Kitty and Marshal Matt Dillon. Warm and dry in their spacious cage, the Australian zebra finches didn't seem to notice the dreariness. They hopped from perch to perch, twittering and happy like always.

Amelia sat and enjoyed the show. Virgil once told her watching and listening to birds could reduce anxiety. She rarely felt *very* worried. That must be from watching Kitty and Matt so much, not to mention all the birds flying free outside.

The dogs wandered into the sunroom together, wearing the red-and-white striped sweaters Shasta gave them for Christmas. A battery pack zipped into the seam powered flashing red-and-white lights. The sweaters were identical—except Louise's was much larger than Lokita's, of course. When Amelia stood and headed for the kitchen, the dogs followed her. Blink, blink, blink. Like walking in a parade!

Allison, Macy, and Shasta were in the kitchen eating breakfast. Whole grain toast with fresh avocado, white bread with peanut butter, and an everything bagel with cream cheese, respectively.

Macy rubbed her eyes. "When the batteries die, we're putting away those sweaters. All that flashing gives me a headache."

Amelia shrugged. "I think it's fun. Like having two electric candy canes walking around the house."

Shasta reached to give Amelia a high five. "Electric candy canes. Good one, sis."

At the counter, Amelia fixed herself a bowl of fruity loops cereal with milk.

"Melia, you're dropping crumbs again." Macy said so without even looking up.

Amelia wiped the crumbs into the nearest sink.

"Rinse them down, Melia."

Amelia rolled her eyes at her warden sister, ran the water to sort of wash down most of the crumbs, then headed to the table with her cereal bowl. Sitting next to Allison, she pulled out her phone. "Would it be okay if I make my YouTube channel public now? It's all ready to go."

"I don't know, Aunt Amelia. Maybe we ought to wait a while longer. There's no rush, right?" Allison sounded worried again. Maybe she should spend more time watching Kitty and Matt.

Amelia chewed a bite of cereal and swallowed. "Virgil says people would probably pay to see my videos. I could start making money from them."

Leaning into Allison, Shasta fluttered her eyelashes. "Well, if *Virgil* said so, it *must* be true."

Frowning, Allison stood quickly, her chair scraping the floor. "Let's wait a while longer, okay? Like Aunt Macy says, there's no reason to draw attention to Wren Island."

When Allison had gone, Amelia surveyed her sisters. "Everyone's so mopey these days."

The silver bangles on Shasta's arms clinked as she twiddled first one set of false eyelashes, then the other. "Wonder what's bothering Allison. Do you think she found out about the mice?"

Amelia looked up. "We have mice again?"

Shasta pulled out a compact and checked her lipstick in the tiny mirror. "Ever since Old Man Frost showed up, entire extended families have been moving in. Mouse cousins, brothers, kids, grandparents. All living happily under one roof. Ours."

Macy reached for the jar of peanut butter. "What Allison doesn't know won't—"

"Oh, Mace. Again with the same old mantra. Give it up already."

"Give it up? I could name a few things *you* could give up!"

While her sisters bickered, Amelia collected the empty dishes, rinsed them in the sink, and added them to the dishwasher.

"Melia, you left wet drips all over the floor."

"Amelia, are you going out where people might see you? You wore that same outfit last week."

In the mudroom, Amelia pulled on a raincoat and boots, then called into the kitchen. "I'll be at the commune if anyone needs me."

"The commune again?"

"What have they got that we don't have?"

Amelia didn't slam the door as she left, but she did *imagine* doing it.

57

Halfway to anywhere

In the aviary at the commune, Amelia cradled a feathery bit of life in one hand. With her other hand, she squeezed an eyedropper to offer a dose of vitamins. The injured sparrow had been found in the forest and rescued a week ago. Amelia snugged the bird back into its nest under a warm light.

After sanitizing the equipment and her hands, she moved on to the next cage. Repeated the process with a junco recovering from having lost a leg. Though the canvas walls flapped in the increasing wind, the aviary remained warm and cozy.

"Amelia?" Ed was scrubbing food and water dishes. "Would you go up to the main building and get another jar of dish soap from the kitchen? It's in the counter cabinet to the left of the freezer."

"Be happy to." *You can always count on Amelia Theodore, folks.*

She pulled her hood up against the wind and marked her progress by counting fence posts between the aviary and the main building. The sun set so early this time of year! Because Wren Island was located so far north. That also meant the days were super long in the summer. She could make a video about Wren seasons for her YouTube channel. Not that anyone was going to see the channel anytime soon, with Allison putting the kibosh on the project.

In the kitchen, she found the dish soap just where Ed said it would be, then peeked around. The cabinets weren't labeled like at home, but she could easily find her way around this kitchen on her own.

On her way out, she passed the library, where someone was always monitoring the hydrophone. Such a quiet, relaxing job. Working in a library, listening for whales.

Back in the aviary, she removed her dripping coat and handed over the jar.

"Thanks." Ed smiled.

Amelia helped him finish cleaning, then dried her hands on a towel embroidered with hummingbirds. "How does someone become a member of the commune?"

Ed accepted the towel she offered and dried his own hands. "There's a joining fee, then ongoing dues. Everyone brings skills to share. We all commit to established guidelines. New members must be approved by the current members."

The way Ed smiled at her after he said that last part made it seem like Amelia would be approved, no problem-o. Macy would blow a gasket, though. With so much mopey-ness in the air, even Allison and Shasta might be annoyed.

"For instance," Ed continued, "you have your interest in helping rehabilitate birds. What other interests or skills would you be bringing with you? If you wanted to join us, that is."

Amelia thought. Making shell wreaths? Probably not the whiz-bang kind of expertise they wanted. Exercising dogs on the beach? Again, not so remarkable.

"Did you retire from a career?" Ed draped the towel to dry. Not nearly as straight as Allison would have wanted.

Amelia shrugged. "I never had to work. I always lived with people who wanted to take care of me."

"You were married? Kids?"

Amelia shook her head. Not married. No kids. No need to go into details.

Ed studied her. "Have you got hobbies?"

"I like making nature videos."

When she pulled out her phone and ran a couple past him, Ed nodded. "We've been wanting to jump-start our social media presence. That's definitely a skill you'd be bringing. But you'd need to be a member of the commune for us to use the videos."

Amelia shrugged. Again. Amelia Theodore, now a full-fledged member of the mopey club. "You can have the videos. Pretend someone from the commune made them."

"We wouldn't do that. We'd want you to get credit for the videos."

"Credit?"

"Income. To be used around the commune, or saved for a rainy day, or whatever you want."

"But I'd have to be a member."

Ed nodded again.

Amelia sighed. Halfway between here and anywhere she wanted to be, that's where she was. "I guess I'll head home."

Ed helped her into her raincoat. "It'll be dark soon. How about I drive you in the Polaris?"

Amelia frowned. It wasn't like she was a child. Like she needed a guardian to hold her hand all the time. She could get herself back on her own, for sure.

"Thanks, Ed, but I like walking."

She followed the fence posts until they ended at the forest's edge. Someday there'd be fencing along the main forest trails too. It didn't matter, though. She'd traveled this way dozens of times. Maybe a hundred.

Farther down the trail, a gust of wind loosened a shower of pine cones and small branches, evidence the storm was approaching. The best place to be now was home.

When the trail split, Amelia headed the way she was supposed to, except it turned out it wasn't the right way. The forest looked different when every tree was waving hello at the same time!

She backtracked to the junction and took the other fork, which had to be the correct trail. Except the farther she went, the more certain she became she was taking the long way, not the short way. Oh well. She'd end up at the house from one direction or another.

She trudged along, keeping her eyes on the trail.

58

Spotlight on a mouse

Macy finished her Mountain Dew—the real deal, with maximum sugar and caffeine—and refilled the glass. Sipping part two of the late afternoon pick-me-up, she wandered into the sunroom and scrutinized the world beyond the floor-to-ceiling windows.

Trees waving branches. Pine cones dropping by the basketful. Raindrops falling lightly, then pounding in a flood, then clearing. Another incidental, passing storm. Or the bustling edge of a more considerable storm. One that might not pass over but crash directly into Wren.

Returning to the kitchen, she set a loaf of fresh bread on the cutting board and began slicing. Allison was working at the table, her laptop open and headphones covering her ears. Focused on writing a new ditty. Macy grimaced and corrected herself. A new *song*.

"Glad I started the slow cooker this morning." She lifted the lid and stirred the simmering soup. "If the power goes out, we'll have a warm dinner."

There was no sign Allison had heard.

Macy spotted the mouse when it poked its beady eyeballs around the doorframe connecting the kitchen to the mudroom. After glancing at Allison, who was still absorbed in her work, Macy moved casually toward the broom closet.

Not casually enough, though. Her switch to stealth mode drew Louise's curiosity. Blink, blink, blink. Louise's flashing red-and-white sweater might as well have been a spotlight on the mouse.

Macy shot another look toward Allison. Still completely absorbed.

With a broom, Macy swept the kitchen floor—just like she would any old day, except every sweep sent the mouse tumbling closer to liberty. Macy cracked open the service door and, with one final whisk, sent the creature out to pastures no doubt greener, even if damp. Heaving the door closed against the rising wind, she turned around.

Only Louise showed interest. Blink, blink, blink. Allison was still engrossed in her laptop.

Macy breathed a sigh of relief. What Allison didn't know wouldn't—

Goodness! She put a hand over her heart. Fluttering. Just from the exertion of shooing out another mouse?

Back in the kitchen, she finished her soda and scratched at her scalp, which felt like it had duct tape stuck all over it. She checked the electronic weather station. The air pressure was dropping. A large bank of rain building in the west was forecast to escalate east and obliterate Wren from the radar.

When a blast of wind hit the roof of the house, Macy jumped, then peered into the sunroom. Were those window panes *bending*? This storm was making her entire body feel like—

"Aunt Macy?"

She spun around.

Allison had removed her headphones. "Where's Aunt Amelia?"

"At the commune. Taking care of birds again, probably."

Macy would've really liked to go to bed. Call it a day and sleep through the rest of this wretched weather. But life wasn't about liking things, was it? It was about taking care of things. Besides, if she went to bed now, she'd just lie there and feel jittery. Here in the kitchen, she could at least take care of—

"Do you think we ought to go get her?" Allison again.

Macy sank into a chair, scratching at her crawling scalp. "She'll be fine. There's still a couple more hours of daylight."

"With this storm moving in, there won't be."

"Go get her if you're worried. Or just call and tell her to stay there tonight."

Allison headed for the mudroom with Louise following. Blink, blink, blink. "Want to come along, Louise?" The dog studied the dimness beyond the open door, then backed up.

Macy didn't blame her. "Why not just call and check on Melia?" How far away her own voice sounded, even to herself!

"I could use the exercise." Allison pulled on rain boots. "See you in a bit."

When the door closed behind Allison, Louise padded to Macy's side and leaned against her leg. Macy closed her eyes. Still, the pulse, pulse, pulse continued in her head.

59

Tilting

As she crossed her driveway, Allison zipped up her yellow raincoat. The marine report indicated four-foot swells at eight seconds, building to six-foot swells after sunset. Gray clouds rolled across the sky like a bolt of the fabric batting Mom used to sew inside quilts. At least the rain had let up for the moment.

"Allison!" Ralph hurried up the driveway. His gigantic rain slicker could have sheltered an entire family.

The last thing she needed now was to get in a conversation with Ralph and have to track down Nancy with an update, during a storm, when phone service and internet would be sketchy. All while nighttime, with its stormy darkness, was coming on by the minute. "I need to go get Aunt Amelia. She's at the commune."

"I just want your boathouse key. To lock it up."

She'd already rolled down the large door facing the water. Why bother locking the side door facing the dock? And why would *Ralph* want her boathouse locked?

Something didn't seem right. But what to do with another rattling piece of information to figure out? "That's okay. I never lock it. I was down there yesterday, rolled down the door, checked everything's storm-ready."

"I'll lock it up for you. The key, please?"

Allison gaped. "Did you just say *please*?"

When Ralph focused on pushing streams of raindrops off his coat, Allison took a long breath against the rising sense she was being pulled under an ominous wave. Sinking. Was Ralph still in communication with Hack? Did Ralph have intel about Hack coming back to Wren? Was Ralph *helping* Hack return?

Rule number one—don't talk about this with anyone. There was no way she was asking Ralph about his involvement before she checked in with Nancy. "Like I said—thanks, but I'll take care of it." She turned to go.

"Don't call Nancy."

Allison struggled to put on a straight face before turning back to him. She was *definitely* calling Nancy, as soon as this conversation ended and regardless of the sketchy phone service and internet. Because this was the first time Ralph had ever admitted a connection with Nancy Sterling, FBI agent.

For now, though, she'd follow rule number two—whatever Ralph says, act like you believe it. "I'm not sure I know what you're talking about. Nancy who?"

Ralph stepped closer. "Nancy Sterling. Hack knows you've been talking to the FBI."

Hack knows.

The world seemed to shift.

Tilt.

Go off axis entirely.

Her panic must have shown, because her hand was taken and held, in both of Ralph's warm ones.

"Allison, listen. What Hack *doesn't* know is that I'm helping the FBI too. We set it up so he wouldn't suspect law enforcement was still waiting for him on Wren. But right now, you and I have got to do this on our own."

When she spoke, her voice sounded smaller than it ever had. "Do *what* on our own?"

"Hack's expecting me to pick him up on the mainland in an hour."

"You're bringing him to Wren? Tonight? In *this* weather?" Her voice was getting more shrieky with every question. Rule number three—contact Nancy if you learn anything helpful. "Why can't we contact Nancy?"

"Your phone's been compromised. We don't know if mine's secure or not. I'll send one message via satellite, and agents will know Hack's headed for Wren. All you have to do is pretend you don't know what's going on."

"That won't be hard to do, because I *don't* know what's going on." Remnants of conversations with Nancy floated through her mind. About Hack targeting people he knew, then returning in person. He could have regained access to her financial accounts at any time from a distance. The agents had said they were leaving Wren because they didn't expect Hack to return. "Why would Hack come back now?"

In a flash of transparency, the expression on Ralph's face—showing concern for *her*—revealed the frightening answer. Now that the FBI had pulled out, it'd be easier to get to Allison.

Hack was planning to retaliate in person for the help Allison gave the FBI. She gripped her shaking hands together.

A shower of raindrops slid off Ralph's flapping sleeves. "He thinks I'm helping him. I've told him we'll have easy access to your plastic fantastic. So lock your boathouse or this whole plan goes haywire. Keep everyone inside. Act like nothing unusual is going on. And *don't contact Nancy.*"

Back to rule number two—whatever Ralph says, act like you believe it. What precisely did *act* mean in that rule? Should she take action as if she believed Ralph? Or *pretend* she believed Ralph, then follow rule number three and contact Nancy?

60

Low batteries

"Aunt Macy?"

"Goodness!" Macy twitched alert. Her niece stood in the mudroom, water dripping off her jacket, looking as terrible as Macy felt. Pale and jittery. Was the girl getting sick?

Allison motioned to the key rack. "Can you hand me the key to the boathouse? I don't want to walk in wearing these muddy boots. And can you get me a flashlight?"

Boathouse key. Flashlight. Macy collected them. Her head felt light. Her heart was racing. So why did she feel so sluggish? She should stop drinking so much soda. This far into the new year, and she hadn't drank a single green smoothie. She handed over the key and flashlight.

Allison peered at her. "Are you feeling all right? You don't look so good."

"I could say the same for you."

Her niece paled even more.

"I'm sorry, sweetheart." Softening, Macy glanced at the two electric candy canes nosing around Allison. "Too bad Louise is afraid to go outside in the dark. You could take her with you to light the way."

"Looks like the batteries are finally going to go. After that, no more blinking sweaters." Allison patted the big dog's head, then studied Macy again. "Are you sure you're feeling all right? Maybe you should lie down for a while."

Macy shooed her niece out the door. "We'll have dinner as soon as you and Melia get home."

"I'm heading down to the boathouse first."

After Allison had gone, Macy gave each dog a cookie, the no-crumble kind, then snugged Lokita into her kitchen bed. She checked the soup in the slow cooker, slid the sliced bread into the oven to warm, mixed a green salad, and set a few unlit candles and a book of matches on the table in case the power went out.

Whew! Maybe she'd sit a spell.

When she opened her eyes, it was darker—much darker. It might be that she'd fallen asleep in the chair at the table. Lokita's soft snoring was such a peaceful sound! And lots of people, maybe even superheroes, rested in the afternoon.

She flipped on lights and moved to the sink. Cleaned the knives she'd used and stored them in the block on the counter. Pulled the butter from the refrigerator to let it soften.

She ought to make an appointment with her doctor on the mainland. She'd seen the doctor not *too* long ago, because Allison insisted they all keep up with their regular health checks. With no physician on Wren, the last thing they needed was a medical emergency when getting to the mainland was difficult.

For instance, during a storm like this.

Macy eyed the blackness beyond the windows. First thing tomorrow morning, she'd make an appointment with her doctor. Because what would happen if the caretaker needed caretaking?

Nothing. That's what would happen. Because this caretaker would never need caretaking.

Shasta bounced down the stairs wearing a too-tight tee shirt, short skirt, and striped knee socks. When she slid into the kitchen skateboard style, Louise jumped up and ran in circles. Macy closed her aching eyes against the bedlam.

At a knocking on the service door, Macy and Shasta headed for the mud-room, let in Virgil and Jax, and hung their dripping jackets on wall hooks.

Jax handed Shasta a box filled with board games. "In case the power goes out. The wind's blowing down giant branches. Trees will probably go next!" The teenager seemed delighted with the weather.

Stowing the lanterns they'd brought, Virgil talked over his shoulder. "Ralph suggested we keep you company tonight. Ride out the storm in the company of friends."

Shasta pulled Scrabble from the box. "Ralph sent you? What a sweetie. He's gone to the mainland to get Hack."

"So I heard." From the way Virgil darted his eyes around, it was obvious he was hoping Allison would materialize.

Macy checked the wall with the jackets. Empty pegs. No yellow raincoat. No coat with pink and purple flowers. "I wonder if Allison and Melia might be out there."

"You *wonder* if they *might* be out there?"

Virgil's voice, rocketing up with diminishing restraint, caused a memory to flash through Macy's mind. Virgil steaming back from the mainland hospital, launching himself onto the dock, flattening Lester Locum.

"Now just calm down, Virgil."

"All things considered, I think I'm demonstrating exceptional calm."

More like demonstrating a teakettle about to blow off its lid, but Macy pressed on. "Melia was at the commune this afternoon. Allison went to get her. Maybe they decided to stay there overnight."

It sounded like Virgil might have sworn. Additional evidence emerged when Jax's eyes popped wide open and Shasta giggled. Macy let it go because, circum-stances as they were, swearing might not be altogether inappropriate. Think of Allison and Melia finding their way through the forest in this weather!

Virgil had whipped out his cell phone. "No service."

"None? Not even a—"

"Is your landline working?"

Macy moved to the wall phone and held it to her ear. "Oh dear." She shook her head.

Virgil threw his jacket back on—faster than Macy would have expected of a man who usually took his time about things.

He grabbed a lantern and was gone.

61

Locking the door

Allison aimed her flashlight at the trail. Not much farther, then they'd be home. She held Aunt Amelia's hand and stepped across the fallen branches. "You're just going to have to keep picking up your feet, Aunt Amelia. There are small branches all across the trail. I'll warn you if I see any more large ones."

"Are we almost there?" Aunt Amelia sounded tired.

Allison squeezed her hand. "I can see the house through the trees. The power's still on."

When they emerged out of the forest, the massive house stood glowing and welcoming. But who was outside the service entrance? Allison stopped walking so quickly Aunt Amelia bumped into her and nearly fell. The person moved toward the forest. Toward them.

Could Hack have arrived on Wren already? Why wasn't Ralph with him?

Would Hack be carrying a lantern?

Before she could switch off her flashlight and become invisible, Virgil's voice reached them. Aunt Amelia returned a happy greeting.

Allison nearly sank to her knees. Relieved Virgil wasn't Hack? Or relieved Virgil was Virgil?

He helped them into the house. Allison locked the door. They shed their dripping coats and boots. The kitchen was warm with the smell of dinner and a cheerfully competitive game of Scrabble between Aunt Shasta and Jax. Aunt Amelia headed upstairs to change into dry clothes.

Walking around the ground floor, Allison checked that doors were locked and windows closed tight. Back in the kitchen, she reached for the house phone. No dial tone. She pulled out her cell phone. No service. Maybe they'd be able to email Nancy once Hack was on Wren. In addition to Ralph's covert satellite message.

Why hadn't she asked Ralph for more details about his so-called plan? In the moment, she'd panicked. *Hack knows you've been talking to the FBI.* She closed her eyes and breathed around four sides of a square. A player at the kitchen table slid Scrabble tiles around. Aunt Macy clinked a spoon through the soup in the slow cooker.

When Allison opened her eyes, Virgil was watching her from across the room, his forehead creased. She pasted on what she hoped would pass for a relaxed smile.

"It's still your turn, Dad." Jax elbowed him. Virgil returned his attention to the board and laid down a couple of tiles. A short word.

"Excuse me, chickee." Aunt Shasta nudged Allison. "I need to get into this drawer. The doggeroos need new batteries."

Aunt Macy clattered a serving spoon to the counter. "Can't we be done with the lighted sweaters, Shasta? All that flashing gives me a headache."

"If the power goes out," Jax called from the table, "we can use the dogs as flashlights."

"Use the dogs as flashlights. Good one, Jax-o." Aunt Shasta closed the drawer. Soon, the electric candy canes were wandering around again, brighter.

Allison checked her cell phone. Still no service. She started to check the landline too, then dropped the effort when she realized Virgil was still watching her, practically clicking clues into place right before her eyes.

She could get stuff past the others easy-peasy. Virgil, not so simple.

Aunt Amelia returned from having changed her clothes. "You guys! The house is moving around upstairs!"

"Oh, for goodness' sake, Melia." Aunt Macy wiped her sleeve across her forehead. "Houses don't move around. Dinner's ready, everyone."

After dinner, Allison rechecked windows and doors on the ground floor again. Hack might be at Ralph's place by now. Ralph might be sending the crucial message to the FBI at this very moment. The power was still on, so that was good.

Unless having the power on *wasn't* good. What if Hack was out there, observing them like they were fish in an aquarium?

Allison turned off the interior lights in the main entry and adjacent rooms. The big room with the grand piano became dark except for ambient light from the fireplace and diffused light spilling from the end of the hallway. She inched closer to the fire and peered out one window. Nothing to be seen but darkness.

She didn't have to turn to know it was Virgil who joined her. He gave off a magnetism sometimes. Most of the time, actually.

"Okay. Something's going on." Not *exactly* a question. But the way he said it indicated he wanted to know what that something was. Now.

"The storm has me on edge."

"We've seen storms like this before."

Not this bad, we haven't. It felt like the pieces inside her, all the bits of puzzling information she'd been trying to keep sorted, might come exploding out of her. Then she'd fall into the abyss of emptiness left behind, too worn to do anything but hope for mercy.

All that and maybe more was going to happen if Virgil didn't remove his hand—his steady, anchoring hand—from where it rested on her lower back.

She stepped away. Gave herself distance. Took a breath, which came out more shaky than she would have liked, but might still pass for normal. "Thanks for being willing to come get me and Aunt Amelia earlier."

"Something's bothering you."

"Nothing's bothering me!" It was totally aggravating how much effort it took to convince Virgil things were okay when they weren't! But you could do anything if you put your mind to it.

Virgil tilted his head to one side. "Are you worried because Ralph's bringing Hack here?"

"He's bringing him *here*? To *my* house?" Her voice had gotten shrieky again. Twice in one tectonic day.

The crease in Virgil's brow deepened. Studying her, he spoke deliberately. "Not here to your house. Here to Wren, as I understood it."

Allison turned, ran one finger along the edge of the fireplace mantel. "You talked to Ralph?"

"He talked to me."

"What else did he say?"

"He asked if Jax and I would stay at the house tonight. Any idea why he'd want us to?"

Her hand trembled, even as it rested on the mantel, so she brought it to her side. She wanted to tell Virgil everything. Ask him for help! But there was rule number one—don't talk about this with anyone. Did rule number one still apply when all the other rules were changing?

"Why won't you tell me what's going on?" Virgil put a hand on her shoulder.

"I don't think I can."

He turned her toward him. "You don't think you can?"

"I want to. I really want to, Virgil. But I can't. I really can't." When she looked into his concerned eyes, her breath caught. "Please don't push me. If you push me, I'm afraid I'll end up . . . " *Ruining the whole thing. Not doing what I'm supposed to. Causing someone to get hurt.*

She blinked back tears. She would *not* cry.

Virgil nodded, slowly. "Do you mind if Jax and I stay in a guest room tonight?"

"That would be a-okay."

Lokita wandered in, a tiny electric candy cane. Allison sniffed, then straightened. "I need to let Lokita outside. Walk her around the yard."

"I'll go with you."

"It's usually a one-person job." She hadn't meant to sound so abrupt.

"Yes, but is it a one-person job tonight?" The gentleness in his voice nearly rocked her off her feet.

The house shuddered in a gust of wind, then settled. A muffled burst of laughter came from the kitchen, where someone must have said something funny.

Allison looked at him, couldn't look away, swallowed.

"It probably should be. A one-person job. Tonight."

For a long moment, he held her gaze. The crease of worry changed to crinkles around his eyes and mouth. A tempered smile, as another question formed. "You play checkers?"

"Checkers?" An easy question. "Yeah, I play."

"I'll set up a board in the kitchen." He was heading down the hall.

"Fair warning," she called. "I always win at checkers."

"Not surprised." In his voice, as it floated back to her, amusement.

She collected the dogs in the mudroom and threw on a raincoat. When she opened the door to the fenced area, out went Lokita. Blink, blink, blink. Louise stood in the doorway.

"If you're too afraid to go outside in the dark, Louise, move so I can close the door."

She shut the big dog inside the house and followed Lokita's flashing sweater around the fenced area.

When the forest roared in a gust of wind, she studied the house. No visual sign of structural movement. But Aunt Amelia was right. The house *did* feel like it was moving when the wind blew hard. Allison had felt it herself, many moons ago. A lifetime ago.

Her hip felt unnaturally tight. Probably from searching all over the forest earlier for Aunt Amelia. Allison did one of her therapy stretches, then cinched the hood of her coat. Tucked her chilly hands into her pockets. Resumed following Lokita around.

When Lokita finished her business, Allison sang the blind dog back toward the house. "Little Lokita, come to me."

Inside, she toweled off Lokita. Sent the little dog ambling toward the kitchen. Shed her dripping coat and hung it on a wall hook. Straightened all the other coats.

Verified that the service entry door was closed tight. Locked it.

Breathed a sigh of relief. Everyone was inside now, safe.

She tapped the lock again, to be sure.

When she returned to the kitchen, Hack was bent over at the game table, kissing a giddy Aunt Amelia on the cheek.

62

Body language

"I heard this is where the party's at tonight." Hack left Aunt Amelia's side and came toward Allison, arms out for a hug. Of all the nerve!

Allison engaged well-practiced body language. *Not so fast, mister. But with decent behavior, maybe later.* Over the years, she'd perfected communicating the message giving her safe physical distance and time to think of an out, without antagonizing a guy. It'd been effective many, many times—whenever her ex expected her to fend for herself at a party, bar, club. It worked now too.

"Oho! So that's how it is." Leaning against a counter, Hack gawked at her, eyes lingering. "You look great, Allison. Really great."

She smiled for what she hoped was long enough to convince him she felt entirely confident, then glanced around the kitchen. Where was Ralph?

Aunt Shasta, Aunt Amelia, and Jax had gathered around a game of Monopoly. Aunt Macy was loading plates into the dishwasher. Louise snoozed in her bed—some guard dog!—while Lokita settled into her own. And Virgil?

His hand rested on the table near a checkerboard. Allison didn't dare look him in the eye but swept her attention back to Hack. She needed all her focus to do this right. To keep Hack unsuspecting and at ease, until Ralph came. Or until one of them could get a message to Nancy.

Feigning a fawn, Allison lowered her eyes, raised them, smiled—then aimed straight for Hack's ego. "You don't look too bad yourself."

"I've been working out."

"It shows."

"Bench-pressing three-twenty-five now."

Another area of response where her ex had given her a lot of practice. "That much? Wow."

Hack flexed one arm. "Check this out."

Aunt Shasta hopped up like a relief pitcher. "Let me feel, Hacky-boy. Ooh! Rock solid."

While Aunt Shasta batted her eyelashes, Allison checked her cell phone. Still no service. If she got a moment out of Hack's sight, she could follow rule number three—contact Nancy if you learn anything helpful. That was what she should have done earlier instead of—

"Might as well put that away." Hack pointed at Allison's phone. "Not going to be any cell service for a while."

"Oh, right. Too stormy." But the confidence in Hack's voice caused a new worry to surface. Could Hack, not the weather, be responsible for the service outage? Could Hack do that much hacking?

She returned the phone to her pocket, next to the boathouse key. Why wasn't Ralph here? What if Ralph and Hack were working together? She glanced at Aunt Shasta again, who hung on Hack's arm and winked at her.

"Where's your dad, Hacky-boy?" Truly, Aunt Shasta deserved an award for her acting skills.

"Trouble with *Lucy Jo*. Water in the hatch." Hack laughed. As if the water in *Lucy Jo*'s hatch wasn't an accident.

Allison poured everything she could into a confident, relaxed smile. Froze it in place when Hack touched her hand. His steely voice sent a revolting charge up her spine.

"I came back for a reason, you know. How about you and I get away together?"

"In this weather? I don't think so." Pulling her hand away, she aligned a stack of napkins on the counter. Moved the napkins closer to the knife block Aunt Macy insisted on keeping out for easy access. Realigned the napkins. Tweaked the knife block.

"Shasta will go with me, then."

Aunt Shasta played with the bangles on one wrist. "I'm waiting for Ralph."

Allison shrugged. "I guess it will be just you going. Might want to wait for the weather to clear."

A scattering of clean forks on the counter looked all wrong. She picked them up, one at a time, and nestled them together neatly. Just so. How much longer until Ralph came? She ventured a glance at Hack.

He clenched and unclenched his jaw. Behind him, Virgil pushed his chair away from the table and stood.

Allison's ex would have stayed where he was. Would have teased her for unsociable behavior, propped up his feet, and drank more beer. If there was one thing she'd learned from living with Tank, it was that when life got difficult, she was on her own.

Not so with Virgil. He was closing the distance. Fearless. Suddenly, it was alarmingly clear why Tank had never helped her in these situations. So *he* wouldn't get hurt.

Now Virgil was barreling into a situation he'd underestimated. She should have told him what was going on!

"Time to go, Hack." Virgil used his not-a-question-but-I-want-an-answer-now voice.

"Wait." Allison turned to Virgil. "He can't go now. We should keep him here because—"

Hack's fist struck fast and hard. Virgil crashed backward into the table and chairs, then landed on the floor. Aunt Shasta screamed. Maybe the other aunts screamed too.

Jax shot forward, then wavered to a stop when Hack lifted one finger. "Don't even think about it, junior. I've got a hundred pounds on you and a jab you'll never forget."

Aunt Amelia stood, mouth gaping, and moved to help Virgil. Hack's foot went out at just the right time, tripping Aunt Amelia, who landed near Virgil. "Oof."

Allison felt it then. A piece she'd never known was in her. It hadn't been there when Tank had lied about his relationships with other women. Or when he'd pushed her out of the car and left her in the middle of the night in a strange part of the city, because he didn't want to keep talking about what she felt was important to discuss. It hadn't even been there when he'd said she wasn't interesting anymore, at the very moment she'd been making a massive effort to do something as worthwhile as create a family.

Maybe it had never been inside her before now. Or maybe it had *always* been there, waiting to surface. Waiting for now. The moment when fearsome agony reached no longer only for her but also for people she deeply loved.

Rage.

People said rage was blinding. For her, it was deafening. It screamed around inside her so loudly she could hear nothing else. Except Louise barking her head off.

"Get out of my house. Get *out* of my house!"

Hack moved toward the door. "Come with me, songwriter. Or would you rather I take your dumb dog?"

He scooped Lokita from her bed. Blink, blink, blink. Then he opened the door and ran outside, carrying the little dog.

In two seconds, Allison took in the surrounding mess. Aunt Amelia and Jax were helping Virgil, who was stirring. Aunt Macy, pale and glistening, was sinking into a chair. Aunt Shasta was hollering about not risking harm to Lokita.

Allison moved to the open door. Hack was running through the dune grass toward the beach, Lokita's flashing sweater acting like a homing beacon. Whirling to Aunt Shasta, Allison shouted. "Keep everyone inside!"

Then she was running. Racing to help her dog. Her sweet little blind dog who had never asked for anything but to be loved. To be *taken care of*.

In the open doorway, Louise continued protesting against going out into the dark. The big dog's barking faded as Allison chased Hack through the dunes, down the beach, toward her boat dock.

63

Not a normal day

The firm, damp sand near the water's edge offered faster running. Saltwater spray lifted by wind off the crashing waves coated Allison's face. With every pounding footfall, her hip throbbed more.

Ahead of her, Hack jogged to the end of the dock and set down Lokita. Blink, blink, blink. The blind dog stood there before taking a few confused steps.

"Lokita!" Allison reached the dock and sprinted. With one massive twinge, her hip gave way, and she crashed to the rough, sanded surface in rocking pain.

Lokita wandered more, tentative, unseeing. Toward the edge of the dock and the churning water below.

Allison tried to stand, fell back when her hip and leg burned in fiery pain. Sitting, she took a deep breath. "Lokita," she sang. "Now we're on the dock. So be careful where you walk."

Lokita took a few steps toward Allison before pausing again, disoriented by the sound of Hack ramming one shoulder against the boathouse door.

Allison raised her voice. "Little Lokita, come to me. Here you are, right with me." She pulled the little dog into her lap.

Hack stopped ramming the door and strode toward them. Allison tried again to stand. Failed again. A blur of red-and-white lights galloped past.

Shaking off a snarling Louise, Hack lost his balance and fell to the dock. "Call off your freak dog!"

For a moment, Allison debated not doing so. But Louise could gnaw through a giant chew toy in ten seconds flat. Her powerful jaw locked on Hack's arm or leg would hurt. A lot. "Louise! Come here."

Hack's yowling turned into whimpering as the padding of doggie footsteps came close to Allison and Lokita. Blink, blink, blink. Louise sat with her back to Allison, watching the writhing figure at the end of the dock.

Allison took a breath. What to do now? On a normal day, she hardly got a moment of privacy. Where was everyone when she needed them?

She did tell Aunt Shasta to keep everyone inside.

Hope Virgil wasn't hurt badly. She should've warned him sooner. Hope Ralph was okay. Wherever he was.

She peered at the back of Louise's head. Had Louise finally conquered her fear of being outside in the dark? Or was she afraid and here anyway? Oh, these dogs! Love for them nearly overwhelmed Allison. She kissed the top of Lokita's damp, salty head.

Shivering, Allison shifted on the wet dock. Tested her hip. Standing was still a no-go. The wind carried spray from breaking waves across the dock, coating her with what felt like a million icicles.

A wisp of rumbling turned out to be Louise, working up to an audible growl. Hack had stood and was moving toward them.

"Hold it right there."

Ralph's voice sent a wash of relief over Allison. His gigantic rain slicker flapped in the wind. Out of one sleeve, the end of a gun pointed at Hack.

Relief turned to dread. This was exactly what she'd feared. That Hack wouldn't give up easily. That firearms would be necessary. What if Hack had a gun too?

"Did you stop taking your meds, pops?"

"Don't call me pops."

"You're pointing that thing at the wrong person. Help me bash in this door. You said her boat would be ready to go. Are you getting too old to do anything right?"

Muttering, Ralph rubbed his bearded chin.

Running footsteps stopped when they reached Allison. Virgil placed warm palms on either side of her face, pushed back her wet hair, and came into focus. "You okay?"

At the sound of his voice, Lokita wiggled into a wag. Allison nodded and tightened her hold on the little dog. Louise stole a glance at Virgil, then returned to surveillance mode.

Virgil draped his coat around Allison's shoulders, then steamed over to where Ralph held Hack at gunpoint. Virgil flicked a finger against Hack's forehead. "That was for the tap on the jaw. Which didn't hurt at all, by the way."

Then, before Allison could believe what was happening, Virgil had slammed a single punch to Hack's gut and dropped him to the dock. Folded in half, Hack rolled and moaned.

Virgil straightened. "*That* was for frightening the woman I love. And her dog."

The woman I love?

Virgil strode back to Ralph and nodded toward the gun. "Always handy to have one of those around."

"Hardly go anywhere without one." With his free hand, Ralph dug in a pocket, pulled out a device, and spoke into it. "Ralph to Nancy."

"Go ahead." Above a static background, Nancy's voice was crisp and confident.

"Suspect down. At Allison's dock." Ralph glanced at Louise. "Head for the flashing red-and-white lights."

"I see them. On my way."

Virgil extended his hands to Allison. "Want help getting up?"

The woman I love! Allison offered a weak smile. "It's usually a one-person job." Thanks to her quivering voice, the line she'd thought would sound cute came out sounding pathetic.

Then she was in Virgil's arms. He sat on the dock, adjusted his coat warmer around her, and gathered her close. As if sitting with her, holding her, was something he did every day. As if he expected to continue holding her every day. And every day after that.

The woman I love! And her dog!

Taking a few warm breaths, Allison snuggled Lokita and pulled the dry flannel lining of Virgil's coat closer. "You put on a coat before rushing to save your girl? It seems funny to take time for that."

"Save my girl? Is that what I did?"

Allison couldn't be sure, but it felt like he kissed the top of her head. She relaxed against him. "Are my aunts okay?"

"Jax is with them." Virgil's voice resonated through her. "Are you hurt?"

The woman you love is fine, she wanted to say. Except her hip felt anything but fine. She'd wait to say anything about that until Nancy arrived. Wait right here in Virgil's arms.

She glanced at Ralph still looming over a groaning Hank. When Nancy came, Ralph could put away his gun. Ralph with a gun! "I hope Ralph has a permit for that thing."

Virgil dipped his head close to hers, enfolding her in the circle that was him, and whispered. "No permit needed to carry a T-handle wrench."

First, the revelation washed over her. Ralph had come through for her, for all of them. Brave enough to pretend he was holding a gun when he wasn't. Good old Ralph.

Then, she was embraced by the intimacy of Virgil sharing a secret with her against the roaring world. Not another corroding puzzle fragment she must keep on her own, but a key shining piece he'd borne as his own burden.

Would she always remember Virgil whispering to her like this? Would she always remember those were the *first* words Virgil whispered to her?

Would he stay interested long enough to whisper more secrets?

Ralph shifted and spoke in a low voice. "I see them coming now."

Allison exhaled. "Um, Virgil?"

"Hmm?"

"The people about to arrive are with the FBI."

"Figures."

"But don't worry. They're not after me. They want Hack."

The arms around her flexed, secured her closer, settled again.

Nancy arrived with three other agents. Hack was read his rights and taken into custody. Nancy nodded at Allison, Ralph, and Virgil. "Once the suspect is secured and the agency is notified of events, I'll speak with you three at the house."

With Virgil's help, Allison stood. Wobbly. "I hope I haven't messed up my hip again."

Ralph slipped Lokita into one gigantic pocket of his slicker and supported Allison on one side. Virgil buttoned Allison into his coat and took her other arm. Louise lighted their way off the dock.

Partway up the beach, Ralph pointed at the house. The light outside the front entrance flashed on and off at random intervals. "What do you make of that?"

Virgil stopped walking. "Jax. Sending a message."

"Like Morse code?" Allison moved forward on her own, testing her balance. Her hip didn't feel as painful as when she'd injured it in the motorbike accident. But her entire left side throbbed, and her leg stiffened more with every stride. After briefing Nancy tonight, she'd go to bed and sleep for a week. Maybe a month.

"What's Jax saying?" Allison tested her hip with an increasingly lengthy stride.

"He wants us back at the house."

Allison continued walking. On her own! "He knows we'll come back as soon as we can, right? Why would he send a message—"

"Allison, lean on me and let's keep moving." Virgil took her arm and steadied her.

She matched his stride. Keeping up with Virgil. The man who had dropped Hack with a single punch. Kabam-o! Take *that*, Hack!

Wow, listen to the wind roaring through the trees.

Ralph cleared his throat. "If we're going in this weather, we should probably use my rig."

"Yep." Virgil kept a steady pace.

"Why would anyone go anywhere in this weather? Did Jax say someone needs to go somewhere? Tonight?"

Virgil dipped his head close. "*Now* who's asking questions?"

Ralph maneuvered her around a driftwood log. "I take it you don't know Morse code."

"I don't know Morse code *yet*. I can learn."

Ralph groaned, long and heavy. "God help us all if Allison Theodore learns Morse code."

Virgil chuckled. "Think she'd be more dynamo than the world's ready for?"

Allison beamed, outside and inside. Dynamo! And Virgil said it out loud for the dogs and Ralph to hear. Dynamos were definitely interesting.

She beamed all the way back to the house. Right up to the moment she stepped inside and discovered a frantic Aunt Shasta trying to revive a passed-out Aunt Macy.

64

Basic moves

The mainland hospital's cafeteria was nearly deserted and offered limited options at this time of night. Virgil made his way to the self-serve beverage counter. Found a clean mug and dug through the tea options. Chose Earl Grey because Allison asked for caffeinated, not herbal.

He touched his aching jaw. Fingered the swollen area around his eye. He'd happily get walloped all over again just to see Allison sparkle. At *him*! All that deferential waiting for her to come around. Turns out all he had to do was take a punch and throw a punch. Win the girl with basic caveman moves.

Notice how he'd restrained himself, though. Didn't completely punch the jerk's lights out like he wanted to. Credit Allison Theodore for making Virgil Tagaloa a better man.

Still, there were a lot of things he couldn't do anything about. It was nice that Nancy Sterling was so helpful. Before they'd even arrived at the hospital, she'd pulled rank and arranged for a private recovery room.

The doc said Macy was going to be fine but should be monitored a while longer. Amelia's wrist fracture simply needed time to mend. The big question mark related to the results from the CT scan of Allison's hip. She was supposed to be resting in the room's second bed, instead of letting Amelia use it for a nap.

Virgil thought for sure mentioning a hospital rule would convince Allison to be cautious. A patient wasn't supposed to move around unnecessarily before the full extent of her injury was known. The second bed was meant for the patient with a possible hip injury, not the patient with a wrist wrap. But Allison had melted him with a smile and promised to stay put in the wheelchair—which she'd better be doing, not putzing around risking a fall.

He filled the mug with hot water. Steeped the tea for less than a minute because Allison asked for it to be weak, not strong. Then he stood waiting for the tea to cool. No way and no how was he handing over a potentially scalding liquid while Allison still shook from all she'd been through.

Would she be okay with him holding her hand now? Touching her? He'd go slow. Let her take the lead.

She'd called herself his girl, matter-of-factly, as if she'd always been. He didn't really save his girl, though. Louise and Ralph did the heavy lifting. All he did was arrive—almost too late—and offer backup. Ask a few questions and give a few answers. Tuck her into a warm coat. Let her know she could hand over whatever weight she still carried. The usual Virgil Tagaloa stuff.

And she had rested, finally. Trusted him. A little sigh, a closer snuggle. A miracle happening in his arms.

The most incredible feeling coursed through every part of him, right there in the hospital cafeteria. He couldn't help standing taller at the help-yourself beverage counter, even puffing up a bit.

With the tea cooled to a comfortable—and hopefully comforting—temperature, he strode down the hall. Closer, closer, closer to the woman he loved.

65

A safe place

In the quiet, dimly lit hospital room, Allison pulled out her phone and checked the time again. Twenty minutes to midnight. Eight minutes later than the last time she checked. Carefully, she leaned forward in the wheelchair. Pulled a portable charger out of her bag. Plugged in the phone.

Aunt Macy's breathing was rhythmic, but lying in a hospital bed made her appear deflated. Allison fended off the image of her mom looking the same way just before she died. Aunt Macy's diagnosis wasn't cancer. It was diabetes. Her heart was being monitored as a precaution.

Allison checked the chair's wheels were locked—she'd promised Virgil she wouldn't risk a fall—then she stood, took careful steps toward the bed, and hovered. She reached to smooth a section of her aunt's hair but pulled back. Touch might wake Aunt Macy.

On the other bed, Aunt Amelia slept soundly, her left wrist bandaged against a fracture. She'd been thoroughly checked out, cared for, and discharged from the hospital. But none of them wanted to leave until they knew more about Aunt Macy's condition and the results of Allison's tests. Allison scuffed back to the wheelchair and eased into it.

At a stirring in the doorway, she looked up, hoping for a doctor. Instead, Virgil set a mug on the table next to her. Tea, weak, the way she'd asked for it. He placed a hand on her shoulder and gently squeezed. "Any new updates?"

"Not yet." She sounded dried up, worn out.

Virgil reached for the tea, handed it to her, waited while she sipped. Returned the tea to the table. Then crouched in front of her and held both her hands. "How are you feeling?"

Hospital staff who recognized her from after her motorbike accident had gone out of their way to say they hoped her pain was coming from a muscle or tendon injury rather than a dislodged pin in her hip. That she was young and healthy and had only overdone it. Everyone had sounded exceptionally optimistic, suspiciously optimistic, when they whisked her off for a CT scan.

But if she had to go through another surgery, another grueling recovery . . .

"Mostly, I feel worried."

Virgil moved one hand to her knee and left it there. Warm, steady.

She closed her eyes and felt her heart breaking against the image of Lokita wandering, confused. Abandoned to find a safe place on her own. *Little Lokita, come to me.* The commonplace ditty had become crucially important. Kept Lokita safe. Might have saved Lokita's life.

Forget winning a Grammy. This was enough. More than enough.

Virgil handed over a tissue, and Allison wiped her tears. He handed her the tea and she sipped.

Had she asked Jax to tuck a warm blanket around Lokita at bedtime? Not likely in the near chaos of Nancy using her EMT training to revive Aunt Macy. Nancy's agents taking off with Hack in a helicopter during a brief break in the weather. Aunt Amelia and Jax calming the dogs. Aunt Shasta hollering at Ralph to fire up *Lucy Jo*, which hadn't sustained the damage Ralph led Hack to believe.

After the awful trip to the mainland—Allison's hip seeming to shred by the minute—Ralph headed right back into the storm to return to Wren. But until he got there, Jax would be responsible for the dogs, the house, the grocery market, any storm damage. A lot to ask of a fourteen-year-old boy.

Virgil pulled out his phone, tapped on its screen, and sat in the chair next to Allison. When his phone dinged, he shared Jax's photo showing the dogs curled up together. "Jax says they've all eaten their dinners. The power's still on. Cell service and internet restored. Jax is playing video games. He'll take the dogs to the market with him in the morning."

Allison nodded. It was funny, though maybe not surprising, that she and Virgil had been wondering about Jax in the same moment. Virgil put away his phone and reached for her hand.

When Aunt Macy stirred, Allison began to stand, but Virgil patted her knee. "Not so fast, leading lady." After checking Aunt Macy, Virgil returned to Allison's side, speaking only with a nod. *Don't worry. She's fine.*

The on-call physician, Dr. Sullivan, entered the room with Aunt Shasta twittering at his side. While a nurse helped a now-awake Aunt Macy sit upright, Aunt Shasta sat on the other bed with a bounce that woke Aunt Amelia.

Dr. Sullivan moved closer to Aunt Macy. "Would you like privacy while we go over your diagnosis?"

Aunt Macy shook her head. "They're all going to know everything about it anyway."

"Your heart looks fine, but I want you to wear a monitor for a few weeks. If everything remains stable tonight, you can go home tomorrow. I'm prescribing insulin to help control your blood sugar."

"I'm not going on insulin."

"You might not need to. You could continue monitoring your blood sugar and see if changing your diet and exercise routine helps."

"That's exactly what I'll do. I could have told you there's nothing wrong with my heart. Never has been."

Wasn't that the truth? There was nothing at all wrong with Aunt Macy's unfailingly resilient heart. Allison smiled at her aunt and was rewarded with a confident nod that indicated Aunt Macy planned to be back in charge. Soon.

Dr. Sullivan turned his attention to Allison. "I have the results of your CT scan."

She glanced around the room. At brave but overwhelmed Aunt Macy. Wide-eyed but exhausted Aunt Amelia. Jittery Aunt Shasta, who'd hopped to her side and would benefit from being delegated a productive task. Taking Aunt Shasta's hand, Allison looked back at Dr. Sullivan.

"Can we talk elsewhere? There's enough going on in here already."

"A consultation room's just down the hall."

Allison tugged Aunt Shasta's hand, motioned for Virgil to come along, and thanked the nurse already resettling Aunt Macy and Aunt Amelia. As Aunt Shasta pushed the wheelchair down the hallway, Allison glanced up at Virgil. The overhead lights illuminated the deepening bruises across his face.

"You said that punch to the face didn't hurt."

Eyes forward, Virgil kept a steady pace. "What punch to the face?"

In the consultation room, Aunt Shasta and Virgil settled in chairs. Dr. Sullivan pulled up images of Allison's scan. "The good news is the hardware's still in place. But the bone at the injury site isn't getting adequate oxygen. It's actually a good thing your muscle gave out when it did, because it means we're discovering this problem early."

"Am I going to need surgery?" Allison held her breath.

"With rest and restricted physical activity, the bone should heal on its own. You'll need to resume physical therapy. I want you on an NSAID, preferably prescription strength. In a few weeks, when the swelling has gone down, we'll get another CT scan."

"The pain's not bad at the moment."

"You might do okay with over-the-counter NSAIDs—*if* you stay off that leg and let it heal. You're going home with crutches. Plan to use them for several weeks."

Allison sighed. Crutches for weeks sounded nearly unbearable. But far, far better than needing another surgery.

Dr. Sullivan flipped off the screen and collected his notes. "I'll release you now if you'll come back in a day or two for a recheck. Would you like me to prescribe a sleep aid for tonight?"

She shook her head. "We'll be staying at a nearby hotel, and I'll sleep as soon as my head hits the pillow. Even without a sleep aid, I might not get up again. Ever." She mostly ignored the look passing between Dr. Sullivan, Aunt Shasta, and Virgil. The same look people had passed around throughout her recovery from surgery. *Take care of the invalid. Don't let her do anything she shouldn't.*

Dr. Sullivan squinted at Virgil. "How are those bruises feeling now?"

Virgil turned to Allison and winked. "What bruises?"

66

Past bedtime

With her right hand—the one not bandaged in a splint—Amelia positioned her phone for more complimentary selfie lighting and hit record.

"Hello, everyone! Earlier this evening, we had a little excitement on Wren Island. I apologize for how my hair looks. It's been quite a night, and now it's past everyone's bedtime. But I wanted to show you this super fancy hotel lobby." She scanned the room with the phone. "Look at the chandeliers! And the mirrors! Wren doesn't have anything like this, unless you count Allison's house. That courtyard over there looks like it might be home to birds. Maybe I'll film the courtyard in daylight tomorrow."

Amelia refocused the camera on herself, then zoomed in on the hotel clock on the wall behind her. "Oh look! It's past midnight, so actually I'll film the courtyard later *today*! Bye for now!"

The YouTube channel was still not available for public viewing, no thanks to Hack Wesson, who wasn't really Hack Wesson. Allison said that after Nancy Sterling got things concerning Hack settled, Amelia's channel would probably be all systems go. But Amelia wouldn't start making money from the channel until she got a *lot* of subscribers.

She had a plan, though. Virgil was going to order little cards with QR codes on them so she could hand them out and invite people to watch her channel. He said a QR code was like a bar code. Scanning it with a phone camera would take a person right to the Wren Island channel! The wonderful world of technology.

Tucking away her phone, Amelia waited to be checked in along with everyone else. The hotel provided complimentary toiletries and pajamas—cotton shorts and tee shirts—for guests whose luggage had been lost. Or guests who arrived without luggage for any other reason. For instance, guests who'd just helped capture one of the FBI's most wanted, then raced to the emergency room wearing panda-print pajama bottoms and an oversized pink hoodie they'd put on a lifetime ago, thinking they were in for the night.

Amelia accepted the sundries. "Much appreciated."

They each got a room key. Were told to use the same key for the elevator, because the rooms Allison booked filled an entire floor. As they piled into their private elevator, everyone tried to not bump unsteady Allison and her crutches.

When the elevator door opened, they were in their very own personal lobby. With a giant potted fern and everything!

Virgil used his key card to slide open the glass doors to their suite. If you were expecting guests, you could leave the glass doors open so your friends could walk right in off the elevator. If you wanted guests to knock first, you'd close the doors. Virgil closed them.

Inside, sofas and tables and chairs curved around a gas fireplace. Standing in front of the enormous television, Amelia had to turn her head right and left to see from one side of the screen to the other. The kitchen was nice, but nothing like Allison's kitchen on Wren.

Crutching to the nearest chair, Allison sank into it.

Shasta ran around opening doors and getting the lay of the land before directing Amelia to a bedroom. "Tell me if you're taking a bath, so I can help. We don't want your splint getting wet."

Virgil got his own suite. With his own gas fireplace! And mini kitchen with sink and fridge.

"We'll put you in there, Allison." Shasta waved toward another set of doors. "I'll sleep in the bedroom next to yours, so I'll hear if you need anything."

None of them had anything to unpack, so they were back in the kitchen again in a jiffy, looking at each other and Allison, who hadn't moved and was definitely fading.

"Let's get you another dose of those NSAIDs, Allison." Shasta dug through their pharmacy bags. "And how about a sleeper?"

"I'll take another NSAID, but I don't need a sleep aid." Allison drew herself up. "What I'd really love is a mug of hot water with a squeeze of fresh lemon, if only we had lemons." She sighed. "Just a mug of hot water will be fine."

Grabbing a room key and his wallet, Virgil bounded back to the elevator. "Lemons it is."

While Shasta trundled Allison off to her bedroom, Amelia poked around the kitchen. If Virgil *did* find fresh lemons at this time of night, he'd want a clean knife and cutting board.

None of the cabinets or drawers were labeled, so maneuvering the kitchen was mostly a guessing game. She found the knives, oddly in the same drawer as plastic bags. If Allison spent much time here, she wouldn't be able to resist organizing the kitchen. Amelia moved the measuring spoons to the same drawer as the measuring cups. That one was a no-brainer.

In no time at all, Virgil returned with ten lemons, all the twenty-four-hour mart had in stock. He warmed a mug of water in the microwave, added a wedge of lemon, and passed the mug to Shasta, who disappeared into Allison's bedroom.

Then all of them except Allison were in the kitchen again, looking at each other through bleary eyes and agreeing it was past bedtime. So off they went to their bedrooms, respectively.

And respectably, Amelia would add if she were narrating a video. Wouldn't want anyone to get the wrong idea.

67

The bathrobe

Waking up in the hotel the next morning, Amelia stretched under the covers, listening to the sound of city traffic filtering in. No singing birds like she usually woke up to on Wren. But it was just for one morning. They'd be going home today.

Had anyone asked Jax to look in on Miss Kitty and Marshal Matt Dillon?

Amelia sent a text, and by the time she'd finished brushing her teeth, Jax had replied with a video of the birds twittering around a cup of fresh seed.

Jax was really stupendous. That apple hadn't fallen far from the tree, for sure.

After pulling on her grimy panda pants and hoodie, which smelled like the hospital and maybe seaweed, Amelia found Shasta and Virgil in the kitchen.

Shasta tossed a menu to Amelia. "Allison's still sleeping. I'll order room service."

Virgil headed for the door. "I'm going to hit the gym first." As if the gym needed to be conquered.

Their breakfasts arrived. A big bowl of fruit for everyone to share. For Shasta, a toasted everything bagel with smoked Chinook salmon and herb cream cheese. For Amelia, blueberry pancakes with whipped cream and a topping she'd never heard of called Rogers golden syrup.

While they ate, Shasta read aloud jokes from a book Virgil picked up at the twenty-four-hour mart. She waved a fork toward Amelia's pancakes. "How about I order a case of Rogers and ship it to Wren? Remember, keep your wrist elevated."

Amelia propped her elbow on the table and raised her wrist above her heart. With her free hand, she sorted bite-sized pieces on her plate, each with a different proportion of pancake, whipped cream, and Rogers. The possibilities were endless!

Virgil returned from the gym, showered, and joined them. For him, chicken apple sausage, scrambled eggs, and pancakes with grade A maple syrup. He'd tried Rogers once before and didn't care for it.

Between the jokes Shasta read aloud, Virgil contributed a few of his own dad jokes, which they laughed at to be nice and because there wasn't much else going on. Poor Virgil. The bruises on his face were part red, part purple. Like he'd been cast in a scary movie.

Allison was still sleeping when Shasta got the call Macy was being released from the hospital. After Shasta and Virgil left to bring Macy to the hotel, Amelia watched *The Dick Van Dyke Show* from a chair distant enough she didn't have to swing her head to see the entire screen.

When Shasta and Virgil returned with Macy, Amelia clicked off the television. "How do you feel, Macy?"

"Fit as a fiddle. For goodness' sake, Melia. Why were you watching television in the middle of the day?"

Amelia shrugged. "There isn't much else to do. It's just a city outside. No beach or forest."

"There's always *something* to do." Macy began rinsing breakfast dishes.

Amelia shook her head. "You don't have to do that. It was room service. We can send the dirty dishes back on the cart."

"Send the dirty dishes back? I don't think so." Macy clattered utensils into the sink.

"Don't break anything, Mace." Shasta dumped out the contents of a shopping bag and pulled Amelia close. "Look what I got. New clothes for all of us so we don't have to keep wearing our grimies. And look at this."

Amelia reached to touch the gorgeous red silk in Shasta's hands. "Wow. What is it?"

"A bathrobe for Allison." Unrolled, the robe revealed a hand-painted peacock across most of the back.

Macy glanced at it and sighed. "If that isn't the most impractical purchase ever, Shasta."

Evening rolled around with Allison still sleeping. Going on twenty-four hours! Everyone else resigned themselves to a second night in the hotel.

Amelia went to bed at the usual time and woke early. To traffic noise. Even on a Sunday morning! She ordered two scrambled eggs all on her own. Plus plain pancakes topped with fresh strawberries and whipped cream, extra Rogers. By the time she finished eating, Shasta was calling the concierge with questions about the menu. Macy ordered plain oatmeal and two scrambled eggs.

Before eating, Macy checked her blood sugar.

Amelia watched carefully. "All good?"

"All good." Macy smiled. "What about you? Is your wrist bothering you at all?"

"Not if I keep it elevated." Amelia propped her elbow on the table and raised her wrist.

Virgil returned from hitting the gym again just as Nancy buzzed and asked if she could come up. He sent the elevator down for her.

"Nice place." Nancy took it in. "I was hoping to ask Allison a few more questions."

"She's still sleeping." Amelia glanced to see if Macy was watching, then stowed her dirty breakfast dishes in an inconspicuous spot on the service cart.

"She's been sleeping for thirty-two hours now." Shasta sliced into a lobster benedict.

Nancy squinted. "Are you concerned?"

Shasta shrugged. "Her doctor said rest was the best thing for her. And it's not like she took anything. Just over-the-counter pills for inflammation."

"Maybe you ought to call her doctor." Perched on the armrest of a sofa, the FBI agent used a tone they wouldn't have been able to argue with even if they'd wanted to.

They waited while Shasta talked with a nurse. "She took two ibuprofen and two acetaminophen. A little water with lemon. Just a minute, let me check."

Shasta headed into Allison's bedroom. Then she was back, talking into the phone. "She does look comfy. Real comfy. I mean, I don't know what she *usually* looks like when she's sleeping, but she's breathing easy, all tucked in, and seems happy as a clam."

They waited.

"Okay, thanks." Shasta clicked off the call. "We're supposed to let her sleep. Let her wake up on her own, quietly. We're supposed to call if she's not up by noon tomorrow."

"Noon tomorrow?" Macy clunked her mug to the table. "Shasta, are you *sure* that's what they said? Next time, I think I'd better talk to the nurse myself."

Nancy stood and headed for the door. "Call me when she's up. No hurry."

They hunkered down to binge on *The Dick Van Dyke Show*. Virgil left to hit the gym again—second time in one day!

When he was gone, Shasta grinned at Amelia and Macy. "He's doing that to impress Allison, you know. Bulking up even more."

They all nodded, pleased as punch.

68

Getting ideas

Monday morning, Amelia was studying the hotel menu when Virgil returned from hitting the gym again. He looked real perky—then deflated when he realized Allison still wasn't awake. She'd been sleeping for over fifty hours!

By the time Virgil had showered, Amelia was preparing to order lobster benedict for breakfast. She hadn't seen it on the menu or known it was an option until Shasta ordered it yesterday. Maybe lobster benedict would become her new favorite food. Maybe this breakfast would be the best of her life.

She waited to order, though, because Virgil said he had an idea. "Dr. Sullivan said it was best for Allison to wake up quietly on her own, right? It's almost noon. What if we nudge her along a bit?" He rummaged through the kitchen and held up a bag of coffee beans. "I doubt anyone can sleep through the smell of strong coffee and frying bacon."

"Oh! Could we have croissants with grape jelly too?" Amelia bumped lobster benedict to a lower position on her list of nice things to wish for.

Virgil took off for the twenty-four-hour mart. When Macy and Shasta emerged from their rooms, Amelia filled them in on the plan.

Returning with fresh croissants, grape jelly, and maple-cured bacon, Virgil started the coffee. But when he went to fry the bacon, the stove burners wouldn't turn on. No power to the oven either. Everything was plugged in. He checked this possible problem and that one. Nothing.

"Microwaving would make the bacon soggy, right? Or too chewy." He stood in the kitchen and drummed his fingers on the countertop.

Propping her chin on her good hand, Amelia sighed. "It would be so *nice* for Allison to wake up to the smell of frying bacon and coffee."

Nodding, Virgil eyed the toaster. He tapped out loose crumbs. Positioned the appliance on the counter and studied it. "I think I remember a buddy in college talking about cooking bacon in a toaster. Drop the strips in like slices of bread. Crank up the dial."

He popped bacon into each slot and pushed down the lever.

Shasta turned up the television volume. All four of them watched an infomercial about a sticky substance useful for anything from tacking up posters to making your boat watertight. Super handy stuff! Next thing you know, there were flames in the kitchen and the fire alarm was going off.

Not short beeps like the smoke detectors at Allison's house. This alarm sounded like a fire engine's horn, blaring over and over. Plus, a disturbing white light above every door flashed on and off. Amelia covered her ears.

Virgil put the fire out just as there was a pounding on the glass door to their private lobby. Macy slid open the doors to reveal the concierge.

"Everyone out!"

Virgil pointed to the toaster. "It's my fault. Sorry."

The concierge frowned at the charred appliance. "Never had one of those do that before."

"He put bacon in it," Shasta tattled, breezing past.

"You put bacon in a toaster?" The concierge started to scoff, then registered the bruises underneath Virgil's scowl and distanced himself. "S-sorry, pal. Hotel regulations say everyone's got to evacuate. Use the stairs. No elevator."

While Virgil tried to reason with the concierge, Macy and Shasta collected Allison. One look at her, draped in the hotel's baggy shorts and tee shirt, too sleepy and confused to balance on her crutches, and Virgil erupted at the concierge.

"She shouldn't have to take the stairs!"

The concierge spoke into a walkie-talkie. "Requesting additional help on the VIP floor." He motioned to the stairwell door. "Sir, would you and your party please come with me?"

Down the stairs they went, in a roundabout mess, all of them helping each other except Virgil, who helped Allison. Outside, they blinked in the sunshine with other hotel guests and employees.

Allison tied the fancy peacock bathrobe around herself and sank into a folding chair someone offered. "What time is it?"

A firefighter checked his watch. "11:12 a.m." He handed her a blanket.

"Fun way to spend a Saturday morning." Allison yawned.

The fireman stilled, studying her. "Today's Monday."

"Really? Wow."

Narrowing his eyes, the fireman turned his attention to Virgil, who'd cornered the hotel manager and was talking fast. Every time Virgil punctuated another point of reason, he glanced toward Allison, flashing his bruised face.

The fireman turned to scrutinize Amelia's splinted wrist, which reminded her she was supposed to be keeping it raised above her heart. She did so, smiling. As if she was saying hello, except she didn't wave.

Crouching in front of Allison, the fireman spoke quietly. "Miss? Have you been threatened recently?"

Allison rolled her eyes. "Have I ever. But it's all right now, thanks to you guys. Law enforcement, first responders, and all. Thank you."

Nodding, the fireman threw another glance in Virgil's direction, then returned his attention to Allison. "It's our job, and a privilege, to help people be safe. Will you be pressing charges?"

"You bet I will. I hope the others will too. Aunt Amelia, keep your wrist elevated."

The fireman stood then, all purposeful, and motioned to the chief. Before Amelia had entirely figured out what was happening, the fire chief and a police officer moved to initiate a friendly conversation with Mr. Virgil Tagaloa, fifty-one-year-old resident of Wren Island, no priors. So it really was ideal timing that Nancy Sterling arrived when she did and cleared up the confusion.

After that, Allison became a kind of sensation. Not only was she recently a victim of one of the FBI's most wanted, but she'd also helped capture the suspect.

Add to that the rumor that the dude with the bird's nest for hair, who thought toasters were for cooking bacon, had been slugged by Allison hard enough to produce all that bruising.

The knockout woman at the center of all this was staying in the hotel's VIP suite—she'd booked the entire *floor*—and was wearing what might be the fanciest bathrobe in the city.

It was too much for anyone to ignore.

And since Amelia was standing right next to Allison, it was almost as if all those firefighters were admiring her too. If she'd known how fun that attention would be, she would've added it to her list of nice things to wish for. Maybe she would start a new list. Nice things that happened unexpectedly.

Once the fire chief was certain Virgil's misuse of the toaster was the only reason for the alarm, everyone was given the all clear.

Yawning, Allison stood with Virgil's help, then poked him. "All systems go, finally. No thanks to you."

They took the elevator back to their suite. Scheduled recheck appointments for Allison and Macy. Ate a late lunch at a restaurant because Allison said Virgil should steer clear of kitchens for a while. Burgers all around, except for Virgil, who drank a shake with a boost of protein powder because his jaw couldn't handle a burger yet.

Then they loaded onto Ralph's boat and headed back to Wren, everyone in a happy mood. A *jovial* mood is how Amelia would have described it if she'd had the energy to narrate a video about it.

On *Lucy Jo*'s deck, in the sunshine and out of the wind, Virgil gently bumped Allison's shoulder.

"You're not going to be allowed near *my* toaster anytime soon," she teased.

All casual, he smiled. "Forget the toaster. Things are hot enough on Wren already. Oh, by the way, when will you be wearing that peacock robe again?"

For that, she whacked him on the arm. Undaunted, he pulled her close and whispered in her ear.

"Keep it G-rated, kids." Shasta grinned. "Your little aunties are watching."

Everyone turned at once to smile at Amelia. The only little auntie they would think required keeping life, certainly romance, G-rated.

When they reached the house, Amelia stopped at the concrete lions and patted one stalwart head, then the other. A matched pair who'd never be more than a few feet apart from each other.

Inside, she checked on Miss Kitty and Marshal Matt Dillon, twittering happily as usual.

She patted the dogs. One, the other, then both at once. Until they wandered off, together.

Then she headed upstairs and climbed into bed, alone.

Huddled into only herself for warmth.

When the tears came, she gave in. Today marked forty-nine years since losing the only man she'd ever loved. And today her niece, a lifetime of brightness ahead of her, was falling in love with a man who would adore her forever.

All that happiness, promise, and future.

Stacked on what might have been, should have been, could have been.

If, years ago, Amelia had known she'd stay single, would being left behind then have hurt even more? If, by some odd trickery, either she or Allison had to be abandoned, who would Amelia choose?

She'd choose to be the one left. Absorb the loss herself. Carry the weight of it all these years.

Just to land here, today, and see Allison be offered the world.

69

Graduating

Spring had sprung! Allison opened windows throughout the upper level of her house. A songbird symphony filtered in, along with the scents of pine, fir, and cedar. The thin layer of marine air hovering above the water around her boathouse was already dispersing in the rising sun's radiance. A bluebird day, as Virgil would say.

She maneuvered down the curving stairwell to the main entry. Getting around the house fairly efficiently now. When outdoors, she was supposed to use a cane—but that changed today. Her most recent CT scan showed continued improvement in her hip. And the physical therapist temporarily living on Wren said Allison was ready to graduate. Starting today, no more cane! Just a walking stick and only when she wanted.

Jacob Yoon did wonders with both her and Aunt Amelia's recoveries. Knew when to push and when to back off. A trait also helpful because the young man, interested in nutrition, was often in the kitchen cooking with Aunt Macy. And with energy to spare, he enjoyed helping with chores at the farmhouse bed-and-breakfast.

Also happening today, Aunt Amelia's wrist splint was coming off once and for all. They ought to celebrate with a party tonight—a subdued event, where no one could overdo it and risk getting reinjured.

Allison checked on the dogs and birds, but Aunt Amelia had already taken care of them. Near the birdcage, Allison found a stack of business cards with QR codes. She scanned the code. Got an error message saying the site couldn't be reached. Opened her YouTube app and searched. No channel about Wren Island.

In the kitchen, she found Aunt Macy and Jacob working out a new recipe for vegetable lasagna.

"For dessert, we'll make brownies. Flourless, with avocado in them." Jacob reached for a baking pan.

"Goodness." Aunt Macy chopped yellow bell peppers. "I don't suppose we could make the brownies buzzy? Add frosting and instant coffee?"

Jacob sent Aunt Macy a look that indicated she ought to know better. Allison laughed. Aunt Macy might have met her match.

Aunt Amelia walked in, and Allison pulled her aside. "I found your cards and scanned the QR code, but nothing came up."

"I haven't made the channel public yet."

"Why not?"

"I didn't think you wanted me to. You kept saying we'd do it after this, that, or the other happened. So I finally stopped asking." Aunt Amelia put a hand on Allison's arm. "It's okay. The videos aren't whiz-bang anyway."

The expression on her sweet, uncomplaining aunt's face was one of peaceful acceptance. Aunt Amelia was a real trouper. Allison hugged her. "I'm sorry I've been so distracted. Can I help you get it going?"

Aunt Amelia brightened. "You'd do that? You could write songs for the videos! Like adding a real soundtrack!"

"That's not exactly what I was—"

"That would be so *great*, Allison! *Real* music with the videos!"

How could she possibly say no to a beaming Aunt Amelia? Besides, it wasn't like anyone else was requesting songs written by Allison Theodore. She ought to do this. Have fun with her songs. Her *ditties*. "You know what? You're right. It would be great. We'll work on it together."

At lunch, they celebrated Aunt Amelia's splint coming off by adding whipped cream and a cherry to her brownie. Then Jacob ceremoniously tossed Allison's crutches out the service door, which started Louise barking.

"Quiet, Louise." Allison shushed the dog. "Reminds me of that awful night."

Jacob passed around the brownies. "I'm still not clear about what all happened."

"What happened was a madman visited our house." Aunt Macy reached for the largest brownie, then passed the platter.

"Hack the whack job." Aunt Shasta chewed. "Huh. Avocado in brownies."

Allison rolled her shoulders against the tension that returned every time she revisited the events of that night. "Ralph told me Hack knew I'd cooperated with the FBI. But I don't think any of us realized Hack would retaliate the way he did. When he took off with Lokita as a hostage, I had to follow him."

"Right after that, Mace passed out." Aunt Shasta chewed another bite.

"Right *before* that, I was tripped by one of America's most wanted." Aunt Amelia sounded pleased with herself.

"That madman punched Virgil too. Laid him out flat as a pancake."

"Oh, gee, Aunt Macy. Virgil did okay."

"He sure took off after you. Once he came to." Aunt Macy passed the whipped cream without helping herself to any.

"Virgil didn't go until he'd made sure *you* were okay, Mace." Aunt Shasta dumped spoonfuls of whipped cream on her own brownie. "When Ralph showed up—"

"Wasn't Ralph already around?" Jacob sipped from his mug.

Aunt Shasta waved both arms, sending her bracelets clinking. "He was aboard *Lucy Jo*, supposedly making emergency repairs. Thought he'd convinced Hack to meet at his house so they could get back at Allison together by taking her boat. Instead, Hack came straight here. But Ralph was already signaling Nancy. When Hack didn't show at Ralph's as planned, Ralph came running over here."

Allison rolled her shoulders again. People she loved, sheltering right here in her own house, had been threatened. Injured. The dogs too. They'd been scared, confused, frantic.

"Virgil hollered at Ralph to go after Allison." Aunt Amelia reached for another brownie. "But Louise was already on her way because Macy had bossed her into it. 'Louise,' Macy said, 'put on your big girl panties and go after that madman right now.'"

Allison joined in the laughter, rolling off more tension.

Aunt Amelia pointed at the dogs. "So all Ralph had to do was follow the flashing lights."

"*All* he had to do?" Aunt Shasta's bracelets clinked. "Don't forget he's the one who stood there pretending a T-handle wrench was a gun. And *I'm* the reason the dogs were flashing."

"The dogs were flashing?" Jacob looked confused. Louise wagged her tail, though still keeping a wary eye on the discarded crutches.

Aunt Amelia nodded. "Both the dogs were wearing sweaters with flashing red-and-white lights. Like electric candy canes. So it was easy for Ralph to see where they'd gone. And I made sure Virgil put on a coat before he left, because it was stormy."

"Is that why Virgil arrived wearing a coat?" Allison laughed again. It felt so restorative to be able to laugh, even if only about parts of that night.

Aunt Macy wagged a finger in the air. "Virgil kept saying he didn't like the way I looked. I *assured* him I was fit as a fiddle—that was before I knew I was going to pass out. Who *wouldn't* be pale and sweating when they were about to pass out?" She pointed at Allison. "But at the moment, *you* were the one who needed help. *You* were the one out there with a madman."

Aunt Amelia propped her chin on one hand and sighed. "Here it comes. I never get tired of hearing this next part."

Aunt Macy drew herself up, nodding. "So that's exactly what I said. 'Virgil, I don't care if you don't like the way I look. If you stay here for one more second, I'll never speak to you again. Our Allison is out there with a madman.' That's when Virgil flew out of here. Wren Island is home to our very own Superman. No cape required."

Aunt Shasta giggled. "No tights either. To the great disappointment of us lookie-loos." Aunt Macy rolled her eyes.

Jacob smiled at Allison. "Your man Virgil seems like quite a guy."

Allison beamed. *Your man Virgil.* "Well, that awful night is in the past now. Hack is in prison. We're healing from our injuries. We're all systems go."

Jacob finished the last bite of his brownie. "Shipshape and Bristol fashion."

Allison tilted her head. "Huh?"

Jacob glanced around at them. "It's a nautical term. For folks living on an island, it might be more appropriate than an aeronautical term."

"Shipshape and Bristol fashion?" Aunt Macy set down her fork.

"Sure! People have been saying it for two hundred years. From when Bristol Harbor's tides fluctuated wildly. If cargo wasn't stored properly, it would spill into the harbor. And they didn't have label makers back then." Reaching for his mug, Jacob grinned at Allison. "Or you could use *all systems go*. Airplane pilots use that term."

"Wait a minute." Allison set down her own mug. "Are you saying *all systems go* is a phrase *airplane* pilots use?"

Aunt Amelia shook her head. "We're not crazy about airplane pilots around here. At least pilots who fly private planes. Especially private floatplanes."

Aunt Shasta sighed. "We used to adore airplane pilots. But not anymore."

Jacob sipped from his mug. "So use *shipshape and Bristol fashion* instead. And by the way, you ladies have mice. Everywhere. I'm surprised spick-and-span Allison here isn't more disturbed about it."

All together and all at once, the aunts exchanged horrified looks. Allison worked hard to keep a straight face and let the scene play out. Aunt Macy stammering through explanations about the problem not being as bad as it seemed. Shasta quoting statistics about mice keeping spider populations under control.

"Sorry, Allison." Aunt Amelia patted Allison's hand. "You've had a lot going on. We didn't want to bother you with it."

Allison stood and brought her lunch dishes to the sink. "That was thoughtful of you. Thanks."

Aunt Shasta's voice rose above the sound of the water running into the kitchen sink. "We'll make sure the mice get taken care of once and for all!"

Allison rinsed her dishes. "I'd appreciate it."

"We won't leave any more crumbs around either!"

"That would be fantastic." Allison turned off the faucet. Dried her hands. Hung the towel to dry, nice and straight.

While walking down the hall toward the front stairwell, she could still hear the lowered voices.

"Jacob, did you *have* to mention the mice?"

"Why wouldn't I?"

"She didn't know."

"How could she *not* know?"

"What Allison doesn't know doesn't hurt her."

"Oh pooh, Mace."

It was inevitable that her aunts' mouse secret would slip sometime. Jacob mentioning it so matter-of-factly, when they were all together at once, was an unexpected bonus. The expressions on their faces! Now Allison no longer had to pretend not to know.

She headed upstairs, laughing—but quietly. What her *aunts* didn't know wouldn't hurt *them*.

70

The real soundtrack

In her den, Allison sat at her desk and bumped the mouse—the computer mouse, not a real mouse. *A mouse in the house? Not so fast. A mouse in the house will not last.*

Who would have ever thought she'd be okay with a mouse in the house? Not the old Allison Theodore. The new Allison Theodore wasn't entirely comfortable with it either. But the new Allison was trying to stretch herself. Learning to be okay with quirks that would have driven her nuts before.

For now, it was enough to know the project of removing mice was in progress. Her aunts were doing what they could to help. She, too, would do what she could to help—and accept what she couldn't change. Aunt Macy had taught her that.

When the electronic piano keyboard beeped awake, Allison opened an app and clicked through Aunt Amelia's videos. Daily life on Wren documented as something special. Finding a shell on the beach. Watching the tide recede. Teaching Louise a new trick. Listening to Allison, Virgil, Jax, or Shasta laugh, question, explain, or defend. Watching Aunt Macy pull a hot dinner from the oven.

Throughout the videos, Aunt Amelia's lilting narration was the real sound-track. Anything Allison added would just be mood music.

She watched a video of Virgil throwing a frisbee for Louise. Watched it a second time. Wrote an accompaniment that came out sounding exactly how she felt about Virgil caring for the dogs. A reflection, somehow, of Louise running like the wind with the mighty ocean as a rolling backdrop. She saved the file and fist-pumped into the air for finishing the song.

It had become clear, really quickly, she wasn't going to get any more song-writing done at Virgil's cabin. Midway through the day, Virgil would wander in with the flimsiest of excuses. They'd stroll to an overlook. Sit under an arbutus tree. Talk about everything or nothing at all. Make scrambled eggs, sandwiches, or . . . Anyway, hours later, he'd return to the market, and she wouldn't have gotten any further on songwriting.

Or at least she wouldn't have put any notes on the page. Virgil thought doing things one enjoyed inspired creativity. He still kept her desk and piano keyboard in the cabin. And Jax gave the dragonfly on the stained-glass lamp the fitting name Sapphire Blaze.

Allison clicked through more videos, wrote more accompaniments, saved the files. Wow, Aunt Amelia had recorded a lot of videos.

Maybe the old Allison Theodore needed to win a Grammy. Needed to write a movie soundtrack for an entire orchestra. But the old Allison lived alone. In an empty house on a remote island. The old Allison peeked through a window before opening the door to anyone—even a neighbor!

The old Allison was kind of peculiar, in some ways. In many ways.

Life felt so much more meaningful now. Cluttered with people and stuff (and mice!), yes, but contentment was all a matter of perspective. All a matter of deciding what was *important*. Living alone and trying to make it big time, or living simply with people you loved? Living in fear of rejection, or trusting people you loved? Trusting you were in this life together, forever, because you loved each other so much you'd never *want* to leave.

Louise wandered in. With muddy paws. The old Allison would have rushed the dog to the bathtub. With one hand, she brushed off what she could. Then she vacuumed the carpet. Once dirt like that got ground in, it was really hard to lift.

When she'd finished, she sat and played with the dog's ears. "Where's the rule, Louise? Where's the rule that says you shouldn't trust *anyone* just because *someone* once left you?"

Virgil loved her. He'd said it *and* proved it in all the little ways. And Virgil wasn't the type to walk away. Would *never* leave someone he loved. Virgil was as steady as they came.

71

Her heart's delight

When the setting sun was casting shadows across the smooth gravel of her ready-to-be-paved driveway, Allison left her den for the market. Louise ran ahead, found a patch of fresh dirt where a fence post had been removed, and dug to her heart's delight.

While coordinating the road improvements, Ralph had made certain Allison's driveway was the first to be flattened, dumped with gravel, and smoothed. Paving wouldn't start for another few weeks. Since Ralph was ferrying much of the heavy equipment to and from Wren, he wanted to prepare all the roads first, then do all the paving at once. Reinstalling the fence posts would be the final phase. Wren Island under construction.

Allison's role was easy. She just paid the bills. Weighed in with an opinion here and there. Enjoyed strolling on a smooth driveway, without crutches, a cane, or even a walking stick. On her way to eat an espresso muffin with cream cheese spread, baked by a guy who, among other talents, probably made the best muffins in the world. A guy who also happened to love her. Love *her*!

Calling Louise away from digging at another post location, Allison decided now was as fitting a time as any to do a bit of excavating of her own. There was quite a lot she and Virgil didn't know about each other. Before traveling the road forward together, maybe they ought to discuss where they'd each come from.

Inside the market, she found Jax wearing a ball cap printed with *Wren Island* across the front. "Cool hat."

"Dad ordered them."

"Are there any more like yours?"

Grinning, Jax nodded toward the stockroom, as Lokita ambled out of her cozy bed behind the cash register. She spent most afternoons at the market now.

Allison crouched and patted the unofficial store mascot's soft head. "Hi, baby. Are you having fun? Are you being a most excellent supervisor?"

She kissed the little dog and nudged her back toward the bed. Just enough to get Lokita going in the right direction, so Lokita could experience the satisfaction of having found her bed all on her own.

Standing, Allison found Jax watching her. He sort of smiled, then turned away, busy behind the counter.

Her breath caught as she deciphered the expression on Jax's face. She must look the same way when missing her mom.

Louise bounded in and jumped up on Jax, making him laugh. Allison headed for the stockroom.

Neat, labeled shelves lined the walls. Supplies were grouped in tidy, logical ways. Dry goods and nonperishables together. Emergency supplies, first aid kits, and bottled water together. Allison gaped. "It just keeps getting better and better."

Virgil gave up trying to stuff his hair—all that wonderful hair—under a hat. "I'm not going to be able to wear this. Want it?"

"You're giving me a Wren Island hat?"

"And anything else you want." He pulled her into his arms and set the hat on her head. "Fits perfect. Must have been designed with you in mind."

She settled into his embrace. "Um, Virgil?"

"Hmm?"

"Do you think we ought to talk about stuff?"

"What stuff?"

"Our past relationships. We've never talked about our exes. What went wrong. What we learned."

"Okay. What did your ex do wrong? So I won't make the same mistake."

"That's easy. He was never around when I needed him."

"I can be around. A lot." Virgil wrapped her closer.

"And I never knew if he'd stand up for me. Be there when I needed help."

"You're maddeningly independent. Capable. Resourceful. Totally with it."

"But sometimes I need help."

Virgil chuckled. "Sometimes you do."

She patted his broad shoulder. "So you'll be around? To go after any creeps? Drop them like I know you can? Kabam-o!"

Virgil nodded, tempering a smile. "On the remote chance a creep bothers you before I intercept him, I'll go after him."

She took a breath, needing to say the last thing too. "One other thing went wrong. He wanted out of our marriage because . . . I wasn't interesting enough."

"I think you're interesting." Virgil's lips found her ear. "I think you're fascinating."

She pulled back and met his eyes. "Seriously, Virgil. I really want to know if you think you might, at all, at any time, change your mind about that. I don't want to pressure you. But I really don't want to go deeper with this relationship if it's not going to be forever."

"Allison." He lifted her hand, kissed it, folded it into his own. "Forever is all I'm offering."

When he wrapped her up again, she held on. "So what went wrong with your ex?"

He took a deep breath and exhaled. Releasing her, he sat her next to him on a large box waiting to be unpacked.

"Drugs. It started with prescriptions her friends passed around. She added alcohol. Then cocaine and any combo anyone claimed was better. By the time Jax was two, I'd put her in rehab six times. She was in jail, out of jail, back in again. We separated and I got full custody of Jax. When Jax was four, we moved here. Wren is almost all Jax remembers, except for a few flashbacks."

"I'm sorry. It sounds awful." Allison leaned against his shoulder. "Where'd she end up going?"

"After we divorced, I lost track of her. Sometimes I wish I knew where she was. Sometimes I'm glad I don't."

"How could she give up her baby? Walk away from Jax? And you?"

"I suppose you could say she walked away—when she took her first hit, her first step down that path. But in the end, it was us who needed to walk away if Jax was going to grow up in a home that wasn't in complete turmoil."

Allison fingered a loose string on the bottom hem of her shirt. "So you and your wife decided, together, that separating was best for Jax."

"It's what we needed to do. She knew it when she was sober. Maybe she eventually understood it more. I hope she did."

Allison pressed her shirt hem flat, flatter. "So when she left . . . "

"In rare moments, she'd say she wanted to keep trying. But after so many times of trying and seeing the same pattern . . ." Virgil dropped his head. "She'd be gone for days, weeks. With anyone. Come back and promise to live differently, then not be able to. I wanted her to change back to the person I'd married. I waited, hoping day after day. She just couldn't stop. I decided the only hope for Jax was to live apart from her."

Allison tried to imagine a square to breathe around. Searched in vain for four predictable sides, then attempted to rise above a sinking feeling. "So when she left you—"

"It was the hardest choice I've ever made. Deciding my son would be better off away from his mother. Wondering if I was doing the right thing by leaving or if things might be different tomorrow. Deciding I must give up on her being able to change."

Allison's heart sank. Right down to the pit of her stomach. "Oh no."

Virgil pulled back, his expression questioning.

When the world stopped spinning, she found her voice. "You're saying . . . *you* left *her*."

72

Inexplicable

He should have seen that coming. Her being afraid he'd leave her. How could he have been so obtuse? Entirely unaware he was rambling on about the one thing Allison Theodore might not be able to live with.

Idiot! Blundering on about the divorce. He should have phrased it differently. Made it sound as if his ex left him.

But he couldn't let Allison believe that. It wasn't the truth.

Virgil Tagaloa wasn't the only idiot though. Somewhere in the world wandered a doofus who didn't want to be with Allison forever. Lost interest! Well, major forfeit for the other guy, major win for Virgil Tagaloa. If Allison still wanted him.

He swallowed against the uncertainty. Now that she knew he left his wife, would she be off and running?

Loving Allison Theodore never came with guarantees. She was perfectly capable of taking care of herself. Happy that way. He might not fully understand her reasons for protecting her heart, but that didn't mean those reasons weren't legitimate. Allison was free to make her own choices.

Her choices didn't change his part, though. He'd always be willing to bail her out when she needed a hand. Willing to sucker punch anyone threatening her safety. He'd look after everyone and everything she loved. Make sure she never ran out of essential supplies, even the expensive seed mix for the Australian zebra finches. Keep stocking high-quality dog food, cheesy bratwurst, and lemons. Add trail posts to help Amelia. Forgo alcohol around Macy. Feign interest in Shasta's ramblings about hair dye and nail polish. Fix the vintage arcade games—again. He'd even watch more episodes of *Gunsmoke* if he had to.

In other words, he'd always be around. Always be willing to be a friend.

But if Allison rejected his friendship, what would happen when she was so frightened she couldn't see straight? So discouraged she didn't know which way was up? What would happen when she couldn't handle a problem but was in too deep to back out? When she needed help from someone she could trust with *anything*?

The thought of Allison pushing through any of that, fiercely independent but miserably alone, made his heart feel like it was being ripped in two.

Heading outside to the porch, he breathed deep. Listened to the familiar whistle of a bald eagle. And its mate's answering call.

One time when Allison was in his arms, she said she felt like she could do—or be—anything. He said he wanted that for her too. Then added, with a chuckle, that he'd try to keep up.

Has he always loved Allison? It feels so. Could he love her more than he does today? That doesn't seem possible, but based on how each day has played out so far, he will. Love her even more tomorrow than today. More the next day. Even more after that.

One of the world's greatest mysteries.

More than extraordinary.

Inexplicable.

73

Nautical terms

Amelia dressed in her Monday outfit, no decision-making required. Pink linen dress with short sleeves, a navy cardigan, and beachworthy sandals. While brushing her teeth, she did the little twisting motions Jacob said were beneficial for her wrists. Then she was shipshape and Bristol fashion.

That's right, folks. Here on Wren Island, we prefer nautical terms over aero-nautical terms.

Downstairs, she pulled on the bucket-style Wren Island hat she wore on Mondays. Navy canvas with pink lettering. Matchy-matchy, as Allison would say.

Now that she and Allison were working together on YouTube videos, Amelia's days were filled with decisions. Choosing which song should go with which video. When to fade out the music so her voice could more easily be heard. Which subtitle font wouldn't block images. And, of course, what new activities to record. Predeciding the day's clothing freed her up to think about everything else.

There was just one problem. Hardly anyone was watching her videos. The Wren Island channel on YouTube was live but sitting there unnoticed. A national treasure yet undiscovered.

Virgil said she should be patient. And he was one to know about being patient.

Working with Allison was super fun, whether or not people would ever see the videos. Allison made the world brighter. More colorful. Just with Allison being herself, the world became more fascinating.

Wonder what that felt like. Being the person who made the world more interesting for someone else.

In the sunroom, Amelia fed Kitty and Matt. If she moved to the commune, would they let her bring the finches? Probably. They were all about birds up at the commune. Would they let her bring her stuffed animals? For sure they'd *let* her. But would they think it was odd, a grown woman keeping stuffed animals?

If she had to leave them behind, think how lonely her nights would be!

Another stumbling block about joining the commune was the money. Allison said she'd pay for it, but that didn't seem right. Not if Amelia was trying to make her own way in the world.

She headed outside, Louise tagging along, and decided to take the long way to the commune. And by long way, she didn't mean the wrong trail in the forest that got you all in a dither until someone came to find you. She meant she'd stroll on the beach first, looking for shells and other treasures.

At the beach, stooping to pick up the shell of a butter clam, she disturbed a little shore crab. Before it scuttled off, she studied its tiny toes with her magnifying glass.

Another stumbling block about joining the commune was Ed. Things with Ed had gotten kind of odd. Him bugging her, every time she turned around, about joining the commune. And he hovered. A lot. Constantly asking if she needed help.

Not did she *want* help, but did she *need* help. One little word changed the message. Just because she carried a magnifying glass along didn't mean she wasn't *capable*. Just because a girl carts a few assistive devices around doesn't mean she's *helpless*.

Ed was probably doing his best, though, at showing interest in her. Just not the kind of interest she wanted.

Around the time Amelia had turned sixty, Macy had said Amelia had probably lost any remaining opportunities for romance.

If it hasn't happened by now, Melia . . .

It turned out Macy was probably right about that too.

When the hydrophone gong rang, Amelia pulled out her phone and opened the app. Quick as a wink, Allison, their very own brilliant Allison, was at her side. Amelia handed over her phone, because squinting at the screen had brought on an instant headache.

"Can you see them?" She pulled out her binoculars.

"One orca. Seems to be alone." Allison pointed toward the western point and helped Amelia aim.

"So orcas can go off on their own? Away from their family?"

"They can and do. This one's awfully close to those crab pots."

Amelia watched the orca mill around the buoy bobbing on the water's surface. "Ed mentioned new technology called ropeless fishing gear."

"How on earth does that work?"

"It's not really ropeless but uses much shorter ropes. It can be recalled by remote control."

"Wow."

"So whales and other marine life don't get entangled. They can die from being caught in ropes, you know."

"People can die from it too." Allison's voice sounded sad. Fragile.

Amelia lowered the binoculars and studied her niece. "Maybe ropeless is the way to go."

"Maybe it is." It was clear Allison was really thinking about it.

Simple stuff like thinking together was how Allison made the world brighter. It was nice when she didn't need to have answers and could just wonder about possibilities with you. When she listened carefully. Or asked a thoughtful question. Or laughed at the same thing you thought was funny.

Amelia offered the binoculars. "Your turn."

They watched the orca. Listened to it talk and sing through the app. The wonderful world of technology.

When the orca moved on, Amelia packed her phone and binoculars back into her bag. They strolled along the beach, together, until Allison headed into the dunes toward the house when Amelia took the trail to the commune.

So, really, here on Wren, Amelia had everything she could ever want. Both her remaining sisters within reach. Her beautiful niece blooming each day. Friends—she learned the most from the kooky ones! Critters of all shapes and sizes to care for. Projects she found fun and worthwhile.

And lots of people lived their entire lives without ever falling in love. So she was already ahead of the curve. Because she *did* fall in love, once. Just because that relationship ended so suddenly, so finally, didn't mean it hadn't counted.

Falling in love, all those years ago, had shaped who she'd become now. In a messy, roundabout way, losing that love had led straight to what she had today.

An unimaginably marvelous life.

74

Paying for it

Allison was sitting at the end of her dock, with Lokita snuggled in her lap, when Ralph arrived. She motioned for him to join her.

He sat and dangled his legs over the edge. "Nice hat."

"Thanks." She fingered the ball cap, the one that fit perfectly and was designed with her in mind, then pulled out a tissue and wiped her eyes.

"Shoot, Allison. What's happened now? Do you want me to go knock sense into Virgil?"

She laughed before catching his seriousness. "You'd do that?"

"Of course I would."

She shook her head, tired of revisiting her last conversation with Virgil. Rehashing his words was getting her no closer to clarity.

A flock of buffleheads floated near. Their neatly delineated markings looked as if they'd been painted with tiny brushes. Not a hint of black where white should be or of white where black should be. Tidy, clean lines. Uncrossed. Unconfused.

"Virgil probably already feels like he's been knocked sideways. A few too many times." She straightened, sniffed, and put away the tissue. What she need-

ed was to focus on an entirely different topic. "Looks like the road improvements are moving along."

"So far, so good. I've been able to finish constructing my shed too. Plenty of
room to store Wren's vehicles for road maintenance, once we acquire them. And
my unpaid taxes have been forgiven, thanks to Nancy."

Allison bumped his shoulder with her own. "Thanks to Nancy, yes. Also
thanks to you, for helping the FBI bring in one of their most wanted."

"I wish I'd had the guts to report Hack sooner. His knowledge about details
in my past scared me into thinking I might go back to jail."

"Hack did lots of scary stuff."

Ralph rubbed his whiskered chin. "Now I've got a new idea on the horizon.
From lowdown a buddy told me off the record."

"Uh-oh. Do I want to hear this?"

"Two of the other victims Hack took advantage of are brothers. Young guys
with families and a charter fishing business. They lost their boat, their only
source of income, thanks to the punk we know as Hack. They've got a friend
willing to give them a boat, but it's not seaworthy. They're willing to do the
work, but they can't afford to buy parts, and they're going to need help with
the bigger repairs."

Allison stroked Lokita's warm back. "You want to offer your expertise and
my money?"

"Can you afford it?"

"Ralph, I can afford to buy your guys an entire fleet. But you've done enough
already, you know, by helping capture Hack."

"I'll never have done enough." Dropping his head, he studied the water below
his feet. She looked out at the ocean in front of them.

Crystal blue today. Sparkling in endless sunshine. The buffleheads floated,
dove for fish, resurfaced, dove again.

"Okay, but don't tell your fishing guys I'm paying the bills. Tell them you
took up a collection here on Wren."

Ralph nodded. "Thank you for your anonymous donation."

"My pleasure. But where does that leave us with the roadwork here on Wren? Do you want me to take over its supervision?"

"Do you *want* to take over its supervision?"

The buffleheads dove again. Did she want to jump in as a supervisor now? Play boss to construction workers who might not be inclined to take orders from a woman? Not to mention, she didn't know the first thing about paving roads. Except what Ralph had taught her. She could learn, though. You could do anything if you put your mind to it.

"I'm willing. But . . ." What she'd been thinking was that she would benefit from time away from Wren. A getaway in a *populated place* this time. Just in case she needed help. Which she didn't plan to. "I'd rather not take over supervision of the roadwork."

"That's what I hoped you'd say. We might have another option. A guy I know from years ago. If I can get Wallace to come to Wren, I could go help the brothers fix up the boat. Wallace could supervise the remaining roadwork and manage my freight business."

"I'm definitely paying for whatever costs you incur helping the brothers. And the road improvements are already in the budget."

"We might have to pay Wallace indirectly. With you giving me the money, me giving it to Wallace. He won't want to know he's being paid by a woman."

Allison rolled her eyes. Last time Ralph brought someone to Wren . . . "Are you sure about this?"

"I know what you're thinking. It won't be a repeat of the Hack debacle. I promise. Wren Island with Wallace around will be entirely unremarkable."

"Unremarkable?"

"Isn't that what you want?"

"If *unremarkable* means no one on a wanted list is after my family. FBI agents aren't crawling around. A sleazeball isn't tracking my boat's movements. If that's unremarkable, yes, that's what I want."

"Allison, I'm sorry. I know I'll never be able to make up for all that, but I'm trying."

She linked an arm through his. "No, I'm sorry about my attitude. You were Hack's victim too. I've mostly let the whole incident go. But every so often I feel angry about Hack's threats and their consequences. More than angry. Infuriated. I shouldn't take it out on you. It wasn't your fault."

"I brought him here."

"You didn't know things would turn out the way they did."

"It will be different with Wallace around. I promise." Ralph stood, pulled out his phone, tapped it, and held it to his ear. He walked off, talking. "Wallace? Ralph Wesson. Yep, been a long time."

Allison played with Lokita's ears. Watched the buffleheads float, dive, resurface.

Ralph was grinning when he returned. "He'll do it."

Allison blinked. "Just like that? Where's he coming from?"

"Somewhere in the U.S., probably. I doubt any other country would have him."

"Oh boy." Allison collected Lokita and stood. "I guess you can start making plans to go help that family with the charter fishing business. Where did you say they live?"

"Hawaii."

Allison rocked back on her heels. "Wait a minute. Wait just a *minute*. The family we're helping lives in *Hawaii*?"

75

Not going back

"Come with us, Aunt Macy. We'll all indulge in rest and relaxation."

Macy clunked a cutting board to the counter and made—and held—eye contact with her niece. This message needed to be understood. "I am *not* going to Hawaii. Final decision."

She reached for a knife and chopped vegetables for a smoothie. As if she'd want to return to the place where life had started falling apart! No, thank you. She was staying right here on Wren. Where she knew the ingredients in her glass and how she'd feel in the morning. Where everyone was on the same page about expectations and responsibilities.

Shasta breezed past with a basket of steaming bread chunks meant for dipping in fondue—which Shasta *knew* wasn't on Macy's list of approved foods. Not only because fondue might contain alcohol, but because it wasn't diabetic-friendly.

"Mace went to Hawaii on her honeymoon." Shasta set the bread on the table. "Probably has bad associations with it."

"Insightful commentary, Shasta, though not requested or required." Macy set down the knife and reached for her niece. "Allison, sweetheart, Hawaii is a special place and you'll love it. But it's where I started drinking too much. I have no desire to ever go back."

Allison squeezed her hand. "We could keep a dry house. Like we do here."

"Easier said than done in Hawaii."

Memories crashed over Macy in waves. Midnight strolls on sand sparkling under starlight. Refreshing afternoons in a hammock. Indulging in food and drink at every meal, *sobriety* a foreign word not yet on the horizon. Why should it have been, when all she was doing was letting herself live a little? Following a million smiling others on a common path. How could she have known it led not to happiness but to heartache?

Why on earth would she consider trading Hawaii's temptations for the pleasures that comfortably hemmed her in now? Family, friends. People to care for. Responsibilities. Allison's magnificent house didn't run by itself. If they all packed up and left, even for a short while, who would look after things here? Make sure the mice got taken care of? "The rodent guy will be coming back routinely. Do you want an exterminator prowling around when no one's home?"

Allison shrugged. "Virgil could take care of it."

Virgil could take care of it? As if Virgil should drop everything whenever Allison needed the teensiest bit of help.

Macy dumped vegetables in the blender and let it whirl. A woman who knew what was what—that's who they needed in charge around here.

At the table, Melia doled out napkins. "Allison and I are going to make videos while we're in Hawaii. We might even start a new channel. Stuff we saw in Hawaii that's different from Wren Island."

Shasta inspected her glittery pink fingernails. "I think I'll knit while I'm in Hawaii."

"Knit? In Hawaii?" Macy clunked a glass bowl into the sink—without breaking it, thank goodness. "What on earth will you make? Not scarves or hats. Bikinis?"

"Hey, that's not a bad idea. I could sell them."

"Aunt Shasta." Allison's tone held a warning.

"I know, I know, chickee. Now that you've restricted my credit privileges, I'm on my own for buying and selling. By the way, that budget class you signed me up for is turning out to be surprisingly beneficial. Did you know if I cut my spending in half for just one month, I'll have saved the amount needed to pay for an online course? Imagine me sort of going to college!" Shasta leaned over and smooched Allison on the cheek. "You're fabu-*lo-so*! Yours will be the first bikini I knit."

Macy brought her smoothie to the table and sat. Checked her blood sugar. All in perfect form. Which was how that fondue smelled.

Oh, to be the woman who could drink a glass of vegetables without a pot of fondue screaming at her. To be free from worry when her nearsighted sister wandered toward the surf, her shopaholic sister acted more bizarre than usual, or her niece required help getting out of a romantic funk.

What was up with Allison and Virgil, anyway? Allison seemed unnaturally unsettled, teetering on the verge of tears much of the time. Virgil was proving more steady than ever—an unimaginable feat—yet he'd clearly backed off and was rarely around the house anymore.

Anyway, Macy didn't need to go to Hawaii to relax. She could relax right here on Wren. What would really be nice would be to get up in the morning, feed the dogs, check on the birds, make a green smoothie, do a few up-and-down stretches, and for the rest of the day do whatever. Or nothing at all. One day at a time.

Not for *very* many days. She'd get bored once she ran out of projects to do and people to look after. But having little to do around the house for a short while could be heavenly.

She straightened, the path obvious.

"You all go and enjoy yourselves in Hawaii. I'll stay here and keep the home fires burning. Mark my words. Wren Island is going to be inundated with riffraff once the roads are finished. Virgil's hats aren't helping. As if Wren Island is a tourist destination!"

Sitting back, she studied her niece. "Does Virgil know you're going to Hawaii? I doubt he'll be thrilled with the idea of the woman he loves jetting off to a tropical island without him."

"How could Virgil possibly know?" Allison looked annoyed. "We're only just talking about the idea now."

"Seems like we've pretty much decided to go." Melia reached for a chunk of bread. "Right here, sitting around our new fondue pot."

"Tiddlywinks!" Shasta snatched up the bread basket. "We can't eat fondue! We'll look flabby in our bikinis!"

"Oh, for goodness' sake." Macy retrieved the basket and returned it to the table.

Looking at her two sisters, she saw the gap, as she always did, where she wanted their sister Anne to be. Looking at her niece, pretty and courageous and stunningly individual, she saw Anne still with them.

If Macy Johansson hadn't landed in a safe place with these girls, then where else in this world could hope be found?

But just to be certain, she'd better confirm. "Did any of you add wine or beer to this fondue?"

"Of course not!" The words rang out as a chorus around the table.

Sticking a fork in a chunk of bread, Macy handed it to Shasta and motioned to the fondue pot. "Then load up, Shasta. You, me, all of us. As you're so fond of saying, we've got to let ourselves live a little."

76

Spark

Virgil reached for another shipping box, flattened it, and tossed it into the market's recycling bin.

Nearby, Ralph punched another box, avoiding eye contact. "Just thought you might want a heads-up."

Exhaling, Virgil nodded. It wasn't easy for one guy to deliver a difficult message to another. *Your girl's getting ready to run off.* Nobody wants to hear that what they're afraid of is actually happening. Better to know than not to, though.

"I appreciate it, Ralph. Thanks for telling me."

"It isn't any of my business."

"But you knew I'd want to be prepared."

Muttering, Ralph shook his head. "That woman is a piece of work—in the best of ways, of course."

"Yeah, she sure is."

Ralph rubbed his chin. "Maybe she won't like Hawaii."

"It's possible." But who wouldn't like Hawaii? Virgil whacked another box flat.

"If there's anything I can do—"

"I'll let you know." Virgil pitched the box into recycling.

"Virgil?"

Couldn't the conversation be over already? He needed to figure out what to do next. He took another deep breath. Let it out through a clenched jaw. "Yep?"

"Sorry to be the one to put the idea in her head. You know, spark the desire to leave."

Ripping open another box, Virgil hurled it to the recycling bin. The desire to run was already deep inside Allison. That spark had been ready to fan into flame. Might always be. A trait Allison shared with his ex. Ralph hadn't done anything but play a small role in what was already happening.

Virgil walked his friend to the door. "Not your fault."

After removing his baking apron, Virgil hung it on a peg. He left Jax a note. Checked the café's ovens and burners—all off.

Then he strode off the porch. Barreled across the road. Fast-walked up Allison's driveway, building momentum as he passed her walnut tree—still a safe haven for wrens. Always would be as long as Virgil Tagaloa was around.

Wrens, dogs, aunts, trees. A new song, another muffin flavor, labeled shelves, whatever. *Count on Virgil Tagaloa to care about it. Help you get it just so. Grocery guy at your service. Whether or not you're here on Wren.*

Gaining speed as he blazed along, he nodded, cementing where he was going with this. If Allison needed space, okay. If she thought she needed thousands of miles of ocean between them for a while, okay. But no way and no how would he let Allison leave without her first hearing how *he* felt about it.

If she wanted to run, she was free to! But he wouldn't let her run from something that wasn't a threat. Wouldn't let her be afraid he'd leave her—not while he was standing firm right next to her, holding on. She couldn't go anywhere in this world where he wouldn't still love her and long for her to be in his arms.

So he'd tell her to go ahead. Enjoy a vacation. Take as long as she wanted.

But then come *home*. To the one still loving her, still waiting for her, same as always.

77

Choosing

Walking up her driveway, Allison found Virgil steaming toward her. On reaching her, he held up one hand. "Let me guess. You're running off to Hawaii."

"I'm not *running off*. I'm just going away for a few weeks." It came out sounding defensive. Probably because Virgil was right. She *was* running off. Not to Hawaii, but to the safest place she knew. Self-reliance. A place that held—had always held—bewitching appeal.

Virgil reached for her then, and she moved into his embrace. His voice resonated through her. "To you, it will be a few weeks. To me, it will feel like a lifetime. What can I do to convince you to stay? Reorganize the checkout lane? Alphabetize the baking supplies? Label the spice shelves?"

She laughed. "If only it were that easy, right?"

At his anguished look, she softened against him. Let him hold her as if he'd always be holding her. Every day. And every day after that.

Was this how it would feel? If she trusted him with all she held dear?

She huddled closer and made herself smaller. Felt him tighten his hold. He'd said forever was all he was offering. Had he said the same thing to his wife? The woman he walked away from?

Trusting him today wouldn't be worth waking up tomorrow and finding out she'd become less than enough. Getting away, untangling from this, was crucial. She straightened, patted his shoulder, aimed for lighter conversation. "How could you already know about me going to Hawaii? I just now decided."

"Ralph gave me a heads-up."

"Not much gets past Ralph."

"Not much gets past me."

Her breath caught. She knew that tone. He was going to spell out the truth of their situation. Because he was Virgil, and when he'd landed on the truth he always, *always*, put the pieces together in a way that finally, *finally*, made sense to her.

Did he know, right now in this moment, how she longed for it all to make sense?

He reached for her hand. "I know you're afraid to be left. I know you think giving all of you isn't safe. That you'll somehow become less interesting. But you can't become less you, and I love all of you. I'm interested in all of you and want you close to me." His voice lowered to a whisper. "Is this how it's going to be? My heart aching for you? Your heart holding back?"

His hold loosened. Enough for her to move away if she wanted.

She closed her eyes against the risk of going all in. Against the fear of eventually blurring into unimportance. "Do you think you'll still love me tomorrow?"

"I know I'll still love you tomorrow."

"How can you know?"

"I've loved you for ages. I can't imagine a world where I didn't find joy in loving you more and more."

He placed a warm palm on either side of her face and kissed her forehead.

"I'm also *choosing* to love you. *Choosing*. To love *you*. Today, tomorrow, the next day even more. And whenever you pull away, I'm hoping my love will draw you back. Help you, somehow, make it home."

78

Same as always

Allison checked her navigational equipment and veered *Buttercup* to the north, where billowy white clouds puffed across a sapphire sky. Look at that. A bald eagle flying the same direction as her.

She glanced at the dogs, both in their life jackets. Everything was shipshape and Bristol fashion. Opening the throttle so *Buttercup* could breeze across the water's surface, Allison resumed the conversation.

"So I ask you again, Louise, where's the rule?"

The dog thumped her tail.

"Where's the rule that says you shouldn't trust *anyone* just because *someone* once left you?"

When Wren Island came into sight, Allison angled *Buttercup* around the island's forested western point. Gave the boulders a wide berth as she approached the dock. Breathed a sigh of contentment at having made it home again.

Louise waited for her life jacket to be unfastened, then launched over the gunwale and took off, scattering seagulls. Allison removed Lokita's tiny jacket and snapped on a leash.

"That freewheeling run on the beach is exactly what I'm talking about, Lokita. Why not let yourself fly into the unknown? Especially if someone wants to go there with you. Taking a chance on love, as they say. Hey, that could be a song."

Allison smiled. "Actually, it *is* a song. We're late to the party on that one. But we've got our own little songs, haven't we? Now we're on the dock. Careful where you walk."

On the beach, Allison let Lokita choose her own slow route around driftwood, rocks, and clumps of seaweed. Soon Louise was barreling back to them at full steam, barking, happy.

Up at the house, Virgil was waving. Allison waved back, her heart somersaulting. Louise ran in circles, then raced up the beach, across the dunes, toward Virgil. He laughed at the dog's antics and sent her galloping back to Allison.

She picked up Lokita and climbed through the dunes. At the concrete lions, she set down Lokita and sent her wandering into the house, Louise nudging her from behind. A muffled burst of laughter came from the kitchen. Voices of people she loved.

Virgil opened his arms, smiling in welcome, the same as always.

She moved toward him.

The air shifted in a soft breeze. The forest stirred. Overhead, a whisper of swaying branches, the dripping scent of pine.

Reaching for her, Virgil wrapped her close, the same as always. Whispered, the same as always. "I missed you."

"I missed you too." Her response was muffled in his shoulder.

"I've loved you for ages." Virgil, still whispering.

She smiled into him. "I believe it."

"Do you believe you'll still be loved tomorrow? Loved then even more?"

She caught her breath. Did she believe it? Did she trust him that much?

The forest hushed, as if waiting for her answer.

Aunt Amelia's voice broke in. "Oh! There you are, both of you. Super. Macy wants to know if you'll pull the bicycles out of the storage shed." Aunt Amelia made her way down the steps to the concrete lions.

Aiming for propriety, Allison tried to pull away. Virgil would have none of it. He wrapped her closer and spoke over her shoulder.

"Amelia? Do you mind if, before we tackle the bicycles, your niece answers my question?"

"Question?" Aunt Amelia giggled. Allison flushed.

A whisper in her ear. A secret spoken against the roaring world. "Darling Allison, do you believe I'll still love you tomorrow? Even more than today? Please say yes."

Held by arms unwilling to let go—he'd say unable—she answered.

"Yes."

Aunt Amelia's squeal broke in. "Oh my gosh! She said yes! You guys are getting married!"

"That's not what just happened, Aunt Amelia." Laughing, Allison pulled back. "Virgil and I aren't getting married."

"You're not?"

"We're not?" Even Virgil sounded surprised.

Allison eyed him. "Are you kidding me? I'm not getting married again."

"Ever?" Aunt Amelia sagged.

Virgil looked like he'd been knocked sideways. How could he not know she wouldn't want to marry again? Far too entangling. No room for escape.

"We never talked about getting married." She searched his face, hoping to find understanding. And acceptance.

"Oh. I see." Studying her, he nodded.

She drew herself up. "I suppose we could talk about it, down the road. But fair warning, I'm not going to be convinced."

"Hmm." More nodding.

"Not convinced easily, that is."

"Hmm."

"Virgil. Will you please say something more than *hmm*?"

"How about I ask a question?"

"In addition to the one you just asked?" Then it hit her. Was he going to propose right now? In front of the house, next to the concrete lions? Before they'd even talked about it?

"Wait a minute, Virgil."

Shaking his head, Virgil put a finger to her lips. "Not asking *that* question. Not until I know you're ready to say yes. Which you will be, eventually."

His eyes met hers. Loving. Trusting and offering trust. His grin became so endearingly confident she nearly kissed him. If she did, would he take it as a promise, one she wasn't ready to keep?

Swiveling her head between them, Aunt Amelia squinted. "You guys are confusing me. Are we still maybe marrying Virgil?"

"We're waiting to hear Virgil's next question." Allison poked him. "Go for it."

"Oh, I see how it is. A new level in our relationship. Questions on demand now." He tweaked the Wren Island hat on her head. Then he lifted her hand to his lips and kissed it. "Funny, but I seem to have forgotten the question."

"You did not."

Shrugging, Virgil released her hand. "Guess we'll have to wonder about it. See if we can't figure out what my next question would've been. I'll go get the bicycles."

Watching him walk off, she held her breath. He'd turn to gaze back at her. He always did whenever he was leaving, even for a nearby task like bringing bicycles out of the shed.

He'd turn and give her one of *those* looks, assuring her he was walking away because he must and only temporarily. Promising he'd return soon—even sooner. Reminding her that while he was away, he'd miss her—and hope she missed him—until the moment, the very first moment, they were together again.

Halfway to the shed, he turned, grinning. Caught her eye, winked.

She flew into his arms.

A Note from the Author

Dear Reader,

One day not long ago, this writer imagined inviting people to influence a story she was writing in real time. When a few brave souls came on board to offer ideas, opinions, and inspiration, an adventure in interactive serialized fiction began. The story developed in directions *readers* wanted. Fictional characters made in-the-moment decisions determined by real people.

The heartbeat of all this gloriousness? A previously unsung place called Wren Island.

You won't find Wren Island on any world map, but it does exist. We find it whenever we imagine what could be. Whenever we reach for courage, anticipate joy, trust in love, hope for something better.

On Wren Island, there's always "more" to the story—behind-the-scenes and yet to come. Remember Ralph mentioning his friend Wallace in Chapter 74? Wallace is the star of the *next* book in the series. Wren Islanders (people like you who subscribe to receive my emails) have and will continue to influence Wallace's story as I write it.

Subscribe today to receive email updates and your free copy of *A Wren Island Companion*, chock full of interesting tidbits and behind-the-scenes peeks. Then watch your inbox for opportunities to influence what happens next. Created with you in mind, Wren Island becomes even more marvelous when you're here.

Gratefully,

Laura

laurajoylloyd.com

Coming Soon

A Wren Island novel featuring seventy-year-old Wallace Bernard.

Book 2 in the Make It Home series by Laura Joy Lloyd.

Summer 2026

laurajoylloyd.com

Share the Wren Island Spirit

"You won't find Wren Island on any world map, but it does exist. We find it whenever we imagine what could be. Whenever we reach for courage, anticipate joy, trust in love, hope for something better."

-Laura Joy Lloyd

Here are a few easy-peasy ways to share the Wren Island spirit:

- Invite a friend for a walk and look for interesting treasures.

- Be honest when talking about life's disappointments.

- Celebrate someone else's achievement, big or small.

- Ask a friend to help you try something new.

- Write an encouraging note on social media.

- Review *Interesting Enough* on Amazon, Goodreads, and elsewhere.

- Tell your book club about Wren Island.

- Bring Allison's buzzy brownies to a potluck.

- Listen to Laura's podcast and the Wren Island music playlist.

- Tell someone about your list of nice things to wish for.

- Look for ways to be extra kind, in your own unique style.

- Whenever and wherever you can, give life your best.

Find more ideas on the author's website. Thanks for sharing Wren Island! laurajoylloyd.com

Discussion Guide

Whether you're pondering the story quietly in your own head, chatting with a friend, or engaging in a lively book club event, may these questions be launching points for endless inspiration.

1. Allison talks out loud to her dogs. Have you known someone who did this?

2. Allison recalls her mother saying "You can do anything if you put your mind to it." In what ways do you agree or disagree?

3. Allison has difficulty envisioning what doing something important or being interesting might look like for her. In what ways can you identify, or not, with her feelings?

4. If you, like Allison, were presented with estranged family members needing a place to call home, how would you respond?

5. After not being able to see real whales as clearly as she liked, Amelia imagines an extraordinary encounter with orcas. Do you remember a time when imagination served you similarly?

6. Macy admits to being "mostly annoyed with herself." What do you

think she means?

7. In a moment of overwhelm, Allison says she's "getting lost in all the clutter." Can you identify? In what ways?

8. Allison justifies borrowing an acquaintance's motorbike by reasoning that islanders often band together to share resources. Would you have felt comfortable borrowing the motorbike? Why or why not?

9. After a harrowing experience, Amelia worries Macy won't allow her to walk alone on the beach anymore. Do you think Macy's concern is warranted? Is Amelia's?

10. At the commune, Amelia learns about simplifying her wardrobe, reducing single-use plastic, and the risk of entanglement from fishing gear. What are your thoughts about these concepts?

11. Did it surprise you that the usually brusque Macy used peaceful imagery to help her fall asleep? Why or why not?

12. When Allison goes missing, Macy regrets saying—and not saying—certain things. Have you similarly second-guessed a conversation with someone you love, especially when separated by physical distance?

13. In what ways does the relationship between Allison and Macy improve? How might their relationship become more complicated?

14. Amelia's experience finding whole sand dollars does not go as she expected. Were you surprised by her response? Why or why not?

15. Amelia has the goal of living independently. What approaches for doing so would appeal to you if you were in her situation?

16. Do you think Allison should have been more cautious about getting involved with Ralph's plan to help a family in need? Why or why not?

17. Virgil waffles between wanting to respect Allison's privacy and push for more transparency. What advice would you give him?

18. Do you think the relationship between Allison and Virgil will last? Why or why not?

19. If you were visiting Wren Island and heard the gong ring, indicating whales could be heard through the hydrophone, what would you do?

20. Do you keep a list similar to Amelia's, of nice things to wish for? What's on it?

Acknowledgments

Wren Island would not be the glorious place it is without the influence of incredibly wonderful people. Some know they've played a role. Others are going about life doing their beautiful thing, never realizing their impact. I'm sure I've missed naming someone here. Please know you, too, have made or are making a difference.

A very special group of people influenced every part of this story from the beginning. My marvelous email subscribers! Thank you for opening my notes on Saturday mornings, for filling out surveys and voting, for contributing your own ideas and dreams for Wren Island. This adventure in interactive serialized fiction would not exist without you.

Is there a hall of fame for editors? J. B. Wilson deserves to be in it. Jill noticed emerging themes before I did. Polished tidbits right up to the end. Held my hand when it would have been easier to let go. She did all this with consistent professionalism and liberal kindness. Errors in the final version are entirely my own. Thank you for being you, Jill.

Steve Kuhn of Kuhn Design Group created a cover I absolutely adore. He exhibited exceptional patience every time I changed my mind only to change it back again.

Tessa Burns was my go-to whenever I wasn't sure if Wren was flying like it should, mostly because I knew she'd come up with something nice to say. Like listening to the podcast was the highlight of her day. Or testing a Wren Island ball cap would be a privilege, especially if the colors were matchy-matchy with *Buttercup*. Tessa is also the creative force behind our enchanting Wren Island map.

Julie Little sacrificed time away from her own extraordinary writing to read messy drafts, clarify confusion, and ask pertinent questions. Without fail, she followed up with a message reminding me I'm loved for who I am, not what I do.

Ginger Kauffman suggested we catch a ferry (à la *Lucy Jo*) to Guemes Island (a Wren-like place) and enjoy lunch at the general store (resembling Virgil's market). Plus, Ginger shared her own tender love story, inspiring much of what transpires between Allison and Virgil.

Sarah Marie Sonoda was always eager to read the latest from Wren Island. She spent most of one evening listening to my ramblings about metaphors, then revisited the conversation the following morning—quelling my fears it'd only been late-night loony talk.

Cheri Gregory of Sensitive & Strong offered me a safe place to discover who I *really* want to be, then cheered my efforts to strengthen my new wings.

Ginny L. Yttrup of Words for Writers encouraged me, always, to up my game. Somehow, she did this while simultaneously affirming I was already enough.

Cynthia Ruchti of Books & Such Literary Agency suggested a story from Wren Island, situated a stone's throw from Reclamation Island, might float on its own. And it did!

Eileen Grafton and Lauraine Snelling took an interest in a wacky idea about letting readers influence a novel while it's being written, then helped me overcome my fear of talking about it.

Community strategist Tonya Kubo offered concrete ways to transform Wren Island into a place worth visiting again and again.

Jonathan and Melanie Ross (Romeo-Oscar-Sierra-Sierra) clarified endless boating-related details and offered thoughtful perspectives. Melanie was the first to invite me to speak at a book club and the first to photograph herself wearing a Wren Island hat while sailing in British Columbia.

Erin Johns Gless of Pacific Whale Watch Association answered my questions about our local orcas swimming near crab pots and introduced me to the remarkable concept of ropeless fishing gear.

Andrew Culbertson of Culbertson Marine Construction always knew where I could view an LCM-8 (like *Lucy Jo*) or SAFE boat (like *Incremental*) in local marinas. He sketched out Ralph's ingenious use of a T-handle wrench, let me tag along for a workday, and even trusted me with 350 tons.

Retired FBI Agent Ray Lauer answered a slew of off-the-wall questions, then cleverly suggested it'd be okay if I included a few unlikely details, because fiction is often more interesting than real life.

In the nick of time, Linda Avellar and Lori Singaraju offered beneficial insights.

Years ago, Aleta Ferrel spent hours with me searching for whole sand dollars. Who knew those sunny afternoons would make their way into this story? Plus, Aleta is the reason we have hats printed with *Wren Island*.

Thank you to the many friends who prayed for and encouraged me! Marlene Anderson, Shelley Cramm, Judy Davidson, Kelly Fernlake, Jeremiah Friedli, Sheri Gates, Joan Husby, Bart and Elaine Jeffress, Deanne Johnson, Wendy Miller, Ann Neumann, Curtis and Nicoline Payne, April Ray, Tim Riter, Barb Robinette, David and Trina Robinson, Raoul and Lynda Robles, Linda Sammaritan, Kolleen Smith, Sylvia Stewart, Amy Lynn Taylor, Essea White, and so many more. Group hug!

Jeannette Anderson and Bill Davidson prayed about my writing efforts for years, then got called home before seeing this novel published.

My dog Moki was always ready with a snuggle, just like Lokita. Rosie was my gorgeous walking partner and didn't mind being accidentally called Louise. Their paw prints will forever crisscross Wren Island. Claiming their vacated spot under my writing desk, Clair de Lune established herself as the world's most reliable foot warmer.

My parents, Robert and Connie Russell, encouraged me from the beginning and never stopped. My sister, Linda Fraught, was the first to read to me. Plus, Linda taught me to love libraries.

Thank you to my husband, Roy, for saying I'm a good writer even while reading novels by *really* good writers. And thank you for letting me daydream, uninterrupted, about Wren Island.

Looking at each of these names, I'm brought to tears. How did so many incredibly wonderful people end up in *my* life?

Thank you to my Lord and Savior. For this life. For everything.

About the Author

Laura Joy Lloyd writes uplifting contemporary stories set on Pacific Northwest islands. Through an innovative style she calls *interactive serialized fiction*, Laura invites readers to influence many of her projects in real time as she writes. Laura also enjoys swimming, knitting, keeping company with creatives, and organizing whatever feels messy.

Connect with Laura!

Website: laurajoylloyd.com

Facebook: facebook.com/laurajoylloyd

Instagram: @laurajoylloyd

www.ingramcontent.com/pod-product-compliance
Lightning Source LLC
Chambersburg PA
CBHW030240120726
47903CB00005B/1554